☑ **W9-BYB-852**

Tears
/ of

F R E M O N T
~~public library~~
engage • inspire • enrich

Item was damaged prior to checkout. Do not remove
this slip, or you may be held responsible for the
damages.

- —— Broken case
- ✗ Damaged/ Broken Binding
- —— Damaged Cover/ Dust Jacket
- —— Pen/ Pencil/ Highlight markings
- —— Piece missing(specify)
- ✗ Stains and/or moisture damage
- —— Torn pages/wrinkled pages
- ✗ Folded page corners
- —— Other _____
- —— Date/Initials __9/8__KPP_____

Published: Pepper Winters 2013: pepperwinters@gmail.com
Publishing assisted by Black Firefly:
http://www.blackfirefly.com/

Editing: by Lindsey from Black Firefly and TJ Loveless from Cliff Hanger Editing.
French Translation: Louise Pion
Cover Design: by Ari at Cover it! Designs:
http://salon.io/#coveritdesigns
Proofreading by: Robin from Black Firefly
Formatting by: http://www.blackfirefly.com/
Images in Manuscript from Canstock Photos:
http://www.canstockphoto.com

Dedication

This book is dedicated to all the Bloggers, Facebook Friends, Beta Readers, Reviewers, and Amazing People around the web. The success of Tears of Tess belongs to you wonderful people.

A huge, heart-felt thank you.

Prologue

Three little words.

If anyone asked what I was most afraid of, what terrified me, stole my breath, and made my life flicker before my eyes, I would say three little words.

How could my perfect life plummet so far into hell?

How could my love for Brax twist so far into unfixable?

The black musty hood over my head suffocated my thoughts, and I sat with hands bound behind my back. Twine rubbed my wrists with hungry stringed teeth, ready to bleed me dry in this new existence.

Noise.

The cargo door of the airplane opened and footsteps thudded toward us. My senses were dulled, muted by the black hood; my mind ran amok with terror-filled images. Would I be raped? Mutilated? Would I ever see Brax again?

Male voices argued, and someone wrenched my arm upright. I flinched, crying out, earning a fist to my belly.

Tears streamed down my face. The first tears I shed, but definitely not the last.

This was my new future. Fate threw me to the

bastards of Hades.

"That one."

My stomach twisted, threatening to evict empty contents. Oh, God.

Three little words:

I was sold.

Chapter One

Starling

"**W**here are you taking me, Brax?" I giggled as my boyfriend of two years beamed his slightly crooked smile and plucked my suitcase from my hands.

We crossed the threshold of the airport and nerves of excitement fluttered in my stomach.

A week ago, Brax surprised me with a romantic dinner and an envelope. I grabbed him and squeezed him half to death when I pulled free two airplane tickets with the destinations blacked out by a marker.

My perfect, sweet boyfriend, Brax Cliffingstone was taking me somewhere exotic. And that meant connection, sex, fun. Things I sorely needed.

Brax had never been able to keep a secret. Hell, he was a shockingly bad liar—I caught his fibs every time when his sky-blue eyes darted up and to the left, and his cute ears blushed.

But, somehow, he kept quiet on the whole mysterious holiday. Like any normal twenty-year-old woman, I searched our apartment ruthlessly. Raiding his underwear drawer, the PlayStation compartment, and all the other secret hidey-holes where he might've kept the real plane reservations. But, for all my snooping, I came up empty.

So, as I stood in the Melbourne airport, with a crazy happy boyfriend and nerves rioting in my heart, I could only grin like an idiot.

"Not telling. The check-in clerk can be the one to ruin my surprise." He chuckled. "If it were up to me, I wouldn't tell you until we arrived at the resort." He dropped the suitcase and dragged me toward him with a smirk. "In fact, if I could, I'd blindfold you until we got there, so it would all be a complete surprise."

My core clenched as thoughts flared with hot images— sexy, sinful visions of Brax blindfolding me, taking me roughly, completely at his mercy. *Oh, God, don't go there again, Tess. You were going to block thoughts like that, remember?*

Ignoring myself, I gasped as Brax's fingers grazed my flesh. I shuddered, and my sequined top became insubstantial.

"You could do that, you know?" I whispered, dropping my eyelids to half-mast. "You could tie me up…."

Instead of pouncing and kissing me like crazy for offering him the chance to dominate, Brax swallowed and looked as if I'd told him to slap me with a dead fish.

"Tess, what the hell? That's the third time you've quipped about bondage."

Rejection crushed, and I dropped my gaze. The tingles between my legs popped like dirty bubbles, and I let Brax shove me back into the box where I belonged. The box labelled: perfect, innocent girlfriend who'd do anything for him, as long as it was in the dark and on my back.

I wanted a new label. One that said: girlfriend who will do anything to be tied, spanked, and fucked all over rather than adored.

Brax looked so disappointed and I hated myself. *I need to stop this.*

I reminded myself for the three-hundredth time, that the sweet, wonderful relationship I had with this man was far

more important than a bit of sexy play in the bedroom.
I mumbled, "It's been too long. Almost a month and a half." I remembered the exact date when the lacklustre sex, in good ole missionary, took place. Brax worked overtime, my uni course demanded a lot of brainpower, and somehow life became more important than a roll beneath the sheets.

He froze, looking around us at the hordes of people. "Great time to bring that up." He guided me to the side, glaring at a couple that came too close. "Can we talk about this later?" He ducked his head and kissed my cheek. "I love you, hun. Once we aren't so busy, *then* we can have more alone time."

"And this holiday? Will you take me like the girlfriend you adore?"

Brax beamed, enveloping me in a hug. "Every night. You wait."

I smiled, letting anticipation and happiness dispel my angst. Brax and I wanted different things in the bedroom department, and I hoped, prayed, got on my knees and begged, that I didn't ruin what we had because of it.

My blood simmered for things entirely *not* sweet. Things I didn't have the courage to say. Downright sinful things that amped my blood to lava and made me wet— and it wasn't chaste kisses.

Standing in his arms, in a public place, with that sexy smirk on his mouth, and hands on my waist, I trembled with a cocktail of need. This trip would be exactly what we needed.

He brushed his lips against mine, no tongue, and I had to squeeze my legs together to stop the vibrations threatening to overtake me. *Is there something wrong with me?* Surely, I shouldn't be this way. Maybe there was a cure— something to take the edge off my desires.

Brax pulled back, smiling. "You're gorgeous."

My eyes dropped to his shapely mouth, breathing

faster. What would Brax do if I pushed him against the wall and groped him in public? My mind turned the fantasy into *him* pushing *me* hard against the wall, his thigh going between my legs, hands pawing, bruising me because he couldn't get close enough.

I swallowed, battling those far too tempting thoughts. "You're not so bad yourself," I joked, plucking his baby-blue t-shirt that matched his eyes so well.

I loved this man, but missed him at the same time. How was that possible?

Life wedged between us: the university course stole five days a week, not to mention homework, and Brax's boss landed a new building contract in the heart of the city.

Each month trickled into the next, and lovemaking became second fiddle to *Call of Duty* on PlayStation, and architectural sketching for the extra credit I'd signed up for.

But all of that would change. Our life together would improve, because I was going to seduce my man. I'd packed a few naughty surprises to show Brax what turned me on. I needed to do this. To save my sanity. To save my relationship.

Brax's fingers squeezed my waist and he stepped away, ducking down to grab the suitcases again.

If I wanted to seduce him, wasn't it best just to go for it? Planning and dreaming seemed wrong when he stood right in front of me.

I dropped my shoulder bag and grabbed the lapels of his beige canvas jacket, yanking him into me. "Let's join the mile-high club," I whispered, before crushing his mouth with mine. His eyes flashed as I leaned forward, pressing my entire body against his. *Feel me. Need me.*

He tasted of orange juice and his lips were warm, so warm. My tongue tried to gain welcome, but Brax's hands landed on my shoulders, holding me at bay.

Someone clapped, saying, "You attack him, girl!"

Brax stepped back, looking over my shoulder at the

bystander. He dropped his eyes to mine, temper flashing. "Nice spectacle, Tess. Are we done? Can we go check in?"

Disappointment sat like a heavy boulder in my belly. He sensed my mood—like he always did—and gathered me into a hug again. "I'm sorry. You know how much I hate PDA's. Get me behind closed doors, and I'm all yours." He smiled, and I nodded.

"You're right. Sorry. I'm just so excited to go on holiday with you." I dropped my eyes, letting wild, blonde curls curtain my face. *Please, don't let him see the rejection in my eyes.* Brax used to say my eyes reminded him of dove's feathers as the white bird flew across the sky. He could be very poetic, my Brax. But I didn't want poetry anymore. I wanted… I didn't know what I wanted.

He chuckled. "You're right about being excited." He waggled his eyebrows, and together we headed to check-in. The girl who'd told me to attack him winked and gave me a thumbs up.

I smiled, hiding the residual pain that my attack didn't inspire the same reaction.

We joined the queue, and I glanced around. People milled like fish in a pond, darting and weaving around groups of waiting passengers. The vibe of an airport never failed to excite me. Not that I travelled a lot. Before the university course, I travelled to Sydney to study the architecture there, and sketch. I loved to sketch buildings. At ten years of age, my parents took my brother and me to Bali for a week. Not that it was fun going on holiday with a thirty-year-old brother, and parents who despised me.

Old hurt surfaced, thinking of them. When I moved in with Brax eighteen months ago, I drifted apart from my parents. After all, they were almost seventy years old, and focused on other 'important things', rather than a daughter who'd come twenty years too late. A dreadful mistake, as they loved to remind me.

They'd been so horrified at the pregnancy, they promptly sued the doctor for botching my father's vasectomy.

An old enemy: rejection, ruled my life. I supposed the desperation to connect with Brax was a way of confirming that *someone* wanted me. I didn't just want intimacy, I *needed* it. I needed to feel his hands on me, his body in mine. It was a craving that never left me in peace.

I blinked, putting the impossible together. I needed Brax to be rough because I needed to be *claimed*.

Oh, my God, am I that screwed up?

I followed Brax in a daze to the counter, and let him put the suitcase on the scales.

"Morning. Tickets and passports, please," the girl in her smart uniform said.

Fumbling with luggage tags, Brax asked, "Honey, can you give her our tickets? They're in my back pocket."

I reached around and pulled out a travel wallet from his baggy jeans pocket. Although twenty-three years old, Brax still dressed like a grungy teenager. I squeezed his butt.

His eyes flashed to mine, frowning.

I forced a bright smile, handing our documentation to the clerk. I didn't even check where we were headed, too focused on ignoring the twinges of sadness at not being allowed to grope my boyfriend. *Maybe I'm too sexual?* My fears were right. I was hardwired all wrong.

"Thank you." The girl's eyes dropped, showing heavily shadowed lids. Her brown hair, scraped back into a tight bun, looked plastic with so much hair spray. She bit her lip and pulled out a ream of tickets before checking our passports. "Do you want your bags checked all the way through to Cancun?"

Cancun? My heart soared. Wow. Brax outdid himself. I never would've thought he'd travel so far from home. I turned and kissed his cheek. "Thank you so much, Brax."

His face softened as he captured my hand. "You're welcome. There's no better way to celebrate our future, than going to a country that values friendship and family." He leaned closer. "I read that on Sundays the streets come alive with strangers dancing. Everyone becomes connected by music."

I couldn't tear myself from his crisp blue eyes. That was why I loved him, despite not being completely satisfied. Brax suffered the same insecurities. He didn't have anyone but me. His parents died in a car accident when he turned seventeen; he was an only child.

Brax owned the apartment we lived in, thanks to the life insurance pay out, and his dad's husky, Blizzard, came with the bargain.

Blizzard and I didn't see eye to eye, but Brax loved the dog like a tatty teddy-bear. I tolerated the beast, and kept my handbags far from chewing height.

"You're the best." I captured his chin, planting a kiss, not caring he was uncomfortable. Hell, the couple beside us were practically dry humping; a peck on the mouth was PG stuff.

The girl sighed across the counter. "Is this your honeymoon? Cancun is amazing. My boyfriend and I went there a few years ago. So hot and fun. And the music is so sexy, we couldn't keep our hands off each other."

Images filled my mind of twirling around Brax in a new sexy bikini. Maybe a change of scenery would amplify our lust.

I said, "No, not our honeymoon. Just a celebration."

Brax grinned, his eyes sparkling.

An idea ran wild. *Was* this trip special? Was Brax going to propose? I waited for the heart-flipping joy at becoming Mrs. Cliffingstone, but a swell of comfort filled me instead. I would say yes.

Brax wanted me. Brax was safe. I loved him in my

own way—the way that mattered, the long-lasting kind.

Silence descended while the girl tap-tapped her keyboard and printed off our boarding passes. After tagging our bags, she handed everything back. "Your bags are checked all the way to Mexico, but you'll have a stop in Los Angeles for four hours." She circled the gate number and time. "Please make your way through immigration, and proceed to the departure lounge. You board at eleven-thirty."

Brax took the documentation and shouldered his laptop bag. Linking hands with me, he said, "Thank you."

We headed toward the Passengers Only lounge. We had little over an hour before boarding. I could think of a lot of things we could do in an hour, but I doubted Brax would be into them.

We were on our way to Mexico. A different country and a different bed awaited us. I could be patient.

I made up my mind as Brax browsed the tax-free PlayStation games that tonight would mark a new beginning for us. Goodbye contentment, hello lust.

Our relationship was going to rip and roar with love and flame. I would make sure of it.

Yes, tonight things would be different.

I needed different.

Chapter Two

Blue Jay

Somewhere, hundreds of kilometres above earth, I woke to dry, recirculated air, and the sickening smell of over-nuked food.

Brax brushed his lips on my forehead. "Dinner is being served, honey."

I scooted upright in the prison of a chair, wincing at my flat butt. Holy hell, it took a long time to travel across the world.

An air-hostess wheeled a trolley slowly down the aisle, smiling fakely and handing out tinfoil-wrapped trays.

"What do you want?" Brax asked, slapping a hand over his wide yawn.

I knew how he felt. All I wanted was a hot shower, a soft bed, and Brax to spoon me.

I shrugged. "I dunno. What were the options again?"

The air-hostess arrived at our row, beaming. "Chicken casserole or beef stir-fry?"

Both sounded woefully unappealing, but I said, "Chicken, please."

Brax ordered the beef, and silence reigned while we ate. Whenever I thought about arriving at the hotel, a mini montage took over. The movie played in my mind: kissing him, telling him I loved him, then pouncing with need. Brax would push up my skirt and claim me in front of wide-eyed guests. *My libido has left the realm of normalcy.*

Flutters wouldn't stop in the darkest part of my belly. The knowledge that I'd finally confess what I needed sexually, terrified and thrilled me.

Brax smiled, chewing a piece of broccoli. "What are you thinking about? You're wearing that stunned tuna look of yours."

Oh, nothing, sweetie. Just fantasizing about you pinning my wrists and taking me hard. He'd probably throw himself out the plane. I was the one twisting our relationship. *I* was the one who'd changed.

Change, to Brax, was *not* a good thing.

I dropped my gaze, shoving a piece of dried chicken around. "I was thinking how much I love you, and how I can't wait to be in bed. Alone."

His face softened, looking so handsome in the dim interior lights. The glow highlighted his smooth jaw, blue eyes, and floppy brown hair. His strong arms and stocky frame screamed builder. Hell, I loved how he stood so big and strong. He could dominate me so easily... but never did. He treated me like glass. Special cut-crystal—placed me on a pedestal where I had to shine and remain dust free and perfect.

He pressed his forehead against mine. "I love you, too. I'm so happy we're spending this time together." He pushed his meal away, or as much as he could on the tiny table, and awkwardly reached into a pocket. "I have a present for you. To remind you of this amazing holiday."

I couldn't breathe. My tongue turned into a brick and saliva morphed into mortar.

He dropped a black velvet box into my lap then rubbed

the back of his neck. "I know we've been together for two years, and I love you with all my heart, Tess. But each year I spend with you, I grow more and more nervous I'm going to lose you."

Suddenly, the cabin stifled with old demons from our pasts, haunting us. I leaned over and kissed his lips gently, just the way he liked. My heart hurt for him. Would he ever get over losing his parents? The doctors said his night-terrors would stop eventually, but it'd been six years since his folks died, and he still couldn't fall asleep without pills.

I whispered, "You will never lose me, Brax. Never. I swear it." I kissed him again and his mouth opened under mine. His tongue flicked out and licked my lower lip, sending heat shooting like little stars.

I moaned and pressed harder, opening wider, forcing more intensity.

He pulled back, smirking shyly. His eyes darted around the cabin as if we'd be reprimanded by the flight attendants.

I murmured, "Can I open it now?"

His face flashed with confusion. "What?"

Feminine satisfaction swelled, I'd distracted him enough with a kiss that he'd forgotten. "The gift. Can I open it now, or wait till we get to the hotel?" Boldness sizzled and I whispered, "Because I have a present for you, too, but you have to wait till we arrive." My voice, layered with husky welcome, caused his nostrils to flare.

"Y—you can open it now."

I grinned, grabbing the box, happier than I'd been for a while. Brax was responding. Captive audience, I supposed.

I cracked open the box; my heart flurried. "Brax, it's… gorgeous."

"You like it?" His voice heightened to boyish delight as he plucked the bracelet from its cage of velvet.

"I don't like it. I love it." I placed the box on my lap, holding out a wrist. I couldn't tear my eyes off the dainty silver jewellery. It symbolized us: gentle love hearts entwined with silver strands, the occasional glint of diamonds at the centre of each heart.

Brax's fingertips grazed the underside of my wrist, securing the clasp. I shivered, sucking in a shaky breath.

"Tess ... I—"

Tension blossomed between us, like a fast unfurling flower, and I ached. Ached for him. Ached for connection. Ached for his body inside mine. Something hot seared in our gaze, and Brax clenched his jaw.

He dropped his eyes, breaking the spell.

Pretending nothing had happened, I rested my head on his shoulder, inspecting my new bracelet. "I'll never take it off."

He sighed, snuggling closer, kissing the top of my head. "I don't want you to. It's yours forever. Just like me."

I inhaled sharply, breathing in his soft apple scent from our shared body wash. Would he ever stop making me hurt and heal at the same time?

"Forever," I whispered and closed my eyes.

The next time I awoke, tyres bounced on the runway. In a foggy haze, we disembarked. The airport was manic, even at one in the morning, and we let the sea of passengers guide us through immigration and processing.

By the time we headed outside to the awaiting taxis, my scratchy eyes felt like a cat had mistaken them for cat-nip, and my mind was cotton wool.

I let Brax lead the way, following obediently while he searched for our driver to the hotel.

"Stay here. I'm going to ask at the info desk. The hotel should've arranged a shuttle for us."

He parked the suitcases by the curb, and I took his laptop

satchel, blocking it with my feet. I plonked on top of one of the cases. "No problem. I'll guard the bags."

He caressed my cheek. "I'll be right back."

I smiled, capturing his hand as he pulled away. "I'll miss you till then."

With a grin, he turned and headed the way we'd come. I admired his fine butt in his baggy jeans. Just once, I'd love to see him in a nice suit, or at least some fitted trousers. No matter how many compliments I rained on him, Brax acted forever self-conscious. Silly man. He didn't see the way other women looked at him, but I did. My claws unsheathed every time.

Ten minutes passed while I sat in the little oasis our bags created, and my nervousness steadily grew. Mexico was loud, boisterous, and the air hung heavy and wet with humidity. We were used to the heat in Australia, but that was dry heat. The moisture saturated my clothes, turning my curly hair limp.

"Excuse me, *señorita.*"

I twisted on the case, glancing behind me. A good-looking Mexican man took off a baseball cap, bowing slightly. His black eyes assessed, making me squirm on the inside.

"Yes?" I asked, standing upright, looking for Brax out the corner of my eye. Where the hell was he?

"I wondered if you were here on your own? Do you need a lift somewhere? I have a taxi. I can take you wherever you need to go."

A wide smile showed stained teeth and skin crinkled around his eyes in a friendly way. My instincts didn't flare into panic mode; I relaxed a little. "No, thanks. I'm here with my boyfri—"

"Tess?" Brax appeared like an apparition, glaring at the man. "Can I help you?"

The man backed up, putting his baseball cap on. "Not at all, *señor.* Just wanting to make sure such a pretty girl stays safe. This city is not good for women left alone."

Brax puffed his chest, dragging me toward him. My eyes widened as his arm clenched around my shoulders. "She's safe. Thanks for your concern." He turned to me, dismissing the man entirely. "I've found the shuttle. You ready to go?"

I nodded, looking to where the man had been, but he'd disappeared—swallowed by the heaving crowd. I bit my lip; just how safe *was* this country? I'd heard the horror stories, as well as the great regales. Either way, I wouldn't be letting Brax out of my sight again. I wasn't stupid enough to think nothing could harm me.

Dragging our suitcases, we made it to the shuttle bus, and spent the next forty-five minutes bouncing and swerving on Mexican roads. The traffic was psychotic—an accident begging to happen—and my heart remained in my throat most of the way. Traffic lights meant nothing, and scooters were given right of way. Pedestrians and cyclists threaded like a massive, living organism at two in the morning. If it was this crazy now, what the hell was it like during normal hours?

It seemed life never slept here. Every bar we passed, pumping with Salsa dancers and spicy tunes, dispelled my sleepiness. I wanted to dance, to rub against Brax, to drink yummy cocktails, and enjoy ourselves.

I immediately loved Mexico.

I'd gone my whole life thinking I was timid, brow-beaten, and unwanted by my family, only to find I was a lust-filled dancer with so many dark desires. This trip would allow me to inspect who I truly was, to be honest, and find the real me. To stop being Tess, the girl who hadn't stood up for anything in her life—the girl who morphed into what others wanted— and evolve. *I'll find the true Tess.* My stomach twisted. What if the real me wasn't worthy of Brax?

We pulled up to a sweeping resort with huge carvings of sombreros and tropical fruit. A fountain jetted water so high it almost touched the three storey ceiling.

A bellhop took our luggage and Brax checked us in. I

wandered in bliss and wonderment. The resort was a living jungle: palm trees, ferns, and exoticness in every corner.

I thrummed with anticipation. I didn't care we'd been awake for twenty-four hours. I wanted to explore and walk along the beach I heard in the distance. The soft slap of waves on sand enticed skinny-dipping and making love under the moonlight.

Arms banded around my waist, pulling me backward. I gasped, landing against hard muscle and wrinkled clothing. Brax kissed my collarbone; I shuddered. "Ready for bed, hun?"

Oh, yes, I was definitely ready for bed. More than ready.

I nodded breathlessly.

Brax swivelled me in his arms, taking my luggage at the same time. A bellhop stood behind, smiling indulgently. "Please, go ahead. I'll bring your bags."

We entered the lift, and the bellhop squeezed in, too. The mirrored interior reflected in every direction. My hair was a tangled bird's nest, my sheer blouse crumpled and ready for a wash, and my grey-blue eyes sparkled with lust and love.

I hoped Brax saw what twinkled in my soul. How much I cared for him.

His blue eyes were warm and content as we disembarked the lift, making our way to our room. The corridor was a wide balcony, open-air with huge potted ferns and little cosy seats arranged for privacy.

"This one, if you please, sir," the bellhop said, pointing to a door as we walked.

Brax grinned and inserted the key card. Once he placed the card in the little holder by the door, soft light illuminated. I moved forward in a trance.

The room was decorated in a perfect Mexican décor of carved wood and bright paintings. The bedspread was a fiesta of colours and textures. Hand woven rugs in purples, reds, and yellows littered the hardwood floor.

I squealed in childish amazement and dashed to the balcony. The gloom of darkness whispered magically as I listened to the waves hissing on the shore.

Heaven. *I'm in heaven.*

Brax tipped the bellhop and closed the door. I twisted to face him; my breathing accelerated. We were finally alone after a crazy long journey.

My new bracelet tinkled, overflowing my heart with joy. I stepped toward him. Brax held out his arms, looking tired but happy.

Fitting me into his embrace perfectly, he rested his chin on my head. "Sorry I couldn't afford five stars, Tessie."

My eyes widened. We were in the middle of a dream and he worried he couldn't give me more. Couldn't he see this was perfect?

I didn't respond. Instead, I captured his face in my hands. He froze, staring deep into my eyes. I sent messages of hunger and hot swirling need. I wanted to crawl inside his soul and light a fire to match the flames licking me.

I kissed him.

Brax tilted his head, allowing my tongue to slink between his lips, but he didn't gather me closer. *Come on. Please, need me, too.*

I kissed harder, pressing against him with an urgency growing out of control. I was too hot. I needed him too much, for far too long. I should've spoken sooner—told him how badly I needed to be possessed. For months, I'd felt cast adrift, like he was no longer my anchor. I needed him to remind me I belonged to him, just like he belonged to me.

Brax chuckled beneath my kisses, twisting his lips. "What's got into you, Tess? You can't keep your hands off me."

My stomach twisted; I blushed. "Is it so bad I want you? Need you? We're in a new country. Can we celebrate our first night?" My eyes flew to the bed and back to his gaze. "We could have a shower together, then I can show you my present."

My present consisted of dressing in fishnet tights, garter belt, and the ridiculously expensive push-up bra I'd bought. I'd planned it all. I'd strut my stuff, and Brax would gawk, making me feel like a goddess. I'd massage him with strawberry body oil, until he couldn't stand it any longer and secured my wrists with my knickers. He'd take me from behind, our bodies slip sliding intoxicatingly, arousing me beyond belief. I'd even been to the beauticians and had some rather painful waxing in my nether regions especially for the occasion.

I trembled at the thought of Brax's gaze darkening, his body becoming feral and possessive.

He pecked my lips, groaning, "I'm super tired. Can we rain check till the morning?"

Disappointment flooded my bloodstream, dousing my need like ice water. Even though it killed me and tears tickled, I dropped my arms, releasing Brax from my embrace. "That's okay. I understand."

He sighed. "Okay, okay. If you need me so badly, I'm game." His voice was resigned, but he smiled tiredly.

Are we really this stale?

Passion fizzled to fear. I couldn't show him. Not now. Not when he seemed happy with vanilla and missionary every other month. I didn't want him thinking I was a sexual deviant, or ruin our holiday before it'd even begun.

I made up my mind not to spill my secrets. It was a mistake to think I could. "No, you're right. It's late. We should go to sleep," I muttered.

Moving away, I didn't get far before Brax captured my elbow. Groaning, he ran a hand through his brown hair. "Why did you do that?"

I blinked. "Do what?"

"Lie. You never lie."

Shame shimmered over my skin; I looked at the bright rug on the floor. "I'm sorry, Brax. I just—I don't want to show you anymore."

He straightened, sucking in a breath. "Why? What's changed?"

Useless tears invaded my eyes. *Stop tearing up!* It wasn't bad—just different. But I no longer wanted different. I wanted to please Brax. I hated being selfish. *I'm a horrible person.*

He ducked, looking into my watery gaze. "Hey, Tess. What is it? Tell me." He pulled me to the bed and into his lap. I huddled into his chest.

What if I told him and he hated me? He'd pull away and leave me alone, just like my parents. I'd be another *mistake.*

I didn't answer, letting him rock me, trying to untangle my jumbled thoughts.

Brax murmured, "Remember how we met? What you said to me?"

Of course, I remembered. He'd made me bleed. Our first encounter didn't exactly conform to first meeting etiquette. I giggled quietly. "I called you an arse."

He laughed. "Not that." Stroking my back, he dived into past memories. "I was walking Blizzard on the beach and threw a stick for him. Out of nowhere, this girl careened like a fallen angel, completely out of control I might add, on a kite board. She bounced along the surf, splashing and spluttering, before a huge gust of wind catapulted her out of the water and right into the face of my husky."

A phantom injury twinged at the memory. I'd been a flipping idiot to think I could kite board. It had been a 'get outside my comfort zone' attempt. It failed. Rather drastically.

Brax continued, "I couldn't believe it when your kite took off down the beach, dragging you and my dog with it. I managed to pounce on you, but it took a good half an hour to untangle you from Blizzard with all those strings and harnesses." His gaze darkened. "I was so worried when I finally got you free. You were bleeding pretty bad from your shoulder and had a black eye. My poor dog had a sore paw and a broken stick." He ran a finger along my cheekbone.

The broken stick had caused the bleeding shoulder. Freakin' stick.

"I asked if you wanted to go to the hospital, and you asked if it was really that bad. I didn't want you to freak out, so I lied. I said it was just a scratch, when in reality it was a gaping hole, gushing with blood and bits of bark sticking out everywhere. I lied 'cause I didn't know what to say."

I flinched. It had been pretty bad. Earned me eight stitches, but Brax never left my side.

"I lied and you said—"

"Never lie. The truth hurts less than fibs and fakers." I remembered that day as if it happened two hours ago. I'd been hurt, because it was my eighteenth birthday and my parents forgot.

"The truth hurts less than fibs and fakers," Brax repeated. "That's always stayed with me because it's so honest and raw. It told me so much about you and made me fall in love. So many people lied to me about my parent's death. Glossing over the darkness, and hiding the gnarly truth."

His arms latched tighter, pressing me hard against him. "Not having the chance to say goodbye will haunt me forever. And not knowing the truth about why they crashed eats at my soul."

His eyes burned into mine. "So, Tess. Don't lie to me. The truth is the only path for us."

I nodded; he was right. I should never have brought it up if I didn't have the guts to follow through.

"Let me go. I'll show you." *Please, please like it. Like*

me.

He reached for my hand, squeezing my fingers. "I'd like to see whatever you want to show me."

I bit my lip. His eyes changed from crisp blue to smouldering cerulean. Hot happiness scorched me, and I kissed him. "You have no idea what this means to me."

He ducked his head, looking through half-lidded eyes. "I think I do." Helping me off his lap, he tapped my butt. "Go. Be quick, so I don't fall asleep."

My new confidence deflated. *Can I really ask him to change?*

Brax groaned. "Tess, you're over thinking it." He pulled me back, wedging me between his spread thighs. "I'm never letting you go. So whatever it is, don't be afraid." He dropped his hand, capturing the silver bracelet. "I hope you know this isn't just a bracelet to me." His fingers stroked the underside of my arm; I shivered. "It's a promise of more. When I can afford what you deserve, I'll make you mine."

I leaned in and hugged him tight. "I'm already yours."

His breath turned shallow and he leaned up to kiss me. It started innocent, sweet, but slowly, he tilted his head, kissing deeper. His hand dropped to my waist, closing the remaining distance. His tongue licked mine in gentle invitation.

I clenched my hands on his shoulders as I warmed, shedding fear and uncertainty. I moaned as he nibbled my bottom lip, reaching behind my neck to make me bend into his kiss.

Everything clenched, revved, and grew slick with need. *Do not attack him. Do not attack him.*

Brax stopped kissing me, and our breathing rasped. "Show me."

He pushed me away gently, and I went to my suitcase. Unzipping the side pocket where I'd tucked the vibrator, I took the plastic bag with my new lingerie, and hid them behind my back. Sucking in a deep breath, I said, "I'll be right back."

Brax nodded. "I'll be right here.

I retreated into the bathroom and flicked the lock. Placing the bag in the sink, I stared at my reflection. After a long flight, I was a mess, but I wanted to get it over with. I couldn't stop feeling like it was a huge mistake.

You can do this. Just be honest. Everything else…we can work through it. It could turn out to be a good thing, the next step in our relationship. It might make us stronger.

I shed my clothes and stepped into the lacy purple G-string and matching push-up bra. The bra may have been über expensive, but it made my boobs look a million dollars, turning my C's to generous D's that spilled over the top.

I wanted to feel sexy and hot, but I really felt like a fraud. My snowy skin looked virginal against the smutty underwear—*God, I look like a wannabe idiot dressed in her mum's lingerie.*

My fingers trembled as I unrolled the fishnets up my leg, and snapped the garter belt clips to keep them in place. *Even more ridiculous.*

I sighed, scowling at my reflection. I wanted sexy and crude and dirty—what I got was insecurity and regret.

Dammit, this wasn't how I wanted to feel. New lingerie promised empowerment and sauciness. All I wanted to do was put my flannelette pyjamas on and forget the whole fiasco.

I met my eyes in the mirror. *Just get it over with.*

Ruffling my hair, I sucked in my belly and stepped out of the bathroom.

Brax was sprawled on the bed. He sat up on his elbows the moment I came into the room. His jaw dropped open, gaze raking over me. Desire exploded in his eyes, sparking something deep inside, overriding the fear of rejection.

Feminine power replaced self-consciousness.

Brax scooted higher, sitting on the edge of the bed.

He shifted, adjusting his shorts. "Wow—"

Heat flashed with radioactive intensity, and I rushed ahead before he could say anything else, before my confidence could falter. I pulled the vibrator from behind my back. The little rabbit sticking out from the purple, glittery phallus made my cheeks flame. Oh, God, *why* was I doing this?

Brax swallowed, his eyes locking onto my most personal possession.

"I want us to be more adventurous," I mumbled, hating my tongue twisting into knots. "I love you, and I love our sex life, but I just thought—well, I'd like to see—if, um...."

Brax slid off the bed, coming toward me slowly. He ripped his t-shirt off at the same time, leaving me to gape like a love-struck moron.

His face was unreadable as he murmured, "You want more?"

More. Such a dangerous word.

I shook my head. "Not more. Different."

Pain flashed in his eyes before disappearing just as quickly.

"Not all the time. Only, sometimes..."

His hand shook as he reached for the vibrator. "You use this?" His finger hovered over the sliding power button. I couldn't swallow—mortification closed my throat.

Sure, Tess, showing him your vibrator will be sexy and fun. I wanted to slap myself, but stood completely still, horrified by what he might say. I'd flayed myself open, bared my desires, only to risk ruining Brax's feelings for me.

I wanted to yell—I'm joking! This isn't the real me. But my lips glued shut; I couldn't tear my eyes away from the vibrator in his grip.

Stupid. So stupid.

Brax slid the power switch upward and a battery powered whir filled the room. I looked away as he pressed the power higher. The phallus sprung to attention, screaming all my secrets.

"Different?" His voice echoed with loss and confusion as he stared at the vibrator. No doubt visualizing me writhing in abandon, using an object to get off instead of him. How could I explain not being intimate for weeks on end was torture? My heart shattered. This was no longer about my needs. It was about his. I'd made him doubt, made him think he wasn't good enough. Shit.

I grabbed the vibrator, hating it in that moment. I turned the power off, ripped out the batteries, and threw it all in the bin. "Forget it, Brax. It was a stupid idea. I just want you, okay? Please, don't hate me." *I'm the biggest bitch in history.*

He shook himself, hands falling to his sides. His gaze clouded as he stared at the floor. I knew that look. It was the same look when he awoke from a nightmare— terrified of waking up alone. "Tess, you have me. But if I'm not enough—"

"No!" I charged into his arms, tugging him to the bed. "You're more than enough. I'm so sorry. Forget it. All of it. Please?" Now, I was the one petrified of being alone. If he didn't think I wanted him, he'd push me away.

Panic made me fumble, and I lay down, pulling him on top. "You're enough. More than enough. Brax, please—" Tears burned my eyes, chest straining with emotion.

His eyes dropped to my breasts, biting his lip. Ever so slowly, he caressed the soft mound of flesh. "It's killing me to think I'm not giving you what you need." His finger dipped lower, finding my nipple inside the bra.

My breath hitched, even though so many emotions rioted within me, my body blazed for his. I needed to connect, to put this mess behind us.

"You're stunning. I always knew you were out of my

league, and seeing you in this underwear makes me realize how sexual you are." His voice dropped with husky undertones as he continued to touch me. "I'm not sure I can keep up with you. I love you, Tess. I love being with you, but I don't need to fuck you to be a man. I need you as a friend, as my support. Do you understand?"

His hand dropped from my breast, skirting my stomach, dragging me into a suffocating embrace. I let him squeeze the life out of me—I needed it. I needed him to convince me he wasn't leaving, that I didn't just ruin our relationship.

"All I need is you. Honestly, none of that matters. I'm content, so happy, when I'm with you," I whispered.

My chest ached so badly. Could he hear the words we'd used? I was content and he used me as support. No mention of passion or unbridled lust.

It doesn't matter. Stop being so foolish. That's for movies, this is real life.

Brax pulled away, eyes turbulent with embarrassment and need. I reached up, pressing my lips against his. He kissed me back like I always wanted him to—with ferocity, violence bordering on pain.

I moaned, wrapping my hands in his hair, tugging closer. That's what I needed—passion laced with pain.

He broke the kiss, breathing hard. "So, all of this? Can we pretend it never happened?"

Relief ballooned in my chest. Gone was the disappointment that I would never be possessed or owned by Brax in bed. I hadn't ruined us. I couldn't be more thankful. "Already forgotten."

He exhaled in a huge gust, smiling crookedly. Kissing the tip of my nose, he said, "Thank you for loving me enough to take what I can give."

My entire body vibrated with remorse. I couldn't reply.

Brax reached behind and undid my bra. He drew it off my breasts slowly, dipping his head to suck my nipple. Heat exploded in my core.

Brax still loved me. That's all that mattered. Nothing else. Not kinky sex, or spicing up the bedroom. I was a very lucky girl. *I am so lucky. Lucky.*

I bit Brax's collarbone and he groaned. He shifted so his rapidly hardening erection pressed into my belly.

Trembling, I eased his jeans down his hips. He arched upright, helping me get them off. Once he sprung free, he ripped off the fifty dollar knickers I'd worn for all of ten seconds, and threw them to the floor.

Brax settled between my thighs, his gaze locking with mine. I bit my lip as he pressed inside. I wasn't as wet as I should've been and the invasion was pleasure as well as pain.

His eyes snapped closed as he settled deep inside. His erection, stretching and filling, sent waves of safety rather than mind-shattering passion.

We rocked together, and he peppered me in delicate kisses, sweet affection. I grew slick around him, warming, building.

My nipples ached for attention, and I wished he'd bite me just a little, maybe then I might be able to climax.

"Tess—" he breathed in my ear, picking up speed. His hips pressed harder and I fought the urge to touch myself, to help reach an orgasm.

With another thrust, Brax moaned, his back shuddering as his butt clenched hard. He came inside, wave after wave of ecstasy for him and simple acceptance for me. I stroked his chest, so happy he was able to find release after everything I put him through.

He collapsed on top, sandwiching me between his bulk and the mattress.

I stared at the ceiling, battling so many thoughts, not all of them making sense. Brax huffed, snuggling his face into my breasts.

Within moments, he was fast asleep, leaving me lonely and confused.

Chapter Three

Robin

"Sign here, please."

The concierge handed us the compulsory waivers. I gulped, reading the fine print. If we injured, maimed, or killed ourselves while using the hotel provided scooters, the hotel would not be held accountable. If it was such a good idea to rent these things, why the huge disclaimer?

I glanced at Brax. "You sure you want to explore Cancun on a two-wheeled death machine?"

Brax bit the top of the pen, frowning at the hire contract. He flashed me a grin. No residue of fear or sadness from yesterday lingered in his face. Thank God.

"You promised this morning. You agreed today was all about what I wanted to do, and tomorrow is all about you."

I smiled. "Fine. But, tomorrow, you are so going to put up with getting a massage with me. No moaning."

He drew a cross over his heart and signed the paperwork with a flourish. He laughed, excitement glowing in his blue gaze. "Do you want your own bike, or dinky on the back of mine?"

No way in hell did I trust myself to weave in crazy, unchoreographed traffic in a foreign country. "I'll go on the back of yours. You do know what you're doing, right?"

Images came to mind of us being impaled on the bike rack on the front of a bus, or run over by a truck carrying piñatas. I shuddered.

Brax scoffed. "I've driven a Harley. How hard can a moped be?"

Pretty damn hard, especially with maniacs driving circles around us.

I scowled playfully. "You drove the Harley for all of ten minutes."

Bill, a building colleague, encouraged Brax to join the local motorcycle group. Brax tried, and promptly said no, which I was super happy about, as driving without doors and a roof freaked me out.

Brax rolled his eyes, tapping the signature bit of my contract. Sticking my tongue out, I signed.

The concierge beamed and walked around the desk. We were in the lobby and more guests had arrived, a wave of shuffling bags and smiles. The soft murmur of excitement weaved around us, layered with holiday vibes.

"Follow me, please." The concierge, in his crisp white shirt and bright orange waistcoat, led the way.

Maybe it wasn't such a bad idea. Hell, we might even get off the beaten tourist track and find something local and new.

I looped my arm through Brax's, doubly glad I'd put on leggings and my large cream t-shirt today. The outfit offered the best protection of all the clothes I packed. I hoped the frail fabrics would protect me a little if we happened to topple.

We followed the concierge out of the hotel and into the basement car park. He unlocked a canary yellow scooter and retrieved two helmets. "Please make sure you keep these with you at all times. It's a one hundred US dollar fine if you lose them."

Brax nodded, fastening mine with dexterous fingers. His touch sent my heart thrumming. Giving me a soft smile, he fastened his own helmet and straddled the bike.

I stood there, feeling like a ridiculous, overripe pineapple. The helmet weighed a ton.

The concierge handed me an A4 map, and drew a red oval, which I assumed was the hotel.

"This is where you are." His minty breath wafted over me as he leaned closer, stabbing the map. "If you get lost, ask a policeman for directions. They are all over the city. And don't separate. It's best to stay together."

My pulse thudded a little. Policemen lurked thick in this city. Not only lurked, but loitered on street corners with weapons and guns. Were the Mexican citizens so ruthless and dangerous?

Don't answer that. Especially when we were about to explore on a contraption offering no safety whatsoever.

Brax patted the seat behind him; I smiled weakly. Throwing my leg over, I rested my feet on the little stirrups and wrapped my arms around his torso like a python.

Chuckling, he turned on the ignition and tested the throttle. "You won't fall off with the death grip you have, hun."

That was the plan. I kissed his neck, loving his shiver. "I trust you." I tried to convince myself, as much as Brax.

The concierge smiled and left us to it. Brax eased off the clutch and we shot forward. My stomach failed to catch up, but after kangaroo hopping a few times, Brax wrangled the bike into submission.

"Ready?" he said over a shoulder.

Lying, I spoke into his ear, "Yep."

We travelled out of the gloomy parking garage and into the blazing mid-morning sunshine. Even with dirty streets, Cancun reminded me of a vibrant party.

Brax put his feet down, stabilizing the bike as we stopped on the edge of the busy road. His heart thumped under my arms, concentration making his shoulders tight.

We watched as speedsters, crazy pedestrians, and vehicles painted in more colours than the rainbow shot past. For the hundredth time, I wondered just how crash hot this idea was.

"Which way, Tessie? Left or right?"

I swivelled my head, wrinkling my nose. No break came in the traffic from either direction. North, south, east, west—it didn't matter when everything looked as death-filled and foreign as the other.

Impulsively, I said, "Right." *Please, let us return to the hotel in one piece!*

Brax nodded, scratching his chin where the strap of the helmet strangled him. He rolled forward, his flip-flopped feet slapping on hot pavement. The bike wobbled while we waited a good ten minutes for courage to join the swarming mass of craziness.

I wanted to suggest flagging and head to the pool—

"Hold on!" Brax sucked in his abs and twisted the accelerator. The bike whined and took off with a skid.

My heart lurched into my throat as we shot forward, narrowly dodging a cyclist with a mountain of merchandise on the back and zipped in front of a smog-spewing bus.

My mouth dried in panic and my arms squeezed Brax so tight, his ribcage bruised my biceps. Oh, my God! I wanted off. *This isn't my idea of fun.*

Brax laughed as we straightened and drove with the mass. His happiness wrapped around us like a protective bubble, and I tried to stop hyperventilating.

My heart softened. He was enjoying this, and I wouldn't ruin it. I trusted him to keep me safe.

An hour later, a waterfall of sweat ran under my t-shirt. The bright sun had landed me with a headache, and my brain felt cooked in the helmet. More than once, I'd tried to pull away from Brax's back, but we were both so hot and sticky, it was disgusting.

We'd relaxed enough to enjoy driving through the labyrinths of streets, exploring side alleys, skirting around markets and peddlers, but now my ass ached, and my thighs had had enough of the vibrations of the scooter.

I needed a drink and somewhere cool—very, very cool.

Almost as if he heard my thoughts, Brax slowed to a stop outside a tiny, decrepit restaurant on the outskirts of the markets we'd driven around.

It looked anything but sanitary, with a sad donkey piñata hanging limp in the sun. The ripped plastic tablecloths didn't encourage one to linger, and the sign was so blackened with filth, I couldn't read the name.

"Ugh—" I exploded into a cough as a cloud of exhaust billowed from a rusty car. *Very hygienic.*

Brax stroked my hands, still clutched around his middle. "You okay?"

I nodded, sucking in a harsh breath. "Yep. I was going to say, surely we can find something better than this dive?"

Brax clambered off the bike, helping me to do the same. My legs were the consistency of rubber. I'd ridden a horse in my childhood and even spread-eagled on a fat animal was better than the scooter. Going over bumps and potholes wasn't good for my lady parts.

"I'm dying of thirst." Pursing his lips, he took in the dank appearance. "We'll just grab a quick drink and leave." Brax unclipped his helmet and tied it to the handlebars. I did the same, almost puddling to the ground in relief to remove the hotbox from my lank hair.

Brax chuckled. "Bad hair day, huh?"

I reached up, running a hand through his sweaty locks. He leaned into my touch, love sparking in his eyes.

I giggled. "A helmet on a hot day doesn't exactly equate to sexy hair."

He pushed his big fingers into my own tangled strands. "I think you look sexy no matter what." Running his touch down my cheek, he kept going, all the way to my hand.

Threading his fingers with mine, he leaned in, kissing me gently. "Hopefully, this place has cold drinks and ice."

My skin was on fire and the thought of ice made my mouth water, but I shook my head. "Not allowed ice, remember? Only bottled water. Our Aussie bellies can't handle the local H2O."

He sighed. "Good point. Alright, I'll just have a beer."

"If you think you're drinking and driving in this mess they call traffic, you have another thought coming, mister." I laughed as we entered the gloom of the little café—if it could be called that—more like a falling down cave. The walls were peeling and tacky posters hung sticky-taped in random places, hiding pockmarking in the plaster. I frowned… they looked just like— *Hell, are they bullet holes?*

Trepidation crawled like icy spiders in my blood. I squeezed Brax's hand as intuition sat up, ringing a loud warning gong. I was a firm believer in listening to my gut—it saved me more than once. "Brax?"

A woman with tobacco stained teeth grinned a holey smile as she appeared. "Well, well, nice to see some customers on such a hot day." Her accented voice rasped across my skin like sandpaper. "What can I get you?"

My heart wouldn't stay still. I wanted to say something. I wanted to leave. But Brax grinned. "Two Cokes, please."

The woman peered at me, her gaze dark as midnight. "No food?"

I stiffened, hating how jittery I was, how much I wanted to run. Before Brax could decide he was hungry, as well as thirsty, I said, "Just drinks. And quickly, we're supposed to be somewhere, we're running late." My snappy tone caused Brax to quirk an eyebrow.

The lady grimaced, shuffling away.

Brax tugged me to a table, and we sat directly under a ceiling fan stirring the hot, stagnant air. Sweat grew tacky on my skin, cooling to a chill. I grabbed a napkin to wipe my face.

"What's gotten into you?" Brax asked, wiping the back of his neck with his hand.

I looked behind, trying to figure out why my spidey senses wigged out of control, but nothing seemed wrong. It was just a shabby eatery. No more. Maybe I was being stupid....

"Nothing. Sorry. I really want to go back to the hotel for a swim, that's all." I flashed a smile.

He grinned, his shiny face pink from the drive. "We'll go as soon as we're done." Laughing, he added, "We must look like such gringos. No wonder the waitress gave us a weird look."

My gut clenched. Somehow, I knew that wasn't the reason. She'd looked at me almost...hungrily.

A scuffle sounded behind; I twisted in the chair to look. Toward the back of the restaurant, near the cash register, a man appeared. His voice was low, angry, as he shook the waitress, fingers digging into her upper arm.

My stomach flipped, kicking out trepidation and blowing it into full-fledged fright. I couldn't stay.

"Brax, I'm not comfortable. Can we can get the Cokes to go?"

He slouched in the rickety chair. "I don't think I can drink and navigate, hun. Just give me ten minutes, okay? Then we'll go." He looked sun-whipped and parched.

I nodded sharply, biting my tongue. I didn't want to seem

like a drama queen, but damn, my flesh rippled with panic. I wanted to be gone. Far, far away, back to the safety of the resort.

My legs jiggled under the table, anxiety pinging in my limbs.

Another man entered the café, wearing a black leather jacket and jeans. His greasy skin shone with sweat, and he had a chunk missing from the top of his ear. Long, stringy hair hung over a gaunt face. His eyes fell on mine; I froze.

It was like looking into a predator's gaze: empty, hungry, black, and evil. It sucked my soul, amping my fear to a full forest fire.

"Brax—"

"Here you go." The gap-tooth waitress deposited dewy, icy cans of Coke in front of us along with pink straws. I broke eye contact with Mr. Leather Jacket, swallowing hard. *Keep it together. Brax is here. Brax will protect you.*

Brax cracked a can open and swigged, groaning. "Crap, I was thirsty." He hadn't noticed my fear, focused entirely on rehydrating.

On autopilot, I opened mine and sipped. The bubbles added to the froth of terror in my stomach. Why was I reacting like this? *Calm down, Tess.* It was a stupid, white girl reaction to being in a dive of a place that was perfectly normal in this over-populated city.

Brax guzzled his drink and stood. "I just gotta take a leak. I'll be right back."

My fear jettisoned into a geyser of panic. "No! I mean, do you have to go here? We can find a McDonald's or some local garage." I twisted my fingers, hidden in my lap. "I doubt the facilities will be clean."

He laughed. "This isn't convenience central. I don't know if we'll be able to find anywhere else, and it will be another hour before we're back at the hotel. I'll just be a tick."

I clutched my Coke until my fingers turned white, trying to stem my panic, and stop being so clingy. I nodded.

Brax blew me a kiss, striding toward the back of the café. His green t-shirt was dark with sweat, showing every curve of muscle. Muscle that could protect me, muscle that was walking away. With every step he took, my heart died a little more. I had no explanation for my behaviour, but some pessimistic part throbbed with grief.

Turn around. Come back.

Brax didn't do either as he disappeared through a door marked *Baño.*

My blood rocketed with adrenaline and my eyes darted around the café, looking for danger. Instincts told me I was in peril. I just didn't know from what.

No one was around. Even the guy in his leather jacket had disappeared.

See, Tess. Nothing to be afraid of.

Something fluffy twined around my legs making me jump so high I knocked my can of Coke over. Shoving my chair back, I looked beneath the table.

A mangy orange cat blinked, meowing. Holy shit, I had to calm down. My heart would combust at the rate it hammered. Every part of me buzzed on high alert.

"Stop staring, kitty." I kept my legs away from the feline and the sticky puddle of Coke.

A minute passed agonisingly slowly; my eyes refused to look anywhere but at the door where Brax disappeared. How long did it take for him to do his business? *Surely,* he should be done by now.

I fiddled with my bracelet. The silver hearts indented my fingers as I pressed hard, using them as rosary beads, summoning my boyfriend to return. My mouth grew dry and chalky, palms slick with nerves.

Come on, Brax. Should I go and wait by the bike? Anything would be better than sitting there terrified. Yes, waiting by the bike was a good idea—in public, in the sunshine.

I stood and turned to leave. My heart flopped into my toes.

Three men guarded the exit. Arms crossed, lips stretched against dirty, rotten teeth. Leather Jacket Man stood in the middle. Our eyes locked and the same evil energy assaulted me, casting oozing black shadows. Unable to look away, my very existence stuttered under the weight of blackness. My instincts had been right.

I was in deep shit.

"Brax!" I screeched, taking off for the door. I didn't care if I over-reacted or if they were there for a casual drink. My instincts screamed, hollered, banged on my ribs to react.

Run!

Flip-flops slapped against linoleum as I bolted.

The men scrambled into action, knocking over a table in the rush to chase me. *No. No. Please, no.*

I hyperventilated as I sprinted through the door, and screamed as a large hand fisted my hair, yanking backward into a stinking hot torso.

"Brax!" I twisted and hissed, holding onto my scalp. Ignoring the burn of torn hair, I turned into something rabid. I bit the man's arm banded across my chest.

He swore in Spanish, dropping me. I fell to my knees, but was running a second later. Nothing mattered but getting to Brax.

"Brax!" I shot to the men's room, only to careen into the solid body of a fourth man. Blood covered his knuckles as he slapped a hand over my mouth, slamming me against the wall. The stench of his palm made me dry heave; I thrashed in his grip.

He grunted, keeping me pinned.

My life shrivelled in hopelessness as I looked over his shoulder. Brax lay sprawled on the dirty bathroom floor, face covered in blood. An arm hung awkwardly and eyes closed. *"No!"*

Rage, passion and horror exploded. I chomped down on the man's palm, tasting rust from breaking flesh.

"Puta!" he cursed as I wriggled, trying to jerk my knee between his legs.

"Brax! Wake up!" I kicked free, only to be captured by Leather Jacket. He hissed something in my ear I didn't understand. His awful fingers squeezed a breast, and dragged me away from Brax.

"No! Let me *go!*" I screamed, too angry and focused on survival to cry. "Fucking bastard, leave me the *fuck* alone!"

Another rancid hand clamped over my mouth and nose, cutting off oxygen. Lungs bucked, kicking in my chest.

I slammed my hip back, connecting with the soft meat between my captor's legs. Leather Jacket howled and shoved me away, hunched over his injured cock.

Run, Tess. Run.

I whimpered, caught in indecision. I wanted to check on Brax but I had to get away. Find help, then rescue him. But no matter how hard I fought, there were always more men. It was like fighting quick sand—a battle I couldn't win.

"Brax! God's sake I need y—"

Leather Jacket took two steps and sucker-punched me in the jaw.

Fireworks exploded behind my eyes, and I fell. Falling, falling, heavy and useless. The floor welcomed with a teeth-rattling embrace. Colours danced in front of my eyes as sickness tried to claim me.

Someone pressed into my lower back, wrenching my arms behind me, and wrapped something coarse and tight around my wrists.

He jerked me upright. The world swam with vertigo, leaving me upside down, back to front.

Leather Jacket's evil eyes glinted with pleasure as he smothered me with a black hood.

Chapter Four

Dove

My sense of smell returned first.

Touch, taste, sound, sight, all remained dormant. But smell. How could I ignore the *reek*?

Stale sweat and the ammonia of piss. Musk, body odour, and garbage.

My stomach flopped, turning me into a pretzel of horror.

Brax!

Oh, God, Brax. Was he okay? Was he dead? All that blood. My lungs went on strike. Brax was back there—wherever there was, alone and in pain. Would I ever see him again? Thoughts rammed like dodgems in my skull. My head pounded with a nasty headache.

Fear, rank and cloying, crawled up my throat. That bastard had been so eager to hit me, as if he lived to be violent. I had no hope against men like that. I knew it was weak, but I wished they'd killed me rather than take me. Who knew what brutality existed in my future.

Another whiff of ammonia; I gagged behind my hood, hoping I didn't throw up and drown in vomit. I panted, forcing the urge away.

Just remain calm. I'd relied on myself all my life. If I got into trouble, my parents were too busy with my brother to offer a shoulder to cry on. I turned to myself in happiness and in terror. I would get out of this. No one was going to take my freedom.

I slid to the side suddenly, gravity extracting a toll as we careened around a corner. Wits came back, battling the foggy pain. I must be in a vehicle.

My sense of hearing returned.

A whimper sounded. I jerked, trying to move away, only for the whimper to grow into a wail. The plea was undoubtedly feminine.

A man cursed, followed by a thud and a cry.

How many victims were in here? I didn't want to die. A tragic statistic of another tourist kidnapped in Mexico. Brax and I were so stupid, travelling with the illusion of being untouchable.

More whimpers and gruff commands as the engine hummed and tyres squealed, gripping the road, taking corners too fast.

I wasn't alone. There were others. Others taken. Stolen. Abducted.

I shouldn't have taken comfort in that, but I did. Just the knowledge I might have allies gave me a burst of hope.

My sense of taste returned.

Immediately, the horrible stench coated my tongue, along with the sweet residue of Coke and sharp tang of terror.

The Coke reminded me of Brax, and I plummeted into heartache. Even if I did manage to escape, how would I ever find Brax? I had no clue where the café was, or how we got there. Would the hotel come looking when we didn't return with the scooter?

My throat latched closed, tormented by images of Brax dying on the lonely wasteland of a men's bathroom floor. Surely, they wouldn't let him die. Someone would take him to hospital.

They took me. *They took me.*

Oh, God. The realization hit like a ten-ton cruise ship. They took me! I was powerless.

My breath steamed the inside of the hood, melting my ears and eyelashes with panicked heat. My vision remained black and useless. The hood obscured everything, hushing the surroundings with dirty cloth.

A rough hand landed on my thigh, squeezing hard. Jumping, I tried to crawl away, but the bindings on my wrists yanked me to a halt.

A language I didn't understand lilted, twisting my heart, making me wish I could wake up and it would all be a nightmare.

The hand clutched my thigh again, wrenching my knees apart.

Red flashed in my vision. I welcomed the rage and kicked as hard as possible. I screamed as an unwelcome hand groped between my legs. My leggings didn't offer any resistance from the horrible pressure. I suffered a slap to the side of my head as I fought.

The fingers disappeared, and I choked on the sudden rush of relief. I coughed, hacking up every emotion inside. This couldn't be happening.

The vehicle screeched to a stop, and the clunking of doors opening resonated. Heartbeats pounded in my ears like heavy drums.

My legs were grabbed, and my butt scraped along a sharp surface. Someone grunted, scooped me up, and threw me over his shoulder like a dead carcass.

Vertigo rushed to my head, lips pressed against dirty cloth.

The power of terror-filled unknown sucked me into a dark place deep inside—a place full of rapists and murderers and unmentionable monsters. Self-pity oozed, and my will to survive faltered.

No!

I couldn't be sucked into depression and give up. I would *never* give up. I would fight until I died; I'd teach the kidnappers they stole the wrong girl if they wanted meek and broken.

In some sick way, they proved my own self-worth. My parents may not want me, but these bastards sure did. They'd stolen me because they had to.

I was valuable. I had to stay strong and survive.

I hung over the kidnapper's shoulder, being carted to who knew where, and something happened.

My mind fractured, literally unthreaded, splitting into two entities. The girl I was: my hopes and dreams, aspirations and love for Brax all blazed bright and true. My insecurities and need for love saddened me. I saw my own fragility.

But that didn't matter, because the other part—the new part—was fierce. This girl had no brokenness or issues. She was a warrior who'd seen blood, stared monsters in the face, and knew without a doubt her life would be hers again.

Somehow the new part wrapped around the nucleus of the old Tess, protecting, cushioning me from the horrors to come.

At least, that's what I hoped happened.

I truly, truly hoped.

The hood was ripped off my head, taking some hair with it. The rest arched and spat with static electricity. I blinked, light saturating my eyes as everything shone with overexposure.

I was in a room.

Dark, dingy, not a dungeon, but not far off. Bunk beds lined each of the four walls. The lack of windows, and dampness from the floor, settled fast into my bones.

I sat on a threadbare mattress, looking around my new home. Girls huddled on each bed. All of them wore an aura of tragedy, eyes bruised with loss, skin painted with injuries and shadows.

A man loomed over me, his beard black and gross. Reaching behind him, he bared a knife.

I flinched, and tried to crawl away. Some part said he wouldn't hurt me. Not yet. But the other part saw the knife and cowered.

I knew what a knife did. It cut things. *Butchered* things. I didn't want to be butchered.

The man grunted, digging fingers into my shoulder, pressing me into the dank mattress on the bottom bunk. I yelped as he rolled me onto my belly. I kicked and twisted, trying to stay upright, fighting an already lost battle.

The motion of sawing caused the string around my wrists to bite deep into sore skin. The blade was blunt and it seemed to take forever before the bindings finally broke.

The man released me, backing away with a scowl. I slowly sat upright, rubbing my wrists, skin indented and heated with a raw, angry red.

"You. Stay." He jabbed a finger in my face before stomping to the exit. The heavy, black door opened and he disappeared. The room echoed with a loud click as the lock slammed home.

The moment he was gone, I gawked at my new roommates. Only a few girls met my eyes; the rest slouched with fear.

I couldn't stop staring. Eight bunk-beds. Eight women. All of us ranged from early to late twenties. There was no rhyme in our abduction. Some of us were blonde, others black, redhead, and brown. Our skin colour didn't match, either: three Asian, two black, and three white.

Nothing screamed pattern. The police wouldn't be able to work out who'd be the next victim—it seemed any woman easy enough to steal was fair game. Whether we were tall, short, fat, slim. Big breasted, long legged. We were all there for one reason.

A reason I didn't yet know.

A reason I didn't want to know.

Hours passed while we stared at each other. No one talked—we didn't need to. We communicated in our silence, deeper than words. Our souls talked. We comforted one another, all the while sharing grief over what would become of us.

The flickering light bulb illuminated our cage, sending tension rippling around the room.

Some time, hours later, the door opened and a younger man with wonky teeth and a jagged facial scar appeared, depositing a tray of eight bowls in the centre of the room. The stagnant air of our prison filled with scents of food— something stir-fried with a platter of warm bread to scoop it up with. My stomach growled; I hadn't eaten since breakfast.

My heart stuttered, thinking about Brax. It seemed so long ago, sharing our first night in Cancun, enjoying our connection.

I forced myself to stop thinking about him. It hurt too much.

No one moved, but we all stared longingly at the food once the door locked again.

I waited to see if there was a hierarchy.

No one budged.

The scent of dinner overwhelmed, and I couldn't stand it any longer. I needed my strength to fight. I wouldn't sit waiting—who knew when they would come for us.

I moved.

My body creaked and protested, but I stood and collected a bowl at a time, handing it with a piece of flat bread to each girl.

They gave a timid smile, a glassy look, a flush of tears. I took comfort in helping them. At least they weren't alone. We were in this together.

When I delivered the last bowl and took my own, I had to swallow my tears. They threatened to drown me if I let them loose.

Brax. My life. My happy, happy world dissolved and left me in hell.

I didn't belong to Brax anymore. I didn't even belong to myself. I belonged to a bleak, unknown, and terror-filled future.

Swallowing hard, I forced the tears away. Tears were not useful, and I refused to buckle. Taking a mouthful of gruel, I hiccupped and steeled myself.

I would not cry.

Not tonight.

Chapter Five

Fantail

For two days, the little room was my world.

Food came twice a day, giving us something to break up the monotonous waiting. Fear of what would happen siphoned away with every tick of the clock, leaving me devoid, empty.

The remaining hours were spent staring into nothingness, or staring at each other.

A few women chatted in hushed whispers, but I didn't. I sat in a cloak of silence and plotted. My freedom had been taken, but I would take it back.

All my life I'd been meek and a doormat. Even with Brax, I never had the strength to speak the truth. That all changed in the two days I sat in contemplation. I put away my fear of being reprimanded, and embraced ferocity. I conjured anger like magic, nursing it deep within, building on it like an impenetrable cape. Never again would I hide my true feelings, or fail to chase what I truly desired. And what I desired most was freedom.

Our food was delivered by the same young man with the scar running from eyebrow to jaw. Whoever had sewn the injury did a hash job, and skin puckered in such a way I would've pitied him, if not for the fact he was in cahoots with my kidnappers.

He wasn't big, but moved with strength belying his scrawny frame. I watched closely, gauging if I could tackle him, if the other women would help me.

Even if the women did rally together, how far would we get? There were guards outside the door, and I didn't know what was out there. City, forest, urban, or country. No point making a move until I knew. Knowledge was power, and surprise was key.

It was the evening of the second day when the door slammed open. It wasn't dinner time and my heart rabbited when Leather Jacket prowled into the room. Predatory eyes immediately fell on me. All my plotting and scheming evaporated as he grinned nastily, heading straight for me.

Fear sprinted through my blood, flaring my aching body, a reminder danger lurked in every inch of this place. Complacency wasn't a good idea.

"Come with me, slut." Fingers wrapped around my sore wrist, yanking me upright. Licking cracked lips, he dragged me toward the door. *No!* I wouldn't go, not like this.

I locked my knees, bare feet scrambled to find purchase on the old floorboards, but I couldn't get traction. He tugged hard, slamming me against his gross body. The leather jacket reeked of sweat and metal.

The women started crying, a wail of confusion puncturing the once heavy silence. Our little oasis in the madness was shattered.

I squirmed, trying to tear his fingers off my wrist, but he reached back and slapped me. My cheekbone blazed with pain; I squeezed my eyes shut.

"Obey! Unless you want to be knocked out again," Leather Jacket snarled. Readjusting his grip, he dragged me down a rank corridor. My face smarted, but I quickly pushed the discomfort away. Pain was a distraction, and I needed to focus.

Men, all dark-haired and grim, dashed past. A woman cried, then screaming joined the horrible symphony. My heart went out to them. It wasn't just me they'd come for.

My pulse thudded every metre Leather Jacket carted me. We passed door after locked door, until he shoved me forward, sending me tripping into a shower block. Multiple showerheads, cracked white tiles, and well-used soap bars littered the floor, like a gym or a jail.

Oh, God.

Leather Jacket jerked my shoulder, swivelling me to face him. "Strip."

A burst of defiance blossomed, and I spat in his face. No way would I undress in front of him. I couldn't. Only Brax had seen me naked—that was his gift, no one else's.

Fuck you. Fuck all of this. I'd never been so gung-ho or courageous, but everything about me had changed. It was time to embrace the new me.

He chuckled. "So, you like it rough, bitch." Before I could duck, his fist connected with my cheekbone, shattering my vision into pieces. Oh, God, the pain was so much worse than a slap. I moaned, clutching my face. I'd never been hit before, but this was the third time in a matter of days.

His hands grabbed the collar of my t-shirt and yanked. The sound of ripping material echoed in the tiled shower block. I whimpered as fresh air licked my exposed stomach and chest. The haze of pain slowly left, and I feinted to the side, trying to get away. But he wasn't suffering from a punch to the jaw and caught me.

He grunted, slapping me again. "You're a wild one. But that won't save you. It'll just mean you won't get the good buyers, and you'll end up drugged and brain-dead." He leaned in and licked, dragging his foul tongue like a Labrador over my cheek, right into my hairline.

I shivered, repulsed.

"If you want another fist to your pretty face, move again," he coaxed.

Already, a hundred galloping elephants lived in my skull, I couldn't handle more. My soul wanted to fight, but my body stayed still, obeying.

"Good girl," he cooed, reaching for my leggings and pulling them down in one swipe. A sharp tug on my hip broke my knickers, and hands fumbled behind to free my bra. It fluttered to the floor, leaving me the most exposed I'd ever been.

Naked, I stood in front of a rapist, kidnapper, and evil, sadistic son of a bitch.

I trembled, clasping arms around my exposed chest. The man chuckled, eyes raping me with a transfixed stare. "You've got nice tits. You can't hide them forever. Get in the shower and wash your filth." He shoved me toward the soap littered area.

I stumbled, but went willingly. It meant I was away from him, away from his stench, his rottenness. *Don't think about him looking at you. None of this can affect you if you don't let it.*

Holding onto the thought, I stooped to pick up a dry piece of soap.

More women arrived, corralled by hard hands and vile men. Each one was subjected to the same treatment, minus the beating, and I turned away as their clothes fell to the floor. The guy with the scar gathered the belongings and disappeared. The wardrobe of our past lives. Gone—just like that. It symbolised more than just undressing us—it was a message: they owned us. We no longer had the right to wear what we wanted, go where we needed, love who we adored. We were reduced to nothing but naked, trembling girls.

The starkness of our reality hit some women hard, and they crumbled to the floor in tears, only to be kicked in the stomach and forced to crawl into the communal shower.

I swallowed salty tears as I turned on the tap, attempting to froth the age-grimed soap.

The water ran cold, but it was heaven to clean away gunk and hardship. I didn't like to think about the reason we were being made to wash. That was the future—a place I couldn't think about. I focused on the present, keeping sane by not letting my imagination run wild with horror.

Bubbles slowly formed on the soap, and I spent the next ten minutes rubbing it over my skin, lathering my hair. I wanted to wash away what had happened. Wishing the water would take my unhappiness and gurgle it down the drain, taking me, too. Surely, the sewers would be a better existence.

"Enough!" a jailer shouted.

We obeyed, rinsing under the cold spray, and proceeded to where a pile of moth-eaten towels lay on a bench. I wrapped a discoloured towel around myself, and a rope came from behind, noosing around my neck. I jumped, clawing at the tight bondage.

The man with the jagged scar came into view, tugging gently. "You are no longer whoever you were. You are to forget about your past because you will never see it again."

He leaned forward, and I froze. I underestimated him. Because he brought us food, I stupidly thought he was nicer than the others, but he wasn't. The same blackness lived in him, too.

"Follow." He strode off, yanking the rope. My back arched with the pressure, forcing me to trot to catch up. I'd been demoted from human to dog with just one act.

Lowborn reactions rose; I wanted to growl and sink my teeth into his arm. If he wanted me to be an animal, I could be an animal.

The shower block disappeared as I padded behind by leash. *Where the hell is he taking me?* I squeezed my eyes closed. I didn't want to know.

What if, now I was clean, they were going to rape me? Put me in some whorehouse and force me into a sea of chemicals and drugs. I'd never return to who I was. Never get free.

No!

I slammed on the brakes, digging bare feet into the floor. My toes ached as Jagged Scar slammed to a halt. My neck screamed as the rope pulled tight, choking.

"Move!" Jagged Scar glared, pressing his body hard against my towel-wrapped figure. My entire being rebelled at being so close, but I gritted my teeth. I wouldn't step away in defeat. I wanted to hiss and head butt him, but I stood there, glaring into his endless black eyes, standing as regal as possible.

"No. I will not move. You have no right to treat me or the other women like this. Let us go." My voice wavered with fear, my heart wild. I could lose my life by disobeying, but I couldn't go down without a fight. I couldn't give up so easily. I let my family walk all over me—I wasn't about to let these bastards do it, too.

A gathering of shocked murmurs rose behind me. I glanced back, horror widening my eyes. My roommates were roped and standing in line, like sheep to the slaughter.

They were shoved out of the way as Leather Jacket stormed toward me. Jagged Scar dropped the end of my rope, stepping backward.

Oh, *shit.*

Ducking, I threw my arms over my head, trying to protect, but it was no use.

Leather Jacket threw me to the ground and kicked. His steel-capped boots cracked a rib as I collapsed under his abuse; the snap resonated, making me scream and curl into a ball.

I couldn't breathe. I couldn't move. I couldn't even cry, the pain was insurmountable. Kick after kick. My breasts, stomach, thigh, ankle. Each blow exploded with heat worse than the last one.

Another scream erupted as one kick caught my solar plexus, causing the towel to unravel. I was beyond simple agony. I was in hell.

He raged something in his native tongue, fisting a hand in my hair, pulling me upright. My skin puckered in terror as he pulled back, gaining momentum to slam my head into the wall.

"*Basta!*"

I knew that word. Enough.

Leather Jacket released me; I slumped to the floor. Every inch wailed with pain. The chill of wood against bare skin reminded me I was beaten and naked. *So stupid, Tess. So, so stupid. You can't win. Just give them what they want.* I was worse off by disobeying: a shivering mess on the floor, incapable of anything but weakness.

Brax. How I wished Brax was here. He'd know what to do. How to keep me safe. I was such an ignoramus to think I could stand up to these men.

Who *were* they anyway?

I latched onto a word: trafficker. It blared like an angry hurricane, hurling me further into terror. As much as I wanted to deny the realization, I knew.

I was being trafficked. Me and these women were about to disappear around the world, exchanged for money, no regard for us as people—we were belongings.

I'd read enough horrible news to know the window of saving a smuggled woman was very short—only a few days before they were never seen again.

No one but my parents and Brax knew I was in Mexico. My parents wouldn't know I'd ever gone missing—they never called or texted. It would be months before they noticed my absence. And Brax. My heart choked. Brax might be dead for all I knew. Dead and cold and blue under a urinal.

The man with the scar shoved Leather Jacket away,

reclaiming my leash. He tugged the rope, twinging my neck. "Get up."

I wanted to laugh. He expected me to stand when my body was cracked and broken? The beating taught me something, though. Obedience was paramount. Nothing wrong in following orders if it meant I survived another day. So, even though it killed me, I fumbled to my feet.

Breathing hard, my entire body wanted to weep, but my eyes remained dry. These men didn't deserve my tears.

Jagged Scar wrapped fingers around my bicep, holding some of the weight. He gave me a lopsided grin, shrugging. "You can make this easy. It's only temporary. Keep your fight for your new owner."

My mind blanked with shock; I blinked. He confirmed my suspicions and I wished I was wrong.

Jagged Scar pulled me forward, both by his grip and the rope. Injuries screamed, especially the cracked rib, but together we shuffled down the corridor. The line behind started up again, each woman taken into a different room. Would I ever see them again?

Leather Jacket smirked as he opened a door, and Jagged Scar guided me inside. Just like the cell we lived in: a windowless room with only one door.

The lock clicking set off panic in my chest like an atomic bomb.

Everything about the space was non-descript, apart from the torture contraption in the centre of the room, half dentist chair, half gynaecologist table with stirrups and levers.

Beside it rested a stainless steel table full of instruments from my nightmares, all glinting wicked sharp under the huge spotlight hanging above.

My mouth snapped shut, and I huddled, trying to become invisible. *Switch off, Tess. Disappear from this hell.*

Needles, scalpels, glass vials full of crystal liquid, and

leather straps heralded my doom as Jagged Scar pushed forward. I had no energy, zapped with pain, but I spun away. I couldn't get on that chair. I couldn't.

The rope around my neck squeezed tight, and I clawed at my throat with broken nails and anxious fingers. "No!"

Another set of hands from an unknown person wrapped around my nakedness and half-dragged, half-carried me to the chair. Together, they threw me on the squeaky, blood-stained leather and Jagged Scar went behind, jerking the rope, making me lie down or choke.

My skin stuck to the leather, making sucking sounds along with my panicked breathing.

The person who'd helped throw me on the chair appeared above.

My heart squeezed with indignation. A woman—young, cruel, with a glossy curtain of black hair framing her face. Her lips lined with early smoker creases, black eyes as vacant as the men. A surgical mask hung from one ear, and rubber gloves sheathed her fingers.

Rage consumed me. She was a woman involved with trafficking women—a traitor to her own sex. "How can you, bitch? How can you be a part of this?"

Jagged Scar reached from behind, tapping my cheek in warning. The woman didn't answer, but averted her eyes. Not from embarrassment, but to secure the leather straps around my forearms. Once secure, she spread my legs into the stirrups and secured my ankles, buckling them so tight the leather bit into my skin like fangs.

Mortification painted my cheeks at being so exposed, so defenceless. I hadn't even fought.

Through the walls, a scream ripped fast and high, but shut off as quickly as it came. My eyes popped wide. Oh, my God, what was happening?

My breath rasped in the small space, rushed and ragged. The woman secured the mask around her mouth and tore open a sterile packet.

My eyes wanted to close, to avoid knowing what was in the plastic, but I couldn't look away. I stared with sick fascination as she attached the needle to a pen-like contraption, adding a vial of black liquid.

What was that thing?

Jagged Scar grabbed another bottle and doused the underside of my wrist, pushing Brax's bracelet further up my arm. My heart squeezed in painful loss. Brax. The bracelet was the only thing I had of him. They'd allowed me to keep it. Misplaced thankfulness overwhelmed, at least these bastards hadn't stolen that, too.

Using a white piece of cotton, Jagged Scar dried my wrist, before nodding at the woman.

She bent over my arm, placing a carbon transfer she plucked from the table, sticking it to damp flesh. She smoothed it against my skin, making sure the image adhered before ripping it off, leaving a purplish outline of a barcode.

Discarding the transfer, she picked up the pen with the black vial and pressed a button. Whirring mechanical noise vibrated.

Shit, they were going to tattoo me! I'd never been inked before, never fell in love with an image enough to want it permanently on my skin, and I definitely didn't want a barcode.

"Stop!"

Jagged Scar pressed his face close as the sharp nick of the tattoo gun tore into my flesh. Teeny, tiny teeth nipped and sawed.

"Accept that you are no longer a woman. You are merchandise. And merchandise must have a barcode for sale."

I wanted to spit at him, but refrained. As degrading as it was to be treated like stock, I bit my lip and bore through it. I would get it lasered off as soon as I escaped.

The burn grew fiery hot as seconds turned into

minutes.

I was no longer Tess. I was dollar signs.

Finally, the tattoo pen cut off with a snarl. I gasped as the woman smeared some sort of gel over it and wrapped my wrist in plastic.

The black lines looked obscene against my red, swollen skin. My first tattoo and it demoted me from dog to shelf produce. A disposable thing. An item. No more. No less.

My fight deflated, leaving under an avalanche of unhappiness. Every part hurt: my heart, body, and soul. I was sucked deep into the pit where snakes and monsters lived, wallowing in self-pity.

The woman pulled off her gloves and snapped a fresh pair on. She moved to the end of the table, positioning herself between my legs. She turned from tattoo artist to gynaecologist.

Oh, hell, this is too much.

I squeezed my eyes, rolling my head to the side. I willed myself to leave this place, to float and disappear, but her fingers touched and kept me anchored in despair.

She inspected between my legs for an eternity before finally patting my thigh like the good dog I was. I hadn't barked or nipped. I'd let them own me with not so much as a whimper.

The woman unbuckled my legs, and I scissored them tight, locking my knees together.

Jagged Scar chuckled. "Keeping your legs together won't save you. There are plenty of other places to violate."

I gulped, and the clatter of the leather straps hitting the metal table sent goosebumps skittering.

Please, let this humiliating and degrading inspection be over.

I opened my mouth to ask to be released, but the crackle of another sterile packet sky-rocketed my panic.

The woman fumbled with something small before facing me with a cruel smile. The syringe glinted under the spotlight. My heart raced. "No. I'll behave. You don't have to drug me.

Please."

The thought of living a permanent life in a drug haze terrified me more than the rest of it. The woman didn't answer and I jerked, trying to get free from the restraints.

I couldn't look away from the syringe, expecting her to inject whatever it was into my arm, but she didn't go for that part of my body.

Her latex covered fingers swiped tangled hair off my neck, and stabbed the thick needle into soft flesh behind my ear.

I screamed as a hard bullet shot from the needle, stretching, maiming.

Withdrawing, she giggled, saying something in Spanish to Jagged Scar. She threw the syringe into a bin and picked up an iPhone-looking thing. Handing it to Jagged Scar, he waved it over the latest injury. My skin wouldn't stop throbbing.

A sharp series of beeps filled the room.

"Working, and linked to the barcode," Jagged Scar muttered.

No! They didn't. All my courage and hope for escape was ruined. They'd not only branded me, they'd tagged me, too. Even if I did escape, they could fucking *track* me.

Tears rushed, desperate to be shed. I didn't realize how much the thought of escape kept me going. Now, even that had been taken.

I gulped hard, trying to keep my eyes dry. Jagged Scar released my arms, went behind me, and dragged the rope from around my neck.

It took a while to understand I was free, and even longer for my sore body to move.

Jagged Scar helped me upright. I grimaced, holding my ribs, not caring my breasts were exposed.

I sniffed and tried to sit straighter, but settled for huddling with my eyes down cast. This was the worst day of my life. No, that was wrong. The worst day was the day they took me. When Brax was beaten and left to his fate. A sob bubbled but I swallowed it back. I couldn't think about Brax, or the nightmare I lived now.

A brown paper bag appeared on my lap. Jagged Scar captured my chin, guiding me to look into his eyes. "Good girl. Give in to your future. Easier, yes?" He caressed my cheek—the first kind touch since I arrived in this hell. After the abuse from Leather Jacket, I wanted to be hugged, tended to. But that would never happen.

Keep fighting, Tess. Never stop fighting.

Heat seeped into my limbs, dispelling aches and bruises. Fighting was all I had left. I wouldn't give in.

I glared at the woman who'd trapped me so completely with a brand and tag. "I hate you. One day, you will suffer as your victims suffer. One day, Karma will come and bite your ass." I had no idea if my promise would come true, but I'd make it a life's mission to bring the wrath of the law on their heads and save innocent women.

I hated them. I hated everything.

Jagged Scar huffed and stole the paper bag from my hands. Opening it, he grabbed the clothes and threw them at me. "Get dressed."

I caught the items and slid gingerly off the chair. I pulled the brown sweater over my head, wincing and gasping. The white knickers were next, followed by a pair of thigh-high socks. Nothing else.

They effectively dressed me as a doll. A broken doll with no worth.

But I was past caring about superficial things like wardrobes. The clothing offered protection, even if the thigh-high socks itched and the jumper wasn't warm; at least I wasn't nude.

The woman forced a hairbrush into my palm and I took it hesitantly. Was this it? Was I being moved?

I worked through my messy tangles before handing the

brush back. My skin smelled of cheap soap and my hair was brittle with no conditioner, but I felt better. More prepared to face whatever came next.

My new tattoo itched beneath the bandage, and I wanted to rip it off to see the barcode in more detail. Could they scan me now? What details were imbedded in the mark?

They hadn't asked any personal information. They didn't care who I was. Only what I was becoming.

Something to be sold.

Chapter Six

Owl

Three days ticked past.

Our little cell, the routine of food twice a day, and hushed conversations helped numb me into some sort of acceptance. My body was bruised in places I'd never seen and my rib ached. After everything we'd been through, I loathed just sitting there.

Every passing hour, I grew angrier. Sitting on the moth-riddled bunk bed, I welcomed the heat of temper. I wanted something to happen. Regardless of what it was, waiting silently killed me. Boredom itched worse than the new tattoo.

The flickering bulb clicked off, and I stared into blackness. A lot of my roommates drifted into vacancy—conversations few and desolate. I refused to partake. I didn't want to reminisce about the situation; I wanted to focus on a future less bleak. To try and keep hope alive in my heart, even as it was suffocated by anger and rage.

The moment I found a situation where I could run, I would. No hesitation. No second thoughts. I'd shoot and stab. I'd kill to escape, and the knowledge I was ready to spill blood, shed a life, filled me with power.

Brax may have died fighting to save me. Now, it was my turn. I'd find him somehow. I'd find him and all of this would be nasty history.

A sliver of light, then a scuff echoed around the black catacomb of our prison. I froze beneath the musty sheets.

A footstep, then another.

My hands clenched, ready to pummel. It wasn't a woman tiptoeing through the night, heading to the bucket in the corner. It was a jailer. I'd paid attention to their mannerisms and noises. The last week taught me how to use all my senses.

I knew with horrible clarity—Leather Jacket had come for me.

A hand patted my thigh, creeping, trying to locate me in the darkness. I stiffened, letting him grope his way, biding time.

When a hand found my breast, I sucked in a breath. *Not yet. Wait.* I pretended to be dead with terror, letting him think I wouldn't fight. *Idiot.* My mouth watered to make him bleed. Retribution was a fine thing.

Leather Jacket's pungent breath wafted as he pressed one knee on the bed, moving to straddle me.

I burst upright.

My punch flew wild but connected with a hard jaw. My other fist landed where I wanted: right in his balls. Victory was righteous in my veins and I smiled.

He squealed and rolled off, landing with a thud on the floorboards. Cries and rustles erupted around the room. We'd never had an interloper in the night before. Stupidly, we thought we were untouchable, our virtues kept for our new masters, whoever they would be.

I shot out of bed, kicking in the direction I thought Leather Jacket was. My foot connected but not hard enough. Hot hands grabbed my ankle, twisting. I lost my balance and fell, landing in a heap half on top of him. My rib screamed, making me woozy.

Horrible groping trailed up my legs, reaching my hips, waist, and chest. I wriggled and kicked. "Get off me!" I bit his ear as he managed to haul himself on top.

He bellowed, and a flare of metallic rust filled my mouth. I'd drawn blood. It was a flag to a bull.

I went berserk. Everything I'd dealt with swarmed into cataclysmic rage. I screamed and attacked. Nails, teeth, knees, and elbows. I didn't care where I struck, or where it landed. I became nothing but claws and fangs.

Leather Jacket scooted away, leaving me fighting air.

"You want to rape me, you bastard?" My voice wavered with tears and violence. "Come and get me."

Women shouted encouragement as I charged into nothing. I found Leather Jacket stumbling for the door. I caught him and grabbed greasy hair. With strength I didn't know I had, I slammed his nose against the wall.

He screeched as something crunched. Adrenaline drenched my limbs, turning me into a wet noodle, slippery, shaky, but I fought to stay strong. *Stay vicious.*

The light bulb flared on, blinding.

Ignoring the burn of my retinas, I grabbed Leather Jacket's finger and twisted with all my might. He struck out and punched me in the chest. My lungs collapsed; I couldn't grab a breath.

The door wrenched open and a barrier of men marched in, pointing machine guns in my face. Sucking in what air I could, I jumped back, holding up my hands. A trickle of blood ran from my temple and bruises added to bruises, but satisfaction was a welcome bloom when I looked at Leather Jacket.

His stringy hair was all over the place, a cut oozed on his cheekbone, and he heaved as if he'd been beaten by a gorilla. He snarled, *"Vete a la mierda, puta."* He nursed his finger and shoved aside a man with a gun, reaching for me.

I didn't think. My body just reacted. I slapped him as

hard as I could; my palm burned, but it was nothing compared to my happiness at the red handprint I painted on his cheek. I'd caused grievous bodily harm and enjoyed it.

I was more dangerous than I thought.

He glared. *"Estás muerto."*

I knew that word: die.

Before Leather Jacket could touch me, two men grabbed him, carting him out of the room. His voice raged as they disappeared.

The remaining men backed out of the room, pointing guns until the lock snapped securely.

I spun slowly in the centre of the dungeon, looking wide-eyed at the women. Some held sheets to their throats, some gawked open-mouthed.

What did they see when they looked at me? A feral woman who'd signed her own death sentence, or a fierce warrior who'd saved herself from rape?

The pretty Asian girl with long, black hair, dropped her sheet and clapped. "I've wanted to do that since they stole me from the nightclub with my friend." Her voice trembled but the glint of fire in her eyes reminded me of myself. "We'll be free again," she added.

I stared, startled and silent, as a voluptuous black girl joined her clapping. One by one, the ladies clapped and smiles stretched unhappy faces.

One by one, fire lit in their gaze.

One by one, they rallied, and I knew we wouldn't be passive anymore.

We were right, and they were wrong.

Righteousness would set us free.

The next day, I was taken by rope leash to shower again. I'd learned to live with the pain in my joints and muscles—they reminded me of victory, not weakness. A badge of honour.

Once I was clean, Jagged Scar pulled me down the corridor and up a flight of stairs. This part of the house, factory, trafficker hotel—whatever it was—was different. Ugly artwork graced the walls, and the room he shoved me into was a normal study. Glass windows with an industrial view, a desk, chairs, and a man reclining, stared at me.

He was as white as me with blond hair, tanned skin, and blue eyes—the same bright blue as Brax.

My heart twisted.

Jagged Scar forced me into a chair, but I never took my eyes off the man in a business suit.

"Who are you?" I rasped.

The man narrowed his eyes, placing palms on the desk. Jagged Scar retreated to lurk by the wall. Tingles of fear darted down my back, but I refused to bow to terror any longer. I'd drawn blood—that counted for something.

"I'm the man who holds your fate in his hands."

"I'm the only one who owns my fate. Not you. Not your guards. Not your sick operation. No one."

He chuckled. "Ignacio was right. You're a fighter." He leaned forward, twirling a pen. "Being a fighter is what gets you killed. You should let go. Let us guide you."

Ignacio? Was that Leather Jacket? I twitched in anger. "Let you guide me to my death by rape and mutilation?"

He leaned back as if I slapped him. "Stupid girl. If you behave, you will be sold to a gentleman who will treat you like a prized possession. Lavish attention on you. Buy you whatever you want."

My mind ran crazy. I was right. I was to be sold into sex slavery, into bondage.

"I am nobody's possession."

He shook his head, smiling. "Ah, but you're wrong. You already are. Sold. Contracted. The deed is done."

My heart tried to claw its way out of my throat, but I sat frozen, brave. "You won't get away with this."

He stood and threw a package into my lap. I caught it on reflex, horrified to find my photograph on a fake American passport, and papers written in Spanish.

"Already have, pretty girl." He came to the front of the desk, stopping in front of me. He trailed fingertips along my cheek, just as gentle, just as adoring, as Brax used to. "What is your name?"

"You're not worthy of my name," I snarled, trying to bite his fingers.

He stepped back, laughing. "Well, I hope you are worthy of the client who bought you. I don't do refunds." He nodded at Jagged Scar, who'd snuck up behind me. "Do it."

My world ended as hands smothered my face, pressing a rag reeking of chloroform against my nose and mouth. I tried not to breathe, fought to get free, but the fumes stung my eyes, entering my bloodstream.

A fog descended, whispering and stealing.

Unconsciousness claimed me.

Chapter Seven

Nightingale

My ears popped on descent.

I instantly recognised the hum of aircraft engines and gentle thrum of metal. I'd been on a plane only a week before. Had it been a week since I'd been a prisoner? It felt much, much longer. I'd changed so much. My life no longer evolved around exams and when I could get Brax naked. Now, all I focused on was survival.

The black hood rested over my head, and I tried to remain calm. Freaking out wouldn't help.

My ears kept popping as the airplane left the clouds, returning to earth. Where was I? They'd given me a passport for a reason, so I must be overseas somewhere.

Time ceased to have meaning as we landed, then taxied a fair distance. Finally, the engines ceased and abrupt silence hurt my ears.

As I sat there, with hands bound and head aching from being drugged, I mentally prepared for the worst. The next stage of my new life. I had to protect myself. Be ready to fight and run.

I couldn't think about regrets and my past. I couldn't think about Brax.

And I definitely couldn't think about what was in store for me.

A sad smile graced my lips. If someone asked me a week ago what I was most afraid of, I'd have said crickets. Those damn flying grasshopper creatures scared the bejesus out of me.

Now, if someone asked me, I'd say three little words.

Three little words that terrified, stole my breath, and made my life flicker before my eyes.

Three little words:

I was sold.

Noise.

The cargo door of the airplane opened and footsteps thudded. My senses were dulled, muted by the black hood, and my mind ran amok with terror-filled images.

Male voices argued and my arms were wrenched painfully as someone pulled me to my feet. I flinched and cried out, earning a fist to my belly. The blow landed on a particularly tender part, and suddenly, everything was too much. I'd been so strong and it hadn't changed my future. Tears streamed down my face. The first tears I shed, but definitely not the last.

The wetness on my cheeks wasn't cleansing; it made me feel worse.

A cold wind whipped, disappearing up the baggy, brown sweater I wore. Icy fingers of winter said I was no longer in Mexico.

I kept moving until one set of hands released and another set secured me tight, dragging me against a hard torso. "This is for Mr. Mercer?"

"*Sí.* Our boss hopes he enjoys this one. She's got spirit. He should have fun breaking her."

My stomach twisted, threatening to evict empty contents. *Oh, God.*

"*Pas de problème.* I'm sure he will."

The French words pricked my ears.

With a harsh pull, my new captor marched me forward. I had no choice but to do as he requested. After a while, he jerked me to a wobbling stop. My rib twinged, but I stood straight and tall. Hunching would show cowardice and uncertainty. I was none of those things. The moment the hood was off, I would run.

A rope looped over my head, catching my ears through the black cloth. I tossed my head, feeling like a prized pony; a thoroughbred ready for the glue factory.

Manly voices murmured, warbling with deep tones and gruffness. I strained to hear, but the wind snatched the vowels before I could comprehend.

The screech of aircraft engines grew louder as another plane landed. We had to be at a commercial airport, but I must've been smuggled in via cargo. I couldn't see anything, but I knew we hadn't been in a cabin with soft seats and air-hostesses. It had been icy cold and dreadfully uncomfortable.

I stood, shivering, while men talked. The tears I shed froze on my cheeks, reminding me to keep my frosty exterior to survive. I had to become an icicle—cool and impenetrable, sharp and deadly.

A hand looped around my bound arm, guiding me forward. I tottered with them, blind and disorientated. The twine around my wrists burned with every jostle.

Why couldn't they invest in handcuffs, or something not as rudimentary? After all, selling women must be a profitable business. What did I fetch? How much for a non-virgin Australian woman with an unfinished bachelor degree in property development?

I'll buy back my freedom. Bubbles of manic laughter tickled. *I'll walk into a bank and ask for a loan to buy myself. Because I'm such a good investment.* I snorted. Oh, God, I was losing it.

We didn't walk far. We stopped and I stood with my heart thumping, waiting, waiting, waiting.

A sharp tug on my wrists, then I was free. My shoulders ached as I brought my arms forward, rolling, working out the kinks.

I was free.

In a wide-open space.

I could run.

Someone behind removed the rope around my neck, along with the hood. I looked left and right, investigating the new surroundings.

Three muscle men stood in a triangle around me. All in black suits, looking very *Men in Black,* dark haired, and rugged. The night sky glittered with a pepper-spray of silver stars. A crescent moon sliced the black velvet. I wanted to stare in wonder.

"Get on board," a man ordered, his eyes hidden by shades, even in the dark. His accent was thick, wrapped in masculine authority. Placing hands on my shoulders, he pushed me toward a private plane.

The white fuselage glowed, looking sleek, modern, dripping with wealth. Initials *Q.M.* scrawled in fancy calligraphy on the tail and wing tips.

Was this the man who bought me? A wealthy owner of a jet who bought women like a pair of new socks? If he was so wealthy, he didn't need to buy willing partners… unless… I swallowed hard. Perhaps he had sick fetishes. Liked to hurt and indulge in sadistic pleasures.

How long would I survive?

I wasn't about to find out.

"Go on. Climb the steps."

It's now or never, Tess.

I bounced on the balls of my feet, pretending to obey. My body revved with energy and I pivoted in thigh-high socks. I'd always been a runner. I used to run track for school, and jogged every day on the treadmill to get in shape for the holiday with Brax.

My body knew how to flee.

I shut my mind off and instinct took over.

I flew.

The cold tarmac bit my feet as I pushed harder. Men burst into action. *They'll probably shoot. I don't care.* A bullet to the head might be a better choice.

"*Arrêtez!*" a man shouted, followed by, "*Merde!*"

I sucked air—it whistled in my lungs. I had no clue where I headed. Hangars loomed like gaping mouths. Sparkling lights of the main terminal looked like the gates of heaven, too far in the distance.

The words *Charles De Gaulle* were bright and gaudy, taunting with hope and safety. Too far. I could never run that distance. Not with the suited hounds on my tail, quickly gaining traction.

Men closed the distance and I added another burst of speed. If only I could truly fly. Perhaps I could get free.

A cannonball of a body came from nowhere, cutting off my trajectory.

We toppled to the ground. The tarmac grated my thigh and I cried out in agony.

My tackler sat up, straddling me. He looked like the other guards—eyes hidden behind dark glasses, his black suit crisp and all business.

My chest heaved with air and regret, stabbing me with pain from my rib. I tried. I failed. The second lot of tears burned, streaking down my flushed cheeks as the man hauled me upright.

I limped, wincing on a sprained ankle. I wanted to wail and shout. My body shackled me with yet another injury; I couldn't outrun anyone.

Head down and hope gone, I hobbled back to the plane under the stern grip of Guard Number Four.

I didn't make eye contact with any of the men, and meekly climbed the steps into the private plane. The men muttered and laughed while I plonked into a white leather chair in defeat.

I tried. I failed. I tried. I failed. It repeated, over and over.

Don't give up. Next time, you could win. Next time, it might work. My hands curled—I would never stop looking for a way out.

Never.

"Get up. We're here." A foot prodded my swollen ankle.

I flinched and opened my eyes. Faking sleep hadn't worked. Every moment we flew in the height of luxury, I seethed with thoughts of how to maim the guards and take the plane hostage.

But I didn't do anything. I sat in the chair, like a blow up doll.

It seemed so long ago I'd hounded Brax for more kinkiness in our love life. I'd do anything to have my old life back, my old love returned. I'd give anything for sweet and pure instead of the dark, sinister, and sadistic ownership that awaited.

If I could press a rewind button, I would, beginning with never going to Mexico.

I stood, and Guard Number Four helped me down the plush, carpeted aisle. Coarse fingers wrapped around my burning wrists, passing me to a colleague at the bottom of the small flight of stairs. The bandage over the tattoo provided very little protection. The pain flared and itched. I hated it.

The moment I was on the ground, I froze. We stood in the middle of a manicured, grassy airstrip, frosty with ice, dark as the depths of hell, apart from the most gorgeous manor house I'd ever seen in the distance. Subtle outdoor lighting illuminated the soft pastel creams, blues, and pinks; French architecture at its finest.

The guard pulled my elbow and we trudged across the grass. I stumbled, stunned by incomprehensible wealth. Who could afford their own plane *and* mansion to house it?

My toes were numb by the time we climbed the front steps. Four story high pillars and intricate plasterwork with cherubs and rosettes welcomed. The three-horse water fountain gurgled and trickled, looking far too perfect to belong to a man who purchased women.

Our breath steamed in the cold as my guard rapped on the huge, silver door, before turning the knob and pushing me through.

Once inside the warm embrace of the house, he took off the shades, propping them on his head. His irises were green and vivid. I searched for evilness—the same vileness from the men who'd stolen me in Mexico, but surprise radiated down my spine. His eyes were compassionate, human.

He bowed his head, looking in front and above.

This was it. My new beginning. My new ending.

"Bonsoir, esclave."

My eyes soared up to the first landing of the giant blue, velvet staircase. Massive works of art hung like armament on gilded walls.

A man in a grey chequered suit, complete with black shirt, silver tie and short, dark hair, watched from the landing.

My entire body ignited as his jaw clenched. His gaze unclothed and terrified me. Everything about him screamed ruthlessness and power. He held himself proud and regal as if this was his castle and I was the latest subject.

Our eyes locked, and something tingled across my flesh. Fear? Terror? Something inside knew he was dangerous.

His lips twitched as I sucked in a breath. He removed his hands from his pockets and placed them on the banister, his fingers long and strong, even from this distance. The way he stared became too much. I felt undone, stripped to my soul.

I stepped back, bumping against the guard behind. He bent his head, whispering in my ear, "Say hello to your new master."

Chapter Eight

Sparrow

The word master echoed like a bad tuning fork.
Master. *Master.*

No, he wasn't my master. Not with his short, sleek
hair and sharp widow's peak. Not with his clenched,
stubble-smooth jaw and trim physique. He was *not* my
master. No one was.

Tears pricked as I thought about Brax. He seemed a
world away compared to this reality. Brax was rough and
boyish, a hard worker through and through. The man,
staring with pale jade eyes and an unreadable, chiselled
face, lived in total contrast. Power radiated like visible
waves, unsettling me more than anything.

He wasn't the fat, repulsive bastard who used wealth
to buy sex slaves. He wasn't gross or any other
monstrous things. *Who* is *this man?*

My eyes widened, drinking him in—the owner of this
house. The owner of... me. *No, never.*

I didn't care who he was, because my life belonged to
me. I stuck out my chin, glaring. I wouldn't be intimidated
by wealth or stature. I didn't care he was tall and moved
like he expected the world to lick his shoes. I would

never lick anything of his.

The man never broke eye contact, ensnaring me in his gaze. Slowly, he pushed off the banister and moved toward the stairs.

I gulped.

He was smooth water—effortless in refinement but just like still water, dangerous if you couldn't swim. Deadly rips and currents lurked deep below the surface. I eyed him, trying to figure out what sick pleasures he indulged in that normal, willing women were hard to come by.

My heart raced with every step he took, descending toward me.

The guard pushed me forward. "Bow to your new master."

I tripped, but regained my footing instantly. My fists shook, I clenched them so hard. My injuries reminded me all of this was wrong. In some warped sense, it seemed innocent like the owner of the house merely welcoming a guest.

"I have no master," I said, putting every ounce of rebellion into the words. "Let me go."

The man stopped mid-step, head cocked. His fingers curled around the banister, showing manicured nails, no calluses in sight. Once again, pale eyes connected with mine, sucking my thoughts into a vacuum.

Up till now, his face had been unreadable, but as we stared, flashes of emotion buffeted me. Anger. Interest. Annoyance. Resignation. And finally, in a blaze of jade…lust.

My breath quickened and I tried to step back again, only to collide with the wall of the guard's chest.

The guard placed a hot, heavy hand between my shoulder blades and pushed, forcing me into a struggling, painful bow. "Do as you're told."

So many thoughts collided. I wanted to spin and steal the gun in the holster under his arm. I wanted to shoot everyone. I wanted to slash at the gorgeous artwork and priceless artefacts around the room. Such things of beauty did not deserve to belong to a man whose goons forced a sex slave to bow.

"Bastard," I muttered, hating I couldn't do any of it. All I could do was obey—for now.

"Stop. If she doesn't want to bow, then don't force her." The masculine voice reminded me of glinting steel, shaped with precision and strength. It was the sound of authority, and despite my best attempts to rebel, I bowed on my own. The sheer weight of his voice compelled obedience.

The guard's hand left my back. He chuckled. "If she doesn't want to bow, perhaps she wants to crawl."

My back snapped upright, and I jumped a mile. My new owner stood directly in front of me. Hands in his slack pockets, head cocked slightly to the side, as if inspecting a piece of art.

"She may crawl if she wishes," he murmured.

"I do not wish," I snapped.

Once again, our eyes connected and I searched for the evil like the men in Mexico, but he guarded himself too well. Nothing gave away what he thought, even the emotions I'd seen before were gone.

We stood staring for moments, before the guard behind me cleared his throat. Shattering the fragile silence and condemning me to whatever would happen next.

"Laissez-nous." The man waved a hand toward the exit. Instantly, the guard left along with a few others I hadn't seen lurking. The rustle of their suits sounded like a death sentence as they siphoned out the door.

Oh, God.

My eyes flicked to the left, where a massive library beckoned. Sultry mahogany, rich maroons, and gold bookcases. A roaring fire beckoned to read a book and slouch in the wingback chairs huddled around the flames.

To the right, a ginormous lounge full of comfortable designer sofas and chairs. Animal hides of zebra and tiger littered the floor, and huge glass doors reflected me standing under the bright lights of the foyer.

The man stood an arm's length away. Tears thickened my throat.

I dropped my gaze, unable to look anymore. Tiredness descended, and all I wanted to do was sleep—to escape this nightmare.

"You won't be able to run," he said, watching closely.

I sucked in a breath. "Who says I'm going to run?"

His lips, smooth and well defined against his five o'clock shadow, twitched. "I smell it on you—the scent of prey. You're looking for a bolthole, somewhere no one can find you." He leaned in, sending a cloud of expensive cologne around me. "You're different, I'll give you that. They didn't break you, but don't think you can fight me. You won't win."

My heart seized. His tone bordered on angry. He was angry at *me*? I was the victim here. My chest swelled with indignation. "What do you expect? I was smuggled here. You *bought* me. I didn't come freely. Of course, I want to run."

His body flinched and mouth pursed. "I'll allow that one indiscretion. Push me again and you'll wish you hadn't." His unusual pale green eyes dropped, intimately following my contours. He stepped forward, so close his body heat tingled. "There are things you need to understand."

I wanted to step back, to keep distance between us, but it would look weak. Instead, I stepped forward, practically pushing my chest against his. "The only thing I need to understand is you're a monster who bought me. You stole my life. My loved ones." My voice cracked, but I plundered on, "You took everything. That's all I need to understand."

His hand reached to touch my cheek. I sucked in a breath as he ran the pad of a thumb along my jaw, then his eyes flashed with amazement as if shocked he'd touched me. Dropping his hand, he wrapped long fingers around my elbow. "Come with me."

My skin flared beneath his touch, heart raced. I twisted,

trying to remove him. "Let me go."

Eyes seared into mine. "You are not in a position to order, slave."

Was it his French accent, or the word slave, making my stomach roll and toil? Nerve endings sparked with rage. Bastard. "I. Am. Not. A. Slave."

He slapped me, not hard, but the punishment put me in my place.

I bit my lip, staunching the flow of unwelcome tears as he carted me into the library. With a heavy sigh, he shoved me into a wingback and sat opposite.

I winced, but held my tongue. I didn't want him knowing I hurt, even if he could grant me painkillers. Not that he would. He was a cold-hearted bastard who wanted broken and weak.

Leaning forward, he clasped his hands between his open legs, so close, dominating the space. Eyes searched my face again, almost imploring to know my secrets.

Discomfort made me wriggle, and I refused to make eye contact, preferring to stare at the licking fire.

We didn't move and I wasn't about to break the heavy silence. I wanted to go home.

Taking a breath, he said, "You are mine. Through circumstances I will not discuss with you, you have come into my possession, and therefore must obey me in all things."

Like hell.

"You are not permitted to use the internet, phone, or any technology of any kind. You may not speak to the staff. You may not leave the house."

He stood, toned muscles glided to the large wooden desk. Pulling a piece of paper free and a small black pouch, he settled back down. "My business partners didn't say where they got you from, what languages you speak, what skills you have. You are no one—a fresh start. We will get along if you remember that." He leaned forward again, encroaching on my space. "You are no one's but mine. Do you understand?" Eyes flashed with excitement as he spoke, as if he loved the idea. Of course, he loved the idea. How many other women did he ruin?

Options ran through my head. I could spit in his face. Try and knee him in the balls. Run and scream. All of those choices ended with consequences and pain.

I stayed mute and still.

The man dropped to his knees, pushing the chair behind in one swoop. My heart raced as he inched forward, his breath hot on my bare thighs. So soon? I hadn't been there for ten minutes and he planned to rape me already? Shit, I couldn't do this. I'd only ever been with Brax. Brax was my first. The one who stole my innocence and my heart.

Breathe. Pretend you're somewhere else.

I gripped the arm rests as he tugged my leg onto his thigh and rolled down my socks. His fingers scorched my flesh all the way down, turning my bruises and sprained ankle into pinpoints of heat. My face scrunched and I gasped as the sock slid off my foot, leaving me bare.

He frowned, glaring at my ankle. Swollen and hot, it looked worse than it felt, but he stared as if my bone stuck out. "Did they do this to you?" His voice was soft, heartfelt as his gaze travelled back up my leg, spotting the bruises, the abrasions, remnants of my captivity and Leather Jacket's hospitality.

My pulse came faster at his concern, then anger followed hot and true. "What do you care? You'll probably do worse."

His eyes snapped to mine and fingers twitched on my calf. "I care, because I don't like damaged girls. And I won't do worse." He lowered his voice, fingers tightening. "Unless you deserve it." His face blazed with protectiveness, followed by heart stopping need. He seemed to battle his interest, whatever sick attraction he had for me.

My heart raced, blood churned. I swallowed hard and waited for wandering hands, horrible fingers, but nothing happened.

The man leaned back, removing his touch. In quick, assertive moves, he pulled a long item from the black pouch and pressed a button at the back. A bright red light flared before muting to nothing.

Shuffling closer until an expensively clad shoulder brushed my knee, he unrolled my other sock and wrapped the item around my uninjured ankle. The cold bite of plastic made me flinch, but it didn't stop him from tightening it. The snap of the twist tie set my heart beating, undoable but for a blade or scissors.

He stood and sat on the edge of the wingback once finished.

I spoke before I thought. "What is that?"

Sitting back, he wiped his hands on his trouser legs. "It's a tracking device." Motioning to my bare legs, he added, "If you're uncomfortable, you may put your socks back on."

Ignoring the fact he'd tagged me again, like the Mexicans, I said, "They aren't my socks. It's what the kidnappers dressed me in." I didn't know what I expected by telling him, but the blank look of disinterest was not it.

Swiping a middle fingertip along an eyebrow, he checked the time on his diamond-encrusted Rolex. "That device informs me where you are at all times. See, slave, no escape."

I had an insane urge to laugh. It was complete overkill. I had a barcode tattooed into my flesh, a beacon in my neck, and a GPS on my foot. I glared, hating him as much as I hated the men in Mexico. What happened to the other women? Did the little Asian girl who was as fierce as me end up in the same circumstances?

The man picked up the paper from the floor and passed it to me. "This is all I have on you. I want to know more."

I took it and my throat closed.

Subject: Blonde Girl on Scooter
Barcode reference: 302493528752445
Age: Twenty to thirty
Temperament: Angry and violent
Sexual status: Not virgin
Sexual heath: No diseases
Ownership guidelines: Recommend strict punishment to break temper. Trim body, fit enough for extreme activities.
History: No living relatives

Oh, God. Brax. Did that mean he didn't survive? No, I'd feel it if he were gone for good. Wouldn't I? Something would break inside; become a void if he was gone forever.

I looked up, wide-eyed, hoping for some sort of compassion, something to latch onto while I swirled in misery, but the man stayed straight and taut, eyes closed off.

"What is your name?" he asked, French accent floating over me. I'd always thought the French accent was sexy, suave. Now, all I wanted to do was throw up and rip my ears off.

Anger dispelled my fear about Brax, and I snarled, "If I'm no one, why do you want to know my name?"

A flash of erotic yearning flickered across his face. "You're right. It's not necessary. However, it's a lonely existence if no one calls you by your name." The way he said it bristled with dark intensity. *Don't try to get my sympathy vote. You don't know true loneliness.*

"Why did you buy me?"

He leaned back, steepling his fingers. "I didn't. You were a gift. An unwanted gift." His lips twitched. "A bribe, if you will."

My stomach coiled like a viper. I'd been given to someone who didn't even want me. At least if someone had bought me, spent a lot of money, they might treat me a little better. Like a prized racehorse or an expensive breed of cat. But this... I was an unwanted present. Like a hand knitted jumper at Christmas.

"What will you do with me?" My voice was barely a whisper.

"That is none of your concern."

"You don't think my future is any of my concern?"

"No. Because your future is mine."

I breathed hard at the unfairness.

He stood, looking down at me. In a flash of movement, he pressed me into the chair, hands over mine on the armrests. I stopped breathing. I stopped everything. I was immobile.

His gaze captured mine, holding me prisoner in their pale green depths. Something dark and urgent flashed, then disappeared. His eyes dropped to my lips and his mouth parted.

The heavy, heated air from the fire seared us. Every crackle of flames made me twitch.

Do not move. Do not move.

Finally, the man pulled back. It looked like it took a lot of effort and he adjusted himself discreetly. "Don't you want to know who you belong to?"

The jump from overbearing to questioning took a while to catch up. Slowly, I shook my head. Why would I want to know his name when I had no intention of using it? "No."

His nostrils flared; he strode away. His suit whispered with every footstep and he paused in the doorway.

"You have to call me something, and I don't want master or owner. You're ordered to call me Q."

"Q?"

He didn't answer. Striding away, he said over a shoulder, "My staff will show you to your room. Remember. Don't try to escape. There isn't any."

Chapter Nine

Blackbird

The moment Q left the library, a silhouette appeared. I jumped a mile, holding my chest.

Images of a dark minion throwing me in a cellar to live with rats, filled me with fear. I tried to stay calm, remembering Q hadn't liked my injuries. I doubted he'd make me sleep in a dank dungeon where I could get sick. After all, if I died of pneumonia where was the fun in that?

The girl, probably mid-twenties, with chestnut hair plaited in a tidy knot, smiled. "I didn't mean to startle you." Her accent was soft and feminine; hazel eyes glowed in dusky skin. Why the hell was she working for a man like Q?

Did she know who I was? *What* I was?

"Please, follow me." She motioned out the door and into the foyer. "Do you have possessions with you?" she asked as we walked awkwardly side by side.

My eyes popped wide, and I snorted darkly. "No, I don't have any possessions."

I *was* one.

The thought snatched me around the throat. I had to stop thinking that. I wasn't anything but Tess. I'd survive.

"Oh, well, that's fine. I'm sure *Maître* Mercer can arrange a new wardrobe."

"Mercer?" I trotted beside her up the flight of stairs. The thick blue carpet was like a cloud between my toes. Hang on, Q told me not to speak to the staff. I paused, weighing if talking to this girl was worth whatever punishment he'd grant. I curled my hands.

Screw it, for the first time in a week, someone wanted to talk rather than order or demand.

"The owner of this household. He's—well, he's the master."

I didn't like the sound of that. I wanted words like fair and a nice employer. Not for the maid to flush and shut up.

In silence, we walked down the longest corridor I'd seen in my life and ascended another twirling staircase before stopping outside a white lacquered door.

"This is yours. I've arranged for new bedding, and prepared it for your arrival."

How long did they know I was coming? Days? Weeks? Fluffing sheets and ironing towels for an unwanted bribe. Who gave a stolen woman as a present, and for what? My mind ran with thoughts of drug dealing, or illegal weaponry, something completely far out to warrant a trafficked girl as collateral. *Underhanded bastard Q.*

I steeled against using his name. Q. What a ridiculous title.

I opened the door and slammed to a halt. I wanted to laugh. Sure, I was surrounded by elegant wealth, but I was a lowly slave and didn't deserve space, or light, or niceties.

Stark and bare, the bedroom did nothing to invite or warm. The single bed, wardrobe, and shelves looked barren and unwelcoming, but the linen smelled clean and the air was fresh.

It was a cell, for all intents and purposes, but thankfulness swelled at having my own room with a hygienic bed. After a week in the Mexican trafficker jail, this was five stars.

My heart plummeted at the thought of Brax. He would hate the thought of me living here. Even our tiny, one bedroom apartment was comfy and designer style. Many a weekend, Brax knocked together a DIY project, the last being a sleigh bed from an old gum tree. This little room rested inside a mansion—owned by someone who wouldn't hesitate to use me, however he wanted.

Oxygen turned to soup and I gave up trying to be fierce. Tears glassed my vision and spilled. My life would never be the same.

The maid tutted in concern, pushing me toward the bed. "There, there. Don't cry. You have your own bathroom, and we can get some personal things to decorate." Her warm arm descended timidly around my shoulders and I rocked.

Now I was here, in the destination of my fate, I lost strength. I wanted to stay angry and strong, but pity and loss swelled.

The simple contact of a caring woman unbuckled me. I sobbed.

Into my hands, into a pillow, into sleep.

The next morning, I was left to my own devices. I showered, and dressed in my sack of a sweater. Not knowing, or caring, if clothes had been bought for me. The rebellion at such a simple thing kept my fire smouldering deep inside.

I left my socks off and padded bare foot down the staircase. I could only assume I'd been put in the staff quarters. The ruckus at five a.m., with people having showers and preparing for the day, kept me up.

Not that I slept. I was foggy-headed with tears and awoke with a splitting headache, but crying purged me, leaving me eerily empty and ready to face my new future.

One thing niggled, though. I didn't have experience in the way of slavery and ownership, but found it surprising Q let me wander freely with no supervision. *Probably some sort of chauvinistic mind game and power trip.*

I couldn't shed my apprehension as I entered the lounge and followed the sounds of cutlery clinking. Scents of freshly brewed coffee coaxed me forward, despite trepidation. My mouth watered for caffeine.

Rounding the corner, I halted as the kitchen came into view. Pale green tiles ran floor to ceiling, acting like a coloured mirror. *They're the same colour as Q's eyes.*

I had to admit my strange new owner had taste. White cabinetry with silver handles glinted like fresh snow, thanks to the sun streaming from the massive skylight. Three stainless steel ovens, a huge cooktop, and a fridge big enough to fit a whole cow completed the huge expanse. Another room, with a temperature gauge and wooden shelving, housed countless bottles of wine. No doubt from a vineyard close-by if we were, indeed, in France.

The girl who'd been so kind to me last night, smiled behind a counter. "*Bonjour.* Are you hungry?"

I didn't think I could eat with all the strangeness, but nodded anyway. I had to keep my strength, and I couldn't remember the last time I'd been fed. No wait, I did remember—the night Leather Jacket tried to rape me. *Fucking bastard.*

My lips curled, thinking how quickly I'd gone from a girl who never cursed, to a gutter mouth. In a way, it gave me strength, being crude and crass.

My stomach growled, taking control out of my hands.

The maid giggled. "Guess that answers the question. But before we can feed you, the master requested you join him. He's in the dining room." She cocked her head at the other end of the lounge. A pair of sliding glass doors blocked a decadent, old English style dining room.

Q sat at the head of the table. A newspaper spread wide, blocking his face.

Seeing him sent barbwire tangling around my stomach. The house lulled me into some sense of acceptance, but I'd never get used to being *owned*—of being someone's slave.

Not that he bought me, only accepted as a bribe. Curiosity rose, wanting to know what I was accepted for, but I shoved it away. I didn't care as I wouldn't be staying long. I'd find a way to run—soon.

I shook my head, looking back at the maid. "I'm not seeing him."

The maid stilled, hands full of pastries. "You have no choice. He summons. You go. That's the law."

"Law?" My eyebrow twitched. I instantly hated the word. The law was something officers upheld. A word implying safety, not rules dictated by a mad man.

"Law." The masculine baritone came from behind. His presence sent chills up and down my spine. I didn't jump. I prided myself on that, but I'd have to get used to how silently he moved. I did not want to be snuck up on, surprised, and taken advantage of.

Keeping my head high and back straight, I turned to face the *master.*

"I obey no such law."

Q growled, rubbing a hand over his stubbly cheek. His dark brown hair was glossy, short, almost like a pelt rather than hair. His wintery green gaze froze me to the core. Dressed in a graphite suit with silver shirt and black tie, he looked distinguished, intelligent.

I cried out as he grabbed me. "I summon. You come. That's the only law you need to understand. I am your owner. You haven't forgotten that so soon, have you?"

He marched me through the lounge and into the dining room. Tossing me into a high backed chair at a table set for twenty people, he breathed hard and leaned over me. "You are mine. You are mine. Repeat that until it gets into your head. You cannot disobey. Unless..." A glint of interest smouldered in his eyes. "Unless you *want* to be punished?"

My heart kicked into high gear, thrumming with hummingbird wings. I shook my head hard. My tongue turned useless, incapable of speech. I'd never been so overpowered by someone's sheer will, but Q flattened me with his intense demeanour. How could I hope to disobey when he only had to threaten with mere words and I turned horribly docile?

"You've forgotten how to fight, so soon?" His accent thickened and fingers captured my chin, pressing painfully. A rumble sounded in his chest, and, fast as lightning, he kissed me.

The force of the attack crashed my head against the back of the chair, radiating pain in my temples. His lips forced mine open, and a tongue darted into my mouth, stealing my will, my fight. He stole everything with one touch.

Growling, his tongue plundered mine ruthlessly, out of control. Fingers trailed from my chin to my throat, circling possessively; an unspoken threat that he could kill me and no one would know or care. I was his—to do with how he pleased.

I moaned and scratched his face with ragged nails.

He jerked back, breathing like an angry bull. His lips glistened from ravaging my mouth, leaving the taste of rich coffee and something darker—a promise of more.

He glared, swiping his cheek with a shirt cuff. It came away with a drip of crimson. His body tensed at the sight of blood.

My heart swelled with pride. He may be able to molest me, but he wouldn't stay whole while he did.

Grabbing a napkin from the table, he patted his

cheek. "You will obey. Don't make me use you like any other buyer would do."

"Isn't that what you mean to do anyway? Rape and ruin me?"

Throwing the napkin down, he stalked back to his chair at the head of the table. The discarded newspaper crackled as he placed hands in front of him. Every move was precise, calculated, as if he knew every nuance illustrated domination.

Four place settings separated us, giving a sense of space. I breathed easier, wishing the taste of darkness and sin would leave. Why did he have to kiss me? A kiss meant intimacy and romance, but that kiss—it claimed me more than any kiss from Brax. It made me hate Q all the more.

Ignoring my question, he demanded, "What is your name?"

I crossed my arms, glaring. *Never.*

"Fine," he barked. "I'll call you Dove, until you answer. Like the grey-blue of your eyes."

My heart tinkled into tiny, irreplaceable pieces. *Dove?* Anger ran up my neck and flamed as memories of Brax swarmed. The soft toy he bought me when I was in hospital. The many times he called me his little Dove.

"No!" I screamed, violence etching my tone.

He didn't even blink at my outburst. Deliberately, he ran a finger along his bottom lip, glaring coldly. His face shadowed with authority, and to my utter shame, my nipples hardened. My body recalled the way he kissed—responding to every part I dare not acknowledge, parts I wished didn't exist. It made me feel as if I led him on—invited all of this to happen with my twisted desires.

Holy hell, *did* I invite this by wanting to be rougher with Brax? Did my fate decide I had a life too perfect and granted my sick desires in the worst way possible?

I couldn't breathe. I stared at the tablecloth as the maid entered the room with a dainty knock, and placed a plate of poached eggs in front of me. She bowed slightly to Q, putting the same in front of him.

Even though my limbs were weak with hunger, I pushed the plate away. How could I eat when I disgusted myself? All of this was *my* fault. I was responsible with my screwed up perversions.

"Eat, damn you," Q ordered, face stoic.

After everything I'd been through, after the breath stealing kiss, and the bloody Mexicans, and my stupid naivety—I could go on and on—I embraced my gutter mouth. "Fuck. You."

His eyes widened and jaw clenched, but he didn't retaliate. He cut a delicate mouthful, chewing carefully. Every bite controlled and precise, as if he kept a tight rein on himself at all times. What did he battle with? Because he battled, I saw that in his eyes.

"If you won't tell me your name, tell me something else about you."

Why did he want to know? He'd already said nothing else mattered but being his.

Swallowing, I stared outside, toward the terrace and the huge bird table swarming with noisy sparrows and blackbirds. The manicured gardens, with perfect hedges and bare flowers, glittered with frost like sparkly lace. From hot Mexico to winter in France, I missed home miserably.

Q put his knife and fork down, placing his hands in his lap. I made the mistake of looking at him, and we engaged in another staring competition. I yelled and screamed silently while he sat and dominated with unsaid threats.

He broke the contest, murmuring, "You have two choices."

My ears pricked, but I pretended insolence. Two choices. Try three. Whatever the first two, the third was escape. I'd make it happen. I'd laser my tattoo off, cut the GPS tag off my ankle, and find a way to remove the node in my neck. I may have brought this on myself, but I would get myself out of it.

Q continued in his deep, accented voice, "One, I rape you, hurt you, do everything you expect of me, and make you live a miserable existence."

I narrowed my eyes, watching closely. His shoulders tensed on the word rape, but excitement heated his gaze, too. Why the two emotions? One hot and wanting, the other repulsed and angry. Lacing my fingers together, I squeezed. Fear threatened to close my throat.

"Or, tell me about yourself, and, if you have a skill I need, I'll put you to work in other ways."

I couldn't help myself. "Other ways?"

Regret flickered across his face so quickly, I wondered if I imagined it. He nodded infinitesimally. "Other ways."

"Like what?"

"Tell me about yourself."

"Tell me first."

He slammed his hands on either side of his plate, rattling the china. "Goddammit, girl, I'm offering you a choice. But it doesn't mean I can't take that choice away." He breathed hard and his anger sent fear spiralling inside.

He called me girl, and yet, I doubted he was much older. Early thirties at the latest. But age didn't matter when he shouted. He scared me more than Leather Jacket did. At least with him, I knew the man I fought. Q, I had no idea.

Trying to focus, I sucked in a breath. Q offered me a choice. If I wanted to escape, I had to bide my time. If Q put me to work, I might have more opportunity than being tied to a bed.

I mirrored him, placing my hands on the table, strengthening my resolve. "What do you want to know?"

His shoulders relaxed a little, but the hardness in his pale green gaze never left. "Where are you from?"

"Melbourne."

"Do you speak any other language but English?"

I shook my head.

He snorted. "That's the first thing to change. I refuse to speak English for long periods. It's a boring language. You will learn French." Waving the comment away, he asked, "What other education do you have?"

I walked a spider's web, one wrong answer and I tickled the wrong strand, inviting choice number one of rape and ruin.

"I'm still at university. I've waitressed and worked in retail."

He huffed, inspecting perfect fingernails. "Nothing of importance. You better have more talent, otherwise…"

I rushed, "I'm training to be in property development. I've almost completed a project managing degree and side line in architectural sketches."

He paused. Interest replaced the hardness in his eyes for a brief moment, before the shutters slammed closed again. "Go on."

There wasn't much else to say. "I've yet to sit final exams, but I studied how to do building budgets, deal with local councils, permits, trade requirements. I'm top in the class for an eco-sustainable village concept for our mid-terms." I fibbed. I came second, but if he wanted me in property, shit, I'd be the best in property I could be.

He leaned back, steepling his fingers again. I fast recognized the trademark move. Q moved with power and the undeniable knowledge of perfect control. "How did they take you?"

The abrupt change in conversation side-lined me.

I thought I'd pushed the terror down deep from being kidnapped, and purged myself last night through a wash of tears, but panic rose and roared, blotting out everything, apart from the agony of seeing Brax bleeding and men knocking me unconscious. Oh, God, would I ever be free?

Q shifted, waiting. He neither cared, nor took sadistic interest as I struggled with memories. Why the hell did he bring it up? *Bastard.*

I answered in a monotone, pretending I hadn't lived it. Surprisingly, it helped distance myself, and a shot of pride filled me. I'd fought and taught Leather Jacket a lesson or two. I celebrated the small win. "I was taken in Mexico. They hurt my boyfriend, knocked me out, and took me somewhere."

"Did they hurt you? Apart from your ankle?"

If he classified being beaten and tattooed, then yes. I nodded.

He sucked in a breath, forehead furrowing. "Did they rape you?"

Leather Jacket tried, but failed. A cold smile tugged my lips. "No. One tried. He wasn't successful."

His hard smile matched mine, and something webbed between us. Understanding? Respect? Something I said changed the way Q thought of me.

My pulse accelerated. Perhaps, if I made him see *me*, not as a possession but as a woman, things might not be so lost after all.

Whatever his feelings, if his respect granted safety, I was all for it.

Whatever happened between us disappeared when Q murmured, "What's your name?" He kept his eyes shadowed by looking at the newspaper on the table. Did he not think I noticed the casual question?

I pursed my lips, not answering.

After a moment, he looked up, glaring. "You will tell me your name."

My breath came faster, hurting my rib, but I remained silent. *What are you doing, Tess? Is another beating really worth keeping your name a secret?* I knew the answer: yes, it was. My name was the only thing I owned. It was sacred.

I jumped as Q called, "Suzette!" His chin rose, showing a

graceful neck and rough-smoothness. Cords of muscle hinted at a rigorous exercise program, yet his body wasn't bulky. In another life, I would've drooled over him. He ought to be on the cover of a GQ magazine. My eyes narrowed. Was that why he called himself Q? So egotistical.

The maid appeared. Her soft smile and adoration for her employer shot me in the heart. How could she be loyal and like this man?

"Oui, maître?"

"Enfermer la dans la bibliothèque. Retirez le téléphone et l'ordinateur portable. Vous avez compris?"

I blinked, wishing I'd stayed with French in high school. Rusty cogs worked hard, shedding dust on a language I knew, but hadn't used in years. Something about a library and a computer.

My eyes flashed between Q and Suzette.

She bowed. *"Oui, autre chose?"*

My mind sped, letting my brain stretch and remember. She'd asked if he wanted anything else. I'd never been thankful for a good memory before, but I wanted to cry with relief—I wouldn't be completely in the dark.

Q froze, and Suzette locked him in her hazel stare. Her stance yelled protectiveness, understanding. Eyes urged him to do… what?

They stared for an eternity, involved in silent conversation, leaving me a third wheel. Finally, Q nodded, sighing, *"Vous savez?"* You know.

She relaxed, face full of sad acknowledgement. *"Elle est différente."* She shrugged. *"Ne la punissez pas."*

She spoke so fast, I only caught different and punishment. My stomach clenched as Q glanced at me, a tortuous mix of lust and hatred in his face.

He nodded sharply, letting his guard down; eyes flared with hunger. *"Oui."* His voice sent shivers across my skin.

Instinct knew before my mind. Something changed in Q. He'd given in to the battle he fought. My heart jumped from its prison of ribs, galloping around my chest. Sinister knowledge coiled through my veins. He gave up fighting. The decision shone in his resigned but tense body. Terror demanded to know exactly what he'd given in to.

Suzette looked at me with pity and hope, before disappearing into the lounge. I wanted to run after her, beg to know what was happening.

Q stood, brushing his immaculate suit and silver shirt. Avoiding my gaze, he said, "Suzette has her orders. Follow them. And, seeing as you refuse to tell me your name, you'll be called *esclave* until you do. If you're going to learn French, let that be your first word."

Now was not the time to advise I knew enough to understand.

He went to walk around the table, but changed his mind. My skin heated as he came closer, and I sucked in a ragged breath as he pressed against me. His hard thigh connected with my shoulder. He rocked his hips, deliberately making me very aware of what was between his legs.

My mind rebelled as everything within flushed to an all-encompassing need. He was so hard and long—rigid and unforgiving. The way he loomed above me sent fear fluttering, mixing with unwanted desire.

I twisted away, wincing from my rib, but the pain couldn't stop the hatred for my traitorous body. How could I even think of desire? That was the thing—I didn't think. My body reacted. Starved of something it needed for so long, coupled with the act of control, triggered buttons despite my terror and repulsion. Tears choked. How could I? *I'm a sick, twisted freak.*

Q interrupted my confusion and hatred. "Do you know that word?"

I didn't have a clue, too involved mentally beating myself

for such a horrid betrayal. *Fight! Think of Brax.* My heart stopped. *No, don't think of Brax.*

Q captured my chin, a flare of heat clenched my stomach. "*Esclave,* answer me. Do you know that word?" His mouth was so close; I couldn't tear my eyes away.

Ordering my brain to work, ignoring my sinning body, I shook my head. I did know the word: slave. But ignorance was a weapon, and I didn't want him to know my arsenal.

I thought fast, thankful when the threads of lust blazed to hate. Yes, hate. That emotion would be my salvation whenever Q managed to turn my body against me.

My voice shook. "I am not an *esclave* and you are not my *maître.* You will never be."

His pupils dilated, and a hand shot from nowhere, wrapping around my neck. We stared nose to nose, him looming in an expensive Gucci suit, me in a tattered jumper. "You *are* my *esclave.* It isn't negotiable. And consider my proposal for two options revoked. I can no longer do so." He breathed hard with unmasked desire. "You're mine, and I chose option one."

I panted. I ached. Every cell erupted, dripping with black, dangerous thoughts. I struggled to remember how much I hated Q, as a carousel of emotions swirled, making me dizzy, hurtling me into darkness. In the darkness lurked heat, fear, intoxication, hyperawareness.

A tear trickled down my cheek; I was ruined already.

Q growled and I liquefied deep inside. My traitorous body swelled and warmed all the while my mind revolted, spewing obscenities. How could I allow my body to betray me so completely? *Why am I so fucked up?*

Q watched my unravelling in wonderment. His mouth parted, pale eyes blazing.

All of this was wrong. So, so wrong. I fell headlong into mourning.

Q ran his nose down mine, breathing deep. Something hard and tight squeezed my stomach. I didn't move. I *couldn't* move.

"I don't want option one," I whispered. I knew what it included: degradation, sexual torture, all manner of things one would do with an unwanted possession. Played with, toyed with, and ultimately thrown out with the trash.

Another rebellious tear escaped, and I hated the droplet with everything. It showed how weak I was, how ruined I already felt.

Q froze, watching the tear trail down my cheek, tickling heated skin. Eyes flashed to mine, and for a millisecond, I saw something human—compassion, remorse, then hunger reclaimed him and he ducked. His tongue swept over my cheek with gentle tenderness, capturing my salty remorse, then ran over his bottom lip.

Maybe because Leather Jacket licked me the same way, or once again instincts knew something I had yet to understand, I relaxed a little. Q didn't lick with sick pleasure, he licked with kindness.

The screwed up, broken part of me, reacted to Q's insolent possessiveness. I wanted so much to believe he would be kind and not hurt me. But he accepted me as a bribe! No one with a soul would do that. I couldn't afford to let his act beguile me.

My eyes snapped closed, protecting all facets of my soul. Ten percent wanted him to deliver his threats—wanted him to be rough and use me. While ninety percent wanted to stab him with the butter knife over and over, until blood decorated the silver wallpaper and pretty tablecloth.

He released me, trailing soft fingertips through my hair. I swayed, broken so easily, confused completely.

His eyes flashed as he whispered, "Until tonight, *esclave*."

Chapter Ten

Swallow

Being a slave was…dare I say…boring.

After Q left, Suzette hovered, never letting me out of sight. She came across as sweet and obedient, but I saw the truth. She was Q's: a head housekeeper who helped keep his slave in line. What had she said to him in the dining room? She'd antagonized, while giving him permission. Q may pay her salary, but she held a power over him I didn't understand.

I didn't think he would've pressed against me or licked my tears if she hadn't encouraged him to give in to the battle inside.

Sometimes, I really hated having sensitive instincts— I sensed too much—painted too vivid futures that I didn't want to come true.

What freaked me out the most was Q listened to her—pushed by his maid to do something he couldn't restrain. My eyes narrowed, trying to figure out their relationship.

Surprisingly, with Q gone, my hunger came back, and I devoured the cold poached eggs. Suzette never left, and once I finished, she guided me toward the library, nonchalantly closing the door.

She left and my ears pricked as the lock clicked.

She may have left with a sweet smile, and my cell might've upgraded to include expensive literature and crystal decanters, but it was still a cage.

My thoughts filled with Q. Where did he disappear to? Probably to run an empire full of illegal activities and debauchery. Only work that danced with unlawful things could grant this sort of wealth. I wouldn't be surprised if he was a major drug dealer.

I threw myself into a wingback and stiffened. His scent enveloped me, sending my heartbeats racing with notes of sandalwood, juniper, and citrus.

My throat closed, connecting the smell of him to unhappiness. I wanted to look out the window, plot my escape, but the library had dark cedar shutters blocking the sun, protecting delicate books within. The air shimmered with dust motes and slivers of light turned the room into a calming grotto.

Despite the relaxing vibe, I couldn't sit still. Q's threat before leaving—until tonight, *esclave*—careened in my skull. I wouldn't wait patiently for whatever he planned to do. I needed to stay active. Find a weapon. Find freedom.

I tested the door, but the lock held firm. I tried the shutters, but try as I might, they wouldn't open. The only way out was the fireplace, and climbing a chimney flue did not inspire me.

Going mad with the need to run, I turned to the books, skimming through signed, first editions of priceless literature, hoping words could take me away. But nothing worked. Slamming a novel closed, I stared at the licking fire. If I burned all his books, would that teach Q a lesson?

I stood, dangling a red leather book above eager flames. *Do it.* My fingers refused to let go, and I slouched in my chair. I couldn't. I wouldn't commit sacrilege on age-old literature, no matter how I hated him.

If I was here for a while they might be my only entertainment.

Hours ticked past on a grandfather clock in the corner, chiming my life away every fifteen minutes and gonging my doom every hour.

How long before Q came back? How long before I could return to my tiny room and hide in sleep-oblivion?

My stomach grumbled as the winter sun set over rolling French countryside. I'd been curled up on the window seat for hours, peering through cedar slats. Mocked by the small slice of the world. Tiny sparrows darted, preening their feathers in the fountain. They were free—I was not.

I'd never longed for the sun so much. Its rays hadn't touched my skin in over a week. I never thought I'd crave the outdoors, especially the cold, but I did. It was an itch I couldn't scratch.

My heart squeezed as a black sedan drove sedately down the long gravel drive and stopped in front of the house. A chauffeur jumped out and opened the rear door.

Q stepped out, smiling reservedly at the man. He straightened his black trench and sucked in a deep breath, as if fortifying himself to enter his own home. The jacket stretched across his chest, showing the powerful breadth of shoulders. He tilted his head toward the library, searching for me no doubt, and fingers loosened the tie around his neck.

A look of depravity and unhappiness etched his features. I huddled on the window seat, hidden by the shutters and gloom, and conjured stories for him.

Who was this man? This conundrum, this enigma. A man so young, but so rich. A man who accepted women, who lived on his own with a galley of staff. A man who had more secrets than I ever did with Brax.

Was he hurting? Did he have a wife? I drafted a fairytale of his faults and flaws granting redemption. Perhaps he was kind under the gruff exterior. Perhaps I could appeal to a sensitive part locked far below and encourage him to release me willingly?

Perhaps.

Perhaps.

Perhaps.

I smashed at my eyes, warning them to stay dry. All my stories were just that: fiction. I had to stay in the real world. A world where focus and the preparation to bolt would save me.

My mind latched onto other things. Things like an escape pack. I needed warm clothes, a stash of food, and a knife to remove the GPS anklet. Those things would keep me alive when I found opportunity.

I could somehow make it to the Australian embassy—wherever the hell it lurked. Would they save me? Send me home. Home to Brax, and parents who didn't care. Parents who hated that I stole their retirement.

The front door swung wide as Q stepped into his home. The glass of the library doors showed him regal and proud, like a magistrate returning to his castle. All aura of confusion lining his face, gone.

He didn't pause, heading straight to the library and unlocking the door.

I tensed and wrapped my arms around my knees. I sucked in a breath as he strode into the room.

It took him a moment to find me, looking in the wingback, by the bookcases. His body coiled tight as he hunted the room. When he found me, he froze.

Something snapped between us, arching with awareness, temptation. I mentally fought it, cutting the connection.

His nostrils flared as we glared from our sides of the room.

"Come," he demanded, holding out a hand, fully expecting me act docile and follow. *As if.*

I bared my teeth, hugging myself hard. I didn't grace him with an answer; my body language screamed all he needed to know: I despised him.

He didn't demand again. Instead, he gritted his teeth and charged. With strength I feared, he plucked me from the seat as if I were an errant child. Fingers bit into my upper arm as he dragged me over plush carpeting and out of the library.

I squirmed, but couldn't dislodge him. "Get off me."

He didn't answer as we almost jogged through the house. I didn't see anyone. No noises of life, no visions of help.

Q headed straight behind the sweeping, blue velvet staircase. My breath caught as he punched the dark wood panelling.

I jumped when it popped open, revealing a door. Fear exploded in my veins. Upstairs in the house, I had the illusion of civility. If he took me down there, it symbolised a lack of constraint. My horror-filled visions might come true.

"No!" I twisted my arm, causing Q to grunt. He had no choice but to release me or earn a broken wrist.

I bolted, but Q was faster. He crashed against me and we collided into the wall. My rib roared and I panted, battling with pain. Turned out, I already forgot the lesson Leather Jacket taught me: obedience may be key, but I couldn't walk willingly down those steps. I'd rather bleed and know I tried to save myself.

Q pressed hips into mine, sandwiching his entire body against me. "Stop fighting, *esclave!*"

He managed to capture my arms, pinning them in his hands. My tattoo burned, along with rope injuries. A knee forced my legs apart, effectively trapping me.

I whimpered as my body once again disobeyed and grew hot beneath his touch. My heart rabbited as Q pressed his forehead against mine. His eyes blazed me to the core. *"Arrête."*

I stopped breathing, suspended by the hard-edged yearning in his voice.

I cocked my chin. "No."

He sighed heavily, pushing away, but keeping hold of my wrist. My muscles trembled as he dragged me through the hidden door and down the steps. He tugged too hard and I tripped.

I landed against his back, causing him to almost fall. His arms came up, wrapping around, pressing us against the banister, stabilizing.

"Merde," he muttered. "Can you not even walk? Is that why they gave you to me? Were you the reject? The one they couldn't sell for top dollar?"

His words slapped, sharp and stinging.

Is that what happened? I'd disrupted their sick operation by standing up to Leather Jacket, the weak bastards removed me before I screwed everything. Anger as well as happiness heated. Anger that they dismissed me as the reject, happiness at standing up to them.

Thank God, I fought. I didn't know how much danger I faced with Q, but I knew in my bones it was better than Mexico. I could've been drugged, raped repeatedly, and left to die in my own vomit. Now, I had to deal with a millionaire with issues.

See, Tess. Whatever happens, it's not as bad as it could've been.

Perversely, I took strength in that. I still had wits, and consciousness. I was still fundamentally me, if only hidden beneath my gutter mouth and fierce persona.

When I didn't answer, Q pulled me down the remaining stairs. The narrow flight ended, depositing us in a shadowed cave of a gaming room. To the right, an apple velvet pool table glowed beneath a low-hung, red chandelier. To the left, a sparkling bar with cut crystal sprinkled rainbows against the wall under spotlights. Wood panels on the walls and ceiling entombed us. All it needed were wisps of cigar smoke and the smell of hard liquor.

The air was hushed, private. A man's heaven.

Q threw me to the side, almost like he couldn't touch me any longer. I stumbled with momentum, toward the pool table. Balls clacked together as I disrupted the neat triangle with an elbow.

I made to turn, to face him, but his hot length folded over me, pushing me hard against the felt. I cried out as he forced my face against the table and ground hips into my ass.

I thought I'd been afraid up till this point. But I wasn't, not really. Being trapped beneath his body, with hot breath on my neck, reminded he was the predator and I was his prey. It degraded, put me in my place, all the while my blood flowed faster, breath turned cloying in my lungs.

I fought.

Wriggling, I tried to buck him off. "Let me go!"

His fingers tightened in answer, pinning me harder in place. I turned feral; my hands grabbed a heavy pool ball and tried to smash his head behind. "Motherfucker, take your hands off me."

Q moaned, sounding tortured and lost, but didn't say anything. Heavy breathing disrupted the quiet tranquillity of the den.

His silence disconcerted me. I had no clue what he thought, or planned. The quiet amplified other senses, heightened my pain in bruises, and the worst horror, the wetness between my legs.

If Brax ever did this—treated me with such ferocity—I'd have come in a moment. I read the mind turned sex from good to great. Being forced would ruin me, so why did my body ignore my fear and soften?

I'd gone from fighting to primed, ready, even as my heart stuttered and panicked.

Q seemed to sense my acquiescence. He rocked

gently, causing more heated blood to rush. He sucked in a breath, then a soft, slightly trembling hand landed on my hair, stroking, petting. Ever so slowly, he tucked blonde strands behind my ears, worshipping me with touch.

My heart unwound a little, soothed by gentleness. He forced me to surrender and accept his warped kindness.

Minutes of stroking turned my bones to molten and his touch dropped to caress my shoulder, my spine, never more than a whisper, but threatening just the same.

I expected roughness, yet he showed tenderness. How could I compete with that? Stay strong and fight when every animalistic part reacted to him.

I whimpered as his fingers trailed down my ribcage, slinking to the side and the swell of a breast.

He hummed in his throat, a sound full of restraint, but also a warning. Slowly, his fingers stroked, running circles over a tender breast, arching closer to my nipple with every touch.

My nipples tightened, puckering with need. The knowledge he was about to touch me so intimately made me pant. My reaction flared Q, and he fisted a hand in my hair, tugging my torso off the felt. His hips kept mine pinned between him and the table.

I yelped as my scalp smarted, but at the same time pleasure radiated, fiery and hot. My entire body burned.

One hand cupped my breast, squeezing a nipple. His hot mouth descended on my neck, biting with sharp teeth.

I couldn't control my body, but I didn't want him thinking I wanted this. I didn't. Not at all. "Stop. Please, don't."

I squeezed my eyes, wishing my mind could fly free from the overwhelming guilt crushing my soul. Guilt for reacting. Guilt for desperately wanting more. Guilt for wanting to kill him.

Q murmured something in French. Minty breath drifted over highly sensitive skin. His hand kneaded my breast, firmer, harder than Brax ever did. He rolled my nipple between dexterous fingers and an unwilling moan crawled up my throat.

Q tensed, pressing a hard cock firm against my ass. "*Putain*, I want you so fucking much."

He pinched my nipple and the flair of pain twisted my stomach. The pinch signified something—a claiming. "What is this?" he whispered darkly.

Q no longer bound himself to whatever rules he played by. Knowing sent aching need between my legs. I tried to stop lust from swarming, fogging, but I couldn't.

I couldn't breathe. Brax's blue eyes filled my mind. What was I *doing*? Brax would hate me for eternity if I let this happen. It didn't matter if I had no choice…I couldn't return to him after being used by another. Tears bruised, hating my weakness, hating my body.

Q bit my neck again, pressing lips along my collarbone, his expensive suit rasped against my back. "Tell me, *esclave*. What am I touching?"

My mind whirred with white noise, detaching itself. He may use my body, but my soul wouldn't be broken. I'd remain untouched. Untouchable.

When I didn't answer, he thrust against my ass, making me cry out. "What is this?"

"M—my nipple."

He bit the shell of my ear, breath gruff and loud. "Wrong. This is mine." He let me go and I breathed in relief, then froze as he touched my ass. His fingers sent fiery trails along my skin in agonisingly soft strokes, working inward, working down.

My legs trembled, breathing quickened, and my traitorous body preened, softening for more.

Q murmured, "Your skin is so soft here." His touch fluttered higher, inching closer.

A tear oozed and dripped onto the felt, turning apple to forest.

Q sucked in a breath. "I'm hurting you so much you need to cry? Have I hit you? Beat you?"

I shook my head, unable to answer.

His touch went from fluttering to branding. I gasped as an invasive hand cupped between my legs. Embarrassment, need, desire, *loathing*, all shot through my heart.

One fingertip brushed against my entrance through damp knickers. "So wet, *ma chérie*." He ran his nose down my neck as his fingertip found my clit. I bucked in his arms. His chest strained against my back. "Your body doesn't lie. It likes it. It likes me."

"I may not be able to control my physical response, but don't confuse anything with me liking you," I half-panted, half-snarled. "I won't. Ever."

He chuckled, sending vibrations. "So determined to fight? Fine." In a sharp move, he grabbed the back of my neck and pushed me toward the pool table again. Bent over, his finger moved firmer against my core. "What is this?" he whispered.

My cheeks flared with heat; I wished to be far, far away.

"Answer me, *esclave*."

"My vagina."

He chuckled, cupping harder. "Wrong again." Expert fingers worked the sides of my knickers, easing them to the left, exposing me. Everything inside tightened, wound, twisted. *Oh, God.*

Why was this happening? Brax. I didn't want to replace memories of him with this monster who thought he owned me. *Don't think.* Tears slipped silently.

The smell of sandalwood and citrus filled my nose as Q settled over me. He didn't touch, which made it worse. His fingers were there; the heat of his skin blazed against my thigh. Anticipation drove me wild as much as it killed, knowing what was to come.

Q fisted my hair, tilting my head to the side. His mouth descended on mine, a tongue opening the seam of my lips effortlessly, despite clamping shut. The moment his tongue entered my mouth, a finger plunged into me, hard and fast.

"Oh, God." My mouth opened wide; I trembled with the onslaught—the act of ownership. He wasn't gentle, he wasn't sweet.

"This is mine. Everything is…"

I knew what he wanted. The word balanced on my tongue but I swallowed. I would never say it.

"Mine," he growled. With no warning, he inserted another finger and fucked me, plunging deep and fast, my body quivering with hunger. My breath was harsh, too fast. I'd never been taken so completely. Nothing else mattered but his fingers inside, and the relentless rhythm he set. The sharp banding of an orgasm sparked in surprise; I moaned. I couldn't climax. That would be the ultimate betrayal.

I jolted, trying to remove his fingers, but he pressed harder, grinding his cock into my ass. "*Merde,* you're so wet. Wet for me." Surprise layered his voice, almost reverent. Had he never made a woman wet before? That couldn't be true, not with the expert way he dragged repulsive need from me. I hadn't gone Stockholmy—I hated him, knew what he did was wrong, but my body, shit, my body didn't care.

Q gave me something I needed since I'd started dreaming of sinful things, started looking at images online of men fucking women with a fine edge of violence.

Q rocked his hips again, and I rocked back, against my will. He sucked in a breath, tickling my neck. Even as I fought to get free, my core rippled with pleasure. His dominance created an unwanted, potent cocktail in my brain. *I don't want this. Stop!*

His fingers thrust inside, drawing more moisture from my body.

He sighed heavily, working a knee between my legs, splaying me wider. I lost balance and his fingers slipped out, gripping my hip.

His legs bent, and he grinded a trouser-covered erection against my wetness. He rocked, hard as steel and hot as a branding iron.

Little stars exploded behind my eyes. Only fabric stopped him from taking me. I hated every thrust. "Please…don't," I cried. Tears ran uncontrollably, joining the stain below.

He struggled to talk, deep and ruff. "You chose option one. Remember?"

Pressing an elbow into my back, he fumbled behind me. His hips disappeared as he unzipped his fly. The sound of metal teeth unzipping terrified me and I snapped. My body may want this, but I sure as hell didn't.

I jerked upright, ignoring the pain of his elbow. I feinted to the side, kicking his kneecap. His leg gave out, but he caught himself on the edge of the table. "Don't fight. You'll only make it worse."

How many times had I heard that? And every time it turned out to be the truth. But I couldn't *not* fight. I'd never be able to live with myself.

I breathed so hard my lungs ached. I looked frantically for the stairs. Where the hell were the fucking stairs?

I made to run, just as Q recovered. He lurched and wrapped his arms around my heaving chest, dragging us to the floor. We landed in a pile of limbs, my rib screaming. Q's fly was undone, trousers hanging precariously on his hips. My knickers were bunched to the side and oversensitive flesh was swollen, needing a release. *No! I'm not turned on. I'm not broken. Not yet.*

Manic possession scorched his eyes, and I slapped him. Q reared back, lips twisting with darkness. Violence bristled as he slammed me down, securing himself above.

I froze, locking my knees together so he couldn't settle between my legs. He clutched my chin, forcing me to look deep into his gaze. "What are you?"

I squirmed, hating the hunger in his voice, echoing the budding need in mine. I was sick to think I ever wanted this with Brax. But I *never* wanted this with Brax. I wanted light role-play, tame bondage, nothing like this. *Please, not like this.*

Q shocked me silent as he kissed my throat. He lingered, breathing deep. My stomach flipped. Pulling back, shock resonated in his face, as if he hadn't meant to resort to being gentle.

A conflict of emotions skittered in his eyes, dampening undisguised lust, twisting it into something else. He sounded regretful, "Say it, and I'll let you go. I · won't hurt you. I won't rape you. Not tonight."

I bit my lip. If I said it, I threw myself at his mercy, but if I didn't say it, I'd be raped and I couldn't handle that. Not after the trauma of everything. Not after my entire world dumped me and left me bereft. Especially not with my body being enemy number one.

"*Esclave,* say it." His mouth tickled my ear again, words vibrating through flesh.

My fight drained, the will to disobey unspooled into meekness. "Yours," I breathed, sick to my stomach, wanting to scrub my mouth out.

He kissed me, so, so softly, smelling like mint and lust—if lust had a smell. "Again."

I shook my head, trying to get free. Q's arms banded tighter, dragging me against his rock hard erection. "Don't test me. My strength to let you go is almost at breaking point. Push again, and I won't be able to stop."

"Why hesitate? That's what you mean to do, isn't it? Ruin me. Keep me captive. A sex slave. Treat me like some animal to use and abuse?" I whispered, but my tone crackled with anger, fierce and bright.

"I don't want to hurt you. I don't want to take from you," he murmured. My heart stopped. His tone hinted his thoughts—remorse.

"What do you want, then?" I raised an eyebrow in confusion.

Q paused, a flutter of fingers caressed my arm, imprisoning me, then stopped as if he did so unconsciously. "You know what I want, *esclave*."

My heart hurt. I couldn't keep up. One moment he touched me as if I were an irreplaceable piece of art, the next he held me as if I was a bitch needing a lesson. He shook me, growling in my ear. "I need you to say it again, then you can go."

Two options. Two decisions. Neither was easy. Both had consequences. But, for now, I chose the one protecting my virtue for another night.

I hung my head and murmured, "Yours."

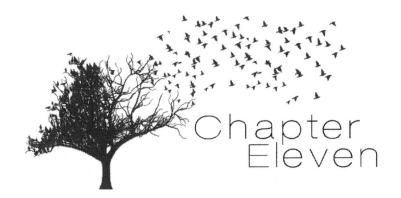

Chapter Eleven

Skylark

The next day, Suzette came for me.

I hadn't slept a wink. The moment Q let me go, I sprinted up the stairs and into my cage.

The elements of a door and walls helped contain the rising panic attack. I pushed the chest of drawers across the door and huddled in the middle of the bed. But I couldn't fall asleep, just in case Q came back to finish what he started.

All night, I battled with repeating nausea and a body too hot. I couldn't evict the fright from my lungs or the shame in my heart. Not because of what Q did—touched me, made me wet against my wishes—but because of the dark part that *wanted* him to take me. I wanted it so damn much.

My eyes remained dry, but my heart wept. Q was my punishment for making Brax so uncomfortable. The bitch, Karma, would make me live my sick fantasies— realize that I wasn't normal, that I needed help.

My rib ached from fighting, but I poked the bone, enticing more pain. I deserved to be in agony, to pay for the sins toward the sweetest man I ever knew. A man I may never see again. Pain confronted all the nastiness harbouring in my soul. *No wonder your parents never loved you. They hated you for stealing their retirement, but also because they saw what you didn't: that you're broken.*

I was a bad, bad person and deserved my fate. I brought this nightmare with my wicked thoughts.

Q was my curse.

When Suzette arrived in the morning, she tried the door, followed by a French slur and a loud knock. "Open up. You aren't allowed to block the entry." She must've leaned into the door as it opened slightly.

My eyes widened as she squeaked the dresser aside, inch by inch. Shit, if a woman her size could break my security, Q could come in whenever he damn well pleased.

Was there no way out? I'd looked out the tiny postage stamp-sized window, searching for downpipes or something to scale to the ground. But nothing could be used—trees grew too far away, and the fall looked at least five stories. Not to mention, once I managed to climb down, guards patrolled and the GPS anklet would alert Q to my location.

Suzette squeezed through the gap in the door, and placed hands on her hips. "You mustn't do that again, *esclave.*"

The word conjured everything from last night: Q's smell, his touch, his aura of power. I shuddered. I should just take my own life. It would stop the internal battle and put me out of my misery. I gulped, hating the hopelessly weak thought. *Never! Shit, Tess never. Whatever happens, you can and will survive.*

Suzette crossed her arms, staring. "It becomes easier." Her voice twisted with anger, her own issues and hurt. It didn't take a rocket scientist to know she'd been through similar circumstances.

My eyes shot to her. "Was it the same for you?" Did Q break her down bit by bit, with his odd mixture of controlling and gentleness?

She shook her head, fingers digging into her forearms. "Not *Maître* Mercer. Another." Her hazel eyes blazed then settled. She sighed, "Q is many things, but never as bad as others."

My ears pricked. Q's name on her tongue sounded strange. I was used to her calling him Master Mercer. What sort of relationship did they share? Not that I cared.

"Let me give you some advice." She moved closer; I watched warily. I didn't buy her friend act. "Let go. It doesn't have to be forever, but allow yourself to relax. It doesn't have to be wrong if he treats you right."

Her words were blasphemous, but some small part of me considered it. How would it feel to forget about Tess for a while? To play a pantomime of the perfect slave. Tess would disappear and *Esclave* would take her place. I'd be the perfect toy, all the while searching for a way to run.

It might be best for her to think I accepted the advice. I stood, bowing my head. "You're right. I'll try." How did other victims get through this? I needed a safety mechanism, something to protect my soul like a suit of armour in battle.

I'd found the protection in Mexico. I'd been ready to do anything to keep my mind whole. I just needed to do that permanently.

She smiled, dropping her arms to clap. "*Super.* Now, have a shower and dress so we can begin the day." Her eyes dropped to my dirty sweater.

I hated the pleasure beaming in her eyes, all because I agreed to give Q a chance. She bounced with happiness because I allowed the horrible new existence to rule my life. Terror iced my spine. Why her vested interest? Mental note: never let my guard down around her. Whatever I said would most likely get back to Q.

"I don't have anything else to wear."

Suzette clucked her tongue, striding toward the free-standing wardrobe. "You obviously haven't looked at what Q bought for you."

Q bought me clothes? *Creepy bastard.* First, he forced me to admit I belonged to him, then expected to dress me like a Barbie doll.

I climbed off the bed and looked over Suzette's shoulder. She was shorter, but her personality made up for her pigmy stature. She pulled out a gorgeous, slinky, silver gown with diamantes across the bodice. "*Fantastique,* this would look amazing on you."

I snorted, forgetting for a moment where I lived and indulged in talking clothes with another female. "There's no way I would wear that." I shuddered to think of the elegant material whispering over my skin, enticing men's attention— Q's attention.

Reaching over, I grabbed a pair of fitted jeans and a knitted cream sweater. They were the least blingy clothes available, but screamed designer and money.

"These will do." I cuddled them, anxious to change the Mexican sweater-dress for new clothes.

She shook her head, giggling. "If you're trying to hide your figure so Q doesn't want you, it will never work. You don't know him like I do. He's…different around you."

My heart swooped and stomach rolled. I hated her tone—the almost maternal love in her voice. What did she mean, different? Perhaps he wasn't normally a horny bastard—just my luck to bring out that side of him.

Before I could ask, she brushed past and hovered by the door. "Come down when you're done. I'll give you some privacy." With a kind smile, she shut the door, leaving me with my thoughts.

Not wanting to be alone to wallow, I quickly grabbed a white lacy bra, and matching knickers, and headed to the bathroom. Funny how, over a week ago, I dressed in expensive purple lingerie in the hope to catch Brax's eye. Now, I wanted a sack to hide in.

The shower helped settle my nerves somewhat. I

should've taken one last night after Q manhandled me, but the thought of being naked in the house, with him lurking somewhere…well, I couldn't do it. I'd rather reek—maybe then he'd be repelled.

But showering in the daytime made me comfortable. Q seemed to leave during the day, and for that, I was thankful. I had alone time—away from his prying fingers and eager mouth.

Once dressed, I headed downstairs and found Suzette in the lounge. The weak winter sun shone patches of brightness on the white carpet like golden pools. Everything about the house looked as if it belonged in a waxworks or museum. Too perfect. Too neat. Where was the haphazardness of life: the pair of shoes by the door, a dirty glass on the coffee table? It was sterile.

I ached for my home with Brax. The roughness, the texture, but most of all the happiness. I'd never find happiness here. Perhaps Suzette was right. Maybe playing a part would be easier until I could be free again.

Shutting my feelings off, I asked, "I'm here. What did you need me for?" I hoped she wouldn't lock me in the library. Q hadn't ordered me to breakfast, but who knew what rules he left her to follow.

Suzette stopped cleaning the windows with a bright pink rag and smiled. "Nothing. I didn't want you upstairs all alone, that was all." She stuffed the rag into her pinafore pocket, coming closer. "I do know what you're going through. You can talk to me. I won't betray your confidence." The look in her eyes wavered with pity and understanding.

Her kindness, and offer of friendship, wrung my heart dry. Tears sprouted, unbidden. How desperate was I for a friend? To have someone to talk to would be beyond wonderful.

You can't. She belongs to Q.

Suspicion replaced hope and I glared. "What did Q order you to do? Befriend me so I'll tell you my name? Tell you things I'll never tell him? Strip me of my only defence?"

Her mouth gaped, face twisted. "No, not at all. I'm only trying to be nice."

Her reaction caused doubt and I slouched. I was a bitch. When I didn't reply, an uncomfortable silence fell.

A woman called from the kitchen, "*Suzette, arrêtez de parler à l'esclave et venez m'aider à faire le dîner de maître Mercer. C'est dimanche; je ne vais pas faire le canard à l'orange toute seule.*"

I strained, deciphering the long string of French. Something like: stop talking to the slave and make dinner for Master Mercer—my torturer. He didn't deserve food.

I raised an eyebrow as Suzette smiled. I'd give anything to know what she thought—it might help figure out what the hell my future held.

"Do you want to come help us cook? *Maître* Mercer has duck à l'orange on Sundays. It takes a while to prepare."

My mouth hung open. She honestly thought I wanted to prepare dinner for the bastard who'd fingered me last night? Did she know what happened in the gaming room? My cheeks flushed. Q hadn't exactly been discreet, dragging me down the stairs.

I laughed with a bitter edge. "Do you want my honest answer? Or the one I should give?"

Suzette dropped her eyes, stepping closer. Her gaze bounced fugitively toward the kitchen. "Come help. Be a part of the household, while he isn't here. He can't stop you from having fun, companionship." Her hand fluttered on mine; I tensed. "If you find connection with others, you'll be able to withstand a lot more."

Stand more? Of what? Erotic torture and mind-warping games? I laughed again, brittle and tear-sharp. "You think I'll be able to have fun? That's an impossibility. Let me go. Let me return to my boyfriend, then I'll have fun." My body shook as anger exploded. I wished it were Q I screamed at, but his minion would have to do. "Brax might be dead because of the men who kidnapped me. All because your sick boss likes to own women. All of this is a mistake." I thumped my chest, buckling with heartache. "Brax might be *dead*. Do you understand? And it's all my fault!"

She nodded, biting her lip, distressed by my outburst. "I'm so sorry to hear about your boyfriend, but you have to forget him. He's in your past, and *Maître* Mercer isn't a bad man. Give him a cha—"

I slapped hands over my ears, like a child refusing to hear the awful truth. "You're heartless to think I could ever forget about Brax." I fought tears with temper. "And stop lying for Q. Stop trying to mould me into whatever he expects slaves to be. Just stop it!"

She touched my arm, tugging lightly so I released my ears. She whispered, "Don't stop living while you endure. And don't let the pain of your past stop you from being happy in this new life." Taking a deep breath, her passion tinged with anger as she added, "Don't do what I did, and pretend it will all go away. I let my owners break me. Not because I couldn't fight anymore, but because it was the easier way to live; you never truly break. The key is not to lie to yourself, even while you fake it."

Breathing hard, I dropped my arms. Her hazel irises were clear and full of wisdom. She'd learned the hard way and wanted to help me cheat on the lessons coming.

I still didn't know why she spoke so highly of Q, but I thawed a little. However, the memory of sitting in Brax's lap, on our last night together, fragmented me. Brax's voice resonated in my thoughts, *"The truth hurts less than fibs and fakers."*

I had to abandon the truth and wrap myself in lies to survive. I had to change completely.

Suzette showed a different reality, and even though she rattled the bars of my jail and confirmed there was no way out, she comforted, too. She was living evidence I could endure and survive.

"Thank you," I murmured. "Surprisingly, that does help a little."

Linking her arm with mine, she tugged me toward the kitchen. "I'm glad. Next time, don't fight him, okay?"

My hackles rose, effectively stomping on my warming feelings toward her. "What does it matter to you?"

She refused to meet my eyes. "Doesn't matter. Come along, dinner won't cook itself."

Hours later, flour dusted my nose, and the citrus tang of orange enveloped the kitchen. The cook, Mrs. Sucre, who was round as a donut and just as doughy, pulled a well-roasted duck from the oven as the front door slammed.

The afternoon spent in the kitchen had been the best since I'd boarded the plane to Mexico. Suzette wormed her way into friendship, and we started a tentative bond which I hoped would keep me sane as long as I remained captive.

But all those relaxed feelings flew away as Q strode into the kitchen.

I froze, holding a pan of roasted rosemary potatoes. Q's presence filled the kitchen, consuming oxygen, awareness…space. He looked like a resplendent peacock in a royal blue suit and crimson shirt. His pelt of hair shone under the kitchen lights, while his pale jade eyes smouldered.

My entire body reacted: nipples hardened, mouth parted. I tried to stop it, but I couldn't ignore his call.

Him. He was back. Here. In the house.

Oh, God. Primal instincts clawed, itching to bolt, while at the same time, I softened with need. Emotions tore me in two and I trembled, almost dropping the potatoes.

Suzette appeared, lightly brushing her fingers against my hip. Her touch was petal soft, sharing some unspoken sisterhood. Calm acceptance tamed my jitteriness, but Q never broke eye contact. He stared with an almost physical connection, causing my heart to race and guilt to swell for no reason.

She smiled happily as Q and I continued our silent war, then she jumped as he stormed closer. His abrupt change from standing to movement unsettled Suzette and me.

We shifted back a step, not that it helped with the powerhouse of Q coming straight for us.

"C'est quoi ce bordel, qu'est ce qu'elle fait ici?" Q snapped, glaring at Suzette, shoulders rippling with temper.

Suzette bowed her head. *"Je suis désolée, maître."*

Dismissing Suzette without a second thought, his eyes looked me up and down in one arrogant sweep. "What are you doing in here? You're a slave, not the hired help. Get out." He leaned closer, brushing my cheek with a hard hand. Electricity zapped from his touch and my core clenched on its own violation.

Not again. Please, stop betraying me! How could I hate him when my body melted every time he touched me?

Q yanked his hand away. He narrowed his eyes as if the spark between us was my fault. "Have a shower; you're covered in flour. *Merde.*"

Before I could argue the word *slave* implied I should cook and clean, Suzette pushed me toward the exit, whispering, "Don't argue. I can see the desire to stand up to him in your eyes. But remember what I said."

The moment we were in the lounge, she rushed, "Have a shower, and dress in one of those beautiful gowns. He'll love seeing you in things he bought." Her eyes grew dreamy, as if match-making us made total sense. "Give him what he wants."

Pulling away, I felt betrayed all over again. I hissed, "Give him what he wants? How about I tie myself up and present myself as the main course? That's what he wants, isn't it?"

Suzette pinched the bridge of her nose, throwing me

an exasperated look. "His fantasies will be shared, I'm sure. It's your job to let him show you without fear or guilt."

My lungs squeezed together. "*What?* You think he suffers fear and guilt? Try the girl who's been kidnapped! Holy shit." The curse fell like a nasty bomb; Suzette frowned in disapproval.

"Just go and dress." She shoved me toward the stairs and I ran.

I couldn't wait to get out of there, but had no intention of obeying. She'd stepped over the line, implying her boss suffered more than I did. Fuck that. I'd show him how much I didn't want to be there. I thought I could do it—pretend and pantomime. I thought I could become something slave-like and meek.

I was wrong.

Hot, terrible anger boiled as I bolted up the steps two at a time. I'd show him. I didn't think of the consequences, focused only on what would make me feel better.

Slamming the door, I headed straight to the wardrobe, and wrenched open the doors. Racks of designer dresses and Victoria's Secret lingerie beckoned with style. My fingers itched to attack the clothes, to take my wrath out on innocent fabric. I may not be able to hurt Q physically, but I could hurt his wallet.

I yanked the first item—a delicious amethyst dress—off its hanger and tore the neckline with my teeth. My heart raced as I gnawed on the silky fabric. It took a few attempts, but I managed to cut it enough to rip it with my hands. It cracked like a lightning bolt and split in two.

The next victim hung on a padded hanger—a cream blouse with prancing black horses. It ripped with a loud snarl. I tossed it to the floor, joining the growing cemetery of clothes.

In a rampage, I grabbed the bras and tore the straps off. They joined the graveyard. Next, I found a drawer full of impractical nylons and laddered them with nails and teeth.

I panted, loving the fierce retribution in my veins. It may only be clothes I ruined, but it gave me an outlet. My skin shone with sweat as I reached for another blouse.

I froze as the door slammed open.

Q stood, fists balled at his sides, posture hard and unmovable. Eyes darted over the pool of ruined clothing. His jaw clenched before glaring at me with every unspoken command possible.

My legs wobbled, wanting so badly to hit the floor, to grovel for forgiveness. I didn't know this owner standing in the doorway. No remnants of the man who fingered me in both pleasure and pain last night resided in his gaze. I pushed too hard.

Oh, fuck.

I hunched, crumpling the grey blouse in my hands. Fear gripped, turning me into an autumn leaf.

Clearing his throat, he cricked his neck. The force of his temper buffeted like a slap to the face. "Care to tell me why you're ruining three thousand euros worth of clothing?" He purred with undisguised lust, and barely held restraint. His face tense with outrage, smouldering need in his eyes.

My body took control as blood boiled to lava. Attraction rolled through my belly and I wanted to punch myself for how wet I became. I had no self-control. He was right to treat me like a slave. I was nothing but a sex hungry woman who didn't deserve Brax's adoration. Who only deserved to be beaten and taken. I was so fucked up, I couldn't get wet with gentle kisses from a man who loved me. But, put a man who wanted to hurt in front of me, with fucking on his mind and bondage in his thoughts, and I unravelled like the slut I'd become.

Tears erupted, and Q growled. "No point crying. You knew I'd be furious, yet you did it anyway." He stalked forward, kicking the door shut. He stopped a metre away. "Tears won't save you."

I sniffed, straightening my back. I wouldn't give him the satisfaction of admitting I cried because of my torment, cried with hatred for a traitorous body. Fear smothered, but the unmasked need swimming in my blood scared me a hundred times more. Would I have reacted this way for any man who bought me? Or was Q different? An unwilling aphrodisiac to my sinful body.

My voice came out whisper-soft. "I won't allow you to dress me like an object. I refuse." I didn't mention most of the items were gorgeous, exactly what I would've chosen given a bigger bank balance. "I'm human, too. Not an object for you to play with."

He chuckled. "An object who'd rather be naked the entire time? That can be arranged."

My heart bucked. I dropped my eyes. "No."

"No?" He inched closer, bringing inferno heat. His entire body rippled with lustful fire. "You say no after destroying things I bought for you?"

"Does it hurt for you to see things damaged?" I dared look in his eyes and his nostrils flared. "Because if it does, then you're hurting me. I have feelings—same as you!"

His hand lashed out, grabbing the nape of my neck. Dragging me closer, I collided against solid muscle, and breath exploded from my lungs.

"You think you're like me? You're not," he snarled, right before his mouth smashed against mine and his tongue darted past my lips. I punched him, but he didn't stop. If anything, it amplified him from ruthless to out of control.

Spinning me around, he trapped me hard against the door, grinding his hips into mine. In one fluid move, he kicked my legs apart with a foot. So quick, so sure.

My lungs couldn't get enough oxygen as he kissed me harder than anyone had before. Blood mixed with his dark taste. Indents of his teeth bruised my mouth, and my thoughts disintegrated. I half-moaned, half-cried as he thrust his cock so hard against me, my feet left the floor.

Ending the kiss on the same brutal note, he panted, "What are you?"

I blinked, completely disoriented. Then fight returned; I shoved him.

He grunted as he stepped back, but it wasn't enough. Landing on me again, his weight pinned my body. His breath hot on my cheek as he rubbed his five o'clock shadow along my jaw. "Don't fucking push me. What *are* you?"

Not this again. In a moment of lunacy, I tried to head-butt him.

His eyes flared wide and lips twitched. The look of alpha possession overshadowed for a moment with sheer amazement. He rammed his thigh between my legs, rubbing against overheated flesh. Even through denim every part of him awoke every part of me and I ached. I burned. I *wanted.*

"You made me say it last night. You broke me. I won't do it again," I seethed.

He growled, moving his thigh. He cupped with me forceful fingers. My head wanted to crash against his shoulder in servitude, but I couldn't. This was wrong. God help me, I'd broken myself with battling two conflicting things. Run. Fuck. Run. Fuck. The trance sent wetness gushing from me. I'd never been so turned on and never hated someone more.

"I'll gladly break you again to hear you say it." His hands captured my wrists, slamming them above my head against the door. Holding me with one hand, his other went back to my jeans. With nimble fingers, he undid my fly and somehow managed to wriggle his hand inside the denim and knickers.

I bucked as a finger pressed deep inside. No soft requests or gentle foreplay, a straight finger fuck.

"Say it," he ordered. My eyes snapped closed as he hooked his finger, pressing against my g-spot. "Your body drips for me, *esclave*. I'll let you have me, if you say it. Say you're mine."

Another finger entered as fierce as the first and my legs turned to jelly. He held me upright by my wrists and fingers rode me deep. I'd never been touched so totally before. Brax…he wasn't a lover of foreplay… *Stop thinking about Brax. Especially now. This would break his heart.*

My mind cracked into shards. I struggled to fight the insane urge to submit; I could *never* submit. Lifting extremely heavy eyelids, I snarled, "Mine. Not yours."

He flinched as if I'd struck him, eyes flashing with a feral edge. "Wrong answer." He ducked and threw me over a shoulder, just like the captor in Mexico. All residual fear rushed to haunt me and my body no longer hummed. It burned for freedom. To end this, to run.

Q dropped me on the bed, immediately yanking my jeans off. I couldn't stop it. One minute they were on, the next they lay discarded with the other torn clothes.

He climbed on top and I kicked. My knee connected with his rib cage and he winced, but a hand grabbed my side, pressing my own broken rib. Everything oozed to greyness with pain. It gave him time to undo his tie and wrap it tight around my wrists.

My heartbeat thrummed in my arms, hating the tight restriction. Shoving my wrists above my head, he pinned me down, trying to wedge between my legs. I fought like an alley cat. Our legs battled, feet grappled with the sheet, and for a moment, I might've won. I lost with one misplaced kick.

Within moments, I lay spread-eagled with him panting above. Smouldering, unwanted lust ignited. Misplaced lust. Lust that drove me mad with confusion and hatred.

Eagerness and longing flamed his face. His smell of sin, citrus, and sandalwood dazzled my senses, flaring every part. My core clenched as Q rocked, breathing hard and rattling. Somehow, the synapses of my brain hardwired to his scent. Oh, God. He successfully owned one of my senses!

Smell. I couldn't let him take more.

Howling, I bit his shoulder. "Let me the fuck go!"

He reared back, rage and hard-edged respect in his eyes. Did he respect I fought? Did it turn him on so damn much? *Sick, sick bastard.*

He raised a hand as if to strike me.

I fought the urge to curl into a little ball, and stared into his turbulent gaze. "Do it. Hit me. At least the pain will leave a physical mark you'll have to see every day."

He opened his mouth, then shut it. His hand hovered, before cupping my cheek. He ran a trembling thumb across my lips. "Say it." Something raw blazed in his gaze, imploring on some deep, psychological level. He seemed desperate to hear me admit I was his.

He reached between us, stroking my clit through my knickers. All the fireworks that'd been smouldering, sparked to life. An orgasm gripped my muscles with sharp ecstasy; I threw my head back.

"Oh, shit." I didn't want the orgasm—even though I did. I didn't want it, as Brax never gave me one, and to me, that made our separation horribly final. As if Q sliced us apart, leaving me ruined for anything but roughness and savagery.

Just as the bands of muscles exploded, Q stopped touching me. He scrambled off, pulling me to a sitting position. My bound wrists drooped into my lap. I blinked, body resonating with the build-up of intensity, smarting for relief. My orgasm dwindled to nothing.

I wanted to scream. He left me deliberately on the knife-edge of pleasure.

"What is your name?" he demanded, as he undid his belt, tore it from its belt loops, and tossed it on the ground. The sound of the heavy belt buckle hitting soft carpet sent heartbeats racing ever faster.

I refused to answer, but couldn't look away as he undid his fly and untucked the crimson shirt. He left the royal blue jacket on, but unbuttoned it so the material flared to the sides.

Placing himself in front, his crotch the perfect height to my mouth, he ordered, "Suck me." Q's gaze sent incandescent fire racing in my blood, but it didn't match the horror I lived with. Suck him? I couldn't. Not a man. A stranger. My *owner*. I'd rather bite.

When I didn't move, Q pushed his boxer briefs down, pulling his raging hard cock from its prison. The tip glistened with pre-cum, his scent of musk and darkness spelled around me.

Fisting his thick length, he bit his lip, stroking. My stomach clenched; I closed my eyes. "Please—" I shook my head. "I can't."

He inched closer, practically pressing his cock against my lips. "You can. And you will, *esclave*."

I tilted my head away, hyperaware of the dampness of pre-cum as he ran his hot erection along my cheek. His hand lashed out, fingers bruising my chin, keeping me in place. "Open. And if you bite, I'll hit you so hard, you won't wake up for days." His voice rasped with excitement, but there was something else, too. Something I recognised, but couldn't place. Heat blazed all emotions to dust.

My body twitched as tears flowed. I needed help. I needed saving. Everything I felt suddenly boiled over, steaming with no outlet…then something happened.

Everything… stopped.

My mind shut down, body turned numb. Everything I battled… disappeared. I was left an empty shell—uncaring, blissfully vacant.

Calm descended as I accepted obedience like a balm against the hardship of fighting. In that moment, I became what he wanted: his.

Q didn't seem to notice the epiphany I experienced, and when he tilted my head to take his cock, I let him.

He pressed the back of my head, entering my mouth with

his long, velvety length. He moaned as I deep throated with no revolt at all.

I let him.

He groaned, flexing his hips as my lips created a suction around hot flesh. He muttered something in French, bending forward, almost brushing my hair with his chest.

I let him.

In my untouchable cocoon, I would let him to anything.

He was male. I was female. That was all there was to it.

My hands moved on their own accord, reaching for him. One hand cupped tight, smooth balls, while the other stroked his throbbing length.

I floated on a cloud of indifference as I pleasured, touched, tasted. Nothing registered—neither scent, nor taste, nor sound. I was a robot, a perfect toy—my only purpose: to make him come.

Why did I ever fight? This was so much easier. Almost drug like. Dreamlike. I wanted to laugh. Freedom. I'd found it, in my mind.

Q stopped thrusting into my mouth; harsh fingers angled my throat to look up. I didn't stop stroking, even as pale eyes delved into mine.

I blinked, not caring. If he wanted to rape me, so be it. If I was to be his for eternity, fine. He might own my body. He would never own my soul.

"What is your fucking name?" he muttered, French accent warbling the curse. He should swear in French. It sounded better.

I never dropped eye contact, still stroking, still working like a good wind-up toy.

He growled, knocking my hands off his cock. They landed limply in my lap.

Q stood, swaying slightly with his erection standing

proud beneath the shirt, trousers puddled around ankles like shackles. My skin prickled with the force of his stare, but apart from that, nothing moved me. I didn't care what he wanted. My name? I didn't know my name.

Oh, I had to answer. He asked a question. I had to obey. "*Esclave*. My name is *Esclave*."

He hissed between clenched teeth as I reached for his cock again, dragging a fingernail up the length, pressing hard against the slit at the top.

Q's fingers threaded through my hair, grabbing a handful. He yanked my head back, lowering his face to mine; we breathed each other's breath.

I sat there, unmoving. I sighed, relief coursing through my heart. I no longer cared. I convinced my mind to leave, and it had. Everything that happened now didn't matter. It wouldn't stain my life as it had been put on hold.

His gaze swelled with urgency, commandments. Then softened, churning into unhappiness, grief. Before I could figure out the puzzle, blankness came over his features and he kissed me.

His tongue plundered, and I opened wider, inviting him to take. I even licked him back, massaging his taste with my own. He groaned. It sounded tortured, as if he wanted to kiss but didn't, like he fought against morals, choices.

My heart stayed an even rhythm, never rising, even as his hand dropped to my breast and twisted a nipple. Like the obedient slave he wanted, I opened like a sun-warmed flower, pressing flesh into his palm, arching my back.

He stumbled backward, as if I'd bit him, tripping over his trousers. With angry jerks, he hoisted up his pants, wincing as he tucked his erection away.

I cocked my head, wondering, but not caring, why he pulled away. I'd done everything right. "Did I not please you?" My voice was odd—dead, lifeless, robotic.

Q froze, running hands over his short hair. His darker skin whitened with what looked like fear. "What are you?" he demanded.

I didn't hesitate. I knew the answer. It was easy. "Yours."

He sucked in a breath, eyes flaring wide. He paced in front, never taking his gaze off mine. "You said you wouldn't let me! You seemed so strong, unbreakable. You lied to me." He bristled with anger. "I haven't even fucked you, yet you're broken." Guilt etched his livid tone.

I stayed unruffled, unworried. He raged because he broke me? Wasn't that his goal? He should be pleased it took such little time. I thought I could last longer, but my mind no longer wished to fight. I refused to scream and cry when I found solitude and calm. Could he only get off on the sounds of distress?

I had no answer so I dropped my eyes, staring at my bound hands, waiting.

He stalked forward, undoing the tie around my wrists in angry movements. "You lied and I don't like liars."

I shrugged. What was there to say? He owned me— he could call me what he wished. "I'm yours. Isn't that what you wanted?"

He shook his head, temper flaring. "You've given up. You aren't mine unless I make you mine!"

My mind hurt. I couldn't unravel that. I was his. Undeniably. He *knew* that. My body screamed it loud enough.

"Take off your sweater." His eyes dropped to the weight of my breasts under the jumper. Rather than excitement, fear, anticipation, I felt nothing—heavenly nothing. He towered above like the god of sex, his erection straining against his trousers, calling to me.

I grabbed the hem and tugged the sweater over my head in one swoop. I stood and reached for his waist. His skin burned as I touched his hipbone.

His breath came faster, looking hungrily at my bra. It

was so nice not to feel. If Brax watched me the way Q did, I'd have hidden my stomach, worried about the birthmark in the valley of my breasts, worried if he loved me even with flaws. Here, I didn't care.

"Give me your bra." He held out a hand, waiting. His jaw worked as I reached behind and unclasped the lacy cups. I dangled it between my forefinger and thumb, passing it to him. My nipples pinpointed and ached. His gaze thrilled my body, heating my vacancy into need.

Not looking away, Q's fingers latched around my hand, accepting the bra. His thumb caught my barcode tattoo; the burn made me wince. The tinkle of delicate silver summoned his eyes and he frowned.

Brax's bracelet.

The void I floated in evaporated. Memories roared back.

Brax.

Mexico.

Pain.

Leather Jacket.

My mind woke, latching onto things I wished I could forget. *No. No, stay. Don't go back.*

Q's jaw tightened as I tugged my hand back, skin crawling. How did I come to be only in my knickers, standing in front of him? Everything was foggy; a dream I couldn't quite grasp.

Q snapped his fingers around my wrist. Leaning forward, he peered deep into my soul. His thumb played with the bracelet, sending the cool silver spinning. "Who gave you this?"

My breathing accelerated; I gulped. *Don't answer.*

But I didn't need to answer. His face flashed with triumph, his body settled into a taunting stance. "Someone you care about gave you this. Do you think I should let you keep it?" He tugged and the metal bit into my skin. Any more pressure and he'd snap it.

Tess, go back. Leave and float. Who cares about a bracelet? He can have it. Brax can buy you another.

My heart stuttered to a slamming halt. But if Brax died back on the bathroom floor, I'd never get another. It was the only thing I had left.

Fight ruptured and I attacked. My nails swiped his cheek as I barrelled into him. I screamed as we fell to the floor. Q yelled something and snatched at my wrist. The silver tried to stay intact, but broke with a tiny clink, landing on the carpet beside Q's head.

Brax!

I yelled and shoved. Q covered his face as I went savage, reaching for the ruined jewellery. Throat tight, I lunged, but Q was too fast. He rolled so I ended up beneath him on the grey carpet. He pinned my arms with effortless power that made me hate him more. How could I think I could beat him when he subdued me like an annoying butterfly?

Licking his lips, passion raged on his face. "There you are. Don't switch off again. I forbid it."

I was back to this horrible life, I fought. My hands curled and bucked, hating how my naked breasts jiggled as I tried to get free.

Q grunted and sat up, straddling me, cupping my breasts. "What is your name?" His lips pulled back from his teeth as he twisted my nipples sending shocks of pleasure-pain through my system. "What is your name, goddammit? Tell me."

I glared with every dagger of hatred inside.

Silence.

My tongue knotted against ever saying my name again. It was mine. Not his. I never wanted to hear him say it. "Never!"

Q shuddered with a mixture of unnamed emotion and slapped me. My eyes smarted as heat hurt with embarrassment, rather than pain. He fucking slapped me!

"Merde!" he swore. Standing, he scooped the bracelet

from the carpet and dangled it above. "This is mine. *You* are mine. Get that through your head if you ever want it back."

I scrambled to my knees, reaching for it. No, he couldn't take it. It linked to my past, linked to Brax, to who I was deep inside—the tame, sweet girl who wanted nothing more than to belong.

Tears caught in my throat. "I told you what you want. I'm yours. Please, give it back. I'm *yours!*"

His powerful body tightened, buttoning his blazer with precise movements. The silver tantalized in his fingers before he shoved it into a suit pocket. "You say the words but you don't believe it. I told you. I don't like liars."

He turned and opened the door, fingers turning white around the doorknob. "Stay up here. Your punishment for not obeying is starvation. Good night."

Swiping his face, he left.

Chapter Twelve

Wren

That night, I dreamed.

I dreamed of red and passion and violence. Of being taken, owned, possessed—of Q filling me with hardness, fucking me over the pool table.

I woke to my fingers sliding in my wetness. Toes curled and back arched as the orgasm Q denied me rippled with an intensity echoing in my teeth.

My heart raced as I came back to earth, uncramping my feet. A damp spot formed below my ass and cheeks pinked with how wet I was. But lying in the dark, stomach empty, heart ruined, I found peace.

My body no longer throbbed, and for the first time in weeks, I slept soundly.

Time slowed.

Seconds crawled into unwilling minutes, turning into tomorrow and next week. Q didn't come find me, and I never saw him return home from work.

But I knew when he arrived, as the house filled with

passionate music. Lyrics thrummed, stroking with warning. He lived in the same house as me—any moment he could come, but never did.

Most of the time, music throbbed with French laments, but then one night, an English song rained from the speakers.

Every second my temper frays, every moment my beast desires
you think you can win, but you're not consumed by sin
delicate and sweet are no match for hell and ruin
I don't want you to see the depth of my blackness
for there-in lie demons and madness
don't look in my eyes, the truth is not for you
you should run, you should flee, you should hide away forever

I couldn't describe the loneliness aching in my bones. The song reached like a plea, freezing me with confusion.

Ever since that night and the painful song, I couldn't shake the feeling Q tried to tell me something in the music he played. But I couldn't believe it, because if I did—what did that mean? I couldn't feel sorry for my captor. I had to remain aloof, distant. *Be that icicle—sharp and deadly.*

Life settled into a rhythm: an unwanted rhythm, but an ebb and flow nevertheless. I drifted along, wondering why Q granted peace and left me alone. Did he grow bored of his new possession already? Or did work demand his time and grace me with a limited amount of freedom?

Whatever the reason, Sunday burned my memory as the day Q twisted my emotions so much, I found a place inside where I could run. In a way, he taught me how to save myself, even as he broke me further.

Five days passed, each one scratched on a calendar of waiting. My life existed to dust and clean, while Suzette helped smooth my rusty French. I stared longingly at the front door, wanting freedom, but the green-eyed guard was never far away. Watching, always watching.

The only bright spot was Suzette. She welcomed me with

open arms into the Mercer household, and became the rock in the turbulent seas I swam.

She never pried, always chatted about nothing and everything, giving me a sense of normalcy. Every now and again, I caught her watching, a frown on her face and curiosity in her gaze. She plotted something, but I didn't know what.

Even Mrs. Sucre tolerated my presence in the kitchen, as I became a permanent feature—helping prepare evening meals and hovering in the welcome embrace of the busy hub.

Suzette supplied rags and brooms and gave me chores. They helped keep boredom at bay; I needed it. Boredom brought thoughts of escape and endangerment. But no amount of scrubbing stopped my heart twinging every time I remembered Q had Brax's bracelet.

A cold sweat would drench my back at the thought of him smashing it to smithereens to teach me a lesson—ruining something of mine to get back at me for ruining something of his.

He hadn't replaced the clothes I slashed. For a week, I scuffed around in the same jeans and cream jumper, but I didn't care. Suzette mourned the items more than I did. To me, they signified a gaudy uniform: an outfit for a toy.

While cleaning the windows in the lounge on Friday, I contemplated hurling myself through the glass. Not to die, but to get outside. The fluttering of birds and gentle thawing of winter taunted. I hadn't been outside in weeks.

The thought of smashing the glass and bleeding to death stopped the urge, but it didn't deflate the need to run. Surely, this mansion had a gym—a treadmill. Running stationary would be better than no running at all. Q kept fit so he must have equipment somewhere.

My anklet buzzed, shocking me. I sat on one of the fluffy couches and hoisted my jeans. Why did it buzz?

The GPS tracker drove me nuts—a constant nuisance when I tried to sleep or dress. I had hoped it wasn't waterproof, and spent an hour trying to drown it in the shower. Turned out, it *was* waterproof.

"*Esclave?*" Suzette asked, appearing in the doorway. "*Maître* Mercer just called. He has a business dinner tonight with prospective clients."

I stood, stretching. The one good thing about Q not coming for me meant my body

healed. The bruises from Leather Jacket faded to an ugly yellow, and my rib ached, rather than screamed.

The slap from Q hadn't caused any damage, unfortunately. I had the feeling he wanted to hurt me, but didn't quite have the balls. I wish he *had* branded me, and it horrified him so much, those feelings never strengthened.

I didn't want to listen, but my gut said he'd get worse. I had to escape before instincts proved true. Suzette was wrong about him—there were no redeeming qualities. And I wouldn't be suckered in by songs with lyrics oozing sadness.

"Do you want help preparing the meal?" I smiled. Cooking with Suzette was a highlight of my restrictive new life. I never cooked a lot, as Brax had been the chef in our family, but I found a flair for it. My heart lurched at the thought of Brax. Memories constantly caught me unaware, and I wanted to mourn, but at the same time, couldn't. I wouldn't accept he was dead, or that I'd never see him again. It wasn't an option.

Suzette came forward. Something changed; she watched with sadness and resignation. My skin prickled as she asked, "Is it easier?"

I knew immediately what she meant and pursed my lips. Easier? It would never get easier.

She sighed, whispering, "Has he taken you fully yet?"

My heart raced to see jealousy flashing in her eyes. She was jealous? Of *what?* Being humiliated and used?

I stepped away. "Why are you asking these questions?"

She dropped her eyes. "I need to know. Tonight…
this business meeting. I need to know how prepared you
are."

Relief coursed. If I could handle what I'd been
through, I could handle a dinner party. After all, a role as
a servant or waitress would be a lot easier than sucking
off a man who forced me. My pulse thudded. Perhaps I
could tell one of the guests Q kept me prisoner. That I
needed the police.

A smile tugged, but I fought it. Suzette mustn't know
my hopes. But then my happiness disintegrated,
rethinking the idea. The men were probably like Q: sick
fucks.

She stared for a moment, before nodding. "You
don't need to help with dinner. We've got it covered.
You need to head upstairs and get ready. The guests will
arrive in an hour."

My eyes flew to outside, gauging the time. The sun
kissed horizon, already giving brightness to shadow.
When did it get so late?

Suzette pushed me toward the stairs, murmuring,
"Can I ask another question?"

I stiffened, but nodded. "Okay."

"Don't you find him attractive?"

I slammed to a stop in the foyer. "Attraction has
nothing to do with it, Suzette. It's the circumstances, the
way he treats me."

She narrowed her eyes. "Q treats you better than all
my owners ever treated me. You're so lucky." Her tone
turned sullen. "You don't even know."

Anger thickened and I couldn't speak. I felt sorry for
her and what she lived through, but to say I had it better?
Hah!

She continued, "Just think of his requests as rent
money, or protection expenses. You give him what he
wants, and he'll take care of you. Q won't ever seriously

hurt you. Not like—" Suzette shuddered and stopped. Hazel eyes flashed with secrets buried in their depths. "Give him what he needs, then you can test the boundaries of your cage."

Curiosity overrode anger. I took a deep breath and asked softly, "What men, Suzette? How did you come to be here? Were you stolen, like me?"

She twisted her fingers, looking at the marble floor. "The day I was sold to Q was the best da—"

The front door swung open and the devil himself stood framed in twilight. His hair was slightly shorter, as if he'd instructed the hair dresser to make it look like an otter's pelt—sleek, shiny, impenetrable. A light silver suit and turquoise shirt made him look like an expensive jewel.

His eyes shot to mine, naked without his normal barriers. In the brief moment, I saw bone weary loneliness, surprise, and protectiveness. My heart ached to see such longing. What if Suzette was right? Q was deeper than I gave him credit for. Something lurked, dark and vile, but there was a human, as well as a monster, inside.

My body was torn between offering to dispel such unhappiness and killing him to end his misery, and mine.

Blank hardness hid his true thoughts, shattering the moment. I hadn't seen him since he stole Brax's bracelet, avoiding me like the plague, as if giving me time to grieve, to get over his thievery.

My fingers rubbed my wrist absentmindedly and his eyes followed. His face shut down, leaving nothing but domineering arrogance. "Suzette, I thought I told you to get her ready?"

Suzette bowed. "*Oui, maître.*" Pushing me gently, she added, "Get dressed into the gown you'll find in your wardrobe."

"And if you ruin that one, the punishment will be a lot worse," Q murmured. His tone rippled across my skin, sending fire into my blood.

I ran up the stairs.

Safe in the cell of a room, I opened the wardrobe and gasped.

The one and only garment was nothing but gold lace. Long, clinging filigree, offering no coverage apart from a thicker weave around the groin and chest. The fabric train whispered against the floor as I plucked it from the wardrobe.

I was dumbfounded.

Oh, my God, he expected me to wear this? To dinner? I couldn't. I *wouldn't*.

The door burst open; I clutched the dress to my throat. The guard, with the bright green eyes, glared. His body, much wider than Q's, intimidated. "Mr. Mercer sent me to make sure you dressed correctly." His gaze slithered over me, and he puffed his chest. "Strip. I'll help, if you require."

I recoiled in horror. Q wouldn't let his guard have me, would he? I didn't think he would, but who knew. The air in the tiny room sucked into nothing. I breathed hard. "I need privacy."

He shook his head. "No privacy."

Gritting my teeth, I didn't move. I deliberated screaming and ramming into him, but realistically, what would it achieve? Q proved to me, I had no power here. As much as it killed me, I had no choice.

My shoulders fell in surrender; his lips curled. I turned away, my hands shaking as I laid the dress on the bed and pulled the jumper over my head. My skin crawled, knowing the man watched.

I shimmied from my jeans, and left them on the floor. Reaching for the dress, I tried to figure out how to put it on when a heavy palm fell on my shoulder. "Take off your underwear. You aren't allowed to wear anything under the dress."

My entire body revolted, and I leaped away, running

to the corner of the room. His touch didn't infect me like Q's. I didn't warm or react; I tightened and crackled with unwillingness.

The guard snorted, holding up his arms. "I'm not going to touch you, girl. That's the *maître's* right." His eyelids dropped as excitement glowed. "However, the guests will also get a turn tonight."

What? My ears rang. *No. Please.* Horrid realization buckled my knees. The dinner party—there would be no dinner. I was to be the main course. Betrayal settled deep in my heart. I hated Q, but never believed he'd be able to let another touch me. Not with the possessive edge surrounding him.

The guard held out a hand. "Give me your bra and panties. The guests will arrive any moment, and you're to be in place before they do."

My hands curled with the urge to punch his ruggedly handsome face—to make him bleed. But again, what would it achieve? Nothing. The result would be the same, just more painful.

I unclipped my bra and threw it. I refused to give him my knickers—those I kicked behind, wadding them against the wall.

He grinned. "I wouldn't sniff them, if that's what's worrying your pretty head. Wouldn't put it past the master, though." He chuckled loudly, way too impressed with his joke.

Keeping my head high, I scrunched the dress and pulled it over my head. I had to wriggle to inch the clingy material down. The spun threads offered no protection from eyes or temperature, and by the time it encased me fully, I felt trapped.

I could only walk with dainty steps, and my breasts strained as filigree designs stamped patterns into my skin.

The train pooled around my feet, looking like a golden mermaid's tail—a poor creature who didn't belong. I related completely.

The moment I finished, the guard grabbed my tattooed wrist, carting me downstairs.

Chapter Thirteen

Finch

I bit my lip as we descended the stairs and entered an entirely new room. It reeked of sex and money and power. Quintessentially Q, his signature scent of lust and darkness permeated the air.

Crimson booths surrounded a tiny pedestal, round and high—for a priceless figurine or statue. Leather straps with cuffs dangled from the ceiling in the centre. Heavy drapery blocked large windows, and thick black carpeting silenced any noise.

The room was a decadent tomb.

The guard let me go, only for me to be caught by Q. Where the hell did he come from? I'd never get used to how silently he moved.

My skin singed beneath his touch; arcs of animalistic hunger scattered across my body. Q sucked in a breath. I wasn't the only one this crazy need affected. I cursed my body for responding. I needed some serious counselling. I shouldn't grow wet when a man who lived to make my life hell touched me. I shouldn't have mixed emotions of hatred and need. I should just *hate*.

He jerked me against his chest, never looking away. "*Esclave...*" He ran his nose along my cheek, dipping to my neck and collarbone. His hot breath increased heart flurries to a million a second. I wanted to run fingers through his hair, to press my hips against his—but I swallowed the diabolical urges. That wasn't what I really wanted to do. *I want to slit his throat so I can run home to Brax.*

Sharp teeth nipped my throat, stealing my balance.

It'd been a week since his last touch, but it could've been a minute or a millennium and I would've exploded the same. I hated him. He turned everything against me and it hurt, so much.

Walking me backward, lips on my neck and hands on my waist, he steadied us when I connected with the pedestal and tripped. Taking my hand, he helped me perch on the platform. He gazed up, face at chest height, lust glowing in lime coloured eyes.

Unexpectedly, he wrapped his arms around me, dragging my breasts against his face. Keeping me prisoner, he licked through the holes of the dress, sending wet trails scorching.

"Stop," I whimpered, cursing my trembling stomach and melting core.

To my surprise, he obeyed and stepped up, joining me on the podium. With a slight smile, he reached above and caught the leather cuffs.

I couldn't look away as he pulled my right arm up and wrapped the leather cuff around my wrist. The buckles tightened and I sucked in a breath. It reminded too much of Mexico, the tattoo, inspection, injection. My fear consumed, and I jerked away. My shoulder bellowed as I tried to get free. I shoved Q in panic, tugging at the cuff, fingers fumbling to undo the buckle.

Q laughed softly, rubbing his lower lip with a thumb. "I'll let you in on a secret, *esclave*. This is a first for me, too." His hand dropped, cupping his erection through his trousers. "And it turns me the fuck on, watching you struggle."

Two things I wanted most in the world: for Q to die a miserable death, and for him to fuck me. Being restrained highlighted all my stupid fantasies; I couldn't stop the building moisture. Wetness coated my inner thighs as Q gathered me closer.

"*Fuck, tu me rends fou.*" Fuck, you make me hot. His voice throbbed, making me ache, *yearn*.

My heart broke a little more. He owned my sense of hearing as well as my sense of smell. I couldn't ignore the baritone of seduction, or the overwhelming need to obey.

Q pushed my left arm up and secured it. My lungs stuck together when he stepped back, leaving me shackled with arms in the air. My ribcage rose and fell with panicked breathing, igniting pain. "You can't do this."

He cocked his head. "I just did."

"You know what I mean." Swallowing back fear, I added brazenly, "You don't want to do this. Something in you doesn't want to abuse me. I can sense it."

He froze, nostrils flaring. We stood, silently glaring, before he fisted my hair. "You don't know anything, *esclave*. I want this. I've wanted this for too damn long, and you're wrong that it hurts." His chest strained in his immaculate suit as he leaned in, kissing the shell of my ear. He whispered, "I'm not afraid of hurting you. I'm afraid of how far I'm willing to go."

If not restrained, I would've collapsed.

"*Maître, vos invités sont arrivés,*" Suzette said. The guests are here.

My eyes flew frantically to her, begging for help. She stood in the doorway with a mix of emotions flickering. The one I read the clearest was want. Her tongue darted between her lips, dropping her gaze.

Q waved toward the corner of the room. "Pull the rope,

Suzette."

Her gaze popped wide, and the need in her face dispelled, leaving shock in its place. "You sure, *maître?*"

He growled in warning and she jumped to obey. Wrapping tiny hands around a thick red cord, she pulled with one swoop.

I screamed as my shoulders wrenched upright and body weight transferred from feet to wrists. My tiptoes pointed, still on the pedestal, but only barely. I'd become shackled well and truly by gravity.

Q stepped off the podium, inspecting me. My breasts stuck out proudly with arms above my ears, the mosaic dress exposing all parts. "Leave us," he demanded, not looking at Suzette.

I couldn't breathe.

Suzette left the room quickly, and all hope of getting away went with her. Q stood below, looking up. Slowly, he inserted a middle finger into his mouth and sucked. Eyes flashed with so much darkness I would never see the night again and not think of him. His tongue licked with intoxicating grace.

My lips parted, mesmerized. Somehow, focusing on him helped dispel panic, a reminder Q might be bad, but he definitely wasn't the worst.

It was almost a relief when he grabbed my hip, holding me steady. His fingers bit into flesh. Slowly, he poked a finger through the fabric of the dress and found the dampness on my thigh.

His eyes shot to mine. "You continue to surprise me. I didn't need to lick my finger after all."

Cheeks pinked as he feathered up my leg and stroked my entrance. His finger slipped into wetness, and a groan rumbled in his chest. He pulled me closer and, like a pendulum, I went—his to move where he wanted. Pressing his face into my chest, his finger thrust inside, making my knees buckle. I swung slightly in the bindings.

His hand left my hip, wrapping around my lower back, securing tightly. "Ah, *esclave*. You continue to lie. Your body tells the truth."

I wanted to curse. I had no control, but he was a maestro and like an unwilling instrument, I came to life.

"Mercer, it seems you've started without us," a masculine voice oozed. Followed by another, "It looks as if he couldn't restrain himself. Look at that delectable morsel."

Chagrin painted my cheeks. Four men stood, watching greedily as Q finger-fucked me. He stroked hard, quick, wrist rubbing against my inner thighs as I tried to squeeze my legs together to stop him. He wasn't gentle, and I couldn't focus on his touch and the men at the same time.

Heavy eyes closed on their own accord as Q hooked his finger, stimulating my g-spot. I jumped as pressure inside built to a crescendo. Oh, God. I couldn't come. Not like this. Not with men watching, hearing, wanting.

As my inner muscles clenched greedily around his finger, Q pulled away, leaving me panting and red cheeked. I swayed in the restraints, scrambling on tiptoe not to spin.

Q backed away, facing me. As he walked, he brought his finger to his mouth and sucked. Sucked the glistening wetness lingering there, sucked my taste, my very essence.

I wanted to weep.

My body pulsed, throbbed, and I resisted the urge to scissor my thighs, to try and find relief. I wouldn't add to the smug look in his eyes. He knew I hurt, and he'd leave me that way. *Fucking French bastard.*

Reaching the four men, he shook their hands. They exchanged pleasantries in English, never taking their eyes off me. I became the centrepiece. The object to gawk over, but not acknowledge.

"I didn't know you'd taken up the family business, Mercer," one man said, rubbing his greying moustache while eye-fucking me.

I expected Q to laugh, to mingle with the men I thought

were his mercurial friends, but I jumped when he stabbed a finger in the man's chest. "Don't you fucking say that. It's completely different."

The man froze; a battle of testosterone took place between them, before he averted his gaze, shrugging. "Whatever you say."

Another man, this one in expensive jeans and black shirt, looked about Q's age. His face reminded me of a 1920's movie star. Hair swept back and oiled, skin so smooth it looked like porcelain. "Q... " he started, gawking at me with fear in his eyes.

Fear? My terror ratcheted up a notch. Why did he fear me? My mind ran wild with nightmares of what Q would do—hurt me, make me wish I were dead.

Q rolled his neck, slinging an arm over the man's shoulders. They walked away from the other men, Q talking urgently in his ear. I couldn't hear a word, but Q kept flicking hard-edged glances at me, while 1920's man nodded as if Q had a valid argument. Finally, fear disappeared from his eyes, regarding me with keen interest.

Q jerked his head once in acknowledgement as the man patted him on the back; he returned to deal with the other guests.

1920's Guy watched Q go, before stepping closer.

My breaths came faster as he stopped below, looking up with sapphire eyes. With a steady hand, he touched my thigh, adding pressure so I wobbled in the cuffs. "So, you're the one to finally break him."

He walked around, running fingers along my ass and other thigh as he did a full circle. When he stood in front again, he reached for a nipple and tugged.

I twitched, lashing out with a foot. I swung precariously as the man laughed. He grabbed my waist, helping me balance on my toes again. I frowned. What the hell was going on?

1920's Man cocked his head, nodding. "I can see why."
With the cryptic comment, he strode back to the group.
Ten minutes passed as egotistical words filled the tomb.
Every syllable shimmered over my flesh, especially Q's deep
tone. I dreaded the future.

How could I stop my body reacting to his voice and
smell? Two senses he owned… leaving me with four: sight,
touch, taste, instinct. One thing I swore, he'd never own my
instincts—never own something so powerful.

Suzette, along with two other maids in frilly black and
white uniforms, entered the room and placed platters of
scrumptious-looking food on the side board. Most of it was
finger food—crackers with salmon and crème fraîche, stuffed
olives, prawns wrapped in prosciutto, and a fondant fountain
with a waterfall of silky chocolate.

My stomach panged, looking at the sweet delicacies to
dip in the chocolate: pineapple, strawberries, marshmallows,
the list went on. I hadn't had anything sugary since I arrived
at Q's tortuous mansion. Suzette wouldn't let me.

The staff ate bland, and frankly, rather depressing food,
considering we were in the heart of a country that prided
itself on cheeses, breads, and wine.

The men stopped talking and helped themselves to the
buffet. Once they'd filled plates, they sat in one of the
crimson booths by my feet.

Q eased into the booth, unbuttoning his silver blazer to
sit comfortably. Full lips opened to plop a stuffed olive into
his mouth. He chewed—the motion of his jaw and the
muscles in his neck caused my stomach to clench.

I looked away, inspecting the men. One had a big nose
and shaggy black hair. His suit didn't fit well and a dark stain
marked a lapel. Compared to Q, he looked as if he came from
the streets for a free dinner and a show. How did Q know
him? Even with his dark erotic desires, he was leagues above
these men.

The other man never took his eyes off me. His gaze was

a dagger, puncturing, making me ooze with fear. He was big. A foot taller than Q—about the size of a professional basketball player and just as wide. His buzzed cut blondish hair, showed pink scalp, and a nasty scar behind his right ear.

He didn't wear a suit. Instead, he favoured a white, tacky jumpsuit, with the number nineteen on the shoulders and back. Everything about him didn't make sense. He didn't fit in Q's world. In fact, the only one who did was 1920's Man. Something linked him and Q: friendship.

While the men ate, my hands turned icy cold as blood stopped pumping so high up my arms. My wrists chafed in the leather, and the barcode tattoo itched like crazy. I tried to tilt my head, to stand on the very tips of my toes to give my shoulders a break, but I couldn't get purchase. I moaned with overwhelming discomfort.

Q didn't look at me once. He kept his attention on Mr. Big Nose and munched his way through the small plate of food.

That left me strangely alone with the man in the white jumpsuit. He devoured the plate of hor d'oeuvres and asked Q in English, "You like our gift. Yes?" He cocked his head, dragging horrible eyeballs up and down my golden-wrapped body.

My ears pricked. His accent was Russian, not French. My mind kicked into gear trying to work it all out.

Q stopped eating, and dabbed his mouth with a napkin. His motions so smooth and controlled compared to Russian Lumberjack. Q's eyes smouldered with barely restrained tolerance. "*Oui*. Very satisfactory." He threw a fleeting glance at me, before adding, "Where did you buy her from?"

The Russian puffed his chest, glowing with pride. Why did he care if Q found me satisfactory? He bought me as a bribe to make Q do something. But what?

"I won't share my contact's name. But I requested a white girl. I know you have preferences."

My eyes shot to Q, but his posture hadn't changed. He took a sip from a chilled glass of wine. "Fine. Consider our dealing complete."

The Russian scowled. "How will I know you'll keep your promise?"

Q shifted ever so slightly; my skin prickled with the change of hospitality. Q seemed to suck shadows from the room, cloaking himself in authority. "You doubt my work ethic?"

The Russian clenched his jaw, looking from Q to me. "When will we see contracts?"

Q played with a cufflink, taking his time. "Three months. That's how long these things take. But you have my word. And that is law."

Russian Lumberjack snorted, rolling his shoulders. He didn't look happy with the arrangement, but I doubted there was anything he could do. Q was clearly the one in control. Just like my situation—the whole sex slavery thing.

I wanted to roll my eyes. I didn't want to go crazy, and that's how I felt dangling there.

After a pause, the Russian stood, making his way to the chocolate fondant. Q watched with narrowed eyes, before turning to speak with Big Nose and Grey Moustache. 1920's Man's inquisitive sapphire eye's bounced between Q and me. Thoughts raced in his gaze, but his face remained blank.

My heart galloped as I looked at Russian Lumberjack. His posture scared me. He flashed a look at Q while he waited for chocolate to spill into a jug. His eyes shadowed with jealousy and a greedy hunger for power.

I turned to Q. Should I warn him the Russian wasn't his friend, but his enemy? *What are you thinking, Tess? It isn't your business. Who cares?*

As much as I didn't want to admit it—I did care. Not for Q's safety, but for my own. If Q submitted to men like the

Russian, my gilded cage would fast become a dank dungeon.

My body swung in the bindings, and I clenched my abs to stay facing Russian Lumberjack. He moved too slowly, as if thinking about something other than getting food.

My skin erupted into goosebumps as instincts kicked in. The same instincts that screamed not to go in the café in Mexico. I didn't like this. *What's not to like? You're mostly naked, hanging from a ceiling for five men to perv at while they eat.*

I hated the whole scenario, but something about the man in the white jumpsuit did not sit well in my gut.

The Russian moved suddenly, carting a plate full of marshmallows and a little pouring jug overflowing with melted chocolate. He made to go back to the table, but at the last second changed his mind, bee-lining for me.

I twisted in the cuffs, trying to back away, but it was no use. My eyes shot to Q, imploring him to pay attention and stop this, but his head was bowed deep in conversation with Grey Moustache.

The Russian stopped at the bottom of the pedestal, gawking at me. Up close, his skin was pockmarked from acne and shone with grease. His buzzed hair looked coarse, and smelled of too much hair product. He shifted, smiling with a few gold capped teeth. *"Privet, krasivaya devushka."* He caressed my knee through the filigree material. "It means, hello, pretty girl." His voice rumbled, sending fear into overdrive. Where he touched, my skin crawled, and if skin could throw up, it would.

Again I looked at Q, disbelieving he'd let the man touch me. He didn't seem to notice or care. His body twisted away, hands clasped tightly on the table as he nodded at something Big Nose said.

He shut me out with a bear of a man who gazed with unbridled horniness. It wasn't a sensual kind of lust like Q; it was a savage need to rut. To cause pain. I had no doubt he'd enjoy my screams.

With a sadistic smile, the Russian reached for the jug of melted chocolate, and with a calculated gleam, dribbled some on my thigh. The chocolate teetered on the edge of too hot; I hissed between my teeth.

Q shifted, but didn't turn to look. I wanted to scream, but I didn't know if I'd be in deeper trouble. Maybe by not looking, Q gave the Russian permission to do what he wanted.

Russian Lumberjack grinned and placed the plate of marshmallows on the floor, but kept the small jug of chocolate.

Oh, fuck.

"Don't. Leave me the hell alone," I demanded, voice shaky.

Q's pale green eyes landed on me and my skin prickled with relief. He wouldn't let this man taunt me.

My mouth parted as something white-hot passed between Q and I, then he turned away.

My heart stopped, betrayal coated my tongue. He cut me out with one twist of his powerful body.

Tears rushed as the Russian chuckled, reaching with fat fingers to grasp my thigh. Holding me in place, his big wet tongue licked the chocolate off my skin, dragging saliva over my flesh and dress.

I shuddered in repulsion, trying to wriggle from his grip, but he pinched harder. "No struggling, pretty girl." With the jug high, he poured another dollop on my foot. With a gross grin, he dropped and sucked it off. I tried to kick, but I needed toes on the ground to stay stable. I didn't want to spin out of control like I did with 1920's Man. At least he'd been kind and secured me. This man would probably make me spin, disorientating, making me sick.

The Russian stood, drizzling chocolate on my stomach. It trickled down my front, hardening quickly, but not fast enough. It oozed onto my lower belly, dangerously low, way too close to my core.

"Not low enough, huh, pet." He grunted, capturing me in meaty arms, pulling me to his mouth. I squirmed as he licked the chocolate, leaving a cold, slimy trail from his tongue. He shifted, ducking his head; one lash of his tongue caught my clit. My entire body wanted to disintegrate from shame and the grossness of being tongued by a gargoyle.

"You're a fucking bastard. You won't get away with this." Images of slicing his neck and throwing him into a roaring crematorium helped endure his touch. All the wetness Q conjured disappeared, leaving me dry, unwilling, completely sick to my stomach.

My eyes widened in realization. My body reacted to Q despite what he did—because of what he did. But I shut down when another touched me. If Q had been the one to lick, I would've shuddered in erotic torture, hating it, but secretly loving it. But the Russian behemoth repulsed me. The very thought of him anywhere near my body brought me out in dry heaves.

The revelation my body reacted for Q, despite everything, brought equal measures of torment and peace. My body wanted Q's, but at the same time it wanted nobody else. Had he trained me so well, without my knowledge? Or had I given him my sense of touch so willingly? *Please don't let him own that, too.*

I hated the Russian with a fire that would never burn out, whereas my hatred for Q seethed and simmered, hot enough to melt my body. I may want to kill Q for ruining my life, but I didn't hate him enough to kill myself so he would never have me.

The Russian's fat fingers pried my thighs apart and his heavy breath wafted me in garlic. He pushed, and I lost my footing, swinging wide. He stepped onto the podium, catching my swinging body when I slammed against him. He deliberately faced me away from Q, putting himself between us.

Facing the other wall, my eyes widened at the most fantastical mural painted in browns, blacks, and shadow. A cloud of sparrows decorated the wall. I could almost feel wind from fluttering wings as they flew from the grips of a black storm cloud. Freedom beckoned in the patch of blue sky by the ceiling. The painting made my heart weep, needing the same freedom. I couldn't count how many little birds, but each one was unique, coming to life with perfection.

Russian's hand grabbed my breast, twisting painfully. His mouth clamped down on my ear.

I opened my mouth to scream, to demand Q to claim me, but an obscenely large palm clamped over my mouth. Blocking my nose and mouth, just like Leather Jacket had done.

My lungs seized, and I fought. He chuckled as my feeble attempts made a repulsive hard cock wedge between my ass cheeks. My eyes flew to the sparrows. I wished I could sprout wings and fly. I tried to lose myself in the painting, willing my mind to leave.

Fumbling between us, he withdrew something, bringing it to my stomach. Something icy cold bit my flesh. I gasped, heart bucking.

"Hush, little whore. This is between us. You cost me a lot of money, you know. I think it's only fair I sample you." A fat hand fumbled on my lower belly, and the loathsome sound of my dress ripping filled me with black dread. My eyes rolled, trying to see below. What was the icy thing slicing through the material?

With another sharp tug, the dress hung ruined and the tightness around my ass softened as filigree strands went from tight to gaping.

He licked my ear, flashing a hunting knife. I groaned and thrashed. The blade was rust-spotted and tarnished, but glinted wicked sharp. "Stop wriggling, little fish. I'm not going to cut you." He flipped the blade so sharp metal rested in a calloused palm and a sweat stained, wooden handle faced upward.

Oh, shit.

Instincts screamed. *He's going to rape you with the handle of a knife!*

I moaned as loud as I could, using all valuable oxygen to call for help. Faintness tinged when Q ordered in a controlled and angry voice, "Victor, let go of my gift."

The words rang with power; I melted with relief. Q wouldn't let anything bad happen. I knew it. I trusted him to keep me for his own twisted pleasures.

"Just having a hug, Mr. M. I'll let her go in a moment." He looked over a shoulder, no doubt smiling at Q. I thrust hips backward, trying to kick him off balance, but he remained unmovable.

Tension knotted, waiting for Q to demand he unhand me, that he'd touched long enough, but nothing came.

Silence reigned; my heart died as the Russian chuckled soundlessly in my ear. "I reckon I have about thirty seconds before I'm made to stop...."

I didn't have time to breathe. He pushed a large boot against the GPS tracker on my ankle, forcing legs to splay. Capturing my weight completely, he positioned the butt of the knife handle against my entrance.

I struggled, I fought, but I was a fly in sticky flypaper... inconsequential.

"I wish this was my cock, but I can make do," he muttered. He bit my throat, slamming the handle inside. I opened my mouth behind his fleshy palm and screamed. My lungs cried but no sound came out. He tore into me, blazing with splinters and violation. My dryness condemned me to feel every ridge of wood, every scrape of awful hardness.

My eyes glazed with grey, trying to pass out, but

anger cannonballed into my blood. Fight and wrath heated and I fought with all my might.

The Russian grunted as I went wild. I twisted and twined. I kicked and thrashed.

I didn't care if I killed myself getting free, I couldn't let him do this. It hurt. It *hurt!* Q didn't save me. He let the bastard thrust a knife deep inside.

A shot rang out, then I was falling, falling, coming to a horrible stop with my arms wrenched from their sockets by the cuffs. I dangled with my head lolling on my shoulders, sucking in gluttonous breaths of oxygen.

The Russian bellowed, falling off the pedestal, taking the rapist knife with him. He clutched a thigh where a river of red bloomed against the whiteness of his jumpsuit.

"Fuck!" he shouted.

Q raged, face etched with livid anger. "Get the fuck out of my house." His arm outstretched, holding a small, silver gun.

My head swam. Q had a gun. He shot him.

The rest of the guests jumped from their seats, rushing to the exit. Everyone apart from 1920's Man; he stayed behind Q, body tense, hands curled.

Q yelled, "Franco! Escort our guests. They're leaving."

The green-eyed guard magically appeared and hustled everyone out, before coming back and hoisting the cursing Russian to his feet. Once they'd left, 1920's Man laid a hand on Q's shoulder.

Q immediately jumped and spun, waving the gun. "*Putain.* Stop! I know what I'm doing, Frederick. Leave."

The guy frowned, clearly not believing him, but after a moment, nodded and strode out the door.

Silence settled, broken only by Q's and my heavy breathing. I swung by my arms, tears glassing my vision. I didn't have the strength to pull myself up and my shoulders screamed. But none of it came close the aching soreness inside. I felt ripped in two, reliving the first hard thrust, the mind-shattering agony, over and over.

How could Q allow this to happen? I was his, goddammit, and he didn't protect me. He let another man hurt me.

I splintered, wanting to crawl back into the silent void that saved me last time, but my mind wouldn't fly away. My mind was broken.

I must have passed out. I came to with my cheek bobbing against a warm shoulder and my body cocooned in strong arms. The scent of citrus and sandalwood hugged me, sending a mixture of longing and panic kicking in my blood.

"Je suis vraiment désolé," I'm so sorry, a tortured voice whispered. Kisses flurried on my hairline, never stopping. I floated through the house in his arms. "I'll protect you. I'll make it right."

His voice confused me. It dripped with aged pain and sorrow, remorse so great, it weighed down with pressure.

Why did he hurt? He allowed the man to do what he wanted. It was his fault it happened and I refused to listen to his pain. My own pain kept me plenty occupied. His apologies weren't worth shit.

I tried to gather enough energy to hit him, scream, tell him he'd successfully hurt me worse than anyone in my entire life, and that was saying something seeing as I grew up a leper in my own family.

But my mind finally decided it'd had enough and went blank.

Chapter Fourteen

Hummingbird

I woke to a gnawing ache in my womb and a smear of blood between my legs. I washed gently in the shower, forcing all memories and horror into a cage inside my mind. I would never think about that night again. Even in nightmares, the night was banned, erased as if it never happened. Some might say running wasn't a good idea; I say it helped me stay healthy and focused, rather than suffocating in self-pity and things detrimental to my sanity.

I buried my head in the sand, but in return gained freedom and immunity against things hurting my soul. My body hurt, but no more than other injuries I sported. What lacerated me most was Q. He let me down.

In the sick hierarchy of owner and slave, my protection and well-being should be paramount, yet he turned a blind eye.

Out of everything he'd done, last night might've broken me beyond repair, but it only strengthened. The time had come to leave. I deserved better. I deserved to live my life without sick bastards raping me with objects, or Q's twisted mind games. Nothing would stop me from busting the hell out and going back to humanity.

Four days passed after the horrible dinner, and Suzette refused to make eye contact. Q did his disappearing act again, turning music so loud, lyrics corroded my fierce decision to leave. French laments full of regret and self-loathing throbbed through the speakers:

Mes besoins sont ma défaite. Je suis un monstre dans la peau d'un homme.
My needs are my downfall. I'm a monster in human skin.

I hated the songs. Soft songs made Q seem human, living with mistakes and anguish, just like the rest of us. I preferred the raging songs. Ones with a heavy beat, heating my blood, filling me with energy to escape.

Et je prendrai ce que je veux et payerai mes propres désirs. Cauchemars de ma solitude. L'obscurité comme ami.
And I'll take what I want and pay for my own desires. Nightmares for my loneliness. The darkness for a friend.

The longer I lived in Q's house, the more my French improved. Rust gave way to smoothness and it happened without my knowledge. I no longer frowned and worked out every word—gist of sentences became clear, no longer fumbling in the language dark.

Although I missed Suzette and her friendship, I didn't care about the isolation. I was left alone; it kept me focused.

Under the disguise of cleaning, I searched the library and lounge for weapons. A letter opener, scissors, something to help me dispose of the GPS tracker. I couldn't run until I removed it. Q would find me too easily.

My escape plan wasn't well thought out. I had no *Mission Impossible* idea of taking Q hostage and forcing him to release me. All I had were my legs, and a few apples I managed to steal from the kitchen. Living in an open home granted the illusion of freedom—to go where I pleased, move around at will—but in searching for weapons, I realised how false the freedom really was.

Guards patrolled the upstairs level, keeping me from entering bedrooms. Black-suited goons patrolled the sweeping grounds outside, their breath sending foggy plumes into late winter air.

I could enter the library, lounge, kitchen, and bedroom only. It was a tiny cage compared to the expanse of the house. If I cared about staying, I would've sneaked and investigated. Where did Q sleep? What other rooms were there? More like the pedestal room where the Russian bastard hurt me, or worse?

But I didn't care. I'd been here long enough. I wouldn't play damsel in distress waiting for Brax or the police to rescue me. They would never come. It was up to me, and I was ready.

I stepped out of the library, wafting a duster, disappointed yet again I couldn't find a sharp implement, and froze.

My heartbeats raced as a whiff of sin and citrus assaulted. Q was close.

"*Je suis allé trop loin,* Suzette." I went too far. Q's voice twisted with unforgiving darkness.

I wanted to crawl into a ball and hide. I hated eavesdropping. Whenever I did as a child, I heard nasty things that cramped my stomach. Things about being unwanted, a nuisance, a hindrance.

My parents even spoke about adopting me out when I fell violently ill with the flu. They didn't want to deal with a sick child, being older and vulnerable. Caring more for themselves than an innocent girl.

Suzette answered, her voice coming from behind the blue

velvet stairs. The place where the hidden door to the gaming room lurked. "She didn't break. You should see her, *maître*. The fire is still in her eyes." The air bristled with passion, they spoke of me. My entire body boycotted. I wanted to move, but if I moved they'd hear me. What would Q do then?

Q muttered something I didn't catch.

"You're not like him. Don't let this stop you. She feels something other than hatred. Believe me. A woman knows when another wants a man."

Q chuckled. "You want me, Suzette?"

She giggled darkly. "You know I do. But I also appreciate your promise, and that's why I think you need to keep going." The sad resignation made me feel sorry for her.

Q was ruthless and closed off; I didn't care what demons he dealt with. It didn't give him the right to do what he did. So why did jealously prick my skin at the thought of him fucking another? I knew nothing about him, yet my body pined for more—against all my wishes.

If Suzette was on my side, why hadn't she talked to me the last four days? If she'd shown she still wanted to be a friend, I might not have shut off—become so remote and focused on freedom.

My eyes widened. *You don't mean that, Tess.* Would I have stayed even after what happened?

I shook my head, anger hot. No way. I couldn't stay. All I needed was a split second opportunity, and I was gone. Just like the sparrows on the wall—darting to heights where Q could never find me.

"Enough. I will not talk about this," Q snapped, different to his previous tone. Clothing rustled and I darted to the library, ducking next to a bookcase. Q's silhouette stalked past the door, heading outside. The quick flash of sunlight beckoned; I wanted to run after him. To sprint into the fresh air and leave this place—

this confusing, horrible place.

A car waited outside, but Q didn't climb in and drive off. Instead, he stalked out of sight.

I didn't dare move, and Suzette shouted. "I'm heading to the village, Mrs. Sucre. It's my half day off, and I need to run some errands."

I didn't hear Mrs. Sucre's response, but it sounded like she argued. My heart galloped. Suzette was leaving. *This is my chance!* I might not get another. A village meant people. And people meant safety in numbers.

Suzette grumbled and stomped away, obviously summoned by the cook. Not wanting to waste a moment, I pushed off the floor like an Olympic sprinter and darted into the foyer. I fumbled with the front door with anxious fingers, then sprinted down the sweeping steps toward the car. *Please, let there be keys.*

Sun burned my retinas even as the cold temperature bit through clothing. The freshness of being outside gave me a burst of happiness. I would save myself. Tess, the survivor.

Gasping with adrenaline, I checked to see if keys dangled in the ignition.

Nothing.

Shit! I couldn't drive to freedom, but I could stowaway while Suzette drove. Not wanting to be discouraged, I tried the back door, almost crying in relief when it opened.

I threw myself inside, huddling as tight as I could in the foot well.

Suzette bounced down the steps. *"Bonjour,* Franco. You'll drive me to the village?"

Oh, fuck. I clamped a hand over my mouth. Why couldn't Suzette drive herself? Were none of Q's staff allowed to go unchaperoned? My heart raced faster. So many things could go wrong—Franco could catch me, Q would punish.

"No problem. I need some cigarettes, so perfect timing." Franco's voice sounded friendly, upbeat, like any man with no care in the world. Obviously, his conscience didn't care what his employer did to women.

Suzette hopped in the front, smoothing her uniform. Franco climbed into the driver's seat and the car settled with his bulk. His crisp, black suit framed his muscles and my hope of running dwindled.

The car started; the loud purr vibrated in my teeth. I curled smaller as Franco put the vehicle into gear and rolled smoothly into motion. The crunching of gravel sounded loud and the three-horse fountain disappeared as we drove away.

The further we travelled, the more I freaked. This could go terribly wrong, but if it worked, I'd never see Q again. Never hear his voice or smell his unique scent. Something deep inside panged uncomfortably. I hated that he owned two of my senses—possibly even three. He was a master at coercing my body's needs, sacrificing my mind for erotic pleasure. I'd had enough of betrayal from my own flesh.

Every roll of tyres brought a cocktail of eagerness and disappointment. My life would belong to me again. My body would return to being dormant, hiding its secret desires. *But I want that!* Q was a monster in human clothing—even he knew it, judging by his song choice. If he let a man rape me with a knife handle, who knew what he'd do next.

My hands curled with fury. I couldn't afford to feel anything but hatred for Q. Suzette was wrong—I didn't feel any more than repulsion. Hopefully, over time, my senses would belong to me again. I would forget about this nightmare.

Excitement bubbled beneath layers of apprehension as we drove in silence away from hell, toward salvation.

Suzette and Franco didn't talk and I breathed as quiet and shallow as possible. It was odd to run with no belongings. How far would I get without money, credit cards, or a passport?

My passport and purse were in the hotel in Cancun. Then again, the hotel probably checked us out when we never returned. Did Brax go back? I was heading home, and refused to entertain the thought he might be gone. I needed him alive. He was my end goal. If I didn't have him, who was I running back to?

You're leaving a life of overwhelming senses for comfort, Tess.

The thought rocked my soul. While being Q's prisoner, I'd never been so alive. Sure, he was a bastard, and the things he did weren't legal, but at the same time he made me *live*.

I brought the nightmare on myself with unwholesome thoughts, but Q showed me the life I lived with Brax wasn't fully… complete. Brax treated me with utmost care, but never made me vibrant.

On the floor of a car, escaping from my kidnapper, I re-evaluated my entire life. I'd lived in denial for so long, it came naturally. I loved Brax, I couldn't deny that. But my love skirted toward sibling love. Friendship love. A love that would never die, but would never consume me either. I loved Brax because he took me in. He wanted me and I settled, rather than have the guts to find a man who made my soul sing.

Guilt crushed, pressing me against the floor. By lying to myself, I hurt Brax so much. A few tears dribbled and I fought the urge to sniff. One thing I knew, if he still lived, I'd make it a lifelong mission to make it up to him. I'd be the princess he always wanted, and take care of him, regardless if he couldn't save me in Mexico.

Suzette and Franco started chatting aimlessly about the weather, and I forced myself to listen, pushing away debilitating thoughts. I couldn't afford to think about sad things. I needed to be ready to run.

Through the window, hedges and shadowy trees flickered past, rolling hills and farm land. So quaint and picture perfect, it was hard to believe Q lived amongst perfect innocence and followed such darkness.

The twists and turns of the tiny country lanes made nausea swell and I closed my eyes.

I didn't know how long it took, maybe twenty minutes, before the car slowed. Suzette asked, "Can you pull up on *Rue La Belle*? I won't be long."

Franco grunted in acknowledgement, and after a few turns, we entered a bustling township. Sounds of chattering voices and traffic thrilled me. So close to being free.

I dared open my eyes. Pedestrians skirted the car, and cute ancient buildings hovered in French glory.

Suzette climbed out. *"Merci, Franco, à plus tard."* Later.

"I'll be back at the car in ten minutes." His voice rasped. I couldn't believe my eyes as Franco locked the door and strode off, swallowed immediately by the bustling crowd.

I lay on the floor, sucking greedy breaths in the empty car. I was alone!

Wait before you run.

My body shook with the need to flee, but I waited an agonising minute. Slowly, I unfolded from the floor, reaching to unlock the door. I tried to clamber out quickly, but my legs cramped and I sprawled in the path of an elderly woman. Pretty cobblestones bit my ass as I looked up.

She frowned, hoisting her bag higher on her shoulder. *"Excusez-moi,"* she said, inching around, continuing on her way.

I bounced upright, commanding my limbs to un-atrophy so I could run.

The busy street looked the epitome of France. Quaint shop signs dangled in front of wonky buildings with flower baskets and fresh fruit in bushels looked waxy and delicious in the winter sun. Everything was written in French, and I knew I'd be lost within a moment. Where the hell was this place? Were we close to Paris?

I blinked in wonderment. I would never take freedom for granted again. After being caged for weeks, the breeze on my skin felt foreign; the sun an old missed friend. My heart flew. *I escaped.*

I didn't know which way Suzette or Franco went, so I kept my eyes trained on the crowd, dashing fugitively across the road to the green grocer.

"Bonjour, ma belle," an elderly man said, tilting his head as I darted past. Rows upon rows of food made my mouth water. Everything was a burst of sensation, colour—a marvel to my senses.

Being in a crowd liberated and intoxicated. I never realised how much I needed to be a part of something. Sure, insecurities of being unwanted stemmed from lack of parental love, but up till now, I never evaluated how much I thrived at university. I had friends. Good friends.

My eyes pricked remembering Fiona, Marion, and Stacey. Women who I'd studied with and sketched the most far out buildings we could imagine. Tree houses. Underwater mansions. And yet, they didn't know me. I never told them what I wished Brax would do. Even when we shared kinky conversation, I never opened up and admitted I wanted to be a submissive, just for one night.

My heart tripped. What would they say if they knew what happened? Would they understand how disobedient my body had been? How the sexual tension, the unwanted boiling, crippling need inside made me wet for a man I hated?

It was so off the realm of normalcy, they'd probably march me straight to the police for a shrink assessment.

Police.

All thoughts evaporated. I wasn't free yet.

I chose the next building—a cute little one story, with a red chicken on the front called *Le Coq.* The rooster.

I paused, hating the thought that Q would hurt Suzette

for letting me escape. I sighed, cursing that I felt loyal to stay, bound by obligation more than ropes and barcode tattoos. I held my breath, heart winging with terror.

Despite my fear for Suzette, I pushed open the café door. The little bell above jingled merrily, reminding I was on my way home. I couldn't dwell on breaking a friendship with someone I barely knew.

Speed was my friend as I charged to the cashier.

The soft, pudgy woman behind the counter beamed. *"Bonjour, que puis-je faire pour vous?"* What can I do for you?

My mouth became desiccated and I blinked. This was it, no going back. "I've been kidnapped. I need a phone and the police."

Chapter Fifteen

*Heron*

Her eyes widened, flying around the establishment as if one of her customers could enlighten her. Surely, this crazy Aussie chick couldn't be telling the truth.

My chest heaved as panic filled. What if she didn't believe me?

I looked around, glancing over my shoulder at a spattering of patrons. They gawked as if I was a chimpanzee escaped from the zoo. The little café would've been homely with its red colour scheme and over saturation of rooster figurines and posters, but to me it felt hostile. As if any moment, the roosters would come alive and peck my eyes out for disrupting a leisurely lunch.

I'd poured my heart out to a stranger and all she could do was stare.

"Can I borrow your phone?" My voice wavered; tears threatened. Being so close to freedom made me jittery.

She nodded hesitantly, clearly not quite understanding. I spied the phone behind the counter and snagged it, leaning over a plate of bagels and muffins.

My hands shook, apprehension tickled my spine. Fingers

hovered over the emergency call buttons, but I couldn't dial. I needed to hear another voice first.

I pressed the number I knew by heart and tears burst forth as the call connected. It rang and rang for an eternity. *Please, pick up. Please, be alive.*

The woman scowled and disappeared into the back of the restaurant, reappearing and dragging an elderly chef. Both of them wore yellow uniforms with white pinafores, and the same 'what the hell' expression.

I bounced, waiting for the phone to connect. My time was running out.

Hi, you've reached Brax Cliffingstone. I'm unable to get to the phone, but you know the drill. Leave your details, and I'll get back to you. Or, if it's life and death, please contact my girlfriend, Tess, and she'll help out. Her number: 044-873-4937. Cheers!

Beep.

Something snapped in my chest. I hadn't heard my name in so long. Hearing it in Brax's voice robbed my fight, and I shrunk into the tame little girl I'd been before Mexico, before Q, before I knew what I was capable of.

I crumbled, sobbing. Brax's voice resonated around my heart, vibrating with longing. Why wasn't he picking up? Was he dead, or just busy? So many questions and I wouldn't get answers from a machine.

Sniffing back tears, I warbled, "Brax, it's me. I'm—I'm alive. I was sold to a man named Q. I'm not hurt and I'm on my way home. If you get this message, I'll be at the Australian Embassy, hopefully working out passports and things."

I sucked in a deep breath. I wanted to tell him so much: how I changed, what I lived through, but I would never be able to tell him what Q did, as I'd never be able to hide the sick, messed up desire in my voice. He'd know Q turned me on, even as I lied that I preferred tameness. I burned that bridge when I showed Brax my vibrator, asking for more.

Urgency itched; I had to get off the phone, time tick-tocked away. I could break down and find myself again once I was home.

"Brax, if—if I don't get home, promise me you'll find a man named Q Mercer in a small region of France. He has a big house, staff. Tell the police. I love you."

Tears streamed anew as I terminated the call, and instantly dialled another number. The chef, covered in smears of sauce and flour, yanked the phone out of my grip.

"Hey!" I glared.

He shook his head, anger blazing. "You spreading lies. I do not believe—" His eyes shot past me. The door slammed open, bell clanging with warning.

I spun in terror.

Oh, my God. Franco stood in the doorway, eyes bugging out of his head. He froze for a millisecond before launching into action. Hands flew to his jacket, fumbling in the inner pocket. What was he looking for? A gun?

I didn't mean to find out.

I ran.

Pushing past the man and woman, I charged into the kitchen and thanked God for the exit. The door rocketed open as I slammed it with a shoulder.

The back street was salvation, and I sprinted with every bit of strength. My sore ankle yelped as I flew over uneven cobblestones, darting down another alley. I zigged and zagged, trying to get completely lost, hoping Franco would lose all sense of direction.

A grunt and shout obliterated the hope; I ran harder. I couldn't go back. I couldn't. Q would punish me, and I didn't know how much more my mind could take. I might never get another chance to escape.

Changing course, I charged for the main street, exploding from the alley into on-coming traffic. People scattered as I careened out of control, panting hard, eyes wild.

Car horns blared as I slammed to a halt in the middle of the road. My gaze darted, trying to find someone, *something*, to save me. I daren't look behind to see if Franco was close—my entire body felt hunted. Any moment, a bullet would tear through my brain, putting me down like the rabid runaway I was.

Battling useless thoughts, I put all focus into finding a saviour.

A car screeched to a halt, missing me by millimetres. My heart catapulted into my throat as the bumper whispered against my knees. *Shit, am I so willing to sacrifice death for survival?*

"*Putain de merde!*" What the hell? The man with browny-red hair opened the car door, waving an angry hand. "I could've killed you!"

I latched onto his eyes, entreating instincts to say if he could be trusted. Could he save me? I ran to the driver's side, and gripped the door with white fingers. "Please. Take me to the police. I've been kidnapped."

I looked behind me, expecting to see Franco within grabbing distance. I was an exposed target, standing in the middle of a blocked road.

The guy looked me up and down, nostrils flaring as he ran a nervous hand through his hair. Brown eyes glazed with confusion, and I suffered a pang of fear. He wouldn't help.

I backed up, bunching muscles to run again.

Just as I was about to take off, he shouted, "Wait! I take. I take." He ran around the front of the car and opened the passenger door.

Hesitation filled me, looking into the small sedan. Was this a case of jumping out of the pan and into the fire?

Who else do you have to save you?

"*Esclave!*"

My heart spurted with terror; I threw myself into the car. "Get in. Get in!" I couldn't breathe as Franco fought his way through lingering pedestrians, eyes locked on me.

The guy jumped into action and ran to the driver's seat. He slammed the car into gear, and we peeled forward with a roar of the engine. Franco slammed the car roof as we zoomed away, bypassing other cars, and jumping the curb.

I peered at the guy—my rescuer. His mouth thinned to a white line, navigating the road at hyper speed. I wanted to hug him, crush him in thankfulness.

Twisting in the seat, I stared out the back window. Franco jumped up and down in the street, yanking his black hair. He yelled something and threw his hands up, before sprinting back to where he parked.

Breathing hard, I swivelled to face the front, trying to calm down. I'd done it. I was free.

We didn't say a word as we drove from the postcard perfect township onto pretty country roads.

Silence lurked like a third passenger. I stared out the window, tension knotting my stomach. I wanted to dance in happiness, but I wasn't free yet. I needed to stay collected, stay wary. I frowned. After three weeks of torture, could it really be that easy? Uneasiness pricked, and I bit my lip. Surely, it couldn't be that simple?

The GPS! In my rush, I'd forgotten about Q's freakin' tracker. *Shit!* I brought my leg up, resting a heel on the seat. My fingers fumbled with my jeans, pushing them up to access the anklet. I tugged hard, trying to wedge my fingers beneath the twist-tie, but it only tightened, cutting off the blood supply to my foot.

I huffed with rage. How the hell would I get rid of it?

The guy looked over, eyebrow cocked. "What are you doing?" He navigated a turn, before glancing again. "What is that?"

We made eye contact. His face seemed kind enough, not handsome, but not ugly. Mid-thirties with early wrinkles around brown eyes. Deciding he seemed trustworthy, I said, "I need a knife, or some scissors. Do you have anything like that?" I fiddled with the anklet. If I could raise my leg to my mouth, I could gnaw it off. The image made me want to laugh —I escaped, only to have chew my own leg off like a starving rat.

I expected him to say no. I mean, this entire thing seemed too perfect. Who could say their knight in shining armour almost ran them over, then whisked them away in a crappy Volvo?

My mind shot to Franco. Had he called Q? Arranged a search party for me? Q wouldn't let me go easily. He'd hunt, but I didn't intend for him to catch me.

Urgency pumped my blood faster; I wished the driver would step on it. I wanted Formula One driving, not sedate Grandma.

The guy shifted, his foot pressing on the accelerator as he fumbled in a pocket. He frowned, wiggling his ass, reaching for something.

I watched with an incredulous expression, trying to figure out what he was doing. After a few awkward moments, he smiled, pulling his hand free.

With a flourish, he passed me a miniature Swiss army knife.

My eyes popped wide, and I accepted it with shaky hands. "Thanks." My voice whispered with awe. From now on, I would carry a Swiss army knife—never know when one would come in handy. Bet he didn't wake up this morning expecting a runaway to use it to cut a tracker off her body.

I took the red case and flipped open a serrated blade. I blew blonde bangs from my eyes, sawing through thick plastic. It took a lot of energy, and my skin grew clammy beneath the jumper by the time it snapped and fell away.

The moment it dropped to the floor, I breathed a huge sigh of relief. The nightmare was almost over, one step closer to Brax.

The guy watched closely. His intense gaze sent flutters of awareness as I returned the knife. I kept my face blank when he palmed it, shoving it back in his pocket.

Perhaps I should've kept it? *You're not thinking clearly, Tess. Don't trust anyone.*

He gave me half a smile, light returning to his eyes. Fingers tightened on the steering wheel. "What happened?"

I managed three words: "Q Mercer happened." Then weariness smothered and the thought of reliving it was too much. I couldn't talk about it; I might not ever be ready to talk, and that was fine by me. It would become an unspoken moment of time and fade into oblivion.

Huddling, my chest clogged with emotion. So close… so close. I grew heavy as the adrenaline in my blood abandoned me. "I just need to get to the police."

He nodded. The afternoon sun dipped through the windshield, highlighting the red in his hair. *"Pas de problème."*

I gave a watery smile and settled back, looking forward to the future.

The sound of tyres on gravel roused me, panic flared like an old enemy. *Gravel—please tell me we aren't back at Q's.*

I shot upright, blinking out the window. Adrenaline and jittery warmth made my breath come fast. I'd become so used to terror overflowing, I wondered if I'd ever feel safe again.

It was dark; no population, no township, nothing in the looming blackness. I glared at the man supposedly saving me, trying to figure it out.

He smirked, slowing to a stop. I stared out the window again, disbelieving. Where were the bright lights of a police station? The comforting sounds of people?

Brakes squeaked and he grinned in the shadows. "Come with me."

"But this isn't a police station."

He chuckled. "No. Not going to the police. But you're home now, just the same."

My world slammed to a halt; I gawked. He wasn't serious. He *couldn't* be serious. It couldn't happen. It just couldn't. Hadn't I dealt with enough in Mexico and with Q?

Ripe anger gushed, and all I saw was red. I wouldn't let this happen. I wrenched open the door and toppled from the car.

"Hey, arrêtez!" The man fumbled with his seat belt, but he was too late. I shot to my feet and ran.

He screamed obscenities, curses licking my heels, urging me faster. My head swivelled, looking for solitude, a place to run to. But all around, rolling country hills and patchwork farmland imprisoned better than any barbwire. I didn't even know where he'd taken me. I could run for miles and never find help.

My heart ached, pushing my body past endurance. I burst past a row of soaring pine trees and my mouth fell open.

A sprawling country estate rested under moonlight. Inviting with arched windows and Tuscany appeal, but instincts beat an uneven tattoo in my chest. *Evil.* The house reeked of evil.

I darted to the right, running as far from the estate as possible. I came to a wooden fence and scaled it. The moment my feet touched ground again, I jerked my arms, propelling forward. Pain from my bruises and ribs were inconsequential—running was paramount.

I stumbled in the dark, the only light came from the silver, pregnant moon. My ankle rolled on a row of potatoes ready for hoeing. I looked around—acres and acres of potatoes, all resting in blankets of dirt.

Keep running!

My breath rasped in the silent night, and legs burned, but I never let up the pace. I bounded over rows of potatoes like a gazelle hunted by a lion.

A little further, then I would be hidden by the night. I could find help elsewhere. But as I ran, my faith in humanity died a fiery death. All my life, I believed in the goodness of people. Never seeing darkness for myself. But now, I hated everyone, suspected everything. Another part was broken: the ability to trust.

A shape blurred in the corner of my eye and I screamed. A hard form slammed into mine, crushing me against soil and produce. The smell of earth assaulted and I flared with pain.

Heavy breathing filled my ear as I fought. We rolled, caking ourselves in dirt; I tried to bite but nothing came within teeth distance.

I was no match for the new brute. A boulder from the night—he loomed twice the size of Q and fear sliced as hands pawed, rough and angry.

He pulled me to my feet, black eyes glinting. "Hello, treasure."

I kicked and snarled. "Let me go."

He threw his head back, laughing. Thinning brown hair and wrinkled face put him somewhere in his mid-fifties. But no middle-age spread covered his body—it rippled with compacted muscle. With barely any energy, he dragged me across the field as if I were a flea. I stopped struggling; this battle I lost, but I'd save my strength to fight again.

The driver waited, slouched over the wooden fence. He leered as the brute picked me up, helping me over the slats. The driver caught me, running his hands sickeningly up my ribcage, brushing the sides of my breasts. "Nice of you to try and run. We always like a chase."

I dropped my eyes, taking in my dirt stained clothing. I prayed for that vacant part again, the cloud of uncaring, but as they pulled me, struggling, into the Tuscan inspired house, it never came. My mind shackled me to endure whatever would come next.

The brute shoved me through the door, and I jumped as

it slammed shut. My throat dried, noticing how many locks braced the exit. It looked like a bunker—someone who didn't trust a dead-bolt but had to have a chain and bar, too. What the hell did he do in here? *Don't answer that.*

I tried hard not to panic, but my breath came faster.

The brute strode fast, fingers bruising my upper arm as he pushed me through the house. Rooms of understated elegance and money greeted, but cobwebs laced chandeliers and dust rested on unused furniture. What the fuck was this place?

"Why are you doing this?" I asked as he opened a room and shoved me through. My jaw fell open.

The ballroom of the dilapidated house had been turned into a sadistic fun-room. Plasterwork of roses and angels on the ceiling smiled down on rows and rows of dusty floggers, whips, restraints, and so many toys it could've been a sex shop. Two expanses of the huge walls were mirrors.

I immediately looked away from the image. I couldn't stand the sight of being entrapped by two men. My life had fallen into the devil's clutches and I'd done this to myself! I ran from Q. I'd been stupid. So, so fucking stupid!

The brute grabbed my chin, making me look into black eyes. "I'm doing this because it's high time that bastard Mercer gave me some pussy. He thought he could stop farming out women? Too bad, he has customers, and customers have needs."

My world fell apart. That couldn't be true. Q was many things, but I couldn't see him sharing women, trading them, renting them out. But some terrified part wondered if that's how he earned his money. Where did he go during the day? Were there other girls, hidden in the house, being used, abused?

I shook my head. Q hated himself for what Russian

Lumberjack did. His apology ached with remorse. He couldn't have those sort of emotions and be a trafficker, too. It didn't make sense!

The driver spoke up. "That cunt Mercer has a lot to answer for, and we're gonna take those answers from you." He licked his lips. "The moment you said he was the one you ran from, I couldn't believe my fucking luck! He lied to us, and now you're the one who will pay."

I whimpered as the Brute grabbed the back of my neck, shoving me toward the massive mattress on the floor. I fell, coughing as a billow of dust surrounded me. My eyes smarted but I refused to let any moisture fall.

The men laughed and punched each other in the shoulder, as if they were about to get lucky on a date. The world was infested with evil. I hated them. Hated, hated, *hated!*

I glared up. "I'm not an object to take your revenge out on. If you have issues with Q, take it up with him!"

Brute laughed, slapping meaty thighs. "Oh, treasure. *You* are the perfect revenge." He removed his brown jacket, shrugging it to the floor. "I am curious, though. How many girls does he have now?"

I clamped my lips closed. Q conned me into believing I was his only slave—his only plaything. Once again, jealousy gripped my heart. Everything Q made me believe was a lie. He didn't care about me. He didn't have emotions, and he trafficked women. He was worse than the men who kidnapped me—at least they wore their true colours. Q was a chameleon, so clever at hiding the truth.

Driver went to one of the racks and chose a flogger. My heartbeats raced as he swatted his hand, testing the sting. He grabbed a couple of packets from a dusty bowl and threw one at Brute.

The man nodded. "*Merci.*" His eyes fell on me and darkness took over. I wouldn't be able to reason as no soul remained. I knew with deadly certainty they would kill me after. I wished they'd kill me now, before they ruined me.

Driver went behind me and I swivelled my neck, hating him being there.

The air thickened and all three of us froze—caught in a tiny window where normalcy reigned—then my life ended for the third time.

Brute threw himself onto the mattress; his bulk crushed, expelling my breath. I yelped as Driver's hands wrapped in my hair, tugging hard, so I had no choice but to lie down against the rank mattress. I always liked my long hair, but now I wished I was bald. My own body fettered me; I couldn't get free. My scalp stung as he pulled harder. "Obey, slut."

Brute wasted no time in clambering on top; his entire body made me retch. His breath reeked of cigarettes and sourness, and he pulled my legs apart as if they were matchsticks. He looked like a giant wildebeest, about to mount and rut to death.

My chest rose and fell; vision flickered with black spots as I hyperventilated. "Stop!"

The men laughed. "Keep begging, treasure. We like it when you cry."

Oh, God. Oh, God. This was really going to happen. No humanity shone in his eyes. There wasn't anyone to save me. No Brax. No Q.

Just me, two bastards, and an empty house.

I whimpered, squeezing my eyes closed as Brute unbuttoned my jeans and yanked them off. He did the same to my knickers as I scratched at Driver's wrists, trying to make him let go of my hair.

Driver growled, letting go with one hand to slap me. The sound of his palm hitting flesh ricocheted around the room. He slapped me again, coaxing tears to stream. Then he reached down, snaking a hand inside my t-shirt, pinching my breast so hard I saw jagged stars.

I wanted to remain mute, to not give them pleasure

by begging. But words sobbed. "Please. I just want to go home. You were supposed to help me!"

Driver chuckled, twisting my hair with an evil flourish. "Oh, we'll help you alright."

I made the mistake of looking into his eyes. There was nothing but animalistic lust and enjoyment at my pain. What had Q done to these men to make them so happy to destroy a woman? Why must I pay for his sins?

Driver placed a hand on my throat and pressed down, choking me.

Tess, disappear. Find that place. Hurry!

Brute spat on his fingers, putting them between my legs. He frowned, muttering, "She's fucking dry as a husk."

My mind exploded with thoughts of Brax. I was always dry for Brax. But Q… Q made me wet. He befriended my body, despite my hate. I'd broken myself—I didn't need men to torture me. I'd done it every night since I hit puberty.

I wilted in terror as Brute forced his saliva inside. Fingers scraped and tore. My dryness granted pain… agony.

If someone offered me a gun or this, I'd take the gun.

How could I think I wanted to be dominated, commanded? The naïve fantasy of rape wasn't fun. It wasn't sexy or hot. This was true rape, and it would do more than just take my body. It would be what finally broke me into tinkling, unfixable pieces.

Brute's fingers thrust harder; dirty fingernails scraped the inside of my core. I thrashed my head to the side, ignoring the ripping of hair.

The tear of foil echoed and my breathing accelerated; a low keening sounded in my chest.

Driver slapped my face. "Shut up. You'll like it, slut. Then it's my turn."

I opened my eyes. Big mistake.

Brute had his cock out, rolling a slimy condom down the length. The smell of latex filled the air, gagging me. I tried to close my legs, to lock my knees together.

Driver laughed, passing the flogger over my head to him. "Use this. Make her ready."

Brute's lips stretched into a cruel smile. "Ah, treasure. You're in for it now." He raised his arm and struck.

The leather bit my naked thigh, welting immediately with angry blood. I bit my lip, trying so hard to pretend I was dead.

Brute hit me again. And again. Each lick eroded parts of me: my hopes, my stupid thoughts of escape, my love for Brax, my hatred for Q—everything twisted into a cauldron of filthy emotions, sucking me deep into the dark. The fight I prided myself on, disintegrated into pieces and I shrivelled. Each beat stripped me bare; I became lost. I no longer knew who Tess was—I didn't want to know.

The flogger stopped and Brute wrenched my legs apart. Spitting on his fingers, he rubbed my entrance roughly.

"Please—" I moaned. "Don't."

Brute laughed, positioning himself between my legs. "Was that a beg, treasure? You want me?"

Driver panted heavily in my ear, pulling my hair in excitement. "I think she's asking you to fuck her. Better give her what she wants."

Please, oblivion take me. I wouldn't survive. My mind rattled like fractured glass already.

Brute shifted, nudging me with his cock. My body revolted, stomach snarled, and tears flurried down my cheeks. *No, no, no.*

Brute grunted, forcing his way inside. My flesh rejected him, burning with violation.

His hips thrust, burying himself deep. His head dropped as he shuddered, grinning at Driver. "She's fucking tight. You'll enjoy this one."

Driver growled. "Hurry up." He forced horrible

fingers into my mouth, tasting of sourness and metal.

While Driver fucked my mouth with his fingers, Brute thrust his hips, bucking with violence. Heavy breathing rained on my face, horrid, rancid.

I tried to shut everything off. I wanted to bite Driver's fingers—I wanted to fight. I'd been reduced to a piece of meat.

My ears rang, and the room swam with delirium. Mirrors reflected Brute's naked ass as he fucked me. My eyes were haunted, and Driver loomed with a manic look on his face.

A loud bang sounded from somewhere in the house; Brute faltered in rhythm. I squeezed my eyes shut. I didn't want to see if more men arrived—if I'd be subjected to endless purgatory. I never wanted to open my eyes again.

Another bang, then empty air. Brute's horrible cock disappeared and his weight flew off. My hair jerked, then released as Driver screamed.

Grunts and shouts amplified around the room and I opened my eyes.

Three men in suits beat Brute where he huddled in a ball with jeans around his ankles and arms over his head. Blow after blow they rained, and I flinched when one kicked Brute's jaw so hard, his head snapped back, and teeth flew.

My hands curled, loving retribution, the pain Brute suffered.

Driver was strung to the mirrored wall on the rack with whips and handcuffs. More guards punched him; his head lolled on shoulders, blood glinting on his temple.

My heart leaped free from my flogged and hurting body as Q strode into the room. He moved with angry grace, hands curled, mouth pursed. But his eyes—I'd never seen such rage contained.

"*Putain de bâtards,*" Q seethed, pulling a gun from his lower back, stalking toward where Brute lay whimpering on the floor. "You fucking touch a girl of mine and think you could survive?"

Brute reached for him, eyes imploring mercy. "We only took what we used to get from your family. Nothing more." Blood and spittle flew from his mangled mouth.

Q closed his eyes, body shuddering. When he glared at Brute, so many things raged in his face, I ached. "Consider this payment for the past and present." He squeezed the trigger and Brute existed no more. The back of his head exploded with red mist and I scrambled away, huddling on the mattress.

Q turned to me with terrifying calmness. "Ah, *esclave.*" He inched closer, tucking the gun away. "This wasn't supposed to happen."

In that moment, in my fragile and broken state, my feelings for Q changed. He morphed from monster to saviour. He did what Brax hadn't done in Mexico: he found me, *killed* for me. He rescued me from horror and protected me from the bastards who hurt.

Q was no longer the devil.

He was my master and I belonged to him.

Chapter Sixteen

Pigeon

Murmuring in French, Q carried me through the house.

He found a blanket and bundled me up, speaking tenderly, as if I'd bolt at any moment. His touch was feather-soft when he scooped me in his arms, but his eyes glinted with fierce anger. His anger petrified, but I allowed myself to be gathered, cared for—kept safe.

In his arms, I found comfort I craved. His heavy heartbeats soothed more than words and I nuzzled into his neck, drowning myself in citrus and sandalwood. Q came for me. Q wanted me.

His guards stayed behind to deal with the bodies, and I started to tremble. Q's arms bunched beneath my weight, holding me closer. "It's over. You don't have to fear," he whispered. "I'll kill anyone who hurts you."

In his voice, the truth blazed bright. I believed him, completely and utterly. Q did for me what no one else had done: protected me. He fought harder than my parents ever did, and put Brax's strength to shame. Q came after me like I meant the world to him, showing just how lonely and adrift I'd been.

Cold night air refreshed as we strode from the house and Franco jumped to attention. He opened the rear car door. Q slid in, with me still in his arms.

No one said a word the entire drive back to the mansion. Q did nothing but hold me, and for that, I was thankful. He let me drench his gorgeous graphite suit with salty tears as I relived what I'd been through. He squeezed tight when my trembling got so bad my teeth chattered.

I hated my stubbornness, my fight. I did this. Because of my stupidity, I ran into a situation that broke me.

The drive seemed both an eternity and a microsecond. When we drove up the sweeping driveway to Q's stunning home, he kissed my temple, murmuring, "You're safe."

The two little words shot deep into my heart, irrevocably changing me. They opened the floodgates, and everything I knew, disappeared. Everything I had been, became nothing. The Tess who loved Brax, who fought to escape, vanished. She wasn't worthy of Q's protection. Wasn't worthy of being rescued by a man who killed for her.

Q was right: I was safe with him. He made it so simple. I couldn't comprehend how I ran before. I ran from Q's safety, and monsters found me in the dark.

My heart wept for what I did, and fear clutched at the thought of leaving Q's name on Brax's answer machine.

I'd been problematic and wilful, but Q claimed me anyway. He was the first to chase me and blissful happiness warmed inside to finally have someone who wouldn't let me go. His reasons were flawed and wrong, but knowing he would find me settled my mind, lending strength to deal with the rape.

Q did many things, but he never broke me. He

offered things my body wanted without me knowing what those things were.

He was my home. My master. My new life.

My past didn't define me. The horrible rape didn't define me. *Q* defined me and he wanted me to be his *esclave*.

Why hadn't I seen so clearly before? A huge weight lifted off my shoulders; I sighed with complete submission.

Q shifted, looking down, but I snuggled closer and didn't look up. I had to make it up to him. To apologise, so he never sent me away at the mercy of the world again.

The car rolled to a stop and Franco opened the door. Q kept me tight in his arms, carrying me into the house.

The moment the door closed, contentment washed over me. Home.

Suzette skidded from the lounge. She looked at me in Q's arms, clutching her chest with profound relief. "*Oh, dieu, merci.*"

He nodded slightly as Suzette came closer, brushing her hand over my blanket clad body. "I'm so happy Q found you. You're part of this family, *mon amie*. Don't run again."

My body twitched. *Mon amie*. Suzette called me her friend.

Fresh tears sprouted for leaving her, for being so selfish. Brax didn't need me anymore, but Q and this new life did.

Q rumbled a noise and strode up the stairs. Suzette watched us go. I expected Q to take me to my room, but on the first floor he slowed, and opened a door. My eyes widened as he carried me into the most amazing space I'd ever seen.

On the walls were life-size stencils of a carousel: a prancing pony, a carriage, a dancing bear, a soaring eagle. It should've been childish to have black and white images of a fair ride but it gave the room elegance, a whimsical edge playing well with the rest of the black and white theme. A four poster bed with white lacquered posts, and silver sweeping drapes welcomed, but Q didn't head for the bed. He stalked to the bathroom, where iridescent tiles, double walk-in shower, and Jacuzzi bath invited.

Q marched straight into the shower, before slowly setting me down. I clung to his shoulders as he let go. I didn't want him to leave. He was the only thing keeping my thoughts centred on him, and not what happened. I lingered in denial, refusing to dwell on what occurred. I shied away from the memory, letting it fester, layering with insecurity, pain, and overwhelming grief.

My life was no longer perfect—I ruined it by running. I throbbed with need for Q to forgive me. To say he would never let me escape again.

Q stared into my eyes. His pale green ones turned to pea soup as sadness glittered. Something silent passed between us. Reaching behind me, he turned the shower on.

Instantly, hot water rained from two massive showerheads, sending needles of heat through my clothes. I tilted my head toward it, letting each drop scald, purging my skin of filth and tragedy.

Q unwrapped the blanket and tossed it from the shower. He tugged the hem of my jumper, pulling it over my head.

His immaculate suit darkened as moisture seeped into cashmere and silk. He'd ruin it if he didn't leave. But he didn't seem to care that his perfection became wrinkled and stained beyond repair. His focus was entirely on me. His hands moved swift and sure, face closed off and concentrated. But his eyes—they glowed with ferocity, an anger sending spasms of fear through me.

He tossed my jumper to the floor, and his eyes fell to my chest. My white bra turned see-through and nipples stiffened under his look. His jaw clenched as he dropped his gaze, down my body, over my nakedness, to criss-crossed welted thighs.

The pain from the flogger hissed under hot water,

and I wished Q would look away. I was damaged—not a pretty slave anymore. He might send me away.

Q ran a whisper-soft fingertip along a welt. I flinched and tears rushed as memories took me hostage. The shower dissolved into the rotting grandeur of the Tuscan house, Q's touch turned brutal and nasty.

I sucked in a breath, trying to stay in the present, refusing to let nightmares suck me into the dark.

Q's face twisted; he captured my cheeks between hot hands. "What are you?" he clipped, face hard and unreadable.

The question anchored me and I looked into his pale ferocious eyes. I knew the answer he wanted. "I'm yours."

He sucked in a heavy breath, body jerking. "Say it again, but not in English."

Q intoxicated me. My lips parted, and I wanted to stay captured by him, forever. An ancient connection linked us together. I looked into his soul—it churned with agony and demons, but he wasn't evil.

Q dropped his gaze to my lips. *"Je suis à toi."* Something feral heated his features; he pressed his mouth against mine in one fast kiss. "It means, I am yours."

My breath stuttered as power sliced, deep and fast, igniting broken parts of me with sparks. His allure, his power, all magnified to fist around my stomach. In the dark recess of my brain, I translated his words to *him* being mine. The power trip the little words gave was indescribable.

No wonder he wanted me to say it. I was drunk on them. He was mine. *Mine.*

What life did Q live, needing to hear such a strong affirmation? What ghosts haunted him?

Q tightened his fingers, biting into my jaw. "Say it."

With his command, I fumbled into the victim I was, the rape survivor, the slave. The brief sense of ownership left me bereft.

Q twisted my nipple under the wet material of my bra. His cruelty reddened my skin and fight skittered into yielding.

He sent me reeling into needful and damaged. I'd been so close to finding strength, but he took it away in an instant.

Fresh tears spilled as I whispered, *"Je suis à toi."*

Q sighed heavily, resting his forehead on mine. "Will you run again? Will you leave the one man who wants you above all others? Leave his protection?" His voice wavered with regret, resignation, as if he expected me to run, and already suffered loneliness.

My eyes popped wide; I shook my head. "No, I won't run again."

He looked with half-hooded eyes. "How can you be so sure? Don't I scare you? Repulse you?"

He never repulsed me, and fear where Q was concerned was an aphrodisiac. But I couldn't tell him. "I will never escape. *Je suis à toi.*"

With a sharp nod, he reached around to unclip my bra. Droplets stuck to his eyelashes as he frowned, throwing the flimsy lingerie from the shower.

The dynamic of him fully dressed in a soaking wet suit, and me naked and beaten, reminded me once again, I wasn't on equal footing. This wasn't a man caring for me
because he loved or wanted me—he was my owner, fixing a possession.

Q pushed me against tiles, and my body panged with pain. He wrapped strong fingers around my throat and panic soared. Q dropped the barrier, unleashing his anger. "You fucking ran, you bitch! Do you know how hard I'm trying to make you happy? To enjoy you while trying not to break you? Have I seriously hurt you? Have I raped you? Have I done untold damage to you?"

He pushed away, as if horrified with what he'd done. He watched with wide, incredulous eyes as I coughed and rubbed my neck. Phantom fingers lingered around my flesh.

I trembled, watching, waiting for another outburst, waiting for him to hit me. After all, I deserved it.

Q growled, running hands over his sleek hair. "Answer me, *esclave*. Is it really so bad to be owned by me?"

I hung my head. I was so fucked up when it came to Q. He hadn't raped me, but put me in situations that raped my mind, turned me inside out, and made me face dark desires despite clinging to the ideology of loving a man like Brax.

He tortured with games, and let a man shove a dagger hilt inside me. So many things he did, but none as bad as Brute and Driver.

I don't know why, but I need you to want me!

I collapsed to my knees, crying out as welts on my legs burned, and tiles slapped against kneecaps. I bowed at his feet, not able to do anything else. He hated me. He would throw me out, then where would I go? Who would want me after this?

"I'm sorry!" I shouted, sucking in large, gulping breaths as something fractured. I heaved as sadness, self-pity, and lostness asphyxiated. "You hurt me, you torment me—" Sobs stopped my words; I wrapped arms around myself. "But I need you!" I couldn't do this. *I can't!*

Q didn't offer comfort; he didn't give me what I needed—he stood there with his aura of power and ruthlessness, watching me dissolve. Where had the man gone who carried me upstairs? That was the man I needed. Not this bastard. This *owner*.

Q crouched, trying to unlatch my arms from round my ribcage, but I fought him and huddled in the corner. Blonde hair tangled around me, offering protection from his livid gaze.

"*Je suis un salaud,*" he muttered, pulling me into his lap. His suit oozed with liquid as he leaned against the wall, rocking me. I wanted to agree, he was a bastard, but the ache in his voice hurt me deep. He truly believed it, on a much deeper level.

So many things ran through my body at being held. I wanted to snuggle, let him whisper and soothe; another part wanted to run because his compassion was false and hurt all the more. But I couldn't do either. I was weak, and tears held me hostage.

Q rubbed my back, long legs splayed on the shower floor. Through glassy tears, I noticed he still wore shoes. Didn't he care about anything he owned? Were we all disposable?

I cried harder.

Q grabbed me tighter, murmuring, "You're mine, *esclave*. Mine to care for. Mine to fix. I'll allow you to cry while I wash you, but the moment you're clean, you're to stop. Do you understand?"

I blinked through tears, shuddering so badly I couldn't answer.

"Everything about tonight will be forgotten, and you'll only remember what I do to you. Is that clear?" He shook me. "Answer me, *esclave*."

I nodded. There was relief in being ordered to forget and I would obey. After all, Q owned my sense of hearing, I couldn't refuse. "I understand."

Nodding sharply, he reached above, to a glass shelf, where an array of crystal bottles rested. Picking one, he dumped a handful of flowery scented shampoo and placed his palms on my head.

The moment his hands massaged, I cracked again. Wracking sobs exploded from my chest and I doubled over with pain. Not from the rape, or Q's anger, but because of his touch. No one touched me so tenderly. Never had my parents cuddled or offered comfort in their arms. I grew up never knowing how to hug or kiss or love. Brax came along, and with his sweetness, helped heal me. Even with his tender-heartedness, he never just held me—never saw the real me or washed or tended.

It had taken being kidnapped, and sold to a man who

didn't want me, to show how much my existence lacked. Q shattered my walls with his uncouth ways. How could I ever go back to a life where my senses lived in limbo? Where no one cared enough to kill for me?

Q stopped washing my hair, gathering me tighter to him. I crushed against his wet, suited chest, inhaling his unique scent.

He let me cry and didn't reprimand or control. He offered comfort in silence. Lips pressed against my forehead, whispering, *"Je suis là,"* over and over. I'm here. I'm here.

In his kindness, he broke me into the perfect slave. I didn't need his anger to become devoted. I needed his softer moments—gentle love was my undoing, not demands or threats. I was pitiful with how I needed compassion, companionship.

Tears turned from depression to release. After twenty years of struggle, I finally belonged.

Water cascaded around us, but Q never stopped rocking, never stopped caring.

Everything I knew about him was wrong. Who was this man who let me break in his arms? Who was this man who cared so much?

Eventually, I cried myself dry, and Q continued washing my hair. I stayed curled in his lap as firm fingers massaged my neck, shoulders, and back, working kinks from my body. His hands showed a level of bliss I never experienced. On the floor of the shower, I was his pet. *His.* Through and through.

After washing my hair, he dropped his hands to soap my breasts. His touch remained platonic rather than lust-filled and demanding. Once my breasts were washed, he lathered my arms, throat, and belly.

He lulled me into complacency, blanketing me in newfound happiness. I froze when his breath caught, hands circling my lower belly. The steam from the shower laced with tension, and I knew his thoughts morphed from caring to need.

Pressing his forehead against my cheek, his wet hair mingled with mine. "Let me make you forget. Let me give you a new memory, *esclave*."

His purr hitched my breathing, and happiness sharpened to need. My body wanted him to replace the agony of Brute. Q wouldn't hurt me. Not like those men. I nodded infinitesimally.

Q's breathing turned harsh, lowering his hand. Agonisingly slowly, he touched my leg, avoiding the lash marks, stroking reverently. Inch by inch, he made his way up my inner thigh, until exploring fingers found my heat.

I jolted as he circled my entrance. More tears erupted, but he kissed them away, adding pressure to his hold, keeping me still. "*Écarté tes jambes pour moi.*" Open for me.

His voice commanded and I obeyed, relaxing tense muscles, my knees fell open slightly. Q took full advantage.

He inserted one finger, ever so gradually, inside. He made love to me with his finger, but I flinched with pain from the abrasions by Brute.

Q dropped his head, biting my collarbone, making me hiss between my teeth. "Only think of me and what I'm doing. There is intimacy in pain, *esclave*. Let me make your pain my pleasure."

I bucked as his finger entered forcefully, pressing against deep bruises, claiming me for himself. I frowned, focusing entirely on his arms around me, his touch inside. He was correct: there *was* intimacy in pain. I'd never felt so stripped bare, so enchanted by someone as I did in that moment.

Q rocked his palm against my clit, finger feathering inside. I became wet for him, arching in his arms. This was the man who called to me. My master.

He sucked in a raspy breath, pressing his face into my cleavage. Licking the valley of my breasts, he inserted another finger, pressing deep. My mouth opened wide, and I tried to pull away from the mind-shattering rock.

"You beguile me when you let go, *esclave*. Let go."

And like the obedient slave, I obeyed. I mewled and cried, rocking my hips to meet his finger-thrusts. I moaned as my womb tightened, warmed, loving the intrusion of his touch.

He bit my ear, growling as I let my legs fall open in his lap, surrendering completely. He breathed hard, breath clouding around me with mint and spice.

Without warning, he withdrew and smeared my wetness around my clit, pinching and rubbing. Sparks of need fizzed and popped, making their way down my legs.

He groaned as I writhed in his lap. His own needs raged, making him tremble as he rocked his hard cock against my hip.

I gasped and pressed back, loving the gift he gave: the gift of sensual power. My letting go turned him on.

He needed me as much as I needed him. The knowledge magnified my lust a thousand fold. With boldness I never knew I had, I captured his wrist, stopping him playing with my clit.

His eyes shot to mine, lips parted and glistening. Never looking away, I guided his fingers back inside, bowing in his arms as I pressed deep. My flesh welcomed and I rode his hand like I always wanted.

It was Q's turn to snap. With fingers fucking me, he pushed me off his lap and onto the cold slipperiness of tiles. My spine complained, and I found it hard to breathe with hot water cascading into my face, but none of it mattered. It didn't matter because Q wrenched his fingers from me, fumbling to undo his belt buckle. He'd reached his breaking point.

I reached for his fly, helping free his hard cock from sodden clothes. We panted and cursed, both consumed with the need to fuck. To connect. To join.

Q pushed his trousers off his hips, followed by black boxer-briefs. His gorgeous cock jutted proudly, and I felt a moment of fear. I swallowed as Q glared with smouldering pale green eyes. "I'll give you what you need. Don't fear me." His voice dropped from deep, to gravel and stone.

I nodded.

He grabbed my hip, sliding me under him, settling between my legs in one quick, possessive move. I panted, looking up. My body was too hot, heart raced too fast, and it felt as though it was my first time. The first time a man managed to fit all my fantasies into one: connection, possession, lust, passion.

Q crushed his mouth to mine, his taste filling me. His sweet, minty darkness decimated the metallic sourness from Driver putting his fingers in my mouth. I moaned, dragging him closer. I willingly gave Q my sense of taste.

I drowned in his scent, touch, taste, and sound. My heart buoyed as his groan vibrated through me.

His tongue fucked my mouth and my vision spaced; I became lightheaded. Saliva mixed with shower water and we drank each other.

Q thrust, pushing his cock inside just a little. He froze and stopped kissing me. "Are you on birth control?"

Wow, how irresponsible could I be? I hadn't even thought about protection. I pushed hair away, hoping Q didn't have any diseases. I dropped my eyes. "I'm on the injection."

"And how many men have you been with?" he demanded, lust blazing.

I wanted to say no one because the answer was a double-edged sword. Brax and been my one and only... until tonight.

Q must've seen the answer in my face as he nodded.

"You don't have to answer. And you have nothing to worry about from me."

It was odd to pause and talk about protection, when we balanced on the fine edge of erratic sex, but it offered peace. It let me tear through self-restrictions, and embrace hot desires. I was truthful for the first time in my life. "I want you inside me. I need you," I whispered.

Q's answer was to kiss so hard, he bruised my lips. With one hard thrust, he impaled himself inside. My wetness accepted him in a smooth, sensual glide—no pain or agony, only pleasure and ecstasy. His suit rubbed against damp skin; my back screamed from hard unforgiving tiles, but I didn't care.

Q grunted, filling me completely, digging his fingertips into my waist, keeping me pinned. "I've wanted to fuck you since you arrived," he panted, rocking, building a burning fire.

I couldn't speak; I could only focus on Q and his heat inside. He fucked with arrogance and power. Every thrust reminded I belonged to him. An orgasm built deep, and I whimpered at the sharpness.

Q rocked harder, pressing me against the floor as we slid all over the place. "That's it. Give me something of yours. You owe me that." Letting restraint drop, he bucked into me, cursing in French, eyes glowing with so many things, and I felt awed by what he let me see.

My body responded: tightening, building, already forgetting the abuse from Brute.

Q bit my ear, pressing his suited chest against mine, cock thickening inside,
heating, scorching. The fine edge of pleasure and violence unravelled me. "Come for me, *esclave*."

His magic words bent me to his will, and my body no longer obeyed me. It obeyed its new owner.

I screamed as an orgasm rippled from toes, up calves, into thighs, and finally detonated inside my core. I rippled around him, banding tight, milking with every wave of release. Fireworks weren't enough, and I climbed higher, pushed on by Q's thrusts and smell and taste and unbridled rapture.

Fireworks jetted to comets and comets thundered to galaxies as Q pumped harder.

He yelled, *"Baise moi."* Fuck me. He reared back, arms locking as he drove into me the hardest I'd ever taken it. Smooth balls slapped against my ass; I burned, blazed, *fired* from his claiming. "Take my come. Take a part of me," he growled.

Deep inside, I felt him spurt, dousing me in warmth, marking me, while at the same time giving up a part of himself.

Shuddering, the last of his climax wrung him dry. He collapsed on top, uncaring about the steam-filled shower, or his ruined suit. The thrumming of his heart matched mine as we lay on the floor, unable to move.

For the first time in my life, I felt a bond. A profound connection, an intrinsic part of me belonged to him. Not just master and slave, but man and woman.

Was he the man to make my heart sing? This overbearing dom who wanted me to submit one moment, then wrapped me in cotton wool the next?

I couldn't deny he gave me a selfish gift. My body no longer trembled from what happened. He gave me a new memory full of heart-breaking brutality. I throbbed with a residual orgasm, eerily vacant thanks to my soul-wracking cry.

Q met my eyes, and his simmering anger made me swallow. "Am I in trouble?" He looked as if he wanted to put me over his knee and spank me.

His lips twitched and he slapped the side of my ass. "Ah, *esclave*, you're in serious trouble. I'll never be able to leave you alone now."

Chapter Seventeen

Quail

I expected Q to shut down and leave after our shower—too many things passed between us, and I was raw. Q avoided my eyes as he pulled out and stood, but he didn't move to leave.

He leaned down, pulling me off the floor, before stepping out of his soaking trousers and throwing them in the bath. The wet material slapped loudly, followed by his blazer. He left his shirt on, long enough to cover his hips but not the thick, heavy cock between his legs. He maintained the hair down there just like he did his head. A subtle shadow of masculinity without any of the wildness.

My body tingled. He screamed man and dynamism. I was a girl with a ceaseless past, no way enough for him, but determined to try.

He took me tonight in a mixture of compassion and anger, but I wanted more. I wanted what he promised when I first arrived. The act of taking from me, even though my body would willingly give up every part to him.

I bit my lip, remembering Q fingering me over the pool table. I'd been turned on beyond anything I could've imagined. Hatred for him added another dimension to an already overwhelming experience. Now, I didn't hate him, but I still wanted to struggle.

I needed Q to take me again and again. I needed him to rule me so Brute didn't win by making me fear sex. I belonged to Q, yet he never stepped over the line from tormentor to rapist.

I huddled into the towel, so confused.

Q stalked out of the bathroom, leaving wet footprints. The cold embrace of rejection made me tremble. Was that it? He took what he wanted, then left me to fend for myself. What happened to his promise of never leaving me alone?

I couldn't let Q cast me off. Without him, I belonged to no one. I no longer had parents or Brax. My old life was over.

Q ruined me for a monotonous grey-toned existence, eclipsing it with techno colour.

The bathroom closed in, dripping with blackness and horror-filled memories. Without Q, my skin itched with terror as demons and monsters crept from shadows.

I knew I needed to deal with my issues, to find my strength. I couldn't use Q as a bandage to forget, but I wasn't strong enough yet.

The sounds of opening drawers drifted into the bathroom, and Q prowled back with arms full of clothes. He placed them in the dry basin and ripped my towel off. I stood, naked, thrilled how his body tensed, eyes glued to my exposed figure.

"Hold up your arms," he ordered, a large white t-shirt in his hands. I complied and he slipped the t-shirt over my head. His five o' clock shadow rasped my cheek as he bent to tug the hem.

"Step." He kneeled with a pair of white knickers, raising an eyebrow. I clutched his wet shoulder for balance, letting him slide the knickers up my legs. The sensual slide, his fingers kissing skin, made my eyes snap closed.

He pinged the elastic around my hips with a small smile. This man who killed for me, fucked me, *owned* me was dressing me. It didn't make sense.

Q leaned forward and hooked fingers beneath my heavy tresses, pulling damp curls from beneath the t-shirt. His fingers caused lust to swirl again. I was insatiable.

His nostrils flared. The bathroom went from steamy to sex-aware and provocative. He stood rigid and aloof; his face hidden behind a mask of inexhaustible control.

"Hello, treasure."

Brute's voice slashed through my brain. My throat dried in panic as the rape replayed at hyper-speed. My soul chilled with ice, reliving what happened. A tremble racked my body and I keened.

Q lashed out, grabbing my chin. "What are you doing? I told you to forget it. You're only to remember me from tonight."

I dropped my eyes, nodding rapidly, wishing I could obey, but thoughts slithered on the edge of consciousness: Brute with his horrible breath and fingers; Driver with his lies and hair pulling.

With Q here, he helped me forget, but every moment he withdrew, returning to a cold master, rather than tentative lover, I floundered.

Ripping his eyes from mine, he opened a vanity drawer and pulled free a tub of arnica. "Sit," he ordered, pointing at a fluffy bench behind the door. I sat, gasping as Q knelt before me. "This will help."

With soft fingertips, he massaged the ointment into lash marks on my upper thighs—the pressure both painful and delicious. Echoes of memories tried to jail me, but Q's touch wouldn't let me linger in nightmares. Not while he rested between my legs, stroking me. His scent of citrus kept me grounded, reminding he might have flaws, but he cared about his possessions. He would look after me as long as I pleased him.

"What did you mean when you said you were frightened about how far you'd go, when I was chained in the sparrow room?" The words fell out; I clamped a horrified hand over my mouth. Oh, my God, what made me say such a thing?

Q froze and his sudden emotional recoil left me freezing. "I'm not in the mood to answer questions, *esclave*."

Glaring, he returned to rubbing in the pungent healing balm, effectively slicing off any conversation. But a core of strength filled me and I had to know. I needed to know more about this conundrum of a man. Who *was* he?

"What did those men mean tonight? Only taking what they'd taken in the past? Do you traffic women, Q? Is that why you're so afraid to do to me what you've done to others?"

I never thought I'd see Q terrified, but he fumbled upright, throwing the tub of arnica in the sink. It spun around and around, clattering to a noisy stop by the plughole.

Q bared his teeth, swiping ruthless hands over his face. "Don't talk to me about that. It's none of your goddamn business. *Merde, ne me demande plus ça.*" Do not ask me again.

I flinched, buffeted by his anger.

He grabbed me, hauling me to my feet. I scrambled for his hands, trying to get free.

Q glared into my eyes and all the connection we built disappeared. Only annoyance, frustration, and deep-seated loathing showed. "What is your name?" His voice rasped my skin, conjuring heat and yearning.

The Old Tess may be dead, but New Tess didn't want to share the secret either. I couldn't remember exactly why, but it was fundamental to keep it.

"Ami," I whispered. A play on the French word of friend. If Suzette wanted to call me friend, who was I to argue? I could get used to it. Tess would be forgotten. The thought made me sad, but I couldn't give Q my name. I'd given him everything else... that small part was mine.

Q growled, pacing in front. "Even now, you don't break. After everything, you're still strong enough to defy me." He stopped abruptly, seething, "Tell me! Give in, *esclave*. Give me your name!" His chest heaved with anger as eyes beat me into submission.

I bowed my head. I would give him anything for saving me, but not that. My name belonged to my past. My past belonged to Brax. Q was something else entirely. He was my new everything.

"Ami," I repeated.

"You are not my friend," he snapped. "Stop lying."

I shook my head. I knew that. I didn't want to be his friend. I wanted to be his everything, too. I wanted what he offered in his touch, in the undercurrent of need. I wanted him to be honest, just like our bodies were honest. I wasn't the only one lying.

Q stepped against me, the harbinger of citrus and crackling lust. "One last time, *esclave*. What. Is. Your. Name?"

My stomach hurt to lie under the force of his demands, but I couldn't bring myself to speak the truth. "Katrina."

"Lie."

"Sophie."

"Lie."

"Crystal."

"Goddammit, stop!" Q exploded. A hand lashed out, fingers diving into my hair, craning my neck. I perished in his greeny gaze. *"Comment tu t'appelles?"* What is your name?

"Esclave."

His eyes slammed shut, preventing me from seeing conflicting emotions darting in their depths: anger, remorse, tangible need.

When he opened them, there was nothing but blankness. He nodded. "I will learn who you are one day. That is a promise. And my promises are law."

For some reason, my heart fluttered. He made a promise to keep trying, and by trying he would have to get to know me. Perhaps I could make him see me not as an object or possession, but as a person—a woman he ensnared just by being him, not by being my master. Every crazy little thing about him weaved a cage more unbreakable than his mansion and guards. What would he do if he knew that? Would he toss me out because I'd begun the journey of giving Q my biggest sense of all, or would he get on his knees and crush me in thanks for giving him something so precious?

I didn't know. And I wanted to know. Everything.

"No! It can't be true. It can't!"

Brax thrashed in bed, kicking, failing, wrapped in a nightmare. Nightmare number four, this week alone, and I was tired. So tired.

"Brax, wake up." I gripped his sweaty shoulder, shaking him.

He didn't respond, face twisted in grief. I knew what he suffered—he told me his dreams, and all of them featured the car accident that killed his parents.

Every night I held him, gave comfort, and every morning I woke tired and drained. But I soothed him because he needed me, and by being there for him, I felt I belonged.

Brax swung wide, a punch landing on my jaw. "Ow, fuck, Brax. Wake up!" I pinched his nose, cutting off oxygen so he'd wake, but shadows at the bottom of the bed gathered—darker, changing, growing.

My heart stopped as Brute and Driver leered above, licking their lips, cocks jutting from trousers, glistening and evil.

They'd come to finish what they started. They would kill me.

"Brax! Help!" I slapped him, but he never woke.

Brute chuckled. "He isn't strong enough for you, treasure. I'm gonna fuck you so hard, you'll wish you were dead." He moved fast, grabbing my ankles beneath the sheets, dragging me to the end of the bed. I screamed.

No, this couldn't happen. "Brax!"

He lay there, wrapped in his own misery, unaware of mine. Driver laughed, ripping off my pyjama bottoms, tossing them to the side.

My body felt weighed down, moving as if drugged. "Stop. Fucking stop!"

They just laughed.

I wished I were dead, tears leaking. Another shadow crystallized behind Brute and Driver, flocking into being with raven wingbeats and murder. But instead of instilling fear, hope starburst through me.

Master.

Q stood, staring at me with unbridled rage and transcendent power. Time slowed as he pulled free a silver gun and shot Brute, then Driver with sharp-edged finesse. Red rain splattered, but I didn't care. I crawled toward shadowy Q, climbing over corpses, focused only on my owner.

"You saved me."

His smile sent a melody of feeling through me. "You're mine. It's my honour to protect you." He gathered me closer and shadows kissed with icy teeth. "Je reviendrai toujours pour toi." I'll always come for you....

I woke in a room of luxury. The mattress cradled like fluffy clouds, and stencils of carousels made me feel young, fanciful. Not like a slave who'd been fucked by two different men last night, then put to bed like a naughty girl because I wouldn't tell Q my name.

A knock sounded and I scrambled upright, wincing at the lashes on my legs. I checked during the night to see how torn and bruised I was, but Q and his attentiveness halted the injuries. They looked ten times better already, but I couldn't wait for them to be gone. Each welt reminded me of Brute and Driver, Q committing murder, every nasty little thing of running away.

Q was right, though. By fucking me, he overshadowed Brute completely. The fear and crippling memories were there, but every time recollections tried to suck me dry, Q would be there. Touching, kissing, ordering me to only think about him. He stopped my sadness and grief, tinging it with lust and acceptance.

Q stole their power, freeing me by fucking me.

The knock came again and the door opened, without waiting for my reply.

Suzette bustled in with a breakfast tray full of homemade jam and warm croissants. She smiled, placing it on my lap. "*Bonjour*, Ami."

I blinked with how happy she was. Hazel eyes sparkled and dusky skin positively glowed.

I narrowed my eyes, female intuition said why she couldn't stop grinning. "You know he took me last night, don't you?" It was strange to be so open, but she couldn't hide her gloat. She'd been waiting for this day for longer than I wanted to contemplate.

She nodded, perching on the end of the bed. "Yes. But mostly I'm glad to see you in one piece." She dropped her eyes, plucking her pinafore. "Running away was so stupid. I could've warned you about some of the locals around here. Franco isn't a guard to keep you in. He's a guard to protect us from them."

I stopped mid-bite of a croissant. "What do you mean?"

She sighed and glanced toward the door, as if expecting Q to storm through at any moment. Before she could speak, I asked another question. "Were you Q's slave, too, Suzette?"

She froze.

I didn't really expect her to answer, so my eyes widened when she said, "Q set me free when I was sold to him. I'll always love him for that." She bit her lip, before adding, "Q has never taken me, not for my lack of trying. When I arrived, I was broken beyond repair. I had things done to me that I can't even think about, let alone talk about, but Q... Q brought me back to life."

I pushed the tray away, breakfast forgotten. Would I finally learn about my mysterious owner? "How did he bring you back to life?"

She looked up, eyes glittering with tears and memories. "He gave me freedom. Gave me everything I needed to get well again. For a year, he put up with me bowing and crawling, until he finally managed to get me to stand. But it took him another year to get me to open, to talk when I wanted, not just when I was asked a question. He slowly broke the brokenness in me."

She gripped my hand, squeezing my fingers hard. "You don't get it, Ami. And you won't until he tells you himself, but he's the best man I know. Out of all of us, he's the one who's ruined. I've never been able to help him. For five years, I've worked for him, never left his side, but nothing I've tried works."

My heart raced. Suzette confirmed my thoughts from last night. Q may be a dominant but he suffered more than anyone. With what? Perhaps he was terribly disfigured. Was that why he refused to remove his shirt? I'd never seen him naked, or touched his skin.

"Tell me, Suzette. Tell me why he's more broken than you or I."

She hung her head. "That isn't my story to tell, Ami. You'll have to earn his trust and show you care to learn about your master."

"And if I don't want to learn?"

Suzette stood, looking overcome with endless sadness. "Then you don't deserve him."

That night, Q came for me.

I spent the day with Suzette and Mrs. Sucre, battling two different emotions. One moment, my body would warm and liquefy, remembering Q's strength, his lust in the shower. The next, I'd freeze and swallow nausea while memories of Brute crushed.

The two extremes never ended, and by the time we finished dinner in the kitchen, my eyes were heavy, body lethargic. I needed sleep and hoped I wouldn't be hounded by nightmares.

I lay in bed, staring at the silver canopy above. I hadn't cleared it with anyone if I could remain in the carousel room, but Franco spotted me opening the door earlier, giving a slight nod. I hoped his nod meant I could remain on the second level, and not banish myself to the cell of a maid's room.

The door creaked ever so quietly, sending my heart into hyper-drive. I didn't need to ask who. My entire body knew the answer—master.

Q padded across the thick carpet, his silhouette proud and stealthy. I wriggled beneath my sheets. What exactly was he doing here at two in the morning on a week day? I knew how hard he worked. I expected him to be in bed. The moment I thought of Q in bed my mouth went dry. Where did he sleep? What did his room look like?

Then again, I *assumed* Q worked hard. I knew nothing about him, and after the comments from Brute about Q's family, I didn't want to know. If I learned the truth, and it was disastrously horrid, I would have to run again.

And I didn't want to run. The world was dangerous; I preferred to live with the devil I knew.

I held my breath as Q padded closer. It seemed with every step, he pulled energy toward him until the gloom sparkled. An image of Q naked and asleep in bed assaulted me. My mouth watered at the thought of seeing him so vulnerable.

He stopped by the side of the bed. I couldn't see his features in the dark, but his breathing was measured and strong.

He stood in faded jeans and a scruffy white t-shirt. I'd never seen him in something so…ordinary. He wore suits like a persona—a uniform amplifying his demands for submission. It worked. It turned him into a sharp, merciless weapon; the female in me licked her lips at his dangerous edge. But Q in jeans and t-shirt showed another side. A clue into the man behind the suits, a man with too many thoughts and no one to talk to.

He didn't say a word, but simply placed two items on the foot of the bed. He paused, lurking in the dark.

I lay, unmoving, waiting to see what he'd do. I wouldn't let him walk out the door without getting what I wanted. I wanted to talk to him, unravel his secrets. I needed to know if he wanted me so much, he came to wake me in the middle of the night.

Waiting in the dark, I ached for an order to serve.

I licked my lips as he ran a hand over his head, deliberating.

Finally, he stepped toward the door, stopped, and turned back. Sucking in a breath, he ordered, "Wake up, *esclave*."

His voice stroked my skin; I embarrassed myself with a small pant. I couldn't help it—my hearing belonged to him.

He chuckled. "Unless you're awake already."

Dammit.

Coming closer, he leaned down and turned on the diamante side lamp, casting a soft glow, an oasis of illumination. "*Bonsoir.*" His lips twitched a little as he stared from above. I grew too hot under the covers but daren't kick them off. I wore a large t-shirt and shorts, but somehow they were insubstantial when Q looked at me. Like I was a chocolate éclair, and he desperately needed a sugar fix.

"Hello," I murmured, loving the thrill of lust and fear. The knowledge I'd give him what he wanted and no longer suffer guilt. I was free from my feelings for Brax—I let him go. It hurt if I remembered his quirks and kindness, but there was no point torturing myself. Q owned me—that was all I needed to remember.

"I have gifts for you." Q sat on the edge of the bed. His warm weight pressed hard against my thigh beneath the covers. I shivered.

He grabbed the sheets, fumbling beneath the quilt. I yelped as his hand found my ankle, tugging my leg out of bed.

I couldn't speak as he rested my leg on his thighs, running a thumb around my bony ankle. "Something's missing."

His touch resonated directly between my legs. I trembled as he bent and pressed a possessive kiss on my shin. Reaching behind himself, he pulled a black bracelet into view, dangling it.

I gulped. Another GPS tracker.

"This saved your life, *esclave*, yet you cut it off to escape. If you'd have thrown it out the window while driving, instead of leaving it in the car, I would never have found you in time." His voice verged on menacing, shooting horror into my heart.

Oh, my God, he was right. If I hadn't thought I'd be free and in police custody, I might be buried with all the potatoes by now…or wishing I was.

In one swift move, I sat upright, stole the tracker, and secured it around my ankle. The snap of plastic echoed around the hushed space; my heart thudded. I'd tagged myself. I willingly admitted I wouldn't run again.

Q sucked in a breath, capturing my wrist when I went to pull away. He traced the barcode tattooed on my flesh. His face flashed with hatred and anger, but his ire wasn't directed at me. My heart warmed, knowing he hated the people who stole me.

His fingers turned harsh, eyes captured mine. "How

bad was it, when they took you?"

I waited for anger and terror for what they did, but I felt nothing. I didn't know if I blocked it out, or if the rape dulled my senses.

Shrugging, I tried to tug my arm back. "It was the worst week of my life, until last night."

"Worse than me?" he murmured. His voice held an edge, almost as if his question meant a lot more than what he asked.

Wanting to give him something, after all he did for me last night, I nodded. "A lot worse."

He shook his head, eyes unfocused. Memories swirled in their depths and I wanted to chase him wherever he went. I wanted to *know* him. Would he ever let me get close? Was a slave allowed to help her owner, while letting him use her body? I didn't know the rules.

Q finally released me, presenting the other package. "This is for you." His jaw clenched as I held my hands out, accepting the large sketchpad and charcoal pencils. I opened it and couldn't breathe. Inside, architectural graph paper—the exact kind I used in my university course—glowed fresh and new.

My eyes widened. "You remembered what I told you…that first breakfast when you kissed me."

He sat straighter, tension rippling in his body. "I remember everything, *esclave*. I remember how you smell, how you taste. I remember how you feel inside and how terrified you were when I found you at Lefebvre's residence. I also know things you haven't told me. You secretly like what I do to you. You think you hide it, but I know that darkness in your eyes. It feeds me, calls to me."

He fisted the covers, throwing them off me, exposing my body. "Why else do you think I can't leave you alone?"

I couldn't look away from his gaze; his intensity trapped me, searing with need and want. When I didn't answer, he ordered, "Get out of bed."

For a moment, I wanted to disobey, to see what he'd do, but some small part was truly scared of him. I hustled to leave the warm nest. Swinging my legs over the edge, I stood.

Immediately, he grabbed my hips, positioning me in front of him. His breathing grew harsh as he ran his gaze over my unsexy ensemble.

He frowned, thoughts running over his face. He pushed away, stalking to the dresser. Opening a drawer, he fumbled inside before withdrawing a lacy G-string. I gulped as he came back, swinging the knickers on his middle finger.

"Stand by the bed post." His voice dropped even lower, yelling intentions in every syllable.

I didn't move, fighting too many complexities to order my legs to work.

Grinding his teeth, he grabbed my arm, tugging me down the bed to stand in front of a white lacquered bed post. "Put your arms above your head."

He was so close; a heavy cloud of sandalwood and spice buffeted, turning my knees to water. I stretched, arching my back against the pillar, deliberately forcing my breasts to touch his chest. He startled, raising an eyebrow, before reaching up and securing my wrists with the G-string. The lacy material bit into my skin, but it wasn't nearly as bad as being chained in the sparrow room. At least my feet were on carpet, and no guests saw my suffering.

Q bent his head, leaning his length against mine. His hips pressed hard, dominating.

I tilted my chin, positioning my lips for him to kiss me. He never closed his eyes and pale green irises made me feel as if I'd entered a wood glen where naughty fairy men took advantage of fair maidens.

I swallowed hard as he came within a fraction of kissing me. But, with a crooked smile, he pulled back.

"You want me to kiss you, *esclave*. That's not how this works."
Reaching into a back pocket, he pulled free a pair of
silver scissors. Fear widened my eyes. What the hell?
"You don't get to choose what I do to you. Because you
want me to kiss you, I won't."
I moaned, then flinched, wishing I could slap a hand over
my traitorous mouth. *God, Tess, way to sound desperate.* I didn't
want to be tied up and abused. *So why do you ache for it?* Shit, I
was sick. The rape must've done something, made me a
danger whore. But that was a lie. The only thing that
happened was Q. He controlled my body like a puppeteer—I
had no will to disobey—I *couldn't* disobey.
Maybe I should try to find the centre of calm from the
day I sucked Q. The safe zone might protect me from more
upsetting thoughts. Save my sanity, stop me from leaping
willingly into a realm of bondage and kink.
I closed my eyes, trying hard to tap into blank safety.
Fear swelled. If I didn't stop my desires now, I might slide
down a slippery slope, never finding my way back to normal.
You were never normal. I pursed my lips, feeling lost and
confused. How could I want two things at the same time?
Roughness, freedom… both taunted with agonising
temptation.
Q took my chin in his thumb and forefinger, hypnotising
me with his gaze. "Don't. Stay with me."
How did he feel me withdrawing? I shook my head,
dislodging his fingers. "What gave me away?"
Q rolled his shoulders as if reigning himself in, bringing
his energy to heel. "I told you—I sense you." His toned
muscles stood out beneath the white t-shirt; I couldn't look
away from the bulge in his jeans.
"Now, stay still and present." His face remained stoic and
cool as he advanced with the scissors, running the cold kiss of
metal along my neck, dipping to my throat. His breathing
quickened as the blade nicked my collar.
With perfect care, he cut my t-shirt right down the

centre. Each snip undid me, thread by thread, until I was sure he opened my chest, revealing a rabbiting heart, and all my secrets.

Everything he did symbolised so much. Q relished in playing me with unsaid words, everything about him a mystery.

He won't be so cocky when I discover who he is. I'd use those secrets to play the same game—a sick circle of mind-trips and power struggles. My core clenched at the thought of going head to head with Q in a battle of wills. I didn't think I'd win, but I didn't care. I wanted him to win. I could allow him to rule me—like I wanted him to.

He swallowed when he snipped the hem, splaying it wide, showing bare breasts and my rapidly breathing stomach. With perfect control, he ran the pinpoint of a blade from my lower lip, down my neck, between my cleavage, to the top of my cotton shorts.

My skin broke out in goosebumps as he pressed ever so gently. The blade puckered my skin, but didn't pierce. The delicate balance of trusting and fearing him made my heart buck out of control.

Q seemed lost in contemplation, twisting the scissors in a circle around my belly button. He told me not to leave, to remain rather than disappearing in my mind, but *he* left. His face shadowed with thoughts and recollections. Things that didn't seem pleasurable, things that made his body tremble. I'd give anything to follow him—to see if he lived in the dark or the light.

I tested the boundaries of the restraints; no give at all. He'd tied the knickers well. I squirmed beneath the blade; his eyes snapped to mine. He blinked, casting shadows away.

Palming the scissors, he leaned closer, wrapping fingers around my wrists as the button of his jeans bit my belly. His clothed chest teased my nipples, making them harden to painful nubs. "You have no idea how much I want to fuck you."

Oh, God. His voice activated every part. I panted breathlessly, "Why don't you then? Or do you enjoying torturing me first?"

He reared back, jaw working. "Do you think this is torture? I could do so much worse, *esclave*. He rubbed his groin against mine, pressing my ass hard against the bedpost with his cock. "I *want* to do so much worse." His accent thickened, muttering, *"Je veux te faire crier."* I want to make you scream. He didn't say it in a kinky, playful way; he said it with passion so nightmarish, I couldn't see anything but whips and pain and blood.

That did it.

My lust switched to fear and I moaned again, but this time, it was a plea. "Please... you don't have to make me scream. You can take me. I'm yours."

He laughed darkly. "You don't get it do you, *esclave?* Your permission turns me off. I need to take from you to feel something. If you think I'm not like those men who raped you, you're wrong. There's something broken in me, and I need your pain to come." He twisted a nipple with angry fingers. I yelped.

Pain coursed to pleasure, warming, making me wet. If Q was hardwired, needing pain to enjoy sex, so was I. I might've gone through my entire life, never knowing the key to my pleasure was pain.

Q, in his brutality, showed me something taboo... showed I liked to be dominated, and not just light role-playing. No, I needed the real thing.

Light shone through my brain at the realization. *I'm not a sweet, innocent girl who wants cotton candy and sonnets. I'm a fighter, a slut, a woman who needed to be taught her own body.*

As I stood, tied to a bed, my owner leering with sin in his eyes and promise of hurt on his lips, I changed again. The chrysalis of who I'd been cracked open, letting me fly free. I unfurled newfound wings, becoming more than Tess. I became a twisted, treasured belonging, revelling in her ownership. Who wanted Q to hurt her.

Fire blazed in my belly; I bared my teeth, snarling. "I won't let you fuck me."

Everything slammed to a halt.

Q. Me. Time.

The world teetered while Q tried to read me. We glared into each other's eyes, reflecting the same fuckedupness, recognizing the same in the other. The bond between us flared tight, reaching with glowing shackles, binding us together. I relished in the binds, accepting my true identity before Q even realized what I offered.

Slowly, Q moved, his entire body predatory, smooth, shark like. "You won't let me fuck you, *esclave?*" Delight shimmered in his gaze, etched with black smouldering lust. "I've already fucked you. What makes you think I want to again?"

I thrust my hips forward, bumping an overheated core against his straining erection. The moment I slipped into unwilling victim, Q raged with hardness. His cock verged on iron, hard and unyielding.

"I don't care if you do or don't. You won't because I say you're not allo—"

He smothered me with his body; the post dug into my back as his mouth captured mine. His tongue speared between my lips.

I whimpered, melted, wanting so badly to kiss him back. But that wasn't allowed in the role I played. The role I *needed* to play.

His lips branded, tearing another moan from me, rather than a curse. His tongue possessed my senses, forcing me to duel, to parry, to taste and savour. Was I returning his kiss? No, I wasn't. I was fighting to breathe, in every sense of the word.

I bucked, breaking the kiss, breathing ragged.

He turned the scissors on me again, hands deathly still as he snipped the waistband of my shorts. He murmured, "You want me to stop?"

God, no. Never.

"Yes, you bastard. I won't let you do this. It's sick. Wrong. Let me go."

His body trembled with some undescribed emotion; keeping eye contact, he cut again.

I squirmed as the metal continued lower and lower, brushing against my core. "You don't have permission. Stop."

Eyes sharpened with challenge, and he deliberately cut slower, dragging out suspense, snipping my clothes away, one clip at a time.

The moment he cut the crotch, the shorts fell away, puddling to the floor in disgrace. If Q touched me, I'd combust. My damp knickers clung to every part. Pretending to fight stimulated my lust to a forest fire.

No wonder missionary didn't do it for me. I needed scissors and threats to become drunk on need.

Q slammed to his knees, wrapping his strong arms around my thighs, jerking me toward him. I screamed as his mouth connected over my knickers, hot breath radiating like a bomb between my legs. He nibbled my swollen clit through the material, dragging more erratic breaths from my lungs.

I wanted to open my legs, to hook them over Q's shoulder and ride his mouth, but that wasn't the character of unwilling slave. Instead, I wriggled, trying to run from his probing, mind-melting tongue.

He rumbled in his chest; it vibrated against my legs. With one hand, he grabbed my ankle, purposely bringing attention to the GPS anklet. His silent touch spoke volumes. *You're mine. I track you. You can't escape.*

It was a red flag to my brain, knowing I could be wild and wanton because he wanted it. I could scream and writhe, and it only excited him. Brax would run if I ever screamed in bed.

Q tongued me, pressing with a pointed tip, licking wet

cotton. I couldn't stop my breath turning softer, feathery, needful.

"You don't want this?" Q murmured again, standing slowly, trailing a finger up my inner thigh, right to my mouth. With a twist of his lips, he forced his finger past my lips.

The primal instinct to suck consumed, but I forced myself to go against instinct and bite instead.

He jerked, yanking his finger away.

I smiled darkly. "Put anything in my mouth and I swear to God, I'll bite it off." My mouth filled with saliva, anticipation making me hungry.

Ever since I belonged to Q, I discovered things I was never strong enough to visit before. This new, dark part wanted to taste his blood. To get real and gritty and deliciously wrong.

Q stepped closer, jeans scraping highly sensitive flesh. A band of release sparked from the contact. *I'm so close. I'm never this close. God, Tess, he's barely touched you.*

It was the mind games—my brain made it raw, wonderful.

His eyes glazed with need and he bit my lower lip, dragging soft flesh between his teeth: a warning he'd bite back.

I shuddered as he let me go. I expected him to cut my knickers off, but he paused, turning the scissors on himself.

Arching his neck, he snipped the collar, cutting down the centre of the t-shirt, just like with mine. Once in half, he shrugged it off, letting it join my ruined clothes on the floor.

My world spun and all I could think of was sparrows.

Q glared, daring me to judge him. And judge I did. His entire torso and right side was covered in fluttering birds. The panic in a sparrow's eyes closed my throat as they flew frantically from brambles, barbwire, and stormy clouds. The clouds roiled on his side, swallowing up unlucky birds, suffocating them to death.

My heart hurt looking at Q's intricate tattoo. There lurked an evilness, a sadness, reminding me of the mural on the wall of the pedestal room. I wanted to run fingers along perfectly inked feathers. I wanted to lick his nipple where one bird had gotten free, the joy in its eyes blazed with hope.

So much was said by the design, but I didn't understand it. I looked into his eyes. He held contact for a moment, before looking over my head. His hands curled and he sucked in a breath, outlining perfectly cut stomach muscles.

He vibrated with tension. My heart fluttered like little sparrow wings, and I gave my last sense to Q. My sense of sight. Standing so erect, standoffish, he filled my vision with everything I ever wanted. He owned everything but instincts and heart.

"Tell me. Tell me the story of the birds."

He clenched his jaw. "It isn't a story you need to know."

"But it means so much to you. I see a reoccurring theme, Q… I want to understand."

His face blackened. "You don't have the right to call me Q when you're tied to the bed. I'm your *maître*. Address me as such."

Anger at being denied made me argumentative. "I'll fight you. You'll have to wrap me up in brambles, same as the sparrows on your chest, if you want to fuck me, *maître*."

My taunt worked; he grabbed my chin with hard fingers. "You think you're so fierce with your threats. My job isn't to wrap you in shackles, *esclave*. My job is to *unshackle* you. And as much as you deny it, I'm doing a damn fine job."

He ran his nose against mine, murmuring, "So shut the fuck up, stop looking at me like I'm some code to be cracked, and let me do what I fucking want to you."

Stepping back, he attacked his jeans. Rather than undoing them, he cut them. Sawing through the waist band, slicing down the legs. Each snip revealed hard thighs kissed by little curls, firm quads, and perfect bare feet. "Let's see how you stick to your threats when I take your body."

Oh, God. My insides were liquid, heated. Embarrassment at being wet painted my cheeks red. I couldn't control my reaction. Q was my master in every sense.

Q stepped from the ruined jeans, closing the small distance between us. I couldn't look away from his tattoo. I related to it and in a way, I knew what it represented, but the conclusion kept leaping from grabbing distance.

Rolling his hips into mine, wearing only boxer briefs, Q murmured, "Tell me again you don't want this, *esclave*."

How could I lie when my body screamed the truth? My mind was lust filled, hazy, but I had a part to play. Q wanted me to fight so... I fought.

I leaned forward, snapping my teeth, coming within a hair breadth of his nose. "Go to hell."

His cock jumped in his boxer-shorts, scalding me. Out of nowhere, his palm connected with my cheek, sending spasms of heat.

I gasped, glaring with watering eyes. "You fucking hit a woman when she says no? You're perverted."

He pursed his lips. "Tell me something I don't know."

Taking him up on his offer, I whispered, "You think you're a monster. You're not."

He grabbed my hair, twisting my neck. Agony flared, and I whimpered in real fear. "Would a kind man do this?"

When I didn't answer, he twisted further until I screamed. "No! Only a monster does that."

Not pacified, he reached for the scissors, quickly snipping my knickers and his boxers. They fluttered to the floor in pieces. Q weighed the scissors in his hand, before tracing my naked stomach with the blade. "Would a kind man do this?" With a flick of his wrist, he nicked me. Blood welled in the tiny cut. I shivered, wanting to put my hand over the wound, to hide it, heal it.

Real tears dripped. I was an idiot to think there was something redeemable in this man.

"No, only a monster would do that." My voice was barely audible.

Q sneered. "Now you know the truth." He bent and licked the blood off my stomach. His tongue lapped; my core clenched, reacting to the tenderness after inflicting pain. His saliva staunched the bleeding and he straightened, licking his lips.

Everything tightened, my mouth parted, desperate to taste his blood. Tasting him was fair. He cut me—a debt must be paid.

Q narrowed his eyes, our souls screamed at each other, unhindered by human words.

I want to hurt you.

I want to own you.

I want to devour you.

I want to make you mine.

I'm already yours.

Who thought that? Me or him? Whose eyes spoke the truth before we acknowledged it in our minds?

Q reached up, and with a quick slice, nicked below his nipple with the sparrow flying free. A droplet of crimson welled. I watched with crippling need.

Taste. I have to taste.

He stood taller, placing his chest against my mouth. I greedily lapped the droplet, moaning as salty metallic fogged my entire being. Once I cleaned him, he pulled away, murmuring, "Monsters find each other in the dark."

I couldn't read his tone, and I didn't like the implication. *Am I a monster?* Compared to Brax most definitely, but Q... there were limits he crossed that I never could. *Had* we found each other in the darkness? I may have black desires, but I loved light, too. I needed tenderness to temper pain and degradation. Was that an option?

Q wrapped a hand around his cock, stroking, looking deep into my eyes. With another hand, he found my centre, easing a finger deep inside.

Even though my body rippled, I never stopped being in character. Q couldn't know how much I wanted this. I had to fight—I *wanted* to fight.

I somehow tapped into a kickass actress, coaxing a tear to fall. "I don't want this."

His nostrils flared. Unwrapping fingers from his cock, he captured a tear on a fingertip. He stared at it, then me, indecision searing in his gaze. The night reclaimed him, shadowing his face. He licked the salty tear. "You'll be crying more before I'm finished with you."

I began a file on what turned my master on. Tears was one, struggles another. What was his ultimate undoing? I wouldn't stop until I found out.

Tears shed again, forcing myself into the headspace of hating him, just like when I first arrived. Before he saved me, killed for me. Q didn't want a meek slave. He loved my unbrokenness.

Another puzzle locked into place. Was that what Suzette meant when she said Q didn't touch her because she was ruined? He touched me, because I fought—I was strong. He couldn't fuck an injured... yet he wanted... what did he want? To tame me? To parry? Something in him wanted to be accused of being a rapist, of being sick and twisted, because that's how he honestly saw himself.

Q flicked a tongue over my cheek, catching tears. I gasped and wriggled, biting my lip as our naked bodies slid against each other. My nipples sprang to an all new hardness, budding with excitement.

His head bowed, forehead to forehead. I breathed him in, gluing myself to the post, making sure no part reached for him. That would ruin the game. I couldn't forget, I didn't want this.

"Ah, *esclave. Tu m'excites comme c'est pas croyable.*" You excite me beyond belief. His fingers shot between my legs, plunging deep. My knees trembled as his hand rocked, hard.

I whimpered, body reacting—swelling, melting, *needing.* I was ravenous for whatever Q gave. I wanted him so badly, but I wanted to fight just as much. The act of saying no did strange things to me, turning sex from mediocre to knee-wobbly and carnal. I became a hungry, libido-driven woman; only Q could scratch my erotic itch.

Q murmured in French, dialects swallowed by the silent night-shrouded room. I panted, but it sounded hushed, like a dream.

His finger was the ultimate ownership. Palpitating my core, he sucked in a breath as I thrust, needing more

I couldn't help it. I moaned.

He pressed his cock against my hip, smearing glistening pre-cum on me. His erection was hot, hard, and tempting beyond belief. His breathing matched mine in roughness. "You can't lie. Not now. Not when your body blares the truth." He moved his fingers, stroking inner parts of me, throbbing with the need to release.

He was right, I couldn't lie and I cried harder.

I wanted to scream: *fuck me, I'm yours.* Instead, I said, "Get your fingers out of me."

"Shush, *ma belle.* You want this." His voice rippled with sensuality. I wondered how much he acted, too. Had he tamed himself on my account? How much darker would he go?

Q stroked harder, withdrawing more moisture between my legs. My breasts ached to be touched, my mouth was empty, needing kisses, but my heart blazed so full, I thought I might disintegrate into fiery fragments.

Q stopped suddenly, withdrawing. "I'm the only one who can give you what you truly desire." His fingers dug into my cheek, spreading my scent. "But I refuse to take it." He stepped between my legs, positioning his cock where I wanted him most. He rubbed with the tip, earning a pant and a cry.

I rocked, imploring him to take me. I trembled with need so extreme, it set my teeth on edge.

"Give it to me, or you'll become nothing."

My eyes narrowed. "I'm giving you everything you ask for. There's nothing left to give."

Pulling back, he stared, unfettered, eyes blazing with overpowering lust. He stepped away, dragging a hand over his short pelt of hair.

My hips moved toward him on their own accord, searching, wanting. Mortified, I pressed against the post, hoping he hadn't seen.

But he did; his lips quirked. "Always lying."

I said nothing.

Q paced. "I'll fuck you anyway you want, if you give me what *I* want."

Delicious anticipation filled, but I frowned. "What do you want?"

"I want to own all of you, *esclave*. Including your name."

My heart raced. Truth rang in his words. He would deny both of us because he wanted to know my name. I didn't have to fake the answer: "You'll be dead before that happens." I was furious with him.

He chuckled—it sounded positively light-hearted compared to the tension charging around us. "No one will be dead, but I might die of pleasure by having you."

I ignored the thrill, staying in character. "Bastard."

His mood shifted to commanding, dominating. "You have no idea." He laughed but it held pain.

My breath hitched. I tried my rusty French. *"Je ne suis pas à toi."* I am not yours.

Grinding his teeth, he reached up, undoing the

knicker restraints. Pulling my body roughly away from the bedpost, he threw me on the mattress. "I dare you to say that again, *esclave.*" Folding himself over me like a living cape, pressing down, almost suffocating me in the covers. My stomach twisted and a small mewl escaped. The overbearing action of lying on me, both thrilled and terrified.

Lips kissed a trail along the back of my neck, all the while fingers tickled the inside of my thigh, moving higher, higher.

Each millimetre he travelled set my blood to boil. I didn't understand how one touch made me shiver with need. Was it Q's domination? The knowledge I couldn't stop him? It couldn't be. The rape cured me of that ridiculous fantasy.

Somewhere in my mind, I knew Q meant me no harm. He wanted me and I was his; there was nothing wrong with him taking me—anyway he chose.

"Spread your legs," he demanded.

I instantly complied. His fingers found my entrance, stroking. Q's breath hitched as he forced two fingers inside, stretching, bruising, but it wasn't enough. I needed more. An orgasm teased, on the brink of release. So close, so fast. I wanted it desperately.

Q seemed to sense my urgency and slid off. Kneeling behind me, his hands curled around my ankles possessively, spreading my stance even more.

I cried out as his tongue licked up my leg, moving with delicious wet pressure, heading to the one place I ached.

When his tongue found me, sucking my clit with the finesse of an experienced lover, my hips bucked over his mouth. I'd never been so needy, so possessed with yearning. I never wanted to think again. This was true freedom—right here, with my master kneeling between my legs.

A long finger entered, thrusting deep as his tongue lapped, conjuring star bright spasms, shooting in my belly. I rode his finger, searching for friction.

I needed him in me. I needed him to claim.

He stood, grabbing my neck, arching me to kiss him. His

chin glistened from my wetness, filling me with my taste.

He bit my lip, positioning himself behind me. "I own all of you, *esclave.*"

I wasn't prepared for the sharp, sudden, shocking invasion of his massive cock. I cried out as he stretched me wide, giving no time to adjust. My stomach knotted into a complex cosmos, gathering power to release.

I groaned as he thrust hard, taking me from behind, spread over the bed. I trembled in ecstasy I'd never felt before.

Q bit my shoulder, fingers digging deep into my hips, jerking me back, thrust after thrust. Each withdrawal and penetration, built and built until I was sopping wet, moaning, whimpering, more vocal than I'd ever been in my life.

"*Putain de merde,*" he growled, fucking me so hard, my knees bashed against the soft comforter.

His voice was everything I needed to release the glowing galaxy in my core. I screamed, literally screamed, as I came harder than I'd ever come before.

The mind games Q played, the connection I felt after a lifetime of being adrift, all exploded, turning my body into a bundle of hyper-sensitive nerves.

Q's sexual domination enlightened me. My good girl barrier was permanently removed, and I revelled in Q's flesh slapping against mine, finding his own pleasure.

The heavy hotness of his balls slapped against my clit as he fucked harder. My hands grabbed the sheets, bunching them with every skin-slap.

Q fisted my hair, arching my back, at the same time, he spanked my ass. "Fuck, I want to make you bleed." He hit me again, again. Each handprint hot, laced with pleasure-pain and erotic torture.

The agony added another threshold to battered nerve endings. "Oh, God," I moaned, shuddering with fiercely building pressure, racing up my legs, into my centre.

Not again. Surely. I never had multiple orgasms.

Q cursed, slapping me so hard, tears rained even as I panted. *It hurts. It feels too good. Stop. Hit harder. Don't. More.*

I shattered into a gazillion pieces, milking Q's cock for a second time.

"Fuck," he groaned, bucking with feral strength, shaking me to the soul. He slapped my ass so hard, I bit my lip, drawing blood. Stinging pain pulsed while Q exploded inside. I felt every ridge, every spurt, relishing in owning some part of him. He gave himself to me.

His come was mine. Just like I was his.

My ass stung but my body was as limp as a ragdoll.

Q pulled out, breathing hard. I rolled painfully onto my back, watching him stalk to the bathroom. He returned, wrapping a towel around his hips.

I sat up, flinching from his abuse, both external and internal. My body languished in sated bliss.

His demeanour was closed off, angry. He didn't even look me in the eye.

Had I been that terrible? I wasn't experienced, but Brax always seemed to enjoy sex with me. Rejection stabbed like daggers; I waited for a sign that Q was satisfied, but he never looked at me.

His seed trickled down my thigh, spreading a damp stain on the sheets. Tears pricked. I must've done something terribly wrong. I had to fix it. If I didn't please Q, he'd throw me back to men like Brute and Driver. He'd withdraw his protection. His comfort.

I didn't know what to do.

Sliding off the bed, I crawled to Q. He never asked me to be anything other than human, but maybe he secretly wanted me to be lowly.

I clutched his towel, looking into tortured pale eyes. He didn't look like a man who'd had explosive sex. He looked like he wanted to commit suicide, or scrub his cock with abrasive soap. A man with ten-tonne regret.

My throat lodged with need and failure. "I'm sorry. I can do better. I promise. Please, give me another chance."

Old Tess sat up in horror. I begged a man who didn't even want me—a man who kept me like an unwanted pair of socks—to fuck me again.

I begged like he could end my life.

Because he could.

I no longer trusted the world. I trusted Q. With everything I had. I couldn't cope if he despised me for something I did wrong.

Q stepped back, his muscles making it seem as if sparrows moved and fluttered. "*Esclave*, stop this. Go get clean. Go to bed."

His orders slapped me in the face. He wanted me to clean so no part of him remained? How could he ask that? We were linked. If I showered, the link would be gone. I would be nothing again.

Oh, God, I was fucked up. So ruined. So broken.

Q looked down, his jaw working under his five o'clock shadow. "I won't touch you again until you tell me your name."

Then he left.

Just like every time.

Chapter Eighteen

Swan

My new life began.

For two weeks, I only saw Q when he returned home from work, and even then, it was only brief.

With a smouldering, unreadable expression, Q would regard me before disappearing to areas of the house I wasn't allowed to go.

Moments after, music erupted through speakers. Songs with laments or curses, lyrics full of rage and threats, rattled the windows.

Q had eclectic taste in music. Heavy metal screamed from the speakers one night and the verse slapped me with debilitating need.

It's awoken and refuses to go back into the dark
every moment, of every second, of every heartbeat, I fight the urge to hurt
my resolve is weakening, my guilt lessening, my needs overpowering
I am not responsible for what happens to you, you provoked me, awoke
me, excited me
my tongue aches for your blood, my heart beats for pain
fear is my calling card and I mean to earn your terror

Q played the song twice, as if pounding the message into me: whatever he'd done was tame compared to what he wanted, and the longer I didn't tell him my name, the more he needed to hurt me.

Withholding my name was my only weapon against Q. It drove him mad, and I loved it. I loved the power of dragging emotion from him.

I lay in bed at night, panting, so ready for my door to burst open and a wrathful Q to claim me. But stubbornness was my friend, and I wouldn't spill my last secret. Either I was crazy to provoke my master, or I'd gone mad with captivity. Either way didn't matter, as I felt alive when I listened to the loud songs. Obsessed with how my body tingled and tensed, consumed with fluttering wings of anticipation—completely bewitched by Q.

So we played our game, waiting to see who'd break first. Nights passed with relentless need, days inched by with excruciating impatience.

For fourteen days, Q stayed true to his promise and never came.

Winter thawed, and spring splattered the countryside with tulips and daffodils.

I accepted I would never know where I lived. Suzette wouldn't tell when I asked, and I doubted Q ever would.

No one would ever find Tess Snow again. She no longer existed. *I am Mon Amie l'Esclave.*

By day, I worked on my French with Suzette, by night I waited for Q. I was wet all the time, and when he didn't appear, dreams consumed me. Nightmares of Q throwing me away because he couldn't stand me any longer. Reoccurring dreams of Driver and Brute, raping me, about to kill, but instead of Q saving me, Leather Jacket stole me back to Mexico. Where he hurt, broke, and ultimately sold me to another. Brax played centre in my dreams, but he never rescued me. He would either sleep through my torture, or simply look on in despair.

My heart twinged. My subconscious blamed Brax for everything that had happened, but at the same time, it was my fault for not insisting we leave the café. I couldn't expect Brax to fight and kill—it wasn't in his nature. I missed his gentleness, but at the time, it had annoyed me. I always wore the pants in the relationship, but remained whiny, needy, and meek because he didn't give me power.

Q hit me, fucked me, and turned me into a possession, yet somehow unlocked power inside me I didn't even know was there.

Q took everything from me, but he didn't so much as steal it, as I gave it willingly. By allowing him to rule, he gave me something tangible. He allowed me to be *me*. To be *real*.

I was no longer naïve and timid. I grew from girl to woman. A woman who wanted a place beside the complex, problem-riddled man. A woman who wouldn't stop until she knew the truth.

"Ami, can you make the cheese soufflé for dinner?" Suzette asked, bumping my hip with hers as she passed. We were in the kitchen, enveloped with scents of fresh bread and baking.

The sliding doors were open to a crisp breeze, welcoming sounds of birds and spring. France had converted me. I missed the bright Australian sun, but I loved France's cool, understated chic.

I smiled, nodding. "I can do that. Have nothing else to do."

Suzette giggled. "You could always go and dress in something provocative to surprise Q when he gets home. I've been waiting to hear you again, little blasphemer. Why hasn't he been to see you?"

Suzette had become overly interested in my love life; every day we had the same conversation. Just because I swore a few times when Q fucked me meant she had a new nickname for me: little blasphemer. I hated that she heard us.

Mrs. Sucre swatted her with a dishtowel. "Suzette, stop being so nosy." To me, she added, "She hasn't stopped grinning since you let the master into your bed."

I swivelled to stare. Mrs. Sucre's large girth guarded the pot of lobster she stirred.

I blew hair from my eyes. "Let him into my bed? Like I had a choice." Turning to Suzette, I said, "Q is the one not coming to me, Suzette. He won't until I tell him my name."

She snorted. "Q is still your master and you are still his slave. Tell him what he wants to know. You shouldn't keep secrets."

I blushed, looking at the soft dough I kneaded. "He may be able to boss me around, but I don't have to share every little detail. Besides, I am no longer that person. I'm Ami." I shot her a smile, dropping my voice. "You don't know anything about his sparrow tattoo, do you?"

I couldn't stop thinking about it. I wanted to trace him like a map, kiss every feather, understand every reason.

Suzette bit her lip. "Um—"

Mrs. Sucre spun around, wiping her hands on her apron. "Suzette, don't you dare. It's not your secret to tell."

I glared, wishing I could torture them for answers. Not being with Q for so long made me rather desperate.

Suzette shrugged and disappeared into the huge walk in pantry.

I huffed and went back to kneading.

That night, after dinner, Q returned home late and turned on French music. The lyrics quavered around the mansion, echoing in my blood. The sorrowful tune left tangled threads everywhere, guiding me through the house.

I didn't know what time it was, but the staff had retired. I was too edgy to sleep. My body restless, needing something only Q could give.

A flash of vivid green eyes startled me as I floated down a corridor I'd never been in before. Franco scowled, but didn't move to obstruct. Ever since the horrid night where Q turned murderer, Franco gave me more freedom. His eyes followed wherever I went, but he didn't stop me. Maybe Q told him to let me wander, or maybe he sensed I wouldn't run again. I was thankful my cage had expanded.

I continued past Franco, moving deeper into the west wing. I often saw Q disappear down here—it was time to find out why.

Opening double doors at the end of the corridor, I followed a long, Persian carpeted room, staring at massive canvases of photography. Not of wildlife or humans, but cityscapes and high-rise buildings. The harshness of concrete and metal seemed out of place, until I saw dates under each photo, a timeline of purchase and location.

These weren't photos of pleasure, but documentation of ownership. *Holy hell, does Q own all of these?*

I spun in place. Countless snaps of impressive architecture, sprawling hotels, apartment complexes… so many types of property dotted the walls. He owned a small country if it were true.

Needing to know more, I kept going. Everything about the house spoke old money and charm, yet I couldn't see Q in the artefacts, statues, or even the exotic plants flowering around the rooms.

Q remained closed off. I hoped by exploring, I'd find answers, but I only found confusion.

The French song chased with every step, soulful moans and hopeful sonnets. I hummed along to the chorus.

Personne ne voit ma situation, quand tout ce que je veux faire c'est me battre,

Tu me dépeins dans une lumière que je ne pourrai jamais être,
Je suis enchaîné dans l'obscurité, consommé par la rage et le feu,
Je suis proche de la rupture, l'envie est tremblante, violente,
Je suis le diable, et il n'y a aucun espoir.

Can't you see my plight, when all I want to do is fight,
you paint me in a light I can never be,
I come shackled with shadow, consumed with rage and fire,
I'm close to breaking, the urge is quaking, raping,
I'm the devil, and there's no hope.

The song dwindled to silence, leaving my heart racing. On instinct, I opened a huge door and entered paradise. A conservatory, the size of a four bedroom home, welcomed with vaulted glass and sky-scraping palm trees. Sounds of a gurgling river and waterfall lilted behind luscious foliage. Stars twinkled above through the endless glass roof—no moon tonight.

My head cocked, listening. *What is that?*

Tweets and chitters, chirps and whistles. I battled leaves until I came face to face with a two-story-sized aviary.

Jewelled birds flittered and sang, happy in their cage. A lot of them roosted for the night, heads tucked under wings, little chests flurrying.

I looked closer. Instead of parrots and budgerigars I expected, clouds of sparrows, quails, wrens, and blackbirds, littered the aviary. Common, every day, winged creatures, but just as intricate and perfect.

I have to know what the birds mean.

My mind shot back to the mural and the sparrows on Q's chest. The most amazing tattoo I'd ever seen.

Countless hours would've gone into the piece, unlike mine that only took ten minutes. Rubbing my barcode, I wondered if it could be changed. I didn't want to be reminded of what happened… it was in the past, and slavery with Q didn't compare.

A wave of guilt blistered as I ran a thumb over the black lines. I couldn't think about the other women, where they ended up, who they now belonged to; it hurt too much.

A sparrow twirled a note, landing on a branch close by. Its black, intelligent eyes assessed me, its little head cocked. *What are you thinking, little bird? Do you know your master? Can you tell me who he is?*

It bobbed on the perch, then flew away, leaving in a gust of feathers.

The speakers crackled as a new song began. A deep, erotic beat, vibrating through the air. The bass so heavy, leaves shivered with the sound.

My body ached, needing a release. My sense of hearing belonged to Q. Did he know the song would frustrate the hell out of me—needing him, wanting him?

I refused to bring myself to an orgasm, but if he didn't come soon, I'd hunt his ass down and make him break his stupid promise. I would win the competition, without revealing my name.

Watching the birds, my fingers trailed downward to where Q nicked me with the scissors. The cut was long gone, but I wanted another. I wanted rough and untamed. I wanted bruises and cuts, amplifying the thrill of pleasure.

I want him to spank me again.

"*Esclave. Qu'est-ce que tu fais ici?*" What are you doing in here? Q's voice vibrated in the conservatory.

Everything immediately tightened, liquefied, responded. I couldn't see through thick foliage, and spun in a slow circle, searching.

"How did you know where I was?" I peered into the dark green haze, trying to see past the leaves.

He chuckled; it was low, gruff. "This entire house has cameras. Nothing happens without my knowledge."

I should've known. Control freak Mr. Mercer kept tabs on his empire. Did my room have cameras? I wanted to

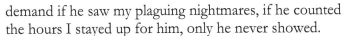

demand if he saw my plaguing nightmares, if he counted the hours I stayed up for him, only he never showed.

Q appeared, emerging from behind a palm-tree. He wore a white linen suit, no wrinkles marring his perfection. The grey shirt looked like a cold winter's day, highlighting pale eyes. He held a black leather folder in his hand, pressing it against a thigh.

My ass stung as a fantasy of being hit with the file charged like wildfire.

I sighed, smiling slightly. Everything was exactly as it should be. My place in the world was by Q's side. I accepted it. It'd been too long. My body warmed, melting, remembering his demands, the way he slapped me as he came. He said he wanted to make me scream. After two weeks of loneliness, I would let him—gladly.

Q came closer, shoulders tense, eyes strained.

I frowned at the stress lines on his forehead and mouth. His gaze met mine, but instead of the usual soft jade, they were faded, like watered down lime, throbbing with pain. I paused. I knew that look—I suffered myself.

Q had a migraine.

"You shouldn't be in here." He sighed, dragging a hand over his short hair, face strained and tired.

My heart sped up. He looked human. Wrecked. The cruel, confusing master was hidden beneath an overworked, hurting man. Tenderness rose; I wanted to care for him, take away his stress. There wouldn't be angry dominance tonight, but I didn't care. Seeing Q this way gave me another piece of the puzzle. It showed the depth of my own feelings. All the normal emotions where Q was concerned were gone: fear, awareness, heat… all hidden under the need to soothe.

Leaving the noisy birds in the aviary, I stepped closer and pressed a kiss ever so softly on the corner of his mouth. "You're not well."

His nostrils flared and he jerked back. "My well-being is none of your concern."

I scowled, crossing my arms. "Your well-being *is* my concern. And I'll tell you why. If you get sick, what happens to me? Where do I go? Who do I end up with?"

Q shifted, eyes going to the cage of birds. Shadows wrapped around him, and I tried to read his secrets. *Why can't he let me see all sides of him?* What the hell was he hiding?

"I'm fine. Nothing will happen to me or you." Anger blazed in his eyes.

I offered comfort, and he didn't want it. I overstepped the boundary from scared slave to equal, and it pissed me off he didn't let me.

I wheeled around, charging for the door. Bloody bastard. If he wanted to lie and wallow in pain, fine by me. Didn't mean I had to stick around and worry. If he wanted me to stay in my little box of possession and didn't want a woman who could help—awesome. I would.

"Wait!" He winced, dropping the folder. I glanced at the exit. I should leave. I no longer wanted to encroach on Q's space, seeing as he didn't want me.

Q moaned slightly, rubbing his temples. "I didn't mean to hurt you, I'm not used to slaves wandering around, rooting through my stuff." He smiled slightly. "You're inquisitive, I'll give you that."

I was insulted and happy at the same time. My feet turned, and I went to stand in front of him. Trying to seem cold and unaffected by his pain, I stooped to pick up the file, passing it to him.

He accepted it with a small nod.

"Did you take some painkillers? Should I find some for you?" I wondered where Suzette kept aspirin. Not that it would help—or at least it didn't for me. The only thing to break a migraine was a head massage with menthol and a nap to dispel the pain.

Q shook his head, motioning for me to walk in front. I obeyed, striding through the over grown conservatory until we stopped in a small seating area next to a large pond, with a gentle waterfall.

Q groaned and slouched in one of the rattan armchairs, sighing heavily. He threw the folder on the matching coffee table, placing his legs on top. With another sigh, he stretched his long body, as if working out the kinks would help his headache.

I didn't know what he wanted—if I should leave or stay, but an enterprising idea popped into my head. Q wasn't as guarded as he normally was. If I stayed and offered support, he might spill something.

Sitting on the chair next to his, I watched while his forehead furrowed and eyes closed.

We stayed silent, listening to the gentle noises of flowing water. Q shifted, rubbing his neck with strong fingers.

I stood, moving behind his chair. I didn't think how he'd react to me touching without permission. I didn't let my mind linger on retribution, only the need to help. *Do you really want to do this?* If I cared, opened my heart to another side of Q, there would be no escaping new feelings for him. If I touched him, it was because *I* wanted to, not because I had to obey. The dynamics of our twisted relationship would shift toward gentler things.

Without his knowledge, Q would give me the very thing I needed to allow him to hurt and abuse me with sex. If he gave me soft, I could give him hard. His leaning on me gave the light I needed to temper the darkness I embraced.

Every thought clambered for space, and I paused trying to figure it out.

Q sucked in a harsh breath, slouching further in the chair. I made my decision. If I cared, he might open. He might see me more than a slave and more as… Tess.

Oh, my God. I wanted to tell Q my name. I wanted

to hear him whisper it with love. To hear him order in his sexy, controlling voice. To yell my name when he fucked me roughly. I no longer wanted to be unidentified.

What's happening to me?

My hands dropped to Q's head, fingers slinking through his pelt-like hair. I moaned with how soft it was. I swayed, wanting to smell, to drug myself with his citrus and sandalwood scent.

He froze, hands covering mine. "What are you doing, *esclave?*"

Tess. My name is Tess.

I added pressure, massaging his scalp with firm strokes. He shuddered under my touch. "Helping rid your headache." Sliding fingers lower, cupping the base of his skull, I leaned forward and brushed his ear with my lips. "If you'll let me?"

Q sucked in a breath, chest straining against his suit. My knees locked as lust kindled hot and twisty in my belly.

He squeezed my hands, bordering on pain, before falling away, granting permission.

The thrill at being allowed made me lightheaded. I pressed harder, swirling with pads of my fingers, adding a touch of nail.

Q moaned, eyes drifting closed as I ran my fingers down to his upper neck all the while pressing, coaxing, stealing the pain through touch. I ran my hands from the base of his skull, all the way to the front of his forehead.

"Ouf, c'est une sensation incroyable." That feels amazing. He groaned louder as I circled around his ears, pressing fingers against his temples.

Butterflies fluttered in my stomach. I cared for my master, and he liked it. Would he reward me?

I smiled softly. Q had won. He won the battle of wills by granting his vulnerability. I would give him my name, the next time he asked—not because he demanded, but because I wanted.

My back ached as I massaged, pressing, kneading. I kept

going—as long as he needed.

Eventually, he covered my hands again, ordering softly, "You can sit now. The pain has broken a little. *Merci.*"

I didn't want to stop; standing over him gave a sense of ownership. With one last caress, I obeyed and perched on a chair.

He watched with half-lidded eyes. The lines on his forehead were diminished, and the tightness around his mouth less prominent. His eyes were still bruised, but weren't glazed and unfocused.

We stared, lust sparking, both unable to look away. Q was the black storm cloud, sucking me toward him like I was a rapidly flying sparrow. The difference between his tattoo, and now, was I wanted to stop flying and let the cloud capture me.

"Thank you, *esclave.*" He dropped his eyes, sitting straighter in the chair.

A shiver danced on my skin, and I reached for the folder, giving myself something to do.

Q watched with unreadable eyes. I sneaked glances at him as I fiddled with the file. I changed our relationship by tending. As his slave, I shouldn't want anything to do with him, let alone nurse him back to health. But the knowledge that my master—my angry, crazy, lusty master—let me care, made me wet and tingly.

My mind pretzeled, trying to figure out my feelings. Why did caring for Q make me powerful and content and lost, all at the same time?

Q didn't say a word as I opened the folder, peering inside.

I frowned at the scrawling French text. I may understand spoken French with ease, but I wasn't very good at reading.

Q inched forward, linking hands between open thighs. Just like he did when I first arrived and he secured the tracking anklet on me. My ankle itched, thinking about the device, funny how I'd grown so used to it. It was my safety blanket—the knowledge Q would always come for me—just like he said in my dreams.

He pointed at the top of the page where a logo stood out: a bird silhouette in flight with a background of sweeping skyscrapers. "*Moineau* Holdings," Q said.

My heart rate quickened. I looked into his eyes. "Sparrow Holdings."

He nodded, opening his mouth to answer, then stopped. He cleared his throat. "You said you knew about property. This is my legacy. I've procured over five hundred acquisitions in under twelve years." His eyes glazed. "I took over when I was sixteen. It rules my life, but I'm thankful for what it gives me in return. What I'm able to do with the money."

He never spoke like this. I couldn't move, in case I broke the spell and he shut down.

Pride filled his gaze; for once, the aura of anger and self-deprecation left, suffocated beneath a powerful CEO who ruled an empire. "It used to be called Mercer Conglomerates when my father owned it." Hate thickened his voice, hands curled. "The moment he died, I changed it. Not only the name, but the entire company's structure."

Silence fell, and I didn't want to speak, move, or bring any attention to myself. Q spoke as if I were more than just a sex toy or belonging. He allowed me to see the passion in his heart for a company I knew nothing about. He hinted at a wealth I couldn't comprehend, and a lifetime of servitude to a company he ran from a teenager.

Q bristled with anger, mentioning his father. Curiosity burned, and I wished I knew what happened. Did his father beat him?

Blinking away memories, he waved a hand at the folder. "Read it. I'd like to know your thoughts on this particular acquisition."

"What?" I couldn't stop my incredulous tone. I stared at the folder as if it stole my slave status and flung me into an employee. I didn't want to be Q's employee, I wanted him equally. *Then answer him... he's asking you as a woman—he's seeing you.*

Heart racing, I looked at the page, tracing the sparrow logo with a shaking finger.

Q breathed hard, rubbing a temple. "I'm asking what you think, *esclave*. You studied property feasibilities at university, didn't you? Unless you lied about that, too?"

His dig at lying about my name irked. *I'm ready to tell you. Just ask.*

Temper filled me, slapping away my nerves. Q wanted my opinion, yet wasn't prepared to give me rights as a human. My eyes flashed. "You're asking me? The slave you'll never let leave the house, or use a phone, or go on the internet. The girl you accepted as a bribe." Horror throttled and I finally knew what I'd been a bribe for.

My lips curled as I looked back at the folder. "I was a bribe for a building contract, wasn't I?" I frantically flicked through the pages, expecting it to give answers. "The Russian gave me to you for something illegal." My tone blazed, self-righteous. "What did you agree to do?"

I couldn't think straight—I'd been nothing but a business transaction, yet Q shot the Russian for hurting me. Where did his loyalties lie? To me—his *esclave*— or the people who made him a fortune?

Q straightened, withdrawing the connection between us. "That is none of your business. I'm asking about this merger. Not another."

I shook my head, unable to let it go. I finally had one answer, and the rest started falling into place. "Is that why you have other girls? You accept women as bribes to allow buildings and things you shouldn't dabble in gain approval?" I breathed hard; it all made sense. "What happened to the other girls?" My eyes flew to the aviary, hidden behind foliage. "Why is it just me in this house? Will you throw me away when you tire of me? Or wait till a better replacement comes along?"

Q glared, sparking with temper.

My hands curled, and I wanted to slap him. "Tell me the truth! What will happen to me?" The fear of the future crippled, turning my lungs into whistling, useless things. I thought if Q came to care for me, he'd keep me, and I'd never have to re-enter the world.

But, once again, he spun a lie. I'd never be able to stay here permanently, as more girls would arrive. More contracts would be signed. Some other slave would spread her legs for Q to hit and fuck and rule.

Blackness tinged my vision as panic rushed. If I used up my welcome, I would be cast out, or killed, or sold to another.

Q sat, deathly still, watching me break apart. He pinched the brow of his nose, trying to find relief from the headache. "You have the wrong idea, *esclave,* and I'm not in the mood to set you straight."

My God, I was *so* happy I never told him my name. It would be worthless to him. He didn't care. I bet he called all his bribes *esclave,* because he didn't keep them long enough to learn their true personalities.

My heart broke. I stood, holding out my hand. "I want my bracelet back. I want you to let me go."

Q chuckled, wincing. "The bracelet is mine. Just like *you* are mine. I thought you'd accepted that."

"Never. You think *I* lie. Everything about you lies. I don't want a master who isn't truthful. I deserve better." The urge to hurt made me yell. "I want a master who buys me! Not accepts me because he has no other choice."

His eyes flashed dangerously; he growled, "Take that back or I'll make your captivity long and full of hardship."

I wanted to laugh, or cry, or both. Somehow, the threat

sounded like a lie. If he meant it, surely he would've done untold terribleness by now. For two weeks, he didn't touch me, while I begged in my dreams for him to tie me up. The songs he played about living with demons and uncontrollable urges were bullshit.

He was a cold-hearted man who teased and cajoled, showing glimpses of the woman I could become, before slapping me down to nothingness.

I was done.

Q tensed his jaw, standing in one fluid move. He slapped me so hard, my neck snapped back. Tears gushed as I cupped my burning cheek. Fear chased away my fight and I cowered.

Q's face raged with anguish and undeniable hunger. He rubbed his palm, smiling darkly. "You can't speak that way and not be punished, *esclave*." Grabbing the back of my neck, he jerked me forward. A tongue captured salty tears. "First sensible thing I've seen you do." His accent was low, exotic, turning his praise into dark and sensual.

Despite my pain and anger, his voice wrapped around my heart. I struggled with visions of fighting harder, pushing him to the floor, straddling, begging him to deliver on whatever sinful promise he hinted.

But my fear of abandonment ruled stronger. I bowed my head. "And what is that?"

Q let me go. "Recognise me. See me. I am your master."

My throat closed, fighting with injustice. He was my master, but for how long? *I don't have a choice in the length of my captivity.* I never did. I never would.

He would never see me as Tess. As a girl. A woman who refused to bow to anyone. A woman who was more than just a fucking bribe.

I glared. "See *me*. I am not yours to torment."

Our eyes clashed, locking with a battle of wills. How

many of these nonverbal fights must we have? My breathing came hard as Q blazed with black desire. The air crackled with monstrous urges; even the birds shut up.

My body warmed, heated, melted. *No, do not betray me.* I couldn't stop slickness building between my legs, or fantasies darting in my twisted mind.

It had been too long since my last orgasm. I'd saved myself for Q, now I never wanted him to visit me again.

Remorse and guilt sucked me into a pit. How could I think Q might be the one for me? He didn't make my soul sing. He made it weep, and scream, and tear itself into pieces.

"I hate you."

"No, you don't. You just don't want to see."

"See what?" I snapped.

Grabbing my barcoded wrist, he jerked me against him. His body infernoed with heat. "You are mine. I can do what I want with you. I can dress you. Fuck you. Send you away. Loan you to others. You *belong* to me. And you've finally realized it isn't romantic, it isn't sexy, or fun. It's something no one should want or desire. You're a captive."

He shook me, his headache etching his eyes with pain. "My role as your master is to debase you to the point of having no feelings, no emotion, no hopes or dreams. I tell you to fuck another man, you ask for how long. I tell you to wear something, you do not fucking chop it up in defiance. You wear it, and appreciate what I give you. You're mine, *esclave*. And it isn't a fucking happy ever after."

He let go, pushing so I stumbled. "How does it feel to face the truth?"

I couldn't breathe. Facing the truth terrified more than anything. In that moment, I fully believed Q would do everything he said. He would debase me to the point of being empty. Happily treating me like a shoe or a tatty suitcase.

I was nothing.

Q advanced, grimacing with pain. "Get on your knees, *esclave*." He pressed a heavy hand on my shoulder.

I was too numb to kick or run. So many emotions in such a short amount of time. What the hell just happened? One moment, I wanted to hear him call me Tess, the next, I wanted him dead. I couldn't keep up.

Q forced me to my knees. "Undo my trousers."

I didn't think I'd ever find numbness again, but as I fumbled with Q's belt, the cloud of indifference swept me away. My heart raced as I undid the zipper, pulling his hard cock free, but my mind went blank.

Q rocked on his feet, fisting my hair for balance. "Suck me. Make my headache go away by other means."

I looked up, circling my fingers around his hot girth. A non-interested thought flickered in the blankness. Either he was really brave, yelling at me then expecting me to suck him and not bite, or just incredibly stupid. I didn't care either way, I'd obey.

I pumped once, shuffling forward on my knees to bring the tip of him to my lips. Q exhaled heavily, pushing his hips forward.

I tongued him, tasting saltiness. The sense tried to shoot me back to reality—I could hold him ransom while I sucked. I could bite and cause immeasurable pain. I could barter for my freedom.

Opening wide, I deep throated him.

He groaned, tugging my hair as his ass clenched. I could bite, but I didn't want to. Even now, my body betrayed. I trembled with lust, tinging vacancy with desire.

I withdrew, fisting him, licking.

"Oh, *merde!*"

I froze; Q scrambled back, holding his wet cock.

Suzette stood behind, mouth hanging open. "I'm sorry! I—eh—" Spinning around, she mumbled, "I didn't mean to interrupt."

I rocked on my heels, keeping my head down. Q was livid, shoving himself into his trousers. He winced when the zipper came exceedingly close to sensitive skin. "*C'est quoi ce bordel?*" What the fuck?

She bounced, looking at the ceiling, fingers fluttering at her sides. "*Je suis désolée,* but there are some men here to see you, *maître.*"

Q breathed hard, smoothing his hair and suit, glaring at me so intensely it felt like another slap. My cheek smarted in response. "Send them away. I'm not prepared to accept guests so late."

Suzette looked over her shoulder, relief on her face. Spinning all the way around, she looked at me with her soul bared.

Heartbeats galloped out of control. Instincts screamed into being and I wanted to block my ears. Looming palm-trees seemed to inch closer, branching with doom. I didn't want her to speak.

"They won't leave, Q. They have a warrant."

He spun to face her. "Warrant?"

I slapped a hand over my mouth. My world imploded. The police. Brax. He got my message. He was alive! *Brax is alive and sent someone to rescue me!*

My heart bucked; I couldn't think. I couldn't breathe. I couldn't do anything but kneel.

Hopelessness squeezed as Q turned to face me slowly. I shrivelled. The consequences of running away, once again ruined my life.

The police had come for Q. *I* ruined his life—just like he ruined mine.

That's not true, and you know it. He gave you back your life. He introduced you to a new life. A better life. I forced my brain to quiet, risking a look at Suzette.

Her eyes brimmed with disappointment and overwhelming sadness. I folded closer to the floor, hating betraying her.

She broke eye contact, looking at Q. "The police believe you're holding a girl called Tess Snow," Suzette whispered, voice breaking.

She took two angry steps toward me, but Q held up his arm, barricading. "How could you? You—you…" She trailed off, mouth twisting with grief. "We all trusted you."

My life shattered for the fourth and final time.

Q froze, all trace of pain and emotion, gone. "That's your name? Tess?"

My body fissured with longing. He spoke my name. Finally, after almost two months of *esclave*.

It rolled off his tongue in one beautiful French twist; I wanted his tongue on me. I wanted to forget everything—to pretend he never said such horrid things or that I brought his life and business to ruin. I wanted to give him my heart and forget.

"Tess…" Q whispered, before baring his teeth. Shadows cloaked him and the look of betrayal flayed more than any whip. "You called the police." His shoulders sagged, and the pain he hid smothered again.

Suzette leaned into him; he welcomed her, tugging her close.

My body rebelled as jealousy glowed bright and green. How dare he find solace in his maid. I was his slave. *Find solace with me—even though I'm the crux of your ruin!*

He nodded once. "So be it."

Chapter Nineteen

Goldfinch

Q and Suzette left.

Without another glance or word, Q turned his back and strode out of my life.

My legs hurt from kneeling, but it was nothing compared to the paralyzing heartbreak.

I should be happy. Brax was alive! But I was dead to my master and didn't know what my future held. The police would arrest him. They'd take me back to Australia, and return me to a half-life—a false life—a life I no longer wanted.

I didn't know how long I rocked, but a puddle of tears dampened the marble below.

You did this. You ran because you knew it isn't right. Q isn't right. I tried to convince myself to stand, to embrace my freedom, and leave this house where so many bad things happened, but I couldn't gather the energy.

Stumbling to my feet, I shivered. The birds were silent and the hushed world of plants made it seem like I was the only one alive. No one wanted me. My abandonment issues crested, swamping with wretchedness.

In a daze, I walked from the conservatory, through the photograph room, and down the long corridor. Every step felt as if I walked to the hangman's noose. I never wanted to see Suzette again—face her rage and tears. She loved Q and I sentenced him to jail. She would never call me *mon amie* again.

I didn't want Q to go to jail. He was many things, but he didn't deserve what I did. He could've broken me, raped me like Brute, but he never did. He fought his desires to ensure I remained whole and strong. He sacrificed everything for a lowly slave.

My stomach cramped and I folded in half. *What have I done?* I evicted myself from a home I wanted, to a world who didn't want me. Back to a man who could never give what I needed. Back to a half existence.

Tears slid down my face. Running away had been a disaster. Anger flared toward Franco. This was all *his* fault. If he kept a better eye, I would never have been able to leave. He should've caught me, before I ruined so many lives.

My thoughts jumped to Brax. Guilt engulfed me. How had the last months been for him? He must hate me for breaking my promise—I said I would never leave, and I did. The first time not on my own accord, but the second time—that was all me. I willingly sliced him from my thoughts, my heart, and made room for my master.

Images of Brax, distraught and heartbroken, made my heart twist. My brain short-circuited refusing to think about him.

Q consumed once again, and I slid down the wall, drawing my knees up to wrap my arms around them. What if the police had taken him into custody already? I would never see him again. Oh, God. Would I be made to testify? I couldn't. I wouldn't.

No doubt, he would hate me for all eternity, wishing he'd let Brute kill and bury me with the potatoes.

My heart died.

I wanted everything from him. I wanted the domination. The anger. But I also wanted love. I needed the connection he offered only half an hour ago. A brief glimpse into a softer side—a side I desperately wanted to know. *I'm a stupid, stupid girl.*

"*Esclave.* What are you doing on the floor?" Franco appeared in his shiny black suit, squatting in front of me.

I couldn't meet his eyes. He would be implicated, too. Why hadn't the police rounded everyone up? I didn't hear sirens or shouts. Suzette said only a warrant had been served... maybe... maybe they wouldn't do anything?

Franco patted my shoulder, vivid emerald eyes sad. "You regret running, don't you?"

I sucked in a sob, wrapping my arms tighter. Franco had been nothing but nice to me. Strict and a prick when I first arrived, but nice just the same. His tough façade hid a man who loved his employer for reasons I was only beginning to understand.

He sighed, brushing tear-damp curls off my cheek. "There, there. It's okay. It's not the end of the world."

I shook my head. "It *is* the end of the world. My world. My master's world. *Your* world. Everything is broken."

"Is that what you were doing? When I found in you in the café? Calling the police?" he asked, no glimmer of anger, just curiosity.

I breathed hard. "No. I called my boyfriend. I was going to call the police, but you turned up."

He tensed. "So, you didn't call them directly?" Light gleamed in his gaze. Guilt pressed ever harder. He wanted to believe I wouldn't turn on Q. He wanted to believe I wouldn't betray them.

I whispered, "I left a message on my boyfriend's machine with Q's name." I looked into his eyes with difficulty. "I would've called the cops, Franco. Don't doubt my desperation to run." But even in my desperation, I was conflicted. I huddled into a little ball, tucking my head into my arms.

Franco stood, pulling my elbow so I had no choice but to rise. "You can fix this." He tugged me down the corridor. "It isn't your fault, *esclave*. You did what you had to do. And now… I believe you wouldn't do it again, and I forgive you."

I looked up, sniffing. I sent his master off to a life of imprisonment and he *forgave* me?

He smiled kindly, green eyes vibrant compared to Q's smouldering pale jade. "Speak to the police. Tell them it was a mistake. You can repair the damage you caused."

The idea blazed with white-hot hope; I threw myself at him, grabbing him into a hug. "Why didn't I think of that?"

Franco chuckled, pushing me away uncomfortably. "You're dealing with a lot, but now you—"

I didn't let Franco finish. I was the key to saving Q's life, his business. I wasted so much time already.

I flew.

Paintings blurred as I sprinted through the house. I wouldn't steal Q's livelihood. My place was by his side. I accepted it. I had to make him forgive me and find a way to stay. I messed up, he messed up. Together, we could fix it.

I darted into the lounge. Empty.

Panting, I pirouetted and dashed across the foyer to the library. The glass was no longer clear but frosted, hiding people within. I didn't care; I burst through the doors.

Q looked up, eyes clouded with pain. Two plain clothes detectives sat opposite on the button leather couch.

I stood, like an idiot, trying to reconcile the image in my head of a horde of police and Q in handcuffs, to the sedate scene.

Small puffs of cigar smoke languished in the air, while the smell of brandy and liquor tantalized. I couldn't make sense of the two older men, both with moustaches—one thin and trimmed, another bushy and grey—sitting relaxed and content, puffing away as if they were there for an after dinner chat, rather than a kidnapping charge.

Q swirled his crystal goblet, amber liquid sloshing up the sides. He watched with hooded eyes. I waited for a wave of hate, a look crippling with betrayal, but nothing came. He was remote, aloof—the perfect, unreadable master.

The moustached men raised an eyebrow, looking me up and down. But no sense of urgency filled them; they didn't stop nursing their brandies and cigars.

What the hell is going on? I barged in to save the day, expecting Q to be beaten and restrained, and they looked as if *I* were the interloper.

I opened my mouth and promptly shut it again. I wanted to ask what was going on, but what could I possibly say?

Shit, I should've thought up a cover story. I was so focused on saving the day, like a dragon- fighting princess saving my tortured knight, I hadn't considered how.

The officer with a thin moustache and heavy wrinkles turned to Q, mumbling in French, "That's the girl?"

Q clenched his jaw, looking at me with a piercing gaze. He nodded ever so slightly. "That's Tess Snow, if you're looking for her."

My womb clenched hearing my name on his lips. I trembled to hear it again. I stepped forward.

Q stood in one fluid move, wincing as the migraine etched his eyes. *He really shouldn't be drinking in his condition.* "Leave, Ms. Snow. You are not welcome."

The order poured salt on already painful wounds. *Not welcome.*

My eyes flickered to the cop with the bushy moustache. He looked like a cuddly father, and a doting husband. How would he react to Q telling a woman he kept captive to leave?

The man sipped his liquor, watching, as if Q and I were a daytime soap opera.

This wasn't going how I expected. "I wanted to clarify a few things, for the record. In case you had the wrong idea," I muttered, ignoring the way Q glared.

The policemen looked at each other, then shrugged. Bushy Moustache scooted forward, leather creaking under his weight. Placing his glass down, and the cigar in a crystal ashtray, he said, "What would you like to clarify, Ms. Snow?"

I fought the urge to look at Q. Holding my head high, I said, "If you can inform me of why you're here, I can let you know the truth." No way did I want to blabber things they might not be aware of.

Busy Moustache nodded with a wry smile. "Fair enough." Pulling a notepad from his breast pocket, he flicked it open. "We are here because the Australian Federal Police contacted us about a missing woman fitting your description. They were advised by a Braxton Cliffingstone of your kidnapping in Mexico."

The officer with the thin moustache spoke. "He gave detailed evidence of how he was beaten and when he came to, you were gone. He also provided us with a phone message from you, implicating Mr. Mercer in your disappearance. As you can imagine, up to that point, Mr. Cliffingstone was incredibly upset, thinking you were dead."

Bushy Moustache jumped in. "He'll be relieved to hear you're alive and well."

Q's fingers tightened around his glass. He never took his eyes off me, flinching at Brax's name.

The police ceased to exist as the library grew smaller, entrapping just Q and I in our own private world. His power reached for me, face harsh and stern, eyes raging with emotion. He watched, not with treason or hate, but loneliness and understanding.

My hands curled, fighting the urge to hurl myself at his feet. Even suffering a headache, Q vibrated with authority and feeling. I glimpsed just how much I meant to him.

His body called to mine and like the obedient slave I was, I went. Q jerked as I touched his fingers, wrapped around the goblet. His nostrils flared, looking over my shoulder at the two policemen who were no doubt watching.

But I didn't care. They had to see what existed between Q and me. They may not understand it—shit, I didn't understand it—but it thrummed in the space.

Q's fingers rose from the glass, capturing mine in one sharp move. Skin sparked and fireworked; I gasped, looking deep into pale eyes.

He straightened and brushed past, going to stand by the fireplace.

My heart raced, hating his withdrawal. Despair replaced my desire and I nodded once. He'd already let me go.

I hated the police for ruining my tentative new existence. I hated Brax for finally coming to find me. I hated myself for being too weak.

Balling my hands, I spoke loud and true. "I'm Tess Snow, and I was kidnapped in Mexico. But this man," I pointed at Q, "Q Mercer, and his household, rescued me and kept me safe. I stayed here on my own accord. The message on Mr. Cliffingstone's voice mail was a mistake. He misheard."

I fell into another realm of awful for lying about Brax, but I was only focused on Q, focused on repairing the unrepairable.

Bushy Moustache stood, nodding. "Thank you for clarifying, Ms. Snow. But now we really must speak to Quincy alone."

Quincy.

Quincy.

My eyes shot to Q. I knew his name.

So enamoured fighting our silent battle of wills, it took outside parties to spill the truth.

I looked at him with such longing, his lips parted. Something arched and sparked and ruptured between us. I couldn't breathe. I accepted everything he said in the conservatory about debasing and owning me.

Q wanted to debase and own me. *Quincy* wanted to share parts of his life with me. It was Quincy who spoke about his business, Q who ordered me to suck him.

I wanted both. Oh, God, how I wanted both.

Images of Q behind bars, with no one to feed his aviary of birds, slammed into me. I almost collapsed to my knees to beg forgiveness.

Every emotion was raw; tears spilled. "Please don't arrest Q—Quincy. He didn't do anything wrong."

Then, I fled.

Chapter Twenty

Tern

I tossed and turned in bed, terrified of what morning would bring.

After running like a coward, I tried to eavesdrop, but voices didn't travel up the staircase.

The unknown haunted me and I couldn't remove the image from my mind of Q in a cell.

I glanced at the clock; my heart stuttered like a faulty object. 2:14 a.m.

No one had come for me. No noise signalled that Q had been forcefully removed from his home. Was he bribing them to turn the other way? I hoped beyond hope this might all blow over, and life would continue. If it didn't, I would latch onto the bedpost and refuse to go. I didn't want to return to Brax or parents who didn't care.

I didn't know how a warrant worked—didn't it give the right to explore the house? How come no one explored?

It didn't make sense. I was still in the man's house, who Brax accused of keeping me prisoner. Somehow, Q kept the law from stealing me or arresting him. *He's more powerful than I thought.*

It was yet another unknown.

At two-thirty, I gave up the pretence of trying to sleep. Pulling the sketchpad Q gave me from my bedside table, I turned on the lamp.

With a painful squeeze in my chest, I cracked open fresh pages and took out a charcoal. My fingers twirled the pencil like an old friend, but I sat staring at the paper, lost.

So many things fought for space inside. I wanted to run, or fight, or scream. I wanted to apologise to Q, then yell at him for making me feel so many things.

Sketching was my outlet, and I wanted to pour everything onto the page.

Slowly, my hand feathered quick strokes, followed by heavier touches here and there. As I worked, I recalled the release drawing gave. It soothed and eased, helping calm my overworked mind. Following lines and contours of buildings from memory, I disappeared into the realm of property and architecture, finding blissful silence from worry and lust.

I frowned as I made a mistake, but kept going. I preferred sketching from a photograph or directly in front of a building, the sun on my face and the world buzzing around.

Sitting in bed, waiting to hear my fate, I sketched Q's mansion. I drew his home on the sketchpad he gifted. His gesture gripped my heart; I throbbed for him. *Please, don't let him be in custody.* My uncertain future tried to steal the oasis of calm and I sighed. Where had Suzette gone? I hadn't seen her since the conservatory. I flinched to think she would've slapped me if Q hadn't stopped her.

Night turned into early morning, yet I didn't turn off the light. I huddled, sketching as if the world would crumble if I didn't. Q's pastel mansion came to life. I added sconces and plasterwork beneath sweeping windows, capturing ruddy cheeked cherubs and intricate architraves.

Normally, my passion lay in crisp lines of concrete and steel, not a historic manor, but the drawing would be one of my best. I wished I could draw humans. Capture Q's face on the page, his sternness, his posture. But nothing, not even a perfect photograph, would capture Q's essential being. Q was vibrant. Q was unique.

Q radiated… as Quincy he turned human. I didn't want human. I wanted my master. A lover who dominated.

Exhaustion warred with sadness, and I sank deeper into pillows.

I fell asleep with the pad on my lap, and charcoal-smeared hands cupping a cheek.

"*Esclave*. I mean… Tess."

My heart catapulted, blood pumping.

Brute. Driver.

Hands. Cock. Pain.

Nightmares shattered, leaving me with breath-stealing fear. A hand landed on my shoulder, hot and heavy. I snapped.

Screaming, I struck, connecting with something solid. Pain blazed in my wrist and I shot upright, yelping. "What the hell?"

A man's *umph* filled the night-silence. The smell of citrus hit, with the reek of bourbon and brandy.

Q stumbled back. "*Merde*. You didn't have t—to fucking hish m—me," he slurred, rubbing his chest, climbing drunkenly off the bed.

Oh, my God. Q.

My body warmed, even as my mind told me to be careful.

He grunted, swaying toward the mattress again, almost tumbling on top.

Hell, my master was inebriated. I knew he shouldn't drink with his migraine. His shoulders rolled, rather than straight and proud, eyes glazed and watery. *Don't tell me he's been drinking with the police all this time?*

I sat up, pushing covers off and climbing out of bed.

Q blinked, shaking his head. He tripped, grabbing hold of a bedpost. I approached him warily, with hands up in surrender and heart rabbiting. "Q... get into bed, before you fall over."

He giggled. Literally giggled like a little girl. "Trying to t—take advantage in m—my intoxicated state, *esclave?*" French accent thickened, slurred. I had trouble understanding.

I stepped closer, my palate catching the smell of booze. He scooted back and swayed like a human tower of Piza. For God's sake, how much did he drink?

I darted forward and caught him, propping him up with a shoulder. The alcoholic whiff tingled my senses. I swear I grew high off the fumes. Or was it his hot, hard, sinful body pressed against mine? Or the deep musky scent of aftershave and sandalwood?

My stomach twisted as Q leaned heavily, turning his head to sniff my hair. He sighed. "Smell so good. So fucking good. Like rain... no, no like frost. Sharp and fresh and icy and cold and...and painful." He closed his eyes, voice trailing into a whisper. "You love c—causing pain."

My heart stopped. *I* hurt *him?* It was the other way around. Completely. I never suffered so much since he owned me.

His eyes flashed to mine, swirling with liquor and lingering headache. "That's what you are. Painful." He thumped his chest. "Painful to me." Closing his eyes again, he frowned and swallowed.

Unable to address the swirling mess of feelings inside, I pushed him toward the bed. "Sit before you fall." Breathing hard, I helped lower him till he lay down.

He moaned, clutching my forearm when I moved

away. His grip was a death trap, and I had no choice but to sit by his side, letting him wrap strong, heated fingers around my barcoded wrist.

Inching closer, I hesitantly ran fingers through his short hair, relishing once again in being able to touch him. I thought I wouldn't see him again—be alone with him again. The fact he wouldn't remember visiting me in the morning didn't matter. He was here. For now. In this window of time, before the sun rose—he was all mine.

He quieted, purring under my gentle touch. Sadness fell as I realized he was about to pass out. So much for having him to myself. He came to hog my bed and left me out in the cold.

His breathing settled, low and even; I pulled away. He was asleep. The moment I moved, fingers tightened on my wrist. "Snow. Snow. You're named after winter... my favourite season."

I froze. He spoke with no holds barred. Voice clearer, but still loose with booze. "Why do you like winter?" I whispered, so afraid he would comatose before answering.

"The season where everything dies, but is reborn better than ever." His eyes flared, and wedged himself upright on elbows, wincing. "That's what I do, you know. I'm winter."

I had no clue what he meant, but stayed as quiet as possible. *Please, keep talking.*

A strange light filled his pale eyes. "Fifty-seven," he mumbled.

Heartbeats raced. Somehow, I knew Q was about to open up. He dropped his guard, allowing me to glimpse inside. I launched into interrogation mode. Trying hard not to look too interested, I linked fingers with his, stroking ever so gently. "Fifty-seven what, master?"

His eyes closed and he moaned, swaying toward my touch. Then his lips twitched and he jerked away. "Not master. Fucking hate that word." Jaw clenched, and he waged a war inside. Smouldering jade eyes entrapped me and I couldn't move.

Drunken glaze stole him again; he sighed with the weight of the world. "Not true. Love that word when I'm *your* master. I love hurting you, fucking you, playing mind games with you. It makes me just like him."

Q curled a fist, and I yelped as he punched himself hard in the chest. "I'm sick. Nothing but evil lives inside." He grabbed me, dragging me close, almost pressing his nose against mine. "You came along, and made me accept the darkness."

I didn't know what he meant. I didn't like the rage and strange glint in his eyes. I felt lost and breakable. Swallowing, I changed the subject. "Why fifty-seven? What does the number represent?"

Q chuckled darkly. "Girls, of course. Fifty-seven little birds I froze in my winter frost and helped thaw."

Girls? He owned and lived with fifty-seven girls before me? Sick jealously rolled, and I froze. *What the fuck does that mean?* My brain hurt. Q's drunken metaphors didn't make sense. No one could have fifty-seven women. It was monstrous.

I wanted to slap him. "You've owned fifty-seven girls?"

He nodded, as if it made perfect sense. "Fifty-seven." A finger connected between my breasts, marking, branding. "You're fifty eight." His eyes dropped to my chest and he cupped my flesh fiercely. "Number fifty-eight, who ruined my life."

I whacked his hand away. "*I* ruined *your* life?" Fierce rage consumed, mixing with jealously, drowning in jittery angst. My heart refused to stop beating a billion flurries a minute. "You sleep with fifty-seven slaves and have the audacity to question how many men I've been with? You're a fucking hypocrite." I shot off the bed, tangling fingers in my hair, inflicting pain to stop the bone-crushing agony of the truth. "You have no idea how fucked up you've made me."

Q flung his long legs off the bed, standing. He promptly sat heavily, holding his head. "Stop screeching, *esclave*. Come here." He kept his head bowed, but a hand outstretched, fully expecting me to obey. Not this time. I'd reached my limit.

I stalked back and slapped him. "I was right to call the police. You're a bastard."

Oxygen cracked with tension as Q looked through heavy lids. His teeth ground and the sloppy drunk morphed into angry drunk. In a flash, Q whipped upright, picked me up, and threw me on the bed. I yelped as he collapsed on top, pinning me to the mattress.

He growled, "I'm a bastard? Isn't that a requirement to being a master? To be cruel and unapproachable? " He traced my ear with a tongue, lacing me in brandy. "I love treating you like dirt. It gets me fucking hard." Q ground his raging hot cock against my flimsy night shorts. "Can you feel that, *esclave*? See what you do to me by fighting? By defying me? I'm a walking hard on needing to punish you, fuck you, remind you that your place is beneath me to take my come and welcome my palm."

He thrust again, a feral shadow on his face. "Every moment with you in my home is delicious fucking torture. Every time I see you, I want to make your skin flush with pain, your breath ragged from pleasure. I want to do everything that I shouldn't want to do. Do you get it? You cause immeasurable pain as you bring alive the sickness in me."

My mind whirled with every word; I tried to push him off. My arms were weak and trembly, body wet and needy. The blackness in his tone warmed, thrilled, repulsed, *terrified*. Not one sense, but everything, sprang to hyperawareness. I wanted to scratch his eyes out—to draw more anger from him for some ludicrous reason.

My core rippled, needing to be taken violently, even as my mind rebelled against the thought of him being with so many others. "Get the fuck off me."

His answer was to kiss me. His tongue darted past my lips, thrusting, claiming with every angry stroke. I wriggled, but it was no use. While he smothered me with taste, he pinned my wrists above my head, breathing hard. Biting my lower lip, he pulled away. "Why didn't you want me to know your name?"

The sudden change from anger to inquisition left me reeling. I pursed my lips, glaring.

Temper blazed on his face, and he kissed me so hard, I cried out with the pain. Q took advantage of my open mouth, plunging his tongue deep, almost choking me with ferocity. When he finally let me breathe, he bit my neck and shook his head like a lion with prey. My skin stung then screamed as teeth punctured my skin.

"Fuck!" I jolted; he laughed.

His tongue lapped the wound, saliva stinging with liquor.

I squeezed my eyes and just lay there. "Why are you being so cruel?"

Tears pressed and my topsy-turvy emotions flicked from lust to lusty hate. "I wish the police arrested you." I could never make up my mind which feeling was true when it came to Q. One moment, I thought I might be able to give him what he needed, be his slave if I got something more in return, other times, I wanted him dead.

He reared back, looking with temper and remorse. My heart stuttered, then raced erratically. He was full of personalities tonight; I couldn't keep up.

Q muttered, *"Tu ne peux pas être á moi, mais je deviens á toi."*

My stomach twisted, filling with frothy bubbles. Our eyes locked and I couldn't look away. Q brushed his lips against mine ever so sweetly, repeating in English, forcing me to swallow the words. "You may not be mine, but I'm fast becoming yours."

Time froze.

His confession tied me up, stole my mind. His drunken state let me see the depth of his feelings. Time began anew, sparkling with new possibilities. My body was no longer mine, it belonged to Q. Everything belonged to Q.

"Goddammit, you don't play fair," I whispered, brushing away a tear that had the audacity to leak.

Q rolled, propping himself on his elbow. One finger traced my nipple through the thin t-shirt. His deep French accent rumbled, "*Esclave*... I can't.... I won't..." he slurred.

My hand reached on its own accord to cup his cheek. Clammy skin burned beneath my fingertips. He leaned into me as if I was a lifeline.

I murmured, "What do you need, master?" My body knew. It had known all along. Q fought more battles than I did, and after his crazy drunk rantings, I began to understand just how deep he went. Just how much he suffered. "Tell me. Anything you want."

"I killed him. I killed him for doing things to girls I desperately want to do to you." He sat on his knees, hazy with alcohol, but still focused, aware.

He sucked in a breath. "Let me have one night where I can do anything I want. Submit to me completely, no more arguing, fighting. Become a perfect slave." He lowered his voice, throbbing with intensity. "For me."

In his request, I saw black need—need so extreme it eclipsed my lust making it seem like a crush compared to a violent love affair.

"You're not just a possession, *esclave*. I could force you to do this, but I won't." He rubbed an unsteady thumb along my bottom lip. "I'm giving you a choice."

The connection between us strengthened, lengthened. By giving me the choice, he showed he cared as much as he may want to destroy.

The rest of the world ceased to exist. The police didn't

matter. Brax didn't matter.

Q and I become our entire galaxy, and I revelled in the gift I was about to give him. The gift I was about to give myself.

I dropped off the bed and fell to my knees. Bowing, I splayed my legs like every image I'd seen of a submissive before her master. I bowed further; hair curtained my face as I whispered, "*Je suis à toi.* Fuck me, master, act out your fantasies. Hurt me. Debase me. Make me yours." Every word I uttered turned on a power inside unlike any other. The fact I willingly gave myself to him, to do whatever he wanted, unlocked new dimensions I'd been too chicken-shit to visit. I needed this as much as he did.

Q unfolded himself from the bed, positioning himself in front of me. His breathing grew harsh and thick, chest pumping with exertion. He stroked my hair before fisting it, jerking my eyes to meet his. Everything about him smouldered: eyes, mouth, body. I could've come just with the pheromones he shot into the air.

"You've made your choice. You can't take it back. I take you up on your offer, *esclave.*" He pulled me upright by my hair. My scalp screamed, and I winced, holding onto his hands.

When I stood, he said, "You can scream. You can cry. But I give you my promise I'll stop if you say the safe word."

"What's the safe word?" I didn't need to ask. I smiled crookedly.

Together, we murmured, "Sparrow."

With another look, singeing my soul, we signed our bargain. Q swelled with dominance and I burned with power of my own. A power I didn't have a name for— power over Q.

"You're mine tonight." Q kissed my cheek.

"Yes," I breathed, and just like that, I became Q's

whore. His doting, willing, eager little whore.

Q vibrated with unbridled sexuality as he grabbed my hand and carted me from the room. I followed my drunken master down the rich corridor and up a set of private stairs only visible behind a wall panel.

Circular steps led up and up, until Q pulled a key from his pocket and unlocked a medieval-looking door.

He practically threw me inside, before slamming it, and locking it with the same key.

My eyes widened as I took in the cylindrical room. It would've been a tower, if the additions to the manor over the years hadn't evolved and hidden it from view. It reeked of masculinity—a dark undertone sending hot need through my veins.

A massive white rug rested in front of a ginormous fireplace. It was so big, I could've stood inside and not reached the mantle. Weapons and ancient paintings covered the walls, along with a bed three times the size of any other.

Q's domain.

The décor screamed hunter; an insight into his wishes, desires to ravage and ruin. The huge room announced how much he loved to control and dominate. He brought me here to do anything he wanted. *How many other girls have been in his space?*

I scowled, ignoring those thoughts. Tonight was about Q and I. Past and future didn't belong in this exquisite present.

Sitting at the end of the monstrous black-covered bed was a mirrored chest. Studded with silver rivets, it reflected my tussled hair and trembling form.

My heart raced, absorbing so much at once.

Q came up behind and slapped my ass. "Stand in the centre of the room." The scent of alcohol warned Q's inhibitions were completely gone. Maybe I shouldn't have agreed until he was sober.

When I didn't move, Q grabbed my throat, sending arcs of fear and want through me. "Obey, *esclave.*"

He let me go and I scampered to the centre of the room. My feet sank into thick, silver-white strands of the carpet. Facing the magnificent fireplace, I noticed carvings of foxes hunted by hounds, and deer impaled on spikes. At first glance, it was pretty and fanciful. But when studied, it writhed with hunger to kill and maim.

A sliver of terror darted down my back; I looked behind for Q. He stood by the wall, pulling on a lever.

Tinkling sounded from above, and I craned my neck as chains with leather cuffs descended.

My throat closed. He wanted to restrain me like he had in the sparrow room. Panic flared, turning my heated blood into a volcanic eruption.

Q's hot form pressed behind mine. I trembled as he rubbed his erection against my ass. "Put your hands up, *esclave.*"

I agreed to do anything he wanted, but I didn't have the courage to go through this again. All I could think about was the Russian and his knife.

Shaking my head, I whimpered, "I'll do anything but this."

He sucked in a harsh breath. "You're disobeying?" His tone held nightmares. "I'll punish you if you don't put your arms up immediately."

I bit my lip. The force of the command buckled me, and I slowly raised my arms. Everything Q was about to do would put my entire mind set to the test. I would either fall head long into love, or break completely. I wanted this to hurt. I wanted to feel every inch. I wanted to remember it for the rest of my life. And if it meant tying me up again, so be it. Perhaps it would replace the memories of the Russian and his knife, just like Q replaced the rape with himself and the shower.

My eyes fluttered closed as Q secured my wrists in the leather cuffs. When the last buckle was tight, I whispered, "I have one request, if I may, master?"

Q pressed his face against my neck, licking the bite he'd given earlier. "One request and no more. Make it count."

I trembled and opened the remaining barriers inside. This request was for me. Only for me. "I want you to call me Tess."

He froze, cock hard against me, chest against my back. A minute ticked past before he murmured, "You want to link your name to this? But you fought so hard to keep it from me."

I nodded, swallowing as he rocked his hips once, causing me to sway forward in the bindings. "I know. But I want you call me by my name. I want to know you own me." My core clenched and I moaned as Q found my breast, twisting my nipple so hard it erupted into flames.

"As you wish, *esclave*. Every time I call you Tess, remember I can do anything I want to you. I fucking own you."

"Yes."

"After tonight, every time I say your name you'll get wet for me. I not only own your body but your identity, too. Do you deny it?"

"No, I don't deny it. I'm yours. Through and through."

With another twist of a nipple, Q strode toward the fireplace. I stood meekly in my cuffs, watching.

He didn't load the fire with logs or fumble with matches. One click and gas flames roared, immediately searing.

Q faced me, running hands over his head. He shed the remaining tipsy haze, cloaking himself with sovereignty. Stalking forward, he pulled silver scissors from a pocket.

I gulped and didn't say a word as he stopped a breath away. Snipping the scissors once with a tight smile, he grabbed the hem of my t-shirt and cut.

The blade tickled my stomach, up between my breasts, until the collar broke apart and it hung in tatters. Q clenched his jaw, cutting away my bra and shorts. With a hot look beneath heavy eyes, he snipped my knickers and watched as they fluttered to the floor.

I stood in naked glory, spreading wings of fearful happiness.

Gathering the ruined clothing, he threw them in the fire. The smell of burning filled the room and the drunken lust on Q's face magnified to desperate proportions.

I couldn't stop how fast I breathed, and hated when Q disappeared behind me. I heard the sounds of latches being undone and a heavy lid creaking open. Things tinkled and clanked sending imagination into overdrive. I strained to look over my shoulder, mouth hanging open at the toys and apparatus in the mirrored chest.

Silence descended, apart from the hiss of flames; I grew more and more uncomfortable. Anticipation played with my mind. *What am I doing? I don't want this. I don't want pain and humiliation.* I should say the safe word and admit this was a huge mistake. I shouldn't be chained, naked, allowing a man to do anything he wanted. He could kill me and there was nothing I could do to stop it.

A slithering sound came from behind, and I tensed. I didn't want to know what it was. Q paced behind, footsteps almost silent on the carpet. "Seeing as I've got you in such a compromising position. I'm going to use it to my benefit." His voice was gravelly with sin.

Oh, God. I wanted to ask what he meant, but he stopped directly behind, a few metres away. Why was he so far?

"How long have you fantasised about being *fucked?* Tortured? Used completely?" He stressed the word fuck; it resonated with erotic waves in my belly. It had to be the most graphic, raw question anyone ever asked.

But it was also a question begging for a lie. I couldn't tell him that ever since hitting puberty I craved something I didn't know. I gave myself orgasms to thoughts of domination and fear. I pressed lips together, not answering.

Out of nowhere, my shoulder blade licked with the pain of a thousand bees. The snap and crack of a whip echoed around the room.

I cried out, jerking in the restraints.

He fucking whipped me! The pain radiated along my back, warm, hot, biting. My stomach tangled with regret. I didn't sign up to be hit and abused. I signed up to be fucked ruthlessly. Tears erupted as another crack and kiss of agony landed. My spine screamed and the wetness between my legs increased.

"Answer me, Tess. How long? How badly? I need to know."

I whimpered, hanging my head. "All along. My mind's been sick for as long as I can remember. It horrifies me. I can't control it. It ruined my relationship with a sweet man, all because I need to be fucked, rather than made love to." The truth cascaded off my tongue in one seamless stream. "I need it. So bad you have no idea."

He chuckled. "Oh, I have some idea." The whip struck again, licking with agony.

"Stop!" I cried, letting tears run free.

"Does the whip make you wet? Make you desperate?"

"Yes! Shit, yes. So much."

Q laughed, it was dark and edgy, and so full of need, my heart twisted. He needed to inflict pain—I couldn't take that from him.

The whip cracked again, but instead of tensing and bracing, I welcomed the lash. My body melted into acceptance and flesh became pliant.

"Tell me your darkest fantasy," he ordered, pacing, the slither of the whip trailing soft footsteps.

I moaned, images flashed into my head of hair fisting, spanking, and bondage. He knew what I liked—he *knew*. But I didn't know what he liked. I curled my bound hands. "Everything you do to me is a fantasy. I want to know yours.

How dark do you want? How much further would you go?"

Q hit lower, licking my lower back and ass. "You aren't allowed to ask questions." Every strike burned, but rather than cripple with abuse, it changed me. I became a phoenix with a flaming back, welcoming the whip's kiss. My body accepted the lash, not on my back, but in my core. Heat cranked to bonfire.

"Please, I need to know. Please…"

Q stopped whipping. I didn't think he'd answer, but his breath kissed my neck, whispering, "You aren't ready to hear the depths of my depravity, *esclave*." He spanked my ass with one firm, biting hand. I groaned.

Even though the pain was multi-dimensional and I equally enjoyed and hated it, I tried to get free. It wasn't the whip punishing—it was being held in perfect submission. I couldn't retaliate. I couldn't twist or run. I could only hang and accept whatever Q gave.

Q backed up, murmuring, "Your skin is beautiful whipped, Tess, blooming pink and red. I think a few more colours are needed. Perhaps a deep maroon."

The crack gave a second warning, before an intense sting buckled my knees; I swung in delirium. The lash held pent up emotion. Fear overrode again. Gone were the tantalizing questions, this was pure violence.

"This is for calling the police on me." Q whipped hard.

"This is for running away." Another agonising kiss.

"This is for making me so consumed by sin, I can no longer think straight." Q grunted as he connected with flesh. I sobbed, wailing for him to stop. The crisscross burns stripped me to my soul.

Q threw the whip at my feet, cradling me in his arms. "It's okay… stop crying." His linen suit rasped against my tender back as he soothed. The throbbing heat kept time with my heartbeats. I sucked heavy lungfuls of air. *Is it over?* "You're fucking with my mind," I breathed through my tears.

Q's hand headed down my belly, inching lower until he cupped me. "No, I'm fucking *for* your mind. I told you, I want to own you—body, heart, everything."

I moaned as he circled my clit, nibbling my ear. "Tell me. Did you like being whipped?" He thrust a finger inside with no warning, arms banding tighter as I bucked in surprise. "Tell me the truth."

I couldn't think straight; I mumbled, "I didn't like it, but I liked giving you what you need. It made me wet knowing you enjoyed it."

"You think you didn't enjoy it... but your body bent to the whip. Listen to what it's telling you. Let it be your master." Q sucked in a breath, finger pulsing inside before withdrawing. He brought his hand to my mouth. "You're wet. So wet. Suck my finger, Tess."

I opened, welcoming. My nose was stuffy from crying and I couldn't get enough breath, but his taste of citrus mixed with me and the pain he caused branded with lust.

I rocked into his erection, silently pleading.

He stepped away, leaving me hanging like the captive I was. Q was wrong when he said being owned by him wasn't romantic or sexy or fun. I'd never felt this way. This uninhibited. This *free*.

The world went black as Q fixed a blindfold over my eyes, tying it securely. His fingers grazed my neck, sending goosebumps and shivers skimming over my nakedness. I grew too hot thanks to the fire and perspiration dotted my upper lip.

"I'm going to take control of you now, Tess."

I nodded erratically, heart beating wildly out of control.

Q grabbed my breast with one hand. Something sharp pinched on my nipple. I wished I could see what it was. Cupping my other breast, the weight of whatever he clamped dangled with an uncomfortable sensation.

Q murmured, *"J'adore tes seins."* I love your tits.

The same pinching weight attached to my other nipple, sending shooting stars of need through an invisible link to my core.

I pulsed in time to blood throbbing in my nipples and whip marks. I whimpered as pain blossomed as more blood rushed.

Q grabbed the back of my neck, smothering my mouth with his. His tongue wrangled mine into yielding, our breaths mingled.

I moaned, becoming drunk on the taste of him.

Breathing hard, he stopped kissing me, and something soft and leathery danced along my stomach. I clenched, trying to figure out what it was. I hated the blindfold—the lack of eyesight. It made everything so much more aware, anxious, and sensitive.

Q sucked in a breath. "Every welt I give you makes me so fucking hard."

I groaned as leather bit into my stomach, right on my pubis. I tried to double over but the restraints kept me arched—available for whatever torture he planned.

"You want to know how dark I'll go? I want blood. I want you sobbing at my feet. I want you in fucking tatters. Does that scare you?"

Another strike, this time just below my breasts. My rib injury flared with pain, and the nipple clamps jiggled as I twisted, trying to run. I couldn't deny the tension of being completely at his mercy made my pussy throb, but I couldn't understand why. Why did being a submissive turn me on? Why did inflicting pain turn Q on?

My voice was barely audible. "Yes, it scares me. Deliciously terrifies." My honesty shocked both of us. Breathing hard, I asked, "Why do you want to hurt me, *maître?*"

Q lashed out, slapping my cheek with a gentle palm. It didn't hurt, but tears oozed beneath my blind fold. "I revoke your permission to speak."

I hung my head, chastised. Guess, I wouldn't know.

Q paced in a circle around me, dragging the flogger over my skin. "It's not about hurting you, sweet Tess. It's about branding you. Your skin is pure as snow, and I get to mark it." He flogged my ass again. It caught a whip mark and blazed with agony. "It's the wrongness, the rightness, I need your pain." He whispered in my ear, "I'm invincible when I hurt you."

Images of dark terror filled me. Every muscle in my body screamed to run. The safe word danced on my tongue. *I'm stronger than this. I invited this. I won't say it... not yet.*

Q hit me particularly hard. It made the bee sting seem like a giant wasp, but I didn't make a sound.

He groaned, tracing a finger over the new injury. "So fucking perfect."

I breathed shallowly, wanting to see. *Needing* to see.

"You deserve a reward, Tess," he said it so sweetly, as if I was a good girl and earned a lollipop. But his domination made me very aware I wouldn't be getting an ice-cream.

The pain once again morphed to tender hooks of passion, and I welcomed the burn. Welcomed the marks Q branded.

He ripped the blindfold off, kissing me, holding my hair so I couldn't move away as he fucked my mouth with a tongue that wouldn't let me breathe.

I gasped and choked, but the moment he left, I wanted more. I wanted to die with him kissing me.

With glinting pale eyes, Q folded to his knees in front of me. "Put your legs over my shoulders," he demanded.

I blinked. "My legs on your shoulders?" I flushed with embarrassment at the thought of him so close to my pussy— spread and exposed. I was so wet it trickled down my thigh. I shook my head, unable to be so vulnerable.

Q reached and slapped my ass. His hand connected with whip marks; I yelped.

"Do as I command, *Tess.*" He stressed my name and it did exactly as he wanted. It reminded he owned me, therefore I had no choice.

Hesitantly, I cocked one leg, placing it on his shoulder. His eyes dropped to my centre, face darkening with need. Self-consciousness painted my cheeks. When my other leg stayed firmly planted on the ground, he glared. "You have two legs. Put them on my shoulders." His voice rasped, chest working hard.

His passion granted a burst of feminine courage. Jumping, I shifted my weight to the cuffs and I straddled Q's shoulders—suspended, completely at his mercy. His arms came up to hold my ass, biceps clenching. He didn't tear his gaze away from my pussy. "You're so fucking beautiful." He kissed my inner thigh in a fleeting move, breath hot. "Here's your reward for letting me hurt you." His voice deepened to brimstone and my head snapped back as his mouth latched onto my clit.

My legs spread on his shoulders gave full access, and he took advantage.

His tongue wasn't shy, swirling around my clit, licking, sucking. Plunging into my wetness, tongue-fucking as if possessed.

It was too much. Too intense. I moaned and whimpered and struggled and wriggled. Little stars shot and fizzled and tormented with every flick of his tongue, every suck of his mouth.

He pressed his tongue so far inside I cried out, wishing it was his cock buried deep. "Please, master...more..." My body was beyond ready to be claimed, bruised, reawakened into passionate pleasure.

The whip marks heated unbearably, my skin rivered with sweat from the fire, and nipples screamed for relief. I rocked my hips into Q, forcing his tongue deeper, demanding him to be rougher.

"Fuck yes," he groaned, fingers digging into my hips

as he dragged me closer. His entire face between my legs. He growled as he bit my clit. Not a simple nip—but a full savage bite.

I screamed as my pussy contracted, thrumming with its own heartbeat. I thrashed, trying to get closer, trying to get away. *I want more. I can't handle more.*

My mind broke completely, ruled by the need to come. "Fuck me, Q. Fuck me. I can't... I can't stand it."

He pushed my thighs, and I melted off him. He stood lightning quick as I swung from the ceiling, trembling. My head lolled, and my eyes were too heavy to keep open. I wanted to scissor my legs to find some relief from the torture. Q turned me from rational woman into a craving addict who needed a fix. I needed his cock. I needed my master.

Q captured my jaw; I opened unwilling eyes. "You can't stand it. Can you?" His sexy five o' clock shadow glistened from eating me out. I swung forward, wanting to lick him, to clean him. My mouth watered at the thought of sucking him. I wanted to bite his cock just like he'd bitten me. I wanted it so much, I'd explode if I didn't get it.

I tried to make sentences form. "I can't stand the thought of not having you fuck me."

His eyes snapped closed before he regained control, murmuring, "You've submitted completely, and you have no idea what that does to me."

I had an idea. The same insane, mind-crippling feeling he did to me. If I wasn't restrained, I'd pounce on him and fuck him till the tingly, urgent, consuming need disappeared. The only problem was, I didn't think it would ever disappear. And I didn't want it to.

"Say it again, Tess." Q let me go, unbuttoning his blazer.

I breathed hard, panting as he ripped the jacket off, dropping it on the floor.

"Fuck me, master. I can't stand not having you."

He groaned, kicking off his shoes as he undid his tie. An evil glint entered his eyes. He slid the cream tie in his fingertips, looking at it then back to me.

My heart lurched as he advanced. "Open."

I shook my head. "No. I won't be able to breathe."

"You'll breathe around it. You can bite down."

I clamped my mouth, moaning as he forced the tie between my lips, tying it. Once secured, he kissed my gagged mouth, running the tip of his tongue along my bottom lip. "You look *incroyable* gagged and bound, *esclave*. I'll suffer the embarrassment of coming in my trousers every time I think of tonight."

Stepping back, he stripped. Not bothering to undo buttons, he tore his shirt open. Pings of plastic sounded as buttons flew wild.

My mouth dried, taking in his perfection. His smooth chest, cut with perfect muscles. Sparrows fluttered, inked in blacks and browns, seeming alive with their feathered detail. He undid his belt, then his fly, and stepped from his trousers.

Standing proud with only black boxer-briefs remaining, Q fondled his thick erection while staring. His eyes zeroed in on my nipple clamped breasts. "Your flesh is so swollen, Tessie."

I jerked. *Tessie.* Brax's nickname for me. Guilt washed over me like a tsunami and I coughed with pain. I'd betrayed Brax in the worst possible way. I was a disloyal bitch.

Q prowled close, looping fingers though the gag. "What did I say? Why do you hurt?"

I looked down, trying hard to push Brax away. I shouldn't care, but I did. It was a mistake to ask Q to call me by my name. Tess might love the sadistic erotic games with Q, but Tessie... she belonged to a simpler past.

Our eyes locked, and Q seemed to understand. "You don't like it when I call you that."

I wished I felt differently but a tear rolled, and I

nodded.

He licked the droplet. "I don't care for Tessie either. You're mine. My Tess."

My eyes glazed and I swooned into him. Guilt evaporated and my lust returned a thousand fold. I came to life under his stare.

And he knew it. He pulled his cock free, wrapping fingers around the thick girth, stroking hard. "Do you like it when I call you that? Mine? All fucking mine."

I shook my head, just to be troublesome. I couldn't look away from Q stroking himself. I arched my back, trying to find relief by rubbing tortured nipples on his chest.

He shuddered, pumping his cock. Reaching with his other hand, he speared two fingers inside, stealing my wetness to smear over the tip, using my lubricant as his own.

I groaned and my body unravelled. My pussy clutched nothing, needing him inside. Nothing else mattered in the world but having him. I wanted to scream at him to fuck me, but the bloody gag turned my words to moans.

He pressed his cock against my stomach, hitting me with it. I moaned and thrashed, trying to get closer.

"Put your legs around my hips." Q held out his arms, ready to catch me.

Finally. *Yes. Yes.*

I jumped, spreading my legs at the same time, using the binds to hoist myself. I fitted snug against him. His hotness against my wetness. His throbbing cock so close, it made me insane.

His eyes flashed as I rocked, smearing sensual liquid all over his cock and balls. He groaned as I thrust unashamedly, providing much needed friction. I could come like this. Humping my master like a dog in heat.

Reaching between us, he pushed me back. Guiding his cock, he angled to meet my entrance.

In one fast move, with hands on my hips, he pulled me onto him. Impaling me completely. His length hit the top of my womb, bruising, stretching. The invasion turned my mind to mush. I went rigid, moaning like the whore I was.

Q's face darkened with savage lust as he thrust once, fingers stabbing into flesh. "Fuck, my cock belongs in you." With one hand, he slapped my breast, activating the clamp to squeeze, sending hurt and spasms of eager dampness between my legs. I wouldn't last long. Shit, I was so close, I rippled with release already. An orgasm teetered on a knife-edge—sharp and deadly.

He rolled his hips, meticulously slowly, dragging every ridge of him along every ridge of me. I wanted to scream. I didn't want slow. I wanted a rampage.

"Raise your eyes," Q ordered.

I guided super heavy eyes from watching his cock fucking me, locking with his. Pale jade fire blazed with demons he kept locked away. They flittered ghostlike, swarming, urging him to lose control.

He growled and thrust once.

Twice.

Three times with ecstasy.

I tossed my head, chewing on the gag, needing to moan, to vocalize just how much he violated me—how much further I wanted him to go.

He bucked again, grinding his teeth. "I hate you for making me break my vow." His face twisted with self-loathing and black delight. *"Qu'est ce que tu es en train de me faire?"* What are you doing to me?

Before I could answer, Q lost all control. Baring his teeth, he dropped the barrier to his demons, pounding into me. There was no rocking, or gentle lovemaking. He pistoned hips into mine, grunting, sweating, a crazed look in his eye. His manicured nails raked my ass, digging deep like rabid claws, inflicting pain in other ways.

The gag barricaded my screams. I bounced in his arms, breasts jiggling with every thrust. The room erupted with the sounds of heavy breathing and slapping sweaty skin. The air temperature was too hot. Q was too much. My body couldn't handle the sensory overload.

Oh, God. Oh, God. I'm coming...

"Tu es à moi." You're mine. Q leaned back, using my weight as a counter leaver, driving upward. His cock so hot and hard, stretching me to breaking point.

My heart sprouted wings, and flew. The build-up of the release rose and rose, never peaking. Fear laced with need. *Too intense.* I didn't think I'd survive it.

The gag blocked air, and the lack of oxygen made my head swim. All I could think about was Q and his nails and his cock and his ragged breathing.

Q leaned back further, head falling as he fucked impossibly harder. His hipbones bruised my inner thighs as he gave me the rampage I needed.

"Fuck, Tess. Fuck yes. Take it. *Putain, ta chatte est faite pour ma bite.'*Fuck, your cunt fits my cock so well.

I couldn't do it. I couldn't hold it any longer. My entire body split in half, but the release *still* didn't crest.

Please, please, God. I need... I can't. I... I...

"Look at me," Q growl-panted.

I obeyed and drowned in his smouldering green. Tension thrummed, consuming, and another element stole us. We were no longer master and slave. We were two rutting animals focused on one goal.

"Master, please..." I begged around the material in my mouth.

Q stiffened with power, thrusting as his eyes flared wide and lips parted. "I'll give you what you want." His body convulsed and a low angry groan ripped from his throat. A hot pulse of semen filled and that was all I needed.

I combusted.

Every atom in my body detonated and fired. My pussy fisted around Q's relentless erection and I screamed. Q's mouth latched onto my neck, biting. I transcended from my mere mortal body, riding wave after wave of eye-popping, brain-splintering euphoria.

Q grunted, thrusting in time to my release; his teeth never let up on my collarbone and a slick trail of blood trickled from my throat where he bit. Some primal part of my brain went wild. I loved that he needed me so bad, he broke my skin. I loved how delicate his tongue was, lapping up my essence.

I shuddered as swell after swell continued, slowly getting less intense. My feet cramped and my entire body felt as if I'd been run over.

With trembling fingers, Q undid my gag, then my wrists. Catching my weight, he cradled me, folding us the floor. We fell in a tangle of limbs onto the thick white carpet, covering it with sweat, come, and drops of blood.

Q didn't withdraw, and somehow managed to twist me so I faced away. Not saying a word, he tucked me closer, spooning me with his hard body.

His heart thudded against my back, matching the erratic pace of mine.

I snuggled closer, blissfully content. Q hurt me, but adored me, all at the same time. He gave me everything I needed. The intimacy between us couldn't be described and I shivered as he unclamped my nipples, rubbing them gently.

He sighed deeply and yawned. The alcohol in his system no doubt left him depleted.

You used me, but you kept me safe. I tried to transmit the thought. My body wasn't capable of speech. Q mumbled something, pulling me closer.

The sun pinked the sky outside and Q twitched, already drifting into oblivion.

Tonight had changed my life. Q may make my soul weep and tear itself into pieces but he made it operatic with joy, too. My soul didn't just sing, it rejoiced.

I finally found a place where my twistedness

belonged.

In Q's arms.

Chapter Twenty-one

Pheasant

Pain and achiness woke me.

Memories of last night swirled, thick and fast. My body clenched, remembering Q's rampant fucking, his drunken ramblings about girls and winter. He gave clues; I just had to figure out the metaphors to understand.

And I wasn't capable right now. My brain was sludge, body hissing with lashes and bruises. I felt used, abused, and entirely adored.

I shifted, trying to get comfortable. The thick carpet cushioned, but also tickled. Q moaned and held me tighter, a muscular arm banded around my stomach. Incredibly, he was still inside, flaccid but still big enough for me to be very aware of the intrusion.

I rocked my hips a little, trying to rouse him.

His breathing changed from deep to shallow. Slowly, he stiffened, filling me like a balloon, stretching until I ached with reminders of how hard he took me last night.

I bit my lip as his nose brushed aside tangled hair, kissing softly.

With a soft groan, he rocked.

My eyes closed as dexterous fingers captured my nipple, rolling tenderly. So different from the angry dominance from last night. Q wasn't the one fucking me this morning. It was Quincy.

I moaned, pushing back, matching his rock. We languished and delighted, not chasing a body-splitting orgasm, but more a gentle glow.

His hand trailed from breast to core, playing with my clit as the rock turned serious, claiming.

I whimpered as Q wrapped his leg around mine, trapping me. With the extra purchase, he thrust, pressing upward, hitting the top of my womb.

"I never thought I'd enjoy vanilla," he mumbled into my hair.

I froze. What did he mean? He'd never shared intimacy before? The gentleness of sex compared to angry rutting?

His breathing caught, not noticing I'd withdrawn, trying to analyse what he meant. His fingers smeared my clit with wetness, rubbing erotically, giving me no choice but to pay attention.

"Come for me, *esclave*." His order was breathless; his leg wrapped around mine, tensed.

He thrust harder, tainted with some of the violence I was used to from Q. Pinching my clit, he forced me to come. My body clenched and quivered, welcoming Q's orgasm as he filled me with his seed. His soft moan sent my heart fluttering, and I smiled.

We must have drifted again. I woke to a knock.

Q flinched, unwrapping himself from around me. Our skin popped slightly as suction tried to keep us together. Q grumbled, holding his head. "*Merde,* how much did I drink last night?"

I laughed softly. "Enough to ramble about birds and girls and…" My voice drifted. Sadness replaced my post conjugal glow. "I'm number fifty-eight."

Air chilled as Q froze. "What?" His eyes flared with panic. "I said that?" He scooted upright, wincing.

I couldn't tear my gaze away from his trim, toned body. His heavy cock still glistened from being inside me. The sparrow tattoo filled me with sorrow for some inexplicable reason.

"Can you tell me now? What do the birds have to do with the fifty-seven slaves you've had before me?"

Q swiped a hand over his face, pacing away. Gathering his trousers, he refused to look at me. Pulling them on, he didn't bother with underwear. I hadn't seen his tattoo from behind, but the cloud looked ominous and evil. A nightmare of thorns and branches trying to devour innocent little birds.

My gaze fell, unable to look any longer. I gasped. Everywhere, my skin was purple with faint bruises and pink with abrasions from the flogger. I twisted, hissing between my teeth to look at my back. Lashes crossed in a lattice pattern, flaming with soreness. He hadn't broken the skin, but damn, it hurt.

Slinging his buttonless shirt on, Q spun around. He passed me a fur blanket from the bed. "You'll have to wear this to your room, seeing as I burned your clothes."

I glared. "Are you deliberately ignoring my question?"

He shut down. Eyes hazy with a hangover, jaw clenched. I couldn't understand his aloofness. His coldness.

The knock came again, interrupting the building tension.

Q sighed, withdrawing even further. "I have to go."

I stood proudly, not covering myself in the blanket. I wanted him to see what he did to me. How I wore the marks with passion. They showed everything I'd become. I was no longer virgin snow. I was claimed. Used.

"You're going to leave in the middle of a discussion?"

His eyes fell to my ruined body, heat and distress flickering over his face. "Don't confuse what happened last night. It was fucking between a drunk master and his slave. You gave me what I wanted. But it's morning, and other things demand my attention."

He couldn't have hurt me more if he tried. My eyes narrowed, stinging with tears. "That's bullshit, and you know it."

He shrugged. "Believe what you want to believe, *esclave.* I'm leaving."

My heart shut down. *Esclave.* Not Tess. He disowned me so simply.

Before I could ask what the hell was going on, he unlocked the door and disappeared.

I took the walk of shame down the circular stairs and into my bedroom. I showered and rubbed arnica into my bruises, before slipping on a beautiful grey dress I found hanging in the wardrobe.

I no longer had aversions to Q dressing me. After what he did last night, a simple wardrobe preference seemed trivial. I let him flay me open in every sense, but instead of feeling treasured and complete, I felt empty and regretful. He did things I never thought I could agree to, yet I never used the safe word. Because I felt *safe* with him.

But that was another lie. He ruined that safety when he left with no explanation. My jaw ached from clenching so hard. Q had no right to shut down and leave. *He has every right. He's your master.*

He's more than that—even if he denies it until he passes out.

I brushed my hair with fierce strokes. Maybe I deluded myself into believing he felt more than he did. He admitted to having fifty-seven women before…what did little ole me matter?

His drunk rambling echoed in my mind. *Winter. Birds. Thawing.*

I dropped the brush.

Holy fuck. Could it be true? Q bought women, not to abuse them, but to *save* them?

My mind couldn't comprehend it. Not after the music of demons inside, not after everything he did to me. But my heart fluttered with hope.

Needing to learn the truth, I bolted from the room.

I found Suzette in the kitchen slicing carrots; she barely acknowledged me. Dark clouds rolled over the spring sunshine, casting shadows.

Mrs. Sucre gave me a half-hearted smile before disappearing into the pantry. My skin pricked with unwelcome. I was a traitor, an outcast.

I moved forward, pressing against the countertop, not entering the massive kitchen. I wasn't brave enough to encroach on Suzette's domain while she glared machetes at me.

Unbearable silence thickened; the house had a weird vibe. Tense, static, as if a storm brewed within.

Whiplashes twinged as I hunched. I had no right to feel ignored. What happened with the police was my fault.

"Suzette... what happened last night? Why didn't the police arrest Q?" I started with an easy question. I needed to break the ice before confirming my suspicions. It made sense though—Suzette told me all along Q rescued her, but I'd been too pig-headed to listen.

She pursed her lips, eyes narrowed. "What do you think happened? The police came and accused Q of kidnapping you."

"But they left. They must've found Q innocent, if they didn't press charges."

Suzette scoffed. "So much you don't know, *esclave.* Things you've lost the right to learn."

My stomach twisted. I didn't realize how much I valued Suzette's friendship. "I didn't call the police. I called my boyfriend and told him about Q, but... that's all."

She stopped chopping. "And you think that makes it okay?" She closed her eyes, visibly forcing away her black mood. When she reopened, her hazel eyes sparkled, but no longer furious. "I know you were terrified when you first arrived. I know you suffered in Mexico. I know you missed your boyfriend—I can't hate you for being a fighter, for running, for being brave. I just wish you'd given us more time before judging and making a bad decision." She picked up the knife and resumed slicing.

Chills darted down my back. She spoke in past tense...

Mrs. Sucre opened an oven, and heavenly scents of cinnamon and sugar wafted as she removed perfectly cooked sweet buns. She placed them in front of me, waving a tea-towel, causing little wisps of steam to curl.

I tried to ignore my racing heartbeats. I hated this feeling. This eerie sense of loss. "Mrs. Sucre. Have you seen Master Mercer? I need to speak with him."

Suzette stiffened but didn't look up.

She shook her head. "No. He left half an hour or so ago. I doubt he'll be home for a while."

Sadness rushed; I gripped the countertop. He left without a goodbye. *What did you expect? Just because you let him whip you last night, you thought things would be different?*

It shouldn't hurt so much... it was to be expected. It was a week-day and he had an empire to run. But he didn't just leave this morning. He ran. Something wasn't right. "Oh," was all I managed.

Mrs. Sucre gave me a compassionate look, sharp brown eyes assessing. With a soft smile, she passed me a warm bun. "Best eat, child. Never know when you'll eat again."

I locked eyes with her, shivers darting down my back. "Why won't I know?" Instincts roared to life and I ran around the countertop to grab her wrist. "What do you mean?"

Suzette watched with wide eyes, anger changing to sadness. She opened her mouth to speak, but a masculine baritone came from behind me.

"She means your stay with us has come to an end, *esclave.*"

No.

Letting Mrs. Sucre go, I spun to face Franco. He stood, crisp and sharp, black shades on his head, the same folder Q first showed me when I arrived from Mexico in his hands. The file the kidnappers created. The file referring to me only as Blonde Girl on Scooter.

My heart convulsed. Q knew what he was doing the entire time. I was unbelievably stupid not to see it. Asking for one night to do what he wished. One night, because that's all he needed. Then he kicked me out. The user. The *bastard*.

Franco came closer; I scuttled back, bumping into the warm, soft body of Mrs. Sucre. By throwing me out, Q tore me from people who cared more than my parents. The maternal comfort of Mrs. Sucre, the strange sisterhood with Suzette. Even my weird connection to Franco.

It was all over.

Franco smiled, but it didn't reach his eyes. He stopped in front of me. Mrs. Sucre placed her hands on my shoulders, offering support as Franco ducked to one knee and sliced through the GPS tracker with a knife. It fell off my ankle, clattering to the tiles.

The symbolism that Q no longer cared slapped like a bitch. He'd removed his protection, his strange affection. He was throwing me back to a world full of Brutes and Drivers.

"That's it then? I have no say?" I fissured, hurting beyond comprehension. Q was too spineless to do this himself. He ordered his staff to remove me like an unwanted pet. I laughed morbidly. "I'm to be put down like some rabid poodle." It might be best if I was shot. How would I cope with everything?

Franco chuckled. "Hardly, *esclave*. You're going home."

Home. The word didn't conjure happiness and belonging anymore. It was foreign and bleak.

Q cast me back to a world I never wanted to return to. Tossing me out like the unwanted Christmas present.

Mrs. Sucre squeezed my shoulders, before dropping her hands and pushing me toward Franco. "Go, now. Put this all behind you."

I dashed to Suzette, capturing her hands. Her eyes flashed to mine; her pity made my heart bleed. "I don't want to go, Suzette. Running away was a huge mistake. You'll explain to Q and let me stay, won't you? You keep saying I'm good for him. That he's a better man than I know. I want to be worthy, Suzette. I want to stay and hear his story."

She unlatched my fingers, stepping back. "I know, Tess, but it's too late. Q brokered a deal with the police. No charges will be brought against him if he sends you home. This is the only way."

My heart ached so much it hurt to breathe. That was how he got the police to stay away. Giving me up to save his own ass.

"No! I can't go. I want to stay. I *need* to stay."

Franco appeared, gathering me in strong, prison-like arms. "Come along. We're on a deadline." And just like that, he carted me from the kitchen, away from Suzette, away from my new life.

As we walked through the lounge, I briefly contemplated hitting him and running. I could lock myself in the bedroom, and wait for Q to tell me himself he didn't want me. But Franco was too strong. It would be pointless.

Franco marched me out the door, chuckling wryly. "Funny, how this began with me pushing you through the door to bow to your new master." He laughed again before adding, "Never had to kick a slave out before."

The lash marks Q gave me last night stood out in stark relief as my skin whitened in panic, reality hitting home. There was no stopping this. "I hated you that day and I hate you now."

He nodded. "I understand, but I'm only following orders."

In the same manicured field, with its windsock and landing lights, rested Q's private plane with his initials. Wind whipped my hair into a snarl; black clouds above built with rain.

Seeing a chance, I said, "Should we really fly in such weather? It's not safe." I dug my heels in, trying to get free from Franco's grasp. "Please, Franco. I want to stay. Call Q. Let me speak to him."

He shook his head, propelling me toward the plane as if I wasn't fighting at all. "Q doesn't want to see you again, *esclave*. I'm sorry to say, but you've caused enough problems in his life." His words stung but his tone was kind, sad.

I hung my head, giving in. Why fight? I couldn't change my fate.

Franco helped me up the flight of steps and into the immaculate jet. Cream leather and honey wood was a prison. I slouched in the same chair as when I first flew. The same horror and grief from that night filled my lungs. *I'm crazy. I'm going home!* I should be excited.

The reoccurring theme in my life happened again. My parents didn't want me. Brax didn't fight to keep me. And Q... Q stole everything and then tossed me back into the shark infested waters of the world.

My hands curled. One thing was for sure, if Q was so heartless to do this, he didn't deserve me. I glared at Franco as he loomed.

"It's been fun, Tess. Just sit back and relax. We'll have you home very soon." He turned, and disappeared into the cockpit.

An airhostess appeared. Her blonde hair in a French twist and white uniform blazed with Q's initials right over her breast. I wanted to hurt her. I wanted to rip the uniform off and steal it. If anyone deserved to have Q's initials branded over her tit, it was me. Shit, he'd owned every part of me last night.

Hot anger flowed and I wished I could tell Q exactly what I thought of him. The low-life coward.

He marked me to the core, all the while knowing he was sending me away. How did I not sense that? How did he lie so successfully?

Tears clouded my vision as the plane taxied, bumping on manicured grass. With a whir of sleek engines, we galloped down the strip, soaring into the air with a gust of turbulence and wind.

I twisted in my seat as Q's pastel mansion shrank from imposing to miniature. Pressing a cold hand on the window, I gulped as black storm clouds swallowed the view, sending me into darkness.

Q stole my hopes and dreams, replacing my feelings with blackness and emptiness.

I was broken.

We crossed timelines in silence. Refuelled in places I didn't care to know.

In a matter of hours, I left behind spring in France, and touched down in autumn Australia.

We taxied toward a private hangar while the moon danced in silver clouds. We left behind a gathering storm to arrive in a perfect, balmy night.

"Time to leave, *esclave*." Franco appeared from the cockpit, holding out his arm to disembark.

My stomach filled with lead; I uncurled from my seat and stepped off the plane. I had no energy to scream or convince

Franco this was a huge mistake. My brain hadn't shut up the entire flight, and I was drained. There was no point rehashing everything when Q no longer cared.

I followed like a good sheep as Franco led me into a building reserved for exclusive arrivals. I looked over my shoulder to stare one last time at Q's plane. It would be the last thing I would see of his.

My heart squeezed and hardened. Calligraphy letters—*Q.M*—taunted me. The plane belonged to a different world. A world I was no longer privileged to enjoy.

I grew from timid girl with secret fantasies, to a fighter who would happily kill her captors in Mexico, to a strong woman who embraced her true desires, to a broken, tired girl who only wanted to sleep and forget—a full, sick circle.

I did the unthinkable: I broke myself, and fell for my master.

Fuck you, Q.

I stared at the floor as Franco spoke rapidly to a customs officer, handing over what I assumed was fake documentation. A conversation later and a nod from both men, Franco placed his hand on the small of my back, pushing me from airside to Melbourne soil.

Warm, dry Australian air swirled with a gentle breeze. Despite the fact I didn't want to be here, I sucked in a lungful. The scents of Melbourne tickled memories and a small wave of comfort descended. Home.

I just have to relearn how to belong. The thought overwhelmed. I had to go back to fibbing to myself and Brax. Go through the motions of living with no excitement or intoxicating thread of sexual fear. Oh, God.

Franco grunted as I slammed to a halt. "Keep going, escl—, I mean, Ms. Snow."

I spun to face him. "Take me back. I don't belong

here anymore."

He scowled. "I can't take you back. The French police will know. That was the deal. Mr. Mercer has a long standing arrangement with the authorities."

My ears pricked. "What long standing arrangement?"

Franco sighed, glaring. "For a slave, you ask a lot of damn questions."

"I'm no longer a slave. Tell me."

He grumbled. "If you'd listened and paid attention, Mr. Mercer isn't in the game of keeping slaves."

The revelation wasn't earth-shattering, I had figured out as much. Q and his frustrating tipsy comments. "Give me something I don't know. I'm number fifty-eight. That means he's had fifty-seven before. That makes him a dealer in women." I couldn't stand it. The thought of Q having so many women made me want to kick and punch and scream. Now I was gone, there would be more. Undoubtedly. "But I know he did it for the right reasons. He helped them… didn't he?" I wanted to hate him, but I couldn't, not for that.

Franco grabbed my bicep, jerking me to the side, away from prying ears. He muttered, "Yes, Mr. Mercer has had fifty-seven slaves. Twelve of those were when he was sixteen. He buys women, accepts them as bribes, but never lays a finger on them." He sighed, "Q rehabilitates broken women, and returns them to their loved ones. He dedicates his money, staff, and home to helping women who've been shattered beyond repair. With some sort of Mercer superglue, he manages to put them together again."

Truth rang sweet. I finally knew.

After two months of living with an unreadable master, I knew the man behind the mask. Suzette hinted all along—the sparrows and birds screamed messages in my face. They symbolized women Q had saved. My eyes widened, finally understanding his tattoo. The black storm and brambles represented the horridness of the world—or him. The birds flapping free were girls he rescued. He wore it as a talisman.

A badge of honour.

If I didn't hate him, I'd love him for that.

I softened, accepting why Q threw me out. He had to protect future women. He couldn't have me ruining his life because he dedicated his time to saving others. I hated that I understood. I would've done the same thing.

My heart wrung dry and I accepted there was no going back. Franco would never betray Q. I had to know one thing, though.

I looked up. "Why me? When he didn't touch anyone else? Why did he try to break me if he fixes broken things?"

Franco looked away, rubbing the back of his neck. "He didn't want to break you. He—" Lips snapped shut, and shame shadowed his face. "This isn't for me talk about."

I grabbed his arm, squeezing hard muscle. "Please, Franco. Tell me. I need to know. I can't deal with anymore. I thought Q cared for me. I care for him, and I made the biggest mistake of my life running and calling Brax." Tears welled and spilled. "If I could take it all back, I would. You owe me the truth."

Franco patted my hand over his. "I know, Ms. Snow, but it doesn't change the fact that for the first time, Q responded to a slave the way a normal master would. He saw your fight and loved you weren't broken. He wasn't trying to break you by doing what he did." He dropped his voice so I could barely hear. "He was hoping you could break him."

Blood rushed into my ears. The songs about needing to fight and claim. I wanted to slap myself for not seeing. Q needed someone who matched his darkness, waged the same war between pleasure and pain.

We were so similar, yet he never let me get close to show him. I ruined it. The police gave an ultimatum, and Q had no choice but to accept.

Swallowing hard, Franco added, "Q deals with a lot. I hoped he finally found the one person who could help him. But then you ran, and it's come to an end."

Franco dropped his arms, stepping back, withdrawing in one swift move. "I'm sorry for what you dealt with in Mexico, and what Lefebvre did to you, but it's time for you to forget about Mr. Mercer, and go back to your boyfriend."

The mention of Brax shot a poker through my heart. What a terrible girlfriend I turned out to be. If Q wanted me, I would never have left. I would've let Brax fumble without me, stomping on my promise that I would never leave. *Will I ever live with myself?*

Franco pushed me toward the taxi stands. Rows of cars waited, bright under glaring lights.

Shoving something into my hands, he said, "This is for your troubles. Goodbye, Ms. Snow."

I wanted to scream as Franco strode away and disappeared. I hated my last name. I missed *esclave*. I missed what the word meant: belonging. Not just to Q, but an entire different existence.

I didn't know how long I stood on the footpath, clutching the envelope Franco gave, but eventually I had no choice but to move. Move forward. Try and forget.

In a daze, I shuffled to the taxi stand.

A driver quirked a bushy, black eyebrow. "No luggage, little lady?"

I blinked. The moment I got in the car, my life would suck me along, and I would never be able to stop it. I would become Tessie again. Fierce Tess would be no more. Q would be no more.

Q was wrong about one thing. Something about me was broken: my heart.

Shaking my head, I mumbled, "No, no luggage."

Get through today, then think about tomorrow. One baby step at a time.

Sliding into the plastic wrapped interior, I gave him my

address. Our address. Me and Brax.
I was going home.

Chapter Twenty-two

Bell Bird

I didn't have a key.

Running fingers along the top of the doorframe, I found the spare. Our apartment resided on the bottom floor of a building of eight units. A one bedroom, chilly box, with no sun or views, but we decorated with bright fabrics and Brax's DIY projects.

Dammit, fit.

The key wouldn't slide into the lock because I shook so much.

I was home. The place where I'd been happy, but clueless as to who I was. Walking through the door meant so much more than just returning. By doing this, I let Q win. I let him disown me.

I hunched, holding my stomach, trying to gather strength. My eyes rested on Brax's steel-capped boots on the door mat, and my heart hung heavy in my chest.

You can't ever let Brax see you like this, Tess... Tessie. This pain is private.

I straightened, sucking in gulps of air. Brax expected a relieved and distraught girlfriend, not a woman vibrating with need for another. Not a woman craving a whip and violence.

I undid the lock and stepped over the threshold.

Fear hit first.

Fear of sameness—the overwhelming homeliness created by Tessie and Brax. It reached like eager claws ready to suck me unwillingly into the past.

My feet stuck to the floor, locking in place, battling an unbearable need to run. The longer I stood trembling with fear, the more confused I was. My mind struggled with two sets of memories: Tessie and Tess. Brax and Q. Australia and France. They wouldn't mesh and in my swirling confusion, the apartment worked a terrible magic. Soothing my terror, making it feel as if I never left.

Q? Who was that? A figment of my imagination.

Mexico? As if, Brax would never travel so far from home.

In a blink, the last two and a half months faded from reality to dream. I grasped at tendrils, forcing myself not to forget. I could never forget. No matter how painful, I wanted to wear the memories like armour, so I never grew weak again. I inched forward, hands curled. Daisy curtains were drawn haphazardly, just like Brax did every time. A dirty plate languished in the sink in our tiny cream kitchen, and his red tool bag blocked the corridor leading to the bathroom and bedroom.

No lights were on, only shadows. I tiptoed through my own home, feeling like an intruder. I didn't belong. I *never* belonged.

A bang came from the bedroom.

I crouched, ready to sprint, instincts on high alert.

Claws clacked on floorboards and a loud bark hurt the silence. Blizzard charged from the bedroom. The husky bounded over the tool bag and crashed against my legs.

The moment his hot, doggy body touched mine, I folded to the floor. I never liked Blizzard, but he signified Brax completely. Eager, happy, loyal to the end.

Dog breath made my nose wrinkle as he slobbered, tail wagging so hard his butt wiggled. "Calm down, Blizzard. I don't need drowning in kisses."

He whimpered as I pushed him away, needing some air. Forcing his massive body onto my lap, he licked with his road-rash tongue. Giving in, I pressed my face into his ruff. "You missed me, huh? You better not have chewed my handbags while I've been gone."

Blizzard yipped.

A loud thud and a muffled curse came from the bedroom.

I froze. Blizzard sensed my mood and clambered off, darting down the corridor to where his master appeared.

My heart churned. *Master.* Blizzard was owned. I no longer was.

Brax stumbled as Blizzard careened into him, then looked up.

Our eyes locked—sky-blue to grey-blue. I was so used to pale green, I flinched.

Brax's jaw hung open and tension erupted.

My insides rippled with complex bewilderment. Old Tess would've flown down the corridor and into Brax's arms, slamming us to the floor. She would've burst into tears and kissed him all over. So, so happy to be back with someone who cared enough to share their life with her.

New Tess waged World War Ten in her heart. Q still held me captive, even though I tried to shrug off his conditioning. Q didn't consider how distraught and lonely I would be. He proved he wasn't a good master. Everyone knows, after captivity, a pet doesn't survive in the wild. He should be punished.

You don't belong to him. Not any longer. But how was I supposed to live after Q? I knew what true belonging meant.

It hadn't been ethical or normal, but I'd been treasured and priceless. I didn't just want to belong. I wanted to be *ruled*. And Brax would never rule me. He couldn't.

Brax shuffled forward, pushing the damn dog out of the way. "Is this real?" His deep voice, full of sleep, rasped with remembrance. Brax. Sweet, comforting Brax. He'd been all alone. Probably suffering ten times what I did.

"Brax." I stepped forward.

Our eyes never left and he moved. "Tessie? My God, Tess."

Then, we were running. We slammed together, wrapping tight arms, squeezing until breathless. Brax rained me in kisses while his bed-warm body, in only singlet and boxers, scalded me with grief.

My heart split into fragments. Q's voice filled me head. *"Smell so good. So fucking good. Like rain… no, no like frost. Sharp and fresh and icy and cold and… and painful."* He closed his eyes, voice trailing into a whisper. *"You love c—causing pain."*

Pain.

It would become a familiar passenger in my heart. Q caused immeasurable agony. I wouldn't survive it. *You will survive it.*

Brax stopped kissing my hair, gathering me in a bone-crunching hug. "Oh, my God, Tess. Tessie? It's really you. Oh, my God." His familiar apple scent and size all overwhelmed, and I did the one thing I swore not to do.

I broke.

Tears waterfalled and I sobbed. Sobbed for my past with this man. The knowledge I had changed completely, and could never go back. I would always live with Q in my heart; there was no longer room for Brax. But I had to pretend. This moment marked the day I locked away my wants and needs, ready to act my ass off. Tessie would be reborn through determination and lies.

Brax pulled back, tears tracking his face. He planted a wet kiss on my lips; I forced myself not to recoil. *He's gone through hell thinking you were dead. Kiss him. Show him you still love him.*

I opened my mouth, expecting a violent tongue, so conditioned to savagery, but Brax kissed sweetly, delicately, so different to Q. So different to what I needed.

He pulled away, grabbing my hands. "Are you okay? Are you hurt?" His eyes flew over me in panic. My grey dress was rumpled and creased, but it looked expensive. It should—it was Prada.

Brax frowned when he noticed the envelope in my grip. I still hadn't had the balls to open it.

Hurt? Yes, in so many ways, but my wounds weren't visible. I shook my head. "I'm fine."

He scowled. "What happened?" He spun me around, running hands down my body. "Are you sure? How did you get here? Did you escape? Maybe we should go to a hospital?"

I laughed softly as his fingers tickled, then winced as he caught residue pain from my rib. "I'm fine. Honest. I just need to go to bed and get some rest. It's been a really long day." *Longest day of my life.*

Brax wrapped his arms around me; together we walked into the dark bedroom. Our queen-sized bed waited, and the cover I made from material scraps depicting the Eifel Tower, cackled with mockery.

I slammed to a halt. Why, why, *why?*

The French romantic symbolism stabbed me over and over; I couldn't take it. I stalked forward, grabbed the edge, and threw it into the corner of the room. I couldn't sleep beneath a symbol of the country where my ex-master lived. I hoped to God he suffered as much as me. Dammit, I wanted his cold heart ripped out—like mine was. *You better be howling in agony, you bastard.*

I vibrated with anger, and jumped a mile when Brax

touched my shoulders. "Tessie… it's okay. I don't know what happened, but we'll get you help. Okay?" He tugged me toward the bed and helped me undress.

I wallowed in thoughts, memories, wishing I could reboot my brain and forget. Forget everything.

Dressed only in the silky slip from beneath the dress, we climbed into bed. The whiff of detergent and fabric softener settled my raging heart, reminding me I used to find peace here. I could find it again, if I tried.

Brax immediately brought my head to lie on his chest. It was a usual position for us and I listened to his heartbeat. Strong and steady, it lulled me into blessed numbness.

Sleep stole my world.

"Esclave, *what do you think you're doing?"*

I froze, looking up at my master. Q stood proud and hard by the side of my bed. He stroked his rigid cock, lips parted with lust as eyes sparked with desire.

"Making myself come thinking of you fucking me, maître."

He stroked harder. A bead of pre-cum glistened. I couldn't stop myself. I shot upright and sucked him. Q groaned, fisting my hair as I lapped and licked and lavished.

"Fuck, esclave. *Your mouth is my entire world. I want to fuck you all day, every day. I can't think straight not fucking you. I want to tie you up and never let you go." His voice ran endlessly as he thrust into my mouth, nudging the back of my throat with force.*

I moaned, slinking fingers between my legs, stroking delicious wetness.

"Stop touching yourself, Tess. That's mine. All mine." He pushed me backward, straddling me. In one quick move, he flipped me onto my knees and spanked me so hard my skin screamed with pleasure-pain.

I pushed my ass backward, begging.

"You're going to take everything I give. You're not going to be able to walk. Do you like the sound of that?" His brutal hand spanked me again; I groaned.

"Yes, master. I love the sound of that."

Q positioned himself behind and—

"Shit, Tessie, you're soaking."

Fingers stroked inside me, smearing my arousal between my legs. Brax lay wedged in my open thighs and dream world dumped into reality.

It's not real.

My heart thrummed, trying to understand. Q wasn't real. Just a dream. I went to run hands through my hair, to pummel the thoughts of Q from my head, but my fingers glinted with wetness. I touched myself in my sleep.

"You were panting and woke me up," Brax murmured, still stroking his finger inside. "You sounded in so much pain, Tessie. Then you started fingering yourself and moaning." His voice ached with hurt, but he kept smiling softly. "I tried to stop you, but you forced my finger inside, and well, you… you woke up."

Shame flamed my cheeks. I looked away, unable to see the turmoil in his gaze. "I'm sorry, Brax."

I breathed deep, battling the urge to cry. I rolled my head, searching for the scent of citrus and sandalwood. My senses were lonely, deprived of everything Q. No longer mine to reprogram, I hated how I couldn't hide. My body gave me away, and Brax was lost and hurt.

I had to fix this. I had to do something.

Brax shifted. His heavy cock pressed against my thigh. Knowledge blazed bright; I leaned up to kiss him.

He froze as I coaxed his lips open. I could give him back his girlfriend. Show I really had returned.

With a harsh groan, he collapsed on top, fingers working deep. His touch didn't flare or sizzle like Q's. Horribly, I found myself growing dry, not wet.

"Tess. God, I've missed you." Soft lips pressed against mine. I wanted to close my eyes, but I needed to reaffirm the man making love to me was not Q Mercer. Not this boy with messy, floppy brown hair and eyes like the sky. This was Brax. And I loved him. *I do.*

I winced as he pressed another finger deeper. I arched my hips, dislodging his touch.

Brax stopped kissing me, looking down. "Is it too soon? I can stop. I just need to know you're here. I have to have you, Tessie, so I know I'm not dreaming." He ran his nose down my throat, sighing. "I've dreamed of you coming home so many times, I don't trust myself that this is real."

I cupped his cheek, tracing his lips with a thumb. Brax was all that mattered. I had to stop thinking and carry on with my future. "I need you, too."

I needed Brax to wipe away Q's claim. Then, perhaps, I could be free.

Silently, Brax eased his hips, pressing inside me. I winced at the bruising and dryness, but held Brax's head against my shoulder as he started to move. I willed my body to respond.

Together, we rocked and reconnected. His body filled mine, and I tried so hard to stay in the present. To let the love for Brax evolve from fizzling to blazing passion, but the spark never rose past a tiny glimmer. Not like the galaxies Q conjured, like the devil-magician he was. *Stop thinking about that bastard.*

Brax moaned, kissing my ear. "Shit, you feel amazing. I missed you. So, so much, you have no idea."

I hate myself.

I hate Q.

I hate my sick fantasies.

I hated I couldn't be the woman Brax thought I was. I hated Brax for complaining about his problems rather than what happened to me.

I churned with black thoughts, sighing in relief when Brax came, shuddering and thrusting hard.

My body never rose past a gentle burn, an orgasm was an impossibility.

Brax pulled out and sat up, looking down. My silky slip had risen above my breasts, revealing nakedness.

"Holy fuck." His mouth plopped open as he scuttled back, almost falling off the edge of the bed. "Holy shit, Tessie. What the hell happened?" Tears glazed his eyes, locked on my flesh.

My heart raced. I looked down. A loud psychotic laugh erupted. Brax looked as if he contemplated taking me to an insane asylum.

Flogger marks, lashes, kisses of red, and smudges of bruises, painted my normally perfect skin.

I shook my head. If Q whipped and branded, knowing he was sending me back, did he know my old lover would see? Did he do this deliberately?

Q, you're a conniving asshole. But in that moment, I didn't care. The marks linked me to him, and as long as they etched my flesh, I was still *esclave*. Whether Q wanted it or not.

Brax stood, pacing naked. "Tell me what happened to you. Why the hell are you laughing?"

My smile dissolved; I dropped my gaze. Because my emotions played roulette, I started to cry instead. I smashed at the traitorous liquid.

Brax hesitantly climbed back on the bed.

Guilt swarmed and I dragged sheets up to my chin. "It's nothing, Brax. Nothing happened. I'm here now. Okay? It's in the past, and no longer matters."

Brax shook his head, panic in his blue eyes. "Do you need counselling? We can go now. I feel so helpless."

The thought of talking to someone was horrid. "No. I'll be fine. Truly."

Brax hiccupped, hunching his shoulders. His voice

cracked as sadness fell from his lips. "Tess, I'm so, so sorry I wasn't able to stop them. I relive that day over and over. I want to kill myself for not being strong enough to stop them, and deserve to go to hell for not listening to you. I forced you to go into the café. This is all my fault."

Panic flared. I couldn't handle it if Brax broke down. I didn't have the strength to soothe him as well as me.

But he dissolved, looking more and more distraught by the second.

I sat up, scurrying to him, making sure my body stayed covered. My knees pressed against his as I took his face in my hands. "It wasn't your fault. No one would have been able to stop them." My body tensed, remembering Leather Jacket. "No one, okay? We were outnumbered. You need to forgive yourself."

Brax hung his head. "Don't you hate me? For not listening? I spent the last two months thinking you were dead. To have you come back to life, wounded, and mentally screwed up…"

I flinched. I was a lot of things, but mentally I was fine. Q wouldn't win. I would get over him.

He looked into my eyes, stricken. "I woke up in the men's bathroom, alone. And you were gone. I don't know how I got back to the hotel, but somehow I did. The police arranged a search party, but no one had hope. They called it off after a week, and the Australian embassy got involved. They sent me home."

He laughed darkly. "They sent me home without you! How did they think I could go on with my life? I wanted to stay and search myself, but the police said they'd been to the cafe, and it was boarded up. No one was there."

Brax took my hand, squeezing painfully. "Where did they take you?"

I was prepared to listen to Brax's story. It was

obvious it ate him alive, but my story… I couldn't. I couldn't tell him the horrible experience in Mexico. I couldn't tell him about the rape when I ran away. I couldn't tell him how much Q meant to me. How much I craved him—even now. I would take it to the grave.

Brax grabbed my wrist, spying the barcode for the first time. Running a thumb over the lines, he murmured, "They did this to you? The low-life wankers." He flipped my wrist as if he could peel it off and make it disappear. "Why did they tattoo you?"

My hand went behind my ear, terror raging. I still had a tracking device in my neck. Q may have taken off his GPS responder, but what if the Mexicans could find me again? Did it automatically fail after time? I needed to find out how to deactivate it, immediately.

Forcing myself to be calm, I said, "Don't worry about me; tell me what happened to you. So you got home? I'm so sorry you were on your own, Brax. I'm sorry they took me from you."

My own tears fell, caused by guilt knowing I made Brax suffer and stress. His nightmares would've been horrific.

"When I got home, I tried everything to investigate where women were taken from Mexico, but once stolen, most girls were never found. Some were located in Spain, and Saudi Arabia, but never alive.

"My heart broke, coming to terms that I'd never see you again." His voice caught, and he looked with such agony, I shrivelled. "Then you called! I wanted to kill myself for not picking up. But my boss had been calling constantly, begging me to return to work, and I put it on silent. When I heard your voice, your panic, the fact that you were alive. Shit, I wanted to break the phone into little pieces for not being able to talk to you."

His chest pumped as his hands curled. "But you gave me a name. A fucking bastard called Q Mercer. You gave me a lead. I had no idea what you were doing in France, but I called the Feds, and they took over. They found a wealthy man living in Blois who owned mega property. I did some research, but couldn't find a single image of him, or what he could be doing with you.

He sighed before continuing, reliving his own nightmare. "The police stayed true to their word. They said they'd investigate, and if they found you, they'd make him release you and put him in jail. I hope to God they hang him."

The thought of Q dead had horror stabbing my heart. The hate in Brax's voice chilled me and I rushed to intercede. "Q Mercer wasn't who I thought he was. I escaped and found myself in worse trouble, but Q rescued me."

I couldn't stop the shiver as Brute shot into my mind. Forcing it away, I added, "He helped me heal, then let me go." Those two paragraphs would be all I uttered on the matter. It was my life, tied with a pretty pink bow.

Brax screwed up his face. "You're saying he just let you go? The police never showed up?"

I smiled. "The police arrived, and thank you for helping them find me. But Q was going to give me up all along." My heart twisted, wishing it wasn't true. "You see, he rehabilitates women who are broken and sold. He buys them, but once they're healed, he sends them home." I couldn't stop the swell of pride in my chest. Q wasn't a monster. He may think he was, but a monster would never do that. A monster would torture and rape and kill. Not offer freedom after a life of misery.

Brax relaxed a little. "So, he never touched you? You were kept safe and protected this entire time?" His eyes dropped to the sheet I pressed against my throat. "What about the marks on your body?"

I sat straighter, hoping like hell I hid the truth. "I got those when I ran away. I lived in luxury, and made friends with his maid, Suzette." I beamed brighter, fighting watery grief threatening to crush. "I'm fine. Honestly. Together, we can get our lives back on track."

He cocked his head, and, for a moment, I wondered if he didn't buy my lie, but then he reached for me. I climbed into his arms.

Brax kissed the top of my head, murmuring, "It's all going to be better now. You're home. I'm never letting you out of my sight again."

I snuggled closer and didn't say a word.

Chapter Twenty-three

Woodpecker

A human is adaptable. A human heart is not.

A month trickled past, and I resumed my old life as if I'd never gone. Two weeks after returning, I called my parents.

Brax told them what happened in Mexico, and they cremated an old stuffed unicorn of mine, then scattered it in the back garden, believing I was dead. In their old, foggy minds, my reincarnation was a messy ordeal, not a happy second chance. The conversation was stilted and hard.

I never called again.

I became addicted to raging songs, just like Q. The lyrics shared my pain, letting it unleash from festering inside.

Your memory won't leave my head
haunting me, hunting me, driving me crazy, I wish I were dead
every time I close my eyes, you're there, ready to suck me into dark desires
reality is where I no longer want to be, my dreams are my salvation
I will cut you out, chop you up, break every bone in my body
if only it meant peace from your dark melody

I never played the songs when Brax was home, but when it was just me and loneliness, words rained with heartache and need.

In my dreams, Q visited, and I woke to shooting stars and orgasms. By day, I forced myself to act and lie and be Tessie. The truth and Q blistered my heart; I became as successful in hiding my feelings as he was.

My secrets stayed locked behind a fortress of blue-eyed innocence. My body healed and the whiplashes no longer showed. But they blazed bright and red on my soul.

Some nights, I twisted my nipples so hard, just to try and recreate mind-tripping lust like Q, but it never worked.

The vibrancy and encompassing life he'd given became a distant, dark paradise. Reality took over. I sat my final exams for uni. They let me take my tests late, due to circumstances, and I passed with flying colours. Brax took me out for dinner to celebrate, but I fumbled through the evening, aware I'd snipped another anchor keeping me here. I had an education now. The only thing tethering me was Brax. And day after day proved it wasn't enough.

I tried to recapture Q's mansion on my tatty sketchpad, but no matter how hard I tried, I couldn't get it right.

I reconnected with Stacey, and friends from uni, and started looking for work in the property industry. I coasted through life in a semi-aware state. Smiling, laughing even, but everything was muted—covered by a filmy screen, never letting me see bright colours, or smell rich scents, or enjoy exquisite pleasure.

Thirty-six days after Q abandoned me, two things happened that rocked my bland world.

Brax subtly changed. I noticed he spent a lot of time putting out the garbage. I didn't care, and only curiosity made me follow one night.

Sneaking outside our apartment block, I found him talking to our neighbour across the hall. She had her face in

Blizzard's fur and a look of adoration in her eyes for Brax.

My fingers convulsed as my heart raced faster—the first spike of emotion in a month.

I never stopped to consider the life Brax led while I played kinky slave with Q. He cared for her—the tentative sweetness he'd shown me when we first met—glowed in his eyes.

Oh, my God, did he resent me for coming back into his life when he thought I was dead?

I was so selfish to never consider it. After the first morning, we pretended as though nothing happened. We never discussed it, and I never complained when we didn't have sex again. I didn't want to admit it, but living with Brax, accepting his kisses and hand-holding, felt like I cheated on Q, which was idiotic and frustrating as hell. But my body hated me for betraying my master. Subsidizing real Q for dream Q, I grew wet while I slept, and trembled for release.

I lingered like a voyeur as Brax helped the girl stand, holding her for a moment longer than necessary. The look of implicit excitement in her eyes made me yearn. Yearn for another.

I waited for green jealousy. I waited for rage. I waited for anything…*something* to show I cared.

Nothing.

Brax laughed at something she said, ruffling Blizzard's head. A smile slowly bloomed on my lips.

Brax liked another. He no longer used me as his crutch, and I no longer needed him as mine. Realization thundered with a hundred drums and lightning bolts.

Happiness. *Freedom.*

Brax didn't need me.

I'm free!

Emotions frothed and stirred. The leash tying me to Brax—the one woven and threaded with obligation and friendship—snipped, leaving me unbelonging.

For the first time in my life, I was mine. Completely alone. No one had a right to me. No one owned or claimed me. Blazing joy blew away my mediocrity, my need for people to care.

I cared for me. *Je n'appartiens qu'à moi.* I am mine. The French affirmation was ridiculously perfect.

I whispered it, tingling with possibility. *"Je n'appartiens qu'à moi."*

The next night, I said goodbye to Brax.

While he went to put the rubbish out and flirt with the neighbour, I pulled an old backpack from under the bed and packed. Turning on the radio, I bobbed to pop music, welcoming a new beginning.

Clothes I didn't like, accessories I no longer cared for, I stuffed in the bottom. For the first time in my life, I was going out on my own. No back-up plan, no safety net. No one to rely on but me.

I didn't have a destination in mind. But I knew I wanted to make good on my promise. The promise I gave to the woman who tattooed me in Mexico. I told her Karma would bite her ass. I wanted to be that Karma. I wanted to hunt and hurt every person involved, and stand up for all the women who didn't have a happy ending like me.

I was done being weak and passive. *I'm done being Tessie.*

Looking at my newly plastic-wrapped wrist, I smiled. Over the past month, I'd had the middle of the barcode lasered off. I embraced the pain; after all, Q taught me pain was pleasure.

He roared into my head.

"Only think of me and what I'm doing. There is intimacy in pain, esclave. Let me make your pain my pleasure."

I shook the memory away, ignoring the clenching between my legs. God, I missed him. Missed his egotistical coolness, his super-hot violence.

But I thanked him, too. Without his cruelty, I would never have found the core of iron deep inside.

Smiling, I traced the small bird in flight trapped between the two ends of the barcode. Beneath the sparrow were the numbers: 58.

It was morbid. Wrong on so many levels to brand myself as slave fifty-eight, but Q was the highlight of my life. The poignant centrepiece who would never come again.

When I was old, married, bored, and drained, I wanted something to remember him by. The tattoo of bird and number would always hold those memories. A lock box of sadistic pleasure available to relive in the privacy of my mind, whenever I needed a shot of fire.

Sighing, I grabbed the last thing in my wardrobe.

The grey dress I'd left Q's home in. A song switched on the radio.

Your touch consumes me, frightens me, beguiles me
you want to capture me
I want to be your victim
you want to ruin me
I want to be your broken
you show me your darkness
and I'll give you my light

The lyrics slapped me around the head, and I stared at the dress for ages. My heart didn't know if it wanted to beat or die. In a horrible moment of disgrace, I sniffed the material. Soft lingers of citrus and sandalwood gripped my stomach with love and hate. Two equal feelings, so different, yet not different at all. They were both one thing: passion.

Screwing the dress into a little ball, something crinkled.

Frowning, I pulled the envelope free that Franco gave me. I'd been too chicken to read it. Instead, I hid it in the dress, hoping I would forget.

I never forgot.

But now, I had strength. I was in control of my destiny. Sitting on the bed, I slipped a finger under the tacky glue to open.

Heartbeats jangled as I tipped the envelope upside down. Brax's silver bracelet fell out.

It landed in my lap and I could only gawk. Q returned my bracelet.

"Merde!" he swore. Standing, he scooped the bracelet from the carpet and dangled it above. "This is mine. You are mine. Get that through your head if you ever want it back."

That was a lie. All of it. He relinquished the bracelet so easily—like I was never his. If he made the commitment to fully own me, I wouldn't have spent the last month in purgatory.

I flung the bracelet away; it landed on Brax's pillow. I didn't want it anymore. It belonged to two identities, who I no longer bowed to.

I will move on, so help me. I would find and rescue women who suffered abuse and hardship. I would become a trafficker's worst nightmare. *Even though you deny him, you're becoming him.*

My eyes widened.

Q saved women, same as I was about to do.

He might save them, but he never brought the bastards who did it to justice. I wanted to go after the monsters, not just the offerings.

I looked into the envelope before tossing it away, and pulled out a small piece of paper. Air refused to enter my lungs.

Esclave,
Tess,

This is for your freedom
Fly high and happy
Je suis à toi
Q

I clamped a hand over my mouth, holding back a wail. Behind the note was a cheque.

Signed with an arrogant swirl of an autograph Quincy Mercer had given me two hundred thousand euros.

I felt faint. Two hundred thousand! Anger blazed. Two hundred. Was that all I was worth? Less than a Bugatti or some other possession he could buy?

Shit, I wasn't for sale!

The money sent two hundred spasms of hot frustration at his audacity. He really was a fucking idiot. I didn't want his money. I didn't want anything from him apart from peace. I wanted him out of my head. I wanted my senses to belong to me again. I wanted my heart to stop weeping. So many things I wanted... and would never get.

Damn him to the depths of hell.

My heart raced. Everything I'd been trying to forget, to run from, grabbed me around the throat, choking with ruthless savagery.

"As you wish, esclave. Every time I call you Tess, remember I can do anything I want to you. I fucking own you."

"Yes."

"After tonight, every time I say your name you'll get wet for me. I not only own your body but your identity, too. Do you deny it?"

I tried to deny it. I tried so damn hard.

But I couldn't swallow the lie. Q still owned me. Owned my body, heart, soul, my fucking everything.

Tears dripped onto my hands. I knew what I had to do.

Rushing to my bedside table, I found my sketchpad and ripped out a page. My hands shook and my stomach tripped into knots.

Brax,
I'll always love you. I'll love your kindness, your generosity, your friendship, your smile. I'll always love the way you made me feel so good about myself and how you kept me safe when I felt so alone. But I know I don't give you what you need. I know I'm selfish with not leaning on you enough and I didn't realize it until now.
Another needs you more than I ever will, and I want you to be happy.
I'm letting you go, Brax, and I wish you so much happiness and jo—

"You're leaving. Aren't you?"

I dropped the pen, sucking in a breath. Brax stood, framed in the door, jaw clenched. He strode to the bed, trying to read my note upside down. His eyes fell to the silver bracelet on his pillow.

I bit my lip as he picked it up, staring, unseeing. The bracelet represented our future and I tossed it away so flippantly.

Leaving a note was cowardly, but face to face, I didn't know if I had the strength. *Find the strength. He needs to know the truth.*

Dropping the paper, I walked to his side. "Yes. I'm leaving."

Brax looked up, holding the bracelet tightly. "You were just going to go, Tessie?" His eyes blazed with hurt. "What about what I want?"

I placed a hand over his heart, looking into blue, blue eyes. "I *am* giving you what you want. What you need. I'll always be your friend, Brax, but we've outgrown each other. I never wanted to hurt you, and by staying, I will."

He hung his head, pressing his forehead against mine.

"That's not true. I need you."

I sighed softly, "I think another needs you more."

When he looked with an eyebrow raised, I added, "The neighbour you've been spending so much time with? I've seen you together, Brax. I know you have feelings for her."

He gulped. "It's not like that. Honestly. She moved in while you were… um… gone, and I've been helping her with some tough shit." He dropped his voice. "Her dad and brother were killed in a house fire. Her mum died when she was a baby, and she's got no one to turn to. I was only being nice."

"What's her name?"

He flinched. "Bianca."

I hated the look in his eyes—the look where he expected me to scream and punch him. He had every right to care for another as lonely as him. Together, they would be each other's everything. I wasn't broken enough for Brax. My courage and strength kept a rift between us all this time.

Kissing him gently, I murmured, "Let me go. You'll be happier, I swear it. The truth hurts less than fibs and fakers… remember?"

He swallowed hard, nodding once. He knew I spoke the truth. "Where will you go?" He gathered me into a hug.

I squeezed him back, but I couldn't confess. "I'm not sure. But know that I'm happy and doing what I need to do." Kissing his cheek, I pulled away. "I hope you're truly content with whoever you end up with, Brax."

He kissed me gently, smiling. "You're going back to France, aren't you?"

I froze.

"I've seen how different you are, Tess. I sleep next to you. I see how you wake up hot and bothered and sexy as hell. Something happened over there, and it changed you. I get it. What happened in Mexico changed both of us."

I battled with embarrassment and awe. Brax saw more than I gave him credit for. Shame made me blush. He was right. I had changed and I couldn't undo it. I couldn't change the fact he lay next to me while I dreamed of Q whipping and fucking me. He suffered in silence as I cried out in need.

Remorse settled heavily. "Brax, I'm so sorry."

He laughed lightly. "Nothing to apologise for, Tessie. I knew we were different ever since you pulled out your vibrator. I'm not comfortable with that sort of thing, and I think I knew we'd go our separate ways that night. It hurt so much at the time, but now… I might be able to breathe with the thought of only having you as a friend."

His acceptance let my heart fly free; I threw myself into another hug. "Stay in touch."

Brax hugged me with endless comfort and kissed my cheek goodbye.

Our two year relationship ended on a friendly note, and I wished Brax the world.

Half an hour later, I strode from the apartment, wearing Q's grey dress.

No belongings.

No trivial items that meant nothing.

Just me, my passport, and note from my master.

With a heart-winging smile, I left my world behind.

Chapter Twenty-four

Kingfisher

The flight to Paris took forever.

The train to Blois an eternity.

The moment I arrived in the village where I ran from Franco, a rainbow of feeling settled. Residual fear from the rape. Excitement at being so close to Q. Nerves at not knowing how he'd react. What if he hated me completely? What if he sent me away again? *Stop those thoughts.* One thing was for sure, Q would hear me out before he tossed me away again. He lived in the darkness? Well, I was about to bring hell on him if he didn't listen.

Deciding to shed memories of running, with recollections of returning, I strode into *Le Coq* and approached the same woman. The roosters on the walls no longer wanted to peck my eyes out. They looked fat and content.

The women who didn't believe I'd been kidnapped gawked as I approached the counter. My skin pricked with phantom panic from the rape, but I forced it away. It didn't define me. It was over.

Her mouth hung open, watching with incredulous eyes.

"*Bonjour.* I'm looking for the *Moineau* residence. Quincy Mercer's estate."

Her jaw dropped further showing unhygienic teeth.

"You…you came here claiming he kidnapped you. Now you want to go back?"

I smiled bright. "Yep. Makes sense, huh?" I didn't elaborate, and tried not to laugh. I couldn't stop bubbles of tentative happiness. I was doing something just for me. It was liberating.

She glared for ages; I didn't think she'd answer, but finally she called into the kitchen, summoning a scruffy boy with hands covered in soapy bubbles. "*Emmène la, à la résidence Mercer.*" Take her to Mercer's estate.

I basked in the lyrical language of French. I'd missed it. I'd grown to love France and its language. Living back in Australia with the twangy accent and heat had never fit. Australia was bright and brash and wonderful. France was chic and refined and smouldered with passion.

The kitchen boy nodded, pushing a black cowlick from his eyes. I thanked the woman and followed the boy to a white van in the back alley. The same alley where I bolted from Franco.

I suffered a pang of terror at the thought of getting in the car with a stranger. I wouldn't survive a repeat of Brute and Driver, but I steeled myself.

We didn't say a word as we drove. Rolling hills and patchwork countryside flurried my heart erratically. Every mile, I was closer to Q. Every mile, I felt more and more confident. This was where I belonged. This was home.

We turned and drove through huge, imposing gates and the sound of gravel pinging beneath the car made sweat pool in my lower back. Nerves skittered, my mouth dry with worry.

Q's pastel mansion came into sight, along with the horse fountain splashing with tiny rainbows in the mid-afternoon sun. Spring gave way to summer, and Q's immaculate gardens rioted with colour. Butterflies fluttered while birds winged. An innocent paradise where a beast lurked. A beast that liked delicate things, but would never kill.

The young boy smiled as we pulled to a halt outside imposing pillars and cherub plasterwork. My heart firmly lodged in my throat. I couldn't move. *What am I doing?* *"Nous sommes arrivés."* We're here. He waved for me to exit.

I stared at the mansion, with everything bared. *I can't do this. Yes, you can.* But what if… what if he refused to see me, or moved onto another slave… or…

The front door swung open.

I ducked in the seat, cowardice taking me hostage.

A very surprised Suzette stepped out, peering through the van's windows. I tentatively waved; her mouth fell open.

The boy laughed, reaching across to open the door. I climbed out, frantically smoothing my grey dress, rubbing my cheeks, wishing I'd taken the time to present myself better.

A slight breeze sent a spritz of water from the horse fountain, dewing my skin, making me shiver.

Suzette and I didn't move for a century.

I doubted any slaves returned once they were released. Then again, I was forcibly removed. I broke tradition by being unpredictable. Our eyes locked and I transmitted everything I felt in my gaze. *Do you see how worthy I want to be? I came back for him. I came back for you. For this life. For everything he made me become.*

Suzette inched forward, her black and white maid's uniform sleek and pressed. Hazel eyes sparkled. "Ami? What… I don't understand." She stepped hesitantly. I closed the distance between us.

I resisted the urge to bowl her over in a hug. She covered her mouth as I smiled. *"Bonjour,* Suzette." The sun burned through late spring haze, warming my skin.

Whatever happened, I made the right decision. Q needed someone to fight. Q needed to be fought for.

I wanted to fight for him. I wanted to *win* him.

The pastel tones of the manor glowed with sun in pale greens, pinks, and decadent renaissance features.

I never wanted to leave.

Suzette squealed, launching herself into my arms. "You came back? Why would you do that? I thought you hated him, us, everything that happened. He threw you away. I thought you'd be plotting murder, not appearing out of the blue."

I ignored the pang caused by the 'throwing away' remark. He didn't. He did what the police told him. I wouldn't hold a grudge... unless he kept being an arrogant asshole, then I'd punch him.

Squeezing her back, I breathed in her scent of lavender and cleaning products. My heart thudded with so many memories. Suzette had been difficult. So loyal to Q, and her hard friendship hurt sometimes, but she was fierce and she'd lived through much more than me.

My respect for her was a hundred fold.

Pulling away, I said, "I've had time to think. Q changed me, Suzette. He took the real me and set me free." I smiled, remembering how fundamental birds were to Q. Speaking in his cryptic language, I added, "He opened my cage and allowed me to fly. I can't help it if my freedom is here."

She pulled back, a sly smile on her face. "You figured him out."

Wrapping her fingers with mine, she tugged me toward the house. I put one foot in front of the other, focusing on breathing so I didn't pass out. My heart hadn't stopped thrumming since I boarded the plane. I felt sure it was nearing expiration.

"I had help from some drunken ramblings and Franco, but yes. I'm beginning to see him. I want to see more." I looked around the massive foyer with its midnight blue staircase and huge works of art. My body spun with a thousand feelings; my stomach wouldn't stop somersaulting.

She pecked my cheek, closing the door behind us, locking us into Q's world. His domain. My future. "What day is it?"

I blinked. Crossing timelines and datelines muddled me. "Um, Sunday?"

A smile split her face. "It's not a weekday."

Oh, my God. My heart winged, soaring around the foyer. "He's here," I whispered. I couldn't wait another moment. "Take me to him?"

Suzette grasped my hand, dropping her voice. "I'm so happy to have you back, Ami."

I smiled. "You know my real name. Call me Tess."

She grinned. "Wait here."

She flew up the staircase, leaving me all alone. I linked my fingers, lost. I was an intruder in this amazing home, asking a hugely successful man to stop being an asshole, and take me back. To show me his ruthlessness. His compassion. To give me the life I truly wanted.

A sound rustled from the lounge. I spun to face a woman in baggy track pants and a sweater three times too big for her. She walked with an air of rejection and sadness. The moment she made eye contact, she whimpered and fell to her knees, bowing.

Time screeched to a halt. I could only stare.

Fifty-nine.

My hands curled. This was slave fifty-nine. My replacement. Where had she come from? Jealously cramped my stomach, but I forced myself to relax. Franco said Q never touched other slaves. I was the first. His last. His fucking only if I had my way.

"It's okay. You can stand," I said softly, inching closer. Brown, straggly hair hung with grease, huge shadows ringed her eyes. Her wrists were brittle thin. Aura beaten and trodden. Everything screamed abuse.

Is this how they all arrive? Was that why Q seemed so

surprised, so intrigued by me? I refused to bow. I swore. I hissed.

My breathing stopped.

I saw myself how Q did that day: a fighter through and through. A woman not stomped into depression or servitude. A flash of brightness in a world of sadness. I was the polar opposite of this poor girl.

I dropped to my knees, holding out a hand. She scuttled away, trembling.

I stood, backing up. "Don't worry. I won't hurt you."

"Sephena. Stand up."

My body clamped and clenched and melted. His voice. *Him*. Master. Controller. Sexy as hell control freak.

I shivered and spun. Facing my master. My chosen fate.

Q stood halfway down the staircase, pale jade eyes blazing with a mixture of amazement, lust, and anger.

The air arched and crackled, tension flooding the space. Goosebumps erupted and nothing else existed but him.

The huddling girl shuffled beside me, climbing to unsteady feet. I tore my eyes from Q as she bowed and went to him.

I followed, drawn like a magnet to Q's power.

Q only had eyes for me; he moved silently down the stairs. His black pin-stripe suit, with aubergine shirt and faded grey tie, whispered with every step. His polished dress shoes shone against blue carpet. I drank in everything about him.

There were lines around his eyes that weren't there before. The knotted tension in his shoulders. His whisper-thin control frayed, showing a less than perfect posture.

He stopped two steps above, glaring. *"Qu'est ce que tu fais ici?"* What are you doing here?

I waged the battle to swoon at his voice. My sense of hearing, so completely owned by him, ordered me to worship. To climb his magnificent hard body, and never let him pry me away again.

I licked my lips, smouldering with need. The spark

between us couldn't be denied. It burned like a tripwire, waiting to explode.

The entire time I lived with Brax, I had no interest in sex. Now, I would *die* if I didn't have him. My legs trembled, body flamed, and wetness melted unashamedly. Q erupted all my longing into a fireball, incinerating my insides.

Poor Sephena was completely ignored.

"I came for you," I whispered. "On my own accord."

His nostrils flared, mouth parted. That mouth, oh, how I wanted to kiss it. Tongue him. Have it all over me.

"Sephena. Go and find Suzette. She'll show you where the swimming pool is." He softened the hard edge in his tone. "Remember, you're free to do whatever pleases you." Q stressed the word free. I fell a little more.

The girl didn't show surprise, but I sure did. How did I not know Q had a swimming pool? What other surprises would I find? I would make sure Q kept me so I could find out. I wanted to help in every part of his life. He needed someone.

I blinked, realizing just how lonely he was. A parade of broken women, sharing his home, never finding solace in them.

He worked and slept and worked some more.

The moment Sephena disappeared, I balled my fists. "We need to talk."

He bared his teeth. "We don't need to do anything. I sent you back. What the fuck are you doing here?"

My palm itched to slap him, to knock some sense into him. Was he clueless to the pain he caused? Or so suffocated by his own, he couldn't think straight? Everything I planned to say flew out of my head; I folded to the floor.

A submissive talking to her dominant. But I wasn't a submissive. I was the woman who would steal Q, just like he stole me. He had no choice. I wasn't going to give him one. "Master...Q...Quincy... "

He sucked in a huge gust of air, suit rustling as he shifted. "My name is Tess Snow. Not Sweetie, or Tessie, or Honey. I'm a woman only now realizing what she's capable of. I'm no one's daughter. I'm no one's girlfriend. I'm no one's possession. I belong to me, and for the first time, I know how powerful that is."

I stared at the marble, laying my heart at his feet. "I came back for the man I see inside the master. The man who thinks he's a monster because of his twisted desires. The man who rescues slaves and sends them back to loved ones. I came back for Q. I came back to be his *esclave,* but also to be his equal."

My voice trailed off as my throat clogged with passion. "I came back to be your everything... just like you're becoming mine."

My heart thudded like a drum, roaring in my ears.

He stepped closer.

Shoes appeared in my line of vision. His voice echoed dark and thick. "You don't know what you're offering."

I lifted my head, boldly wrapping a hand around his ankle. "I'm offering you my pain. My blood. My pleasure. I'm offering you the right to whip and fuck. To debase and harm. I'm offering to fight your needs with my own. I'm willing to join you in the darkness and find pleasure in excruciating pain. I'm willing to be your monster, Q."

I dug nails into his trouser leg, voice aching with truth. "We're the same."

With a snarl, he yanked his foot away, prowling into the library. I looked after him, shocked. Damn, he was hard work.

I stood and followed, locking the huge glass door behind us, flicking the switch to turn the glass from see-through to opaque. Privacy descended and tension threaded between us, exploding into the realm of scary with need. I could see it: hot ribbons of crimson lust, glittering with stars of want and intoxication.

Q bent over his desk, pinching the bridge of his nose. The dark room whispered of sin, compelling wrongness. Books full of erotic stories looked down from dust-free shelves, encouraging me to finish what I started.

I returned to Q. But he had to work, too. He owed an apology, an explanation. He owed me his heart.

Q whirled away, pacing, running a hand over short hair. Eyes flickered to me and I tried to read the burning feelings in his gaze.

"You can't force me to leave, as I came on my own freewill. This may be your house, Q, but you don't have the strength to throw me away twice." I hoped to God I was right.

He growled under his breath, prowling, never stopping.

Standing in the centre of the room, I watched. Letting the beast roam, expelling excess angst. While he paced, I talked.

"That night, before you sent me away, was the best night of my life. The marks you laced me with lasted a full week. Every time I looked in the mirror, or touched a bruise in the shower, I grew slick for you. You visited my dreams. I woke to aching wetness and an empty heart."

My skin grew hot, remembering how many wet dreams I enjoyed under his brutal demands. I loved how his fingernails left faint scars on my ass. "Flashes of memories haunted me at the supermarket, at university. I could never escape you."

He stopped pacing, his gorgeous, angled face frozen in need.

I tiptoed closer, murmuring, "I *ached* for you to dominate. I *throbbed* for you to fuck. I *missed* you. I missed the man I know is in there, but you never let me see." I held up my wrist.

His eyes flashed down and he grabbed me, lightning

quick. "*Merde.*"

I stifled a moan as fingers kissed the bird fluttering in its prison of barcode, whispering over the number fifty eight.

"Why?" His voice was tortured, wavering and gruff.

"Because you set me free."

His eyes locked on mine, angry. "You're insane. I warped your mind. After everything I did... everything you went through because I kept you. How can you speak such lies?"

I cupped his cheek, wincing as sparks zapped my fingertips. I couldn't touch him without pain. It seemed only fitting.

"It's not a lie. You showed me who I truly am." My heart grew warm with steel and iron. "I'm strong enough to fight you. I want to give you everything, but only if you give me what I want in return."

"You really are insane. I hurt you—you should run and never come back." Fingers lassoed around my wrist, tugging me closer. "I'm not something you can tame. I'm not a man who will sprout poems and treat you nice. I'm. Not. That. Human."

I swallowed hard, buffeted with Q's temper and rage. "Did I ask for poems and niceties? No! If I wanted those, I would've stayed with Brax."

Q froze, nostrils flaring. Hardness etched lines around his mouth. "Don't mention that name to me again." His icy cold voice scattered goosebumps on my spine.

I'm losing. He's not seeing.

I slapped him.

My palm smacked satisfyingly against rugged five o'clock shadow. He reared back in shock, then his whole deposition crouched into hunter—killer—monster. "You go too far. Leave before you regret it."

I wanted to stomp my foot like a child. Throw a terrible tantrum to get him to open his eyes. Forcing words between clenched teeth, I said, "I want *you*. I want your complexities, your shadows. I want your whips, and chains, and brutality.

Listen to me! I'm willing to give you a slave who will never break, if you give me what I want in return."

Q cocked his head, finally some shred of amazed compression glowed. "And what do you need in return?" he murmured, so close I breathed his question.

My body went from strong and defiant to fluttering and delicate. "I need you to care for me. Promise you'll share your life and not shut me out. I want to know who Quincy is. I want to belong to Q. I want you to be honest with yourself that I mean something to you, too. Do you have that in you, Q? To care for me completely, so I can give you what you need?"

He dropped his head, suddenly nuzzling my neck. Hiding his thoughts and feeling in my blonde curls. "You're asking for an impossibility. You're asking me to love you."

My heart squeezed at the pain in his voice. His eyes glowed with agony as he pulled away. "I can't. I don't know how. The things I did to you were tame to what I really want. I can't stop it. I can't control it." He pushed me away, hands shoving deep into his pockets. Walking away, he barricaded further connection. "Who wants to hurt someone so much if they're supposed to love them? Who wants to see them writhe in agony and completely submit? No one sane. I'm fucked up, *esclave*. I can't give you what you want."

Esclave.

My body shuddered. Q's face tightened with need, realizing what he said.

"Did you call any other girl *esclave?*" I noticed he called the girl in the lounge Sephena—a name, not a title.

His eyes glinted, shaking his head.

I stepped forward, trapping him by the fireplace. "Whatever you think of yourself, you *do* care. You gave me the sketchpad. You gave me what I needed after I was raped. You're a good person, Q. A saviour to so many women. I want to make you happy."

Q sucked in a heavy breath, watching with unreadable eyes as I reached up, cupping his throat. He stood taller as I squeezed, flaring with power at the thought he let me dominate. I said what I came to say, I needed to hear his proclamation to be satisfied.

Pressing against his larynx, I whispered, "Did it hurt you, sending me away?"

When he didn't answer, I leaned in, tightening my fingers. He swallowed beneath my touch, Adam's apple bobbing with masculinity.

He glared, waging an internal war. I knew he wanted to shrug me off—and he could—there was nothing I could do to stop him, but he let himself be ruled, just for a moment. Finally, something unlocked in his eyes; heart-shattering passion blazed. He nodded. "Yes."

I could barely breathe. "Yes, you hurt?"

He rolled his shoulders, breaking my hold on him. He towered over me, gathering shadows from the room, crackling with energy. "Yes, I fucking hurt. I haven't slept well in weeks. I can't go in my bedroom because I get so hard. I fucking come twice a day remembering how you writhed beneath the whip. How your skin flushed and crested with red." He stopped, breathing hard. His body beseeched mine and I struggled to stay frozen.

Dragging hands over his head, he forced himself to go on as if the confession was the hardest thing he ever had to do. "You're everything I've been looking for and you scare me shitless. You want me to hurt you! You're fucking crazy for taunting me that way." In cobra-strike quickness, he kissed me hard. "I'm terrified I'll end up killing you."

We locked eyes, overcome with truth. My blood thrilled at the thought of his deep desires.

With shaky hands, I unbuttoned his shirt, pushing it aside under his blazer. Every button, he breathed harder, until his chest strained and panted. My own breath matched his.

"Stop it, Tess."

I swallowed. "You won't kill me. You wouldn't go that far." I traced inked sparrows on his skin, following ribs, and hard planes of delectable muscle. "I know you deplore what happened to the women you save. You won't turn me into a broken shadow of myself. Your ferocity feeds me." I ducked to nip his nipple, teeth aching to draw blood. "Whatever you give, I can take... as long as I know how you feel."

My fingers etched brambles and barbwire going around his side, pulling him into me. Q flatly refused to come. Back muscles tensed as he denied my request.

I groaned, loving his strength. His control. But I wanted him closer. Glaring, I pressed against him from toes to chest.

Q ground his teeth, eyes growing heavy with lust. He stood perfectly still, not uttering a word. His power, his rage, filled the library, threatening.

"Tell me..." I murmured. "Speak to me..."

Q sucked in another shuddering breath as I stood on tiptoes, licking his bottom lip.

He softened. The ridges of muscle at the base of his back trembled, leaning into me. "I will never get enough," he whispered. *"C'était la plus grosse erreur de ma vie de te renvoyer chez lui."* It was the biggest mistake of my life sending you away.

Effervescent happiness. Complete sublime joy.

"You're willing to keep me? To hell with the police?" I licked the seam of his lips, capturing his ragged sigh.

"There was no deal with the police. They congratulated me on saving such a strong slave."

Time froze. *What?*

I pulled away, crying out as Q snapped, "You can't tease and expect to get away without paying."

His arms tightened around me, plucking me from

the floor as if I weighed nothing. Q carried me to the desk, swiping the contents off in one swift move. Pens clattered, papers fluttered, and a laptop smashed to the floor.

Practically throwing me on top, he pressed his hips violently against mine.

Heat smoked and words disintegrated to cinders, but I clung to lucidity.

I arched, clawing his forearms. "Stop… what do you mean?" My body swept control away, but I needed to understand. What the *hell* did he mean?

Q groaned, thrusting his hard cock. I automatically wrapped legs around him, thrilling, filling with lava and need.

"The police know what I do. Once the girls are… better… they find their loved ones and return them." His eyes snapped closed as he thrust again, body shuddering with desire. He chuckled darkly, bowing over me. "They've been meddling in my love life since I was sixteen. They thought you were different. Hinting that I'd touched you, rather than helped you." His eyes burned me with hot jade. "It freaked me the fuck out. They saw the truth and I knew I had to get rid of you before I killed you, or worse… turned you into what other sick masters do to their slaves."

He stopped thrusting, the sudden silence chilling me.

"Don't you see? I cared too much to do what I wanted. I made a promise. I won't ever break that vow again."

My world shifted, turned from round to flat. Black and white became colour, night became day.

Finally.

The puzzle of Q Mercer made sense; I fitted the final piece. I wanted to hug and bite and slap and fuck him to death. He gave me up because he cared for me. Even though he swore he never could.

I laughed. Men. Glorious stupid, egotistical men.

My man.

Mine.

He stared deep into my eyes, not moving apart from a

small pulse of his hips, barely detectable. I rocked, moaning as the seam of his fly teased through my dress.

"Break your promise. Now. With me."

Q shook his head, even as his hips pressed harder. "I can't ever let myself free."

He groaned as I shot up and kissed him. Wrapping my arms around his neck, I threw my entire being into the kiss.

He fought for a millisecond, before kissing me back, plunging his tongue deep and violent, taking possession completely. Brain muddled, breathing caught, and I no longer thought. I only felt.

I nipped at his lip, fighting his tongue with mine. We fought our wordless battle, hearts racing to the same beat.

He broke the kiss. Instead of lust and unbridled need, he was… sad, remote.

I spread my legs further. No way would I let him over think this. He hissed as I arched my back, purring against his rigidness. "I need you—I need you to hurt me."

Something dark thickened the air, and I hid my smile. Quincy was losing to Q. Black desires slowly tearing at the cage he locked himself in. *I'm winning.*

"You need me? Or you want me?" he growled, mouth pursed as he thrust hard.

I trembled and writhed, taunting, dangling the wanton little slave in front of a diabolical master. I panted, "Is there a difference?"

In my mind, there wasn't. Both were important. Life and death important with how my body heated and summoned for release.

He grabbed my nipple through the silkiness of the dress, twisting, dragging another cry from my throat.

"Do you need me as a man, or as your master?" he bit the words into pieces, a vein on his neck stood out as he unzipped his pants, pulling his straining erection free. "Is this what you're begging for, *esclave?*"

I nodded, unable to look away from his huge, delicious hard cock. "Yes. God, yes."

His fingers bunched my dress up my thighs, and he pushed aside my knickers. His finger disappeared inside with no gentle foreplay, but I was drenched for him. I bowed around his touch, whimpering with gratitude. So long. So, so long since I felt such rhapsody.

He smeared wetness over my clit. My legs bound tighter, squirming away from the sharp edged pleasure. "Q... Master."

Never breaking eye contact, he curled his fingers around my bird tattooed wrist, locking me in his dominance. His touch oozed sexual prowess, bending my will with nothing more than pressure.

"Do you promise to tell me if I go too far? Do you promise you'll never let me take away your spirit, your fight, your strength? You promise you'll always stay strong." His finger speared deep, stroking my g-spot.

My mind shot blank. He wanted me to promise? Fine. I could promise. I came here to give him everything. If he needed it in blood, I would sign. I would autograph any contract, if it meant Q gave me himself entirely.

His finger thrust, pressing incredibly deeper, dragging dark needs to the surface; I clenched, hungry, desperate for more. "Answer me, *esclave,*" he rasped.

I looked deep into his eyes, imprisoning both of us. Irises were dark and smitten, lids heavy with lust. "I vow to fight you to the death before I let you break me."

Q withdrew his fingers, reaching over my head for a letter opener. The sharp glint of the blade sent my heart winging wild.

"I'm a businessman, Tess. I don't take promises lightly."

I scooted up, pushing my dress to cover myself. My body vibrated for his touch, but I saw how important this was to him. My chest ached. Q was going to agree to keep me. To allow me to share his world. I waited in thick anticipation. I would do anything to put his mind at rest.

"You're asking me to treat you like a slave, but also share my life with you?" His face was closed off, becoming perfectly Q again. "To allow me to control you, but also be an equal?"

I nodded. "Exactly."

His eyes flashed and his fingers tightened around the letter opener. "I almost came to steal you back, you know."

My heart kicked into a higher gear; I fought the soft smile. "You did? Why?"

He snorted, smiling wryly. "You know why. It's been complete and utter hell. *J'étais malheureux sans toi.*" I've been miserable without you. Sighing heavily, he added, "The other girl, Sephena, arrived from some sadistic prick in Tehran a week after you left. All I could think about was you. You bowled through my front door, spitting, and so proud."

He cupped my jaw with angry fingers. "She was carried in by Franco because she passed out from fear of a new master, completely different to your ferocity."

He bowed his head, glaring at the blade in his hand. Determination and acceptance settled in his gaze. "You must never *ever* let me break you so completely. I need your fire, your temper. Your unbreakable will."

I slid off the desk, standing on crinkled paperwork, no doubt for another building merger. "I've already given you my promise, and you didn't have to steal me. I returned."

He swallowed, and his face cleared from confusion and misplaced desires. Vivid excitement gleamed. He stood taller, light tempering his darkness as he finally understood what I offered. Finally understood I was powerful enough to stand up to the beast he lived with and collar it. I would let it hurt me, but never ruin.

"I'll try and give you what you want in return for two things." He tugged a blonde strand, bringing me forward to plant a harsh kiss on my lips.

"You only have to ask."

He murmured against my mouth, "I want you to work for me. I know you finished your exams. You're qualified."

I looked up, mouth gaping. Two things knocked me over. One, he trusted me to work in his multi-billion dollar company, and two: he'd spied on me. My soul flew. He hadn't let me go after all. *I'm happy he stalked and spied.* Damn right, I was. Ecstatically happy.

"And the other?"

"Two others, actually." He straightened, bracing himself. His face thundered with temper, rolling with heavy clouds. "If you *ever* sleep with another man again, I swear to God, I won't be responsible for what I do. You went home to that boy Brax. You shared his bed for a month. That was the worst kind of torture, and I refuse to do it again." He breathed hard, shaking his head, eyes haunted.

I threw myself against him, kissing, climbing him. He crushed me, teeth bruising lips as if he wanted to replace all my thoughts with only him. He didn't need to try. He did it effortlessly. When I could breathe again, I muttered, "That goes for you, too. No other women. I'm the one you whip and fuck." Flashing him my tattoo, I said, "This little bird belongs in your cage. No one else."

He groaned, backing me against the desk again, rocking. I leaned back till my shoulders pressed hard wood. I grabbed his tie and forced him to fold over, warming me. His naked chest teased between the unbuttoned shirt and I ran my fingers up his back, hissing as he bucked into me. Not caring I was wanton and brash and horny and all manner of hot, bothered things. It had been so long; I needed him so bad.

Q nodded. "Sounds like a fair trade."

I smacked him lightly. "And your last condition?" I

panted as his lips trailed down the side of my neck, disappearing between the valley of my breasts.

Q bit my nipple through my dress and jagged lightning erupted through my belly. "I want to commit murder."

My heart stopped beating.

"I'm going to put the bastards down who hurt you. I'll personally make sure their entire operation is burned to the ground."

I jerked back, looking into his furious eyes. I couldn't breathe. *He wants the same revenge I do.* I didn't even have to ask. He saw deeper than he even realized. However unconventional our relationship, it rang with rightness. Q spoke to me on a much deeper level than man and woman.

I fully believed I was made for him and he was made for me. Two halves of the same fuckedupness. Two souls from the same twisted desires, unable to fully be free until we found each other.

Throwing my arms around him, I breathed deep his heady scent of citrus and something darker, something pulling energy from my body. Transcending my soul from my mortal shell, ready to be claimed and taken.

"You're the one, Q Mercer. You were always the one."

Q blushed. The first time I'd ever seen shyness on a man so strong and bold. Pink tinged his perfectly sculpted cheekbones, melting me into a puddle. *Will I ever get used to how much he means to me? Do I ever want to?* I wanted to live my life in seventh heaven. Constantly in awe. Constantly needing.

Q gritted his teeth, pulling the letter opener through a fleshy palm. A small line of blood welled. With his other palm, he grabbed my hand, locking eyes as he sliced my skin the same way.

The burn was nothing. I welcomed it. I knew what Q

wanted to do. It made complete and utter sense. Anyone else wouldn't see how much I needed to mix our essence, our life force. But he did.

This was a contract between two monsters fighting in the dark. Our blood was basic ink for such a deal—a deal of pain and endless pleasure.

We clasped hands. Sonnets and thunder and every element in the universe shot through him to me. I shivered as Q growled, "I promise to protect you, ravage you, hunt those who hurt you, and give you the life you deserve. My fortune is yours. My secrets are yours. And I will give you the corpses of the men who hurt you."

My body hummed with the pact we made.

"I promise to fight you every hour of every day."

His lips curled in a cruel smile. "Welcome to my world, *esclave*. I fight my desires every second."

Unlatching our grip, he smeared our combined blood on my tattoo. "You're the first bird I released who came back. The only bird."

Tears glassed my vision as I caressed his cheek. "I was always running to you. I just didn't know it. My freedom is in your captivity, Q. I fly when I'm with you."

He licked his lips, worshipping awe and rapture in his gaze. *"Je suis à toi."* I am yours.

I shook my head. *"Nous sommes les uns des autres."* We are each other's.

Epilogue

Q Mercer

Twenty years ago

Silence was my friend. Always had been. Probably always will be.

Somehow, the air carried me, killing any noise I made, turning me into a shadow. I moved with stealth—a ghost—a phantom. Never a peep—never a sound.

My parents lost me for two days once, and I never left the house. I disappeared inside the huge, rambling mansion we called home, drifting from room to room.

Stealing food from the kitchen and camping inside giant, unused fireplaces.

Secrets were hard to keep hidden from a silent, inquisitive eight-year-old. I saw the truth of what went on, and it made me sick to my stomach.

My mother knew, but did nothing, preferring peach schnapps and Baileys to my father. And my father preferred slaves to his wife.

I was five when I first heard the screams. Guttural calls for help, full of distress and heartache, followed by a horrible groan of pleasure and ecstasy.

That was the first day I slipped into the forbidden room, and watched my father beat and rape a girl. Her ass blazed red as he pumped into her from behind.

My little heart raced. I knew I shouldn't see this. I didn't understand it. Something bad was happening, but I was too naïve to know. But, on some level, I knew exactly what it was.

My father hurt a woman who didn't want to be hurt. She hadn't been naughty like I was sometimes. All she did was cry and curl into a ball. Yet my father beat her with fists and whips. Enjoying her cries, he turned into a purple-faced baboon with pleasure.

The scene scarred my brain for life, irrevocably changing me. I went out of my way to be kind and gentle to every living thing. The cook caught me, time and time again, feeding birds, mice, and other woodland creatures.

My mother fell more and more in love with fruity-smelling alcohol, leaving me motherless, with a rambling drunk.

All while my father amassed a stable.

He already had a stable full of cars: Bugatti, Audi, Ferrari, and Porsches. He owned a barn full of thoroughbreds and world cup racers. But it wasn't enough. He wanted humans. Girls. *Possessions.*

On my eighth birthday, he brought home his twelfth filly. She kicked and screamed, until he punched her so hard she passed out. A full wing of the house was barricaded for his new acquisitions. No member of staff was permitted.

But I knew secrets he didn't. Hidden passageways in the walls—no lock could keep me out.

I watched from air ducting and wall cavities. My stomach twisted as I saw sick, foul acts committed against fragile women.

Rather than suffer boyhood excitement, a thrill of shame coated my life. I wallowed in guilt. My own flesh and blood ruined lives of others. Stealing their freedom and turning them into broken belongings.

I never loved my father, but day by day, my hatred for him grew. I hated that he'd created me. I wanted nothing to do with him. I wanted him gone.

On my thirteenth birthday, I broke into the stable while my father wasn't there.

The girls all looked up with red-rimmed eyes and fright. I didn't know why I went. To offer sympathy? Comfort? It seemed so stupid, standing there. I offered to bring them anything they wanted—to steal food from the kitchen, anything to take that hopelessness from their eyes. But they wailed and hid; running from a scrawny thirteen-year-old boy.

Their fear stank, and I couldn't stand to be there any longer. But I owed them something, anything—it was my father who ruined them—it was my place to make it right. "Please. I don't mean to hurt you." My balls hadn't dropped; my voice sounded as high as their whimpers for help.

Not one of the girls came near me that day, but I saw their bruises, the shadows under their eyes, the haunting emptiness in their souls. I couldn't stay away.

The next day I returned and uttered the one word I swore I never would. The word my father used a lot. "*Esclave,* obey me."

Immediately, the girls stiffened, dropping to their

knees. All twelve bowed, long hair, all different colours, kissing the ground.

That was the day I learned the word broken. They were broken. Completely. And I couldn't stand it. With one command, they were mine, and I hated their weakness as much as I hated my father for creating such miserable creatures.

I ordered, "Crawl to me."

Sounds of skin rubbing against carpet as the circle of naked slaves obeyed.

"Stop."

They did. Immediately. Total obedience.

Standing in a circle of women, I made a vow. I would help them. No one should be broken beyond repair. No other human had the right to steal their life.

I would become their saviour, and rehabilitate them back to sanity.

Three years passed before I got hold of an untraceable gun. Boarding school in London allowed me to mingle with rich, bored kids with mean connections. Criminals hung around the wealthy like flies to rotten meat, and I took advantage.

I earned a reputation for being closed off and angry, when really, I plotted constantly how to bring my father to justice. My family's reputation preceded him and people feared me. Feared my power, my own legacy of a ruthless tycoon.

I did nothing to disillusion them. Fear was a powerful weapon—I knew. I saw how fear ruled my father's women.

Two weeks later, school holidays came around. I travelled home on the train with my leather-bound suitcase, a heavy black gun in my waistband.

I hated going home. There was nothing there for me. Only the undying need for vengeance.

My mother had died a year before from alcohol poisoning, leaving me vacant. She was my mother, but never paid attention to her only son. I wasn't bourbon or shiraz, therefore I wasn't important.

Mrs. Sucre welcomed me home, and I holed away in my room, cleaning my new possession. Staring at shiny brass bullets, I welcomed anger and rage.

At two in the morning, I went hunting. Night was my father's playtime. I knew where to find him.

I sneaked with the silence, fingers tight around the new purchase.

The whimpers of girls punched me in the chest. *Soon. Soon you'll be free.* I knew they'd thank me for what I was about to do. My own sanity would thank me. Soon, I wouldn't have to live with guilt that I allowed my father to continue hurting so many innocent women.

My father never heard a thing.

I moved right beside him while he fucked a girl, holding her pigtails like handholds; his old man ass wobbling with every thrust. My lips curled in distaste and I snarled. The girl's tears set fire to my stomach.

I raised the gun, testing the weight. My hand was dry—not sweaty or nervous. My heart even and sure.

"Enjoy your last fuck, father. It's the last you'll ever do."

My father, Mr. Quincy Mercer the First, stopped mid thrust, face bright red, jowls trembling.

"What are you doing in here, you little shit? Get out. I told you this part of the house was forbidden."

Girls all around the room, tied up in horrible positions, started to cry. Some with their necks bound to ankles. Others hanging from the ceiling upside down. Tears flowed, but light slowly glowed in their eyes. Hunger, revenge, freedom, infected each like wildfire. Smashing the shackles of brokenness.

I didn't say another word. What was there to say? I

squeezed the trigger.

The red spray was a gruesome firework. My father's brains splattered over the girl he still impaled on his cock.

She screamed and scrambled away, wiping her face with shaking hands.

The entire room rippled with darkness. I flexed my arms, standing in the centre, breathing deep.

My father's reign was over. I was the new owner of the Mercer Empire. At sixteen, I inherited all his belongings, including the stable of women.

For a brief moment, my cock stiffened at the thought of carrying on my father's legacy. It would be so easy to violate a girl who was bound, unable to move or stop me. I could lose my virginity to a slave. I could do whatever I wanted. A ruthless tycoon, just like my old man.

But as I stood, with my mind overflowing with darkness, I knew I could never walk that path.

I wanted it too damn much. I *craved* the feel of submission. I *drooled* for a woman sucking my cock under duress. I *hated* myself with vengeance.

I was my father's son, after all. Somehow, the moment I killed him, his evilness shot into me. I wanted to put a bullet in my own brain as I knew I'd never be free from the monstrous urges.

Needing to run, I quickly freed the women and brought them clothes from my mother's old things.

The girls accepted what I gave. Keeping their eyes downcast, mouths closed.

That night signified a new beginning. For all of us.

A year later, my rehabilitation of the twelve women was complete. Some girls left immediately after I freed them. I gave them money, and sent them back to loved ones. A few remained, needing psychological help. I admitted them to the local hospital, footing all the bills.

I didn't need to lie about how the girls became that way. Everyone knew my father and his sick tastes. He supplied many a sick fuck in the village with toys. Renting them out for thousands, not caring some never came back alive.

I'd been painted with the same brush, even though I resisted the beast inside. I wanted more than anything to keep those girls locked and chained, and subservient to my desires, but I never caved. Always fighting. Forever struggling.

The last girl to leave was a sheik's daughter. She'd been a gift for a lucrative property deal in the east. Captive for six years, she felt some sort of sick loyalty to me for freeing her.

The night before she left, she trapped me in my bedroom. The girls were allowed free reign of the house, slowly acclimatizing to freedom once again.

She closed the door, signifying what she wanted with one click of a lock.

I tried to refuse her. I tried to push her away. She didn't owe me anything, most of all her body, but she took control, and made me do things my father would've been proud of. I lost my virginity, not in sweetness and tenderness, but with spanking and degradation.

The moment it was over, I loathed myself. I kicked her out, put her on my private plane, and sent her home. I couldn't stand to see her. She reminded me how far I'd fallen. How alike I was to the one man I hated the most.

The following years were torture. I needed a release, but normal sex didn't cut it. I needed violence to get off. I needed the feel of complete submission of ownership. My blood was tainted, and I'd never be free.

Then the bribes started. As I grew my father's empire to worldwide domination, people wanted property favours. A building here. Special grants there. I had friends in powerful places and men gave me presents. My father's reputation preceded once again, and instead of gift baskets, I received slaves.

It started slowly, one a year. Then two. Until, finally, I became the king of accepting trafficked women for a business deal. It cost a fortune to accept, and I didn't touch a single one.

They arrived, broken, trembling, sometimes drugged, sometimes completely damaged. I became a father, brother, friend to them.

Most recovered, but others... some I couldn't save.

I enlisted the help of the local police. Together, we worked tirelessly. They made me an exemplary citizen for my 'charity'.

Then Suzette arrived. She had bite marks all over her body. Hair shaved, cigarette burns, and broken fingers. I promptly hired a mercenary to return the favour to the men who broke her.

It took six months before Suzette spoke a word. Another six months before she let me be in the same room with her. Slowly, she started working around the house, throwing herself into housework, as if she could become invisible as a staff member and not the slave she'd been. And I let her.

It helped. Her skin went from pallid to rosy, her eyes lost the panicked hue, and slowly she stopped jumping whenever I appeared, moving with silence.

When I asked if she was ready to go home, she refused. She threw herself at my feet, begging to stay. She had no one to return to, and professed her love for me. She wanted me to love her. Take her however I wanted. But I couldn't. I never could. I couldn't resort to using broken women. I would never find myself in the aftermath.

Instead, I used professionals. Played out dark fantasies with women who gladly accepted ten thousand euros for a bit of pain. It never satisfied. It left my throat coated with dissatisfaction, but that was my sacrifice. I would never touch a slave again.

Suzette became fundamental to helping other girls heal. She befriended them, and they found their way back to happiness quicker.

Our little team worked well for years. I focused more on property than saving women. I expanded the company into South East Asia, Fiji, New Zealand, and Hong Kong.

Then my world flipped upside down.

Esclave fifty-eight arrived.

The moment she stumbled across the threshold, all those dark needs roared and raged inside. I wanted to throw myself down the stairs and take her then and there. I fucking wanted, wanted, *wanted.*

She was different.

She wasn't broken.

For the first time, a slave came to me spitting and alive. Intelligence blazed in her eyes and my cock stirred, unable to be controlled. I knew I wouldn't be able to stop, and hated her almost as much as I hated myself.

I finally met a woman with fire and passion matching my own, and all I wanted to do was break her. I wanted her to be mine in every way humanly possible.

I was a sick, sick bastard and would go to hell for what I fantasized.

After twelve years of battling the beast, it sprang from its cage and refused to go back. The lifetime of urges couldn't be refused. They overtook, held me hostage, and I fell into the role of master so effortlessly, as if it was the true me. The real me. *The monster.*

She was mine.

Present

She shook her head, looking into my black soul with dove-grey eyes. *"Nous sommes les uns des autres."* We are each other's.

Two emotions fought for space in my chest. The beast lurched forward, ready to take her up on the offer to debase and hurt, while the other wanted to gather her gently and lavish every penny I had.

After everything I did. After what Lefebvre did... my heart raced. *That fucking cock-sucking bastard.* Black anger gathered again at the thought of him raping her. I wanted to dig up his unmarked grave and dismember him piece by piece. A single gunshot was too good for that asshole.

But Tess survived. She forged stronger and shone brighter. She never broke.

I pressed against her again, hissing between my teeth at the burn in my cock. I wanted to fuck her so bad, but I needed to tame other urges, too.

"Nous sommes les uns des autres," I repeated, kissing her deeply. Her soft groan sent my sanity spiralling out of control. How did I manage to send her away? Kick her from my room after she let me whip her to the point of drawing blood? I'd been a bloody saint with willpower of an angel.

I sacrificed everything, because I refused to break such a perfect woman. A woman who pranced into my life with spark and fire, threatening to burn my very existence to the ground.

"I can't believe you came back," I murmured, heart galloping, still unable to believe the blood oath we made. I smeared residual crimson on her throat, whispering fingers across her collarbone.

My eyes dropped to the tattoo on her wrist. Holy fuck, what was she trying to do to me? She spoke to the darkness inside, and despite her fear, stood up to me. I wanted to pummel her into the ground to make her obey, but her rebellion was also my undoing.

I'd never be free of her.

Tess Snow.

Tess *esclave.*

Mine.

All mine.

I can't wait any longer. She came back on her own terms. It's my turn now.

I stood, shoving my cock into my trousers, wincing at how fucking hard it was. Damn woman cast a spell on me. Tess blinked, watching with those intoxicating Bambi eyes, begging me to fuck and hurt her.

I groaned. If I did this, there would be no going back. She would become everything I needed. I had to trust in her vow. The promise she would be strong enough. I hoped to God she was right because I gave up fighting.

The monster roared, beating his chest, salivating at the thought of what was to come.

I was done and she was mine, in every sense.

"Come." I grabbed her tattooed wrist, jerking her from the library. Stalking through the foyer, her little pants sent lust into a realm of insanity. Fuck, I needed her. To scream and writhe and *bleed.*

What sort of man needed to make a woman bleed? Not a sane one. *I'm infected. Poisoned. Destined for hell.*

I slammed my fist against the hidden door beneath the stairs, taking violence out on the wood panel.

Tess flinched, but didn't move away.

I raised an eyebrow as the door opened, giving her one last opportunity to admit she made a huge mistake. Not that it would make any difference. I wasn't letting her go again. Willing slave or not. The beast preferred unwilling, because I was sick. So sick.

"Je suis à toi," she panted.

I gritted my teeth. Fuck, yes, she was mine. No one else's. She was lucky I didn't hang and quarter the stupid boy she went home to. Idiot. Sleeping beside her every night—touching her. Couldn't he see the unique treasure he had? My chest swelled with pride. Tess left him for me. She was too much for a boy. She needed a man with a demon inside.

I didn't think I'd ever find a female beast with contorted desires like mine.

But she found me.

My back rippled with tension as I dragged her down the stairs. The lights clicked on automatically, illuminating the dark teak bar, pool table, a music recording studio, and sauna.

Tess didn't say a word as her eyes fell on the pool table, chest pumping. Goddammit, I loved touching her that night. I'd been so ready to rape her, to try and get rid of the sickness inside in one swoop, but she fought too much, made me too hot. I wanted the agony of dragging out the suspense. I wanted to torture myself with the insanely painful urge to fill her with my cock.

I was rather proud of my strength that night. If I had raped her—who knows if she could've handled everything else I did to her.

Tess bumped into me, unable to tear her eyes off the table. I wrapped tight, imprisoning arms around her, growling. "Remember my fingers inside you, *esclave?* Remember how wet you were? Even then, your body knew you belonged to me."

She shivered, tight and tense, but malleable and feminine at the same time. "Are you going to finish what you started that night? Take me over the pool table?" A pink tongue darted between her lips, tempting me beyond belief.

Fuck, I could barely stand, my cock ached so hard.

"No. I have another idea."

She sucked in a breath, pulse strumming in her wrist where I held.

Rational thoughts smashed the horny beast to the side. I panicked. How the hell would this happen? How could I hurt her and then...not? Would the insane urge to beat the shit out of her ever leave? *I'll constantly have to watch what I do, how hard I do it.* I could never resort to being my father. Never.

I spun her, trapping her against my chest, rubbing my cock on her belly. "Your skin is too flawless. I want to scar it." I squeezed my eyes closed. I sounded like a sick fuck, but shit, the thought of marking her permanently did insane things to me.

She wiggled, thrusting hips against my thigh, riding me, deliberately driving me crazy. So brave, so stupidly brave. "You've already scarred me. You just can't see it."

I sucked in a breath. Images of her soul ripped to shreds because of what I did made me flinch.

Forcing the thoughts away, I grunted, "Just so we're clear, I'm your master and you're mine... you're *esclave*. I'm going to hurt you. I'm going to fuck you, and when we're done, I'll try to give you what you want. I'll try and talk, or chat, or whatever you want me to do." I sighed heavily, tensing as blackness claimed me. "But I can't promise I'll be able to." Trying to be semi-human, I demanded, "Do you still want to do this? Knowing I might not be able to do anything but take and take. Until you can't give anymore? Until I wring you dry?"

She nodded, biting her lip, face tight with need. "*Oui, maître.*" Grey-blue eyes hot, full of sex and yearning. She bowed her head, blonde curls hid her face; a dominant thrill shot through my body.

The freedom she granted—to allow my darkness to mix with hers—was indescribable. I wanted to crush her to death in an embrace, and never let go. I wanted to fuck her so hard she broke in my arms. I wanted to kiss her brow and nurse her back to health once I hurt her. I wanted so many things. So many things I never thought I could have.

I couldn't stop staring. She arched up, pressing soft, breakable lips against mine. "*Maître,* punish me. I deserve to be punished for fucking another man while I was away from you."

What. The. Fuck?

My body slammed to a halt. My world spun with brimstone and hell. I wrapped fingers around her throat. "You *dare* admit that? Are you suicidal?" I squeezed until true fear popped into her eyes, and it fed me. Shit, it fed me. The fear, the fragility. A delicate bird I could wipe from existence so easily.

Horror tempered my rage; I forced my fingers to relax. *Get a grip!*

"Not suicidal, but close if you don't touch me. I'm on a knife edge needing you, Q."

Hearing my name on her lips ignited the fuse I tried so hard to stop from exploding. I was done holding back. No more talking.

Grabbing her hair, I dragged her to the crystal bar in front of the pool table. I wasn't in the mood for games. I was in the mood for alcohol and getting wet.

I pressed her over the bar, revelling in her moans, her cries, her sexy pants. "You'll be sorry you said that, *esclave*. You want to see how dark I'll go? Well, you can't. Not until you prove your promise. Not until I trust you're strong enough."

I wrapped my fingers around the base of her skull, placing her cheek against the cold granite countertop.

She writhed, pressing her ass hard against me. Goddammit, this woman.

"Does it make you jealous? Do you want to wipe away the memory of him with your cock? Because I want you to. I need you to. Q... please...Q."

Holy shit, who was this little animal? Did I create her, or was she always this twisted? My skin sparked with tingles. Emotions I never experienced before exploded. Happiness. True, unbridled happiness.

I shook her for good measure. "I'm so fucking jealous of that boy. I was jealous of Franco flying with you back to Australia. I was jealous of Suzette for earning your friendship. I was even jealous of myself when I fucked you. Fuck, yes,

I'm jealous. *Insanely* jealous."

Her mouth twitched. "Good. I'm happy."

Shaking my head, I grabbed the back of her grey dress—the same dress I bought her—and ripped it down the back. She trembled as the loud snarl of fabric echoed. Once it was destroyed, I splayed it open, exposing her back, ass, and thighs.

My palm twitched, and I couldn't stop it. I spanked her. Hard. Probably too hard, but she cried in such pleasure, my cock jerked and I almost came.

Instantly, her white flesh bloomed red with a hand print. I groaned, caressing her, wanting more, always craving more.

When I froze, trembling with the urge to go too far, Tess looked over her shoulder. "One smack? That's all you feel I deserve?"

I literally couldn't take it. I hit her. So. Damn. Hard. My palm fired and stung. Tears sprang to her eyes, and I ground my cock against her ass, throbbing with unshed come.

Needing to give my hands something to do, I opened the mini-bar below and pulled out a vintage bottle of icy champagne.

Ripping off the gold foil and popping the cork, I shuddered with so much pent up need, I couldn't think straight.

Tess watched, tears glittering on her cheeks and eyelashes. Her face pressed obediently against the counter, not saying a word.

Once the sharp tang of alcohol filled the space, I gave her a tight smile, then upended the expensive champagne all over her back, drenching her hair, making her shiver with bubbles and chill.

Tess moaned, writhing, hips bucking for mine. I growled, swigging the last dregs as I thrust against her red slapped ass. Grinding, rocking, I wanted to do so much to her, but my need to come took all control out of my hands.

She wants to see how dark I'll go. We had a future to look forward to, full of sin and debauchery. I would teach her the meaning of blackness, initiate her into my world.

A thrill shot up my legs and into my belly. A future. Together.

My mind raced, unable to stay on one concise thought. She gave me everything so willingly, on a platter of sex, ready for the taking. In return, I owed retribution from her kidnappers. I wanted to lay corpses at her feet and prove I may be a monster but I was *her* monster.

A beast who would turn savage on those who wronged her.

Ducking down, I tore the white G-string off with my teeth, dragging an eager tongue up the side of her back, lapping over ribs.

Her ribs were virgin, no tattoos, unlike mine. It'd taken four years to get it exactly right, adding more and more birds as I saved more and more slaves.

The fact Tess inked herself with a bird told me how deep she already went. How much she wanted me. *All of me.*

The taste of her and champagne fogged my brain. I needed more.

Slamming to my knees, I grabbed her ankles, spreading her legs with force. She slipped, hands gripping the countertop. "Q... God, yes."

Her voice vibrated through me, sending lust into overdrive. I stood back up, yanking my tie off in one swipe. Her eyes widened. "No, don't gag me. I'll be quiet."

I cocked my head, glaring. *"Obéis, esclave."* Obey. She closed her eyes, parting lips slightly, allowing the material to bind her. With the two ends behind her head, it felt like reins. Controlling her completely, ready to be ridden into a frenzy.

Tying the ends quickly, I resumed my position between her legs. Her exposed cunt above dripped with wetness and champagne. It was the most delicious sight I'd ever seen.

Groaning, I licked the bubbles, tracing them up her inner thighs.

She bucked, spreading her legs even more.

Fuck, she tasted amazing. Soft and smoky and hinting at orchids and frost.

When I flicked a tongue over her clit, she spasmed, moaning, tears oozing. I dug my fingers into her thighs, keeping her steady. My cock ached in the confines of my pants. I wanted to shove it inside her.

But first, I wanted to lick and drown in her taste. Without warning, I spurred my tongue into her slit. She screamed, muffled by the gag, inspiring me to lick harder. The sharp tang of champagne drowned in her powdery sweetness. Nectar just for me. A mind-blazing aphrodisiac.

I wanted to bite, to brand, to rape.

I lost track of time as I worshipped her pink flesh. Who needed time when everything I needed was right here. I never wanted to eat again unless it tasted like Tess.

But my cock wept with pre-cum, throbbing with urgency to replace my tongue and fuck. Games would have to come another day. When I wasn't about to spurt like a fucking school boy.

I stood, breathing hard, wiping Tess's juice from my chin. Fumbling with my belt, my eyes widened as violence took me over. I yanked the leather from the loops, weighing it in my hands.

With lust-heavy eyes, Tess looked over her shoulder. Her lips were split and grimaced thanks to the gag, cheeks ruddy red with passion.

I folded the belt in half, palming the metal buckle. I slapped my palm, wincing at the sting, loving how she panted harder.

I cocked my eyebrow. "Is this punishment enough for fucking another?"

For a moment, she paused. I expected a no. A whimper, a plea to run. Instead, with a sharp blue glint in her eye, she shook her head coyly. She cocked her jaw, body language asking me to remove the gag.

I didn't want to, but obliged.

After I untied it, she sucked in a breath as I lay the drenched tie on the counter. For a millisecond, she didn't speak, intoxicating me with her pants. Then that sexy, dangerous glint appeared again. She snapped, "Don't fucking think about whipping me, you monster. I told you, I don't want this. Let me go."

Oh. My. Fucking. God. Denial. Rape. Anger. Delicious delirium.

My eyes snapped closed and the beast raged to life. "Fuck, *esclave*. I told you not to tempt me."

My hands curled around the leather, snapping it tight. This perfect woman was about to get the whipping of her life. Then I'd fuck her. Hard.

She let me do unthinkable things to her. She gave me everything I needed and more. She fed both the man and beast and she would never be free again. She was in my cage and I would never open the door. She was the key. The key to my happiness.

Patting her ass, I raised my hand. The moment of anticipation had us both shivering out of control.

I struck.

The belt whistled through air, connecting with her champagne-damp skin with a loud *smack*.

She moaned and bit her lip, squeezing her eyes tight.

My hips jerked on their own accord, fucking air as I struck again and again. Never in the same place twice, I decorated her ass with stripes of red. I couldn't get enough oxygen; my chest rose and fell with every pummel.

I lost control and hit too hard, a small trickle of blood welled. She yelped, moving her ass away, but I held her still. "I'm not done with you yet, Tess. Ten strikes for running.

Ten strikes for leaving. And ten strikes for coming back to the monster's den when he willingly set you free." I hardly recognised my own voice, it was so thick with need.

"Too many. I can't do that many." Tears dripped and her entire face was grief-stricken.

"You're the one who wanted dark. I'll give you dark."

And I did.

Thirty pieces of dark.

Thirty strikes of delicious temptation that made my life seem cosmically bright compared to the black I lived in.

Tess screamed and sobbed, but beneath it all was an undercurrent of sexual need. Her wetness trickled down her thigh, thicker, creamier than the champagne. She may hate it, but she loved it.

Once the last kiss smacked her perfect ass, I dropped the belt and in the same second, undid my fly, pushed my pants down, and pulled out my throbbing cock. "Spread," I ordered, pushing her lower back, bending her to my will.

She obeyed, whimpering as my cashmere blazer rubbed against sore skin.

Then she wasn't crying anymore.

I plunged so deep, so fast, her feet left the floor and she slid on the champagne wet counter. "Oh fuck, yes," I grunted.

Her back arched as a delighted scream erupted from her. I wrapped an arm around naked breasts, holding her upright. My hips dug into hers, trying to possess every inch. My cock was hungry, desperate, already rippling with the urge to fill.

She's so tight, so wet.

I slid in and out, thrusting deep until my balls slapped against her.

"Oh, God I've missed this," she cried. "Missed you. Missed the pain."

"Shut up and take it, *esclave*." I thrust, twisting her nipple, biting her neck. My jaw trembled with the urge to draw blood again. I went wild for her blood. It was the best drug. The elixir of the beast inside.

Her hot, whipped flesh burned my lower belly; I couldn't think of anything else but fucking her. I lost control. Spreading my stance, wrapping fingers around her hips, I gave myself over to darkness.

"Take me, Tess."

"I've already taken you, *maître*."

I pounded into her, beyond caring her hipbones collided with hard granite, or knees bruised against cabinets. All I focused on was pleasure.

She cried out, thrusting back, urging me to go harder, *harder*.

I couldn't breathe as a sharp band of release throttled my cock, demanding to spurt into this amazing slave. This woman who turned my world upside down. This woman... the key to my undoing.

I growled like a feral beast as I gave myself over to pleasure. Sensation exploded from my thighs, up my balls, and into my cock. I thrust like a monster with only seconds left to live, filling her with come, marking her, making sure she knew who her master was.

The moment I spurted, she clenched around me. "Fuck, yes, Q. Oh, God. Give it to me. I want you. I want all of you." She came and came, fisting, milking, tearing every drop of come I had to give.

I spasmed and twitched as overbearing intensity replaced hot-arching pleasure, but I couldn't bring myself to stop rocking inside her. I never wanted to leave her hot, dark wetness. It was where I belonged.

She went floppy, breathing like tormented blackbird. My legs grew weak and wobbly. I pulled her into my arms, heading to the floor in one jumble of sweaty, champagne sticky bodies.

She laughed as I laid her on my belly, protecting her nakedness from the cool tiles. Even though depleted, my cock never softened and every wriggle fired new life into it.

Would I ever get enough of her? Would I ever show her how dark I could go?

She went to pull away, but I lassoed my arms tighter. "Where do you think you're going?"

"I thought I was crushing you." She wiggled her ass, sending sparks into my balls. After a month of not having her, she wouldn't get away that easily.

I gently smacked her belly, aware her ass was beyond punishment after the belt. "You think I'm done with you, *esclave?*" I nuzzled her ear, licking softly. "I've only just begun."

The End

Continue Tess and Q's journey in Quintessentially Q

Reviews

6 SPELLBINDING ~ TITILLATING ~ SENSUAL STARS!!!--Lady Vigilante, Goodreads Reviewer
6 STARS- Best book/Best Series of 2013--Hook Me Up Book Blog

"All my life, I battled with the knowledge I was twisted…
fucked up to want something so deliciously dark—wrong
on so many levels. But then slave fifty-eight entered my
world. Hissing, fighting, with a core of iron, she showed
me an existence where two wrongs make a right."

Driven by his vendetta against his father, Q swore a vow
he would never touch a slave. Instead, he spent a lifetime
battling dark urges, the need to hurt, and threw himself into
saving broken birds. Dedicating his home and fortune to fix the
wrongs of others.

Until Tess.

After surviving everything life threw at her, Tess emerged
from the ashes as a woman with fire and spirit. Her past didn't
break her, no matter how much Q tried, and in a twist of fate,
she broke him. Together, they fixed each other.

Tess is his completely. Q is Tess's irrevocably. But now,
they must learn the boundaries of their unconventional
relationship, while Tess seeks vengeance on the men who sold
her. Q made a blood-oath to deliver their corpses at Tess's feet,
and that's just what he'll do.

He may be a monster, but he's Tess's monster.

Sneak Peek into Quintessentially Q...

Prologue

I thought I would be her nightmare—her terror and darkness. I wanted to be. I needed her more than food or sunlight. Only when she came into my life did I start to live—intoxicated by her taste, screams, and joy.

But our fucked up fairytale didn't exactly have a happy ending.

Tess.

My Tess.

My *esclave*—so strong and fierce and sexually feral—wasn't strong enough for what happened.

Her cage wasn't me anymore.

It was them.

Chapter One

All I could think was—she's dead. She had to be. All that blood, so bright with a coppery tang, almost sweet.

Her snowy skin was extra frosty, grey-blue eyes closed to me.

Rage and terror strangled as I fell to my knees in the warm puddle of crimson. The whip in my hands was slippery with sweat, and I hurled it away in disgust. I did this. I let myself go and showed my true self. The monster inside ruined the only brightness in my life.

"Tess?" I pulled her into my arms, dragging her cold, lifeless form closer. Blood smeared over us, and her red-welted body oozed with damnation.

"Wake up, *esclave*," I growled, hoping an order would force those dove-blue eyes open. No response.

I bent, pressing my cheek against her mouth, waiting endlessly for a small puff of breath, a signal I hadn't gone too far.

Nothing.

Fear stopped my heart, and all I wanted to do was rewind time. Rewind to a simpler place where I lived with needs and urges, but never let myself believe I could be free. Rewind to the day when Tess arrived, and I promptly sent her back to her silly boyfriend Brax. At least if I did, she would be safe and my life wouldn't have ended.

At least then, Tess would be alive.

My demons killed her.

I killed her.

I threw my head back and howled.

"Q. Q!"

Something sharp bit my shoulder and I flinched. Rolling away, I tried to ignore the call. I deserved to stay in this endless hell. The hell I created for killing the one woman who stole my life and showed me an emotion I never dared dream for: love.

My cheek smarted as if someone slapped me, blazing through the darkness with a bite of pain.

Eyes snapped open to a wild-eyed, blonde goddess on top of me. The debilitating terror wouldn't leave, even though she was alive, and glaring at me with passion I grew to know so well.

"What the hell, Q. That's the third time this week. You going to tell me what you're dreaming about to warrant howling like a werewolf?" Tess pinned my shoulders to the mattress and I couldn't stop muscles from tensing. I liked her on top, but didn't like her holding me as if she was in control. It wasn't how I worked.

"None of your business." I rolled, grabbing her hips to pin her beneath me. I risked a small smile. With her under me, my world righted again. I ran hands over her waist, up her throat, to her lips. Her breath fluttered, coming faster and the rest of my panic receded.

She was still breathing.

I hadn't killed her.

Yet.

Other Books

The Final Conclusion to Tess and Q's story.

TWISTED TOGETHER

"After battling through hell, I brought my esclave back from the brink of ruin. I sacrificed everything—my heart, my mind, my very desires to bring her back to life. And for a while, I thought it broke me, that I'd never be the same. But slowly the beast is growing bolder, and it's finally time to show Tess how beautiful the dark can be."

Q gave everything to bring Tess back. In return, he expects nothing less. Tess may have leashed and tamed him, but he's still a monster inside.

DESTROYED

Reviews

This book enticed & enthralled me completely. Pepper's stories are like a fine piece of art. They are profound, unique, raw and beautiful. --Kristina, Amazon Review

Pepper Winters has a ridiculous level of talent, and I'm in awe of how deeply she delves into her characters. There are not enough stars, seriously.--K Dawn, Amazon Reviewer

If you like a bit of grey in your romance then you need to get this book because it's one of the best books I've read this year.—Bookfreak

USA Today & Top 20 Amazon Bestseller.

She has a secret.

I'm complicated. Not broken or ruined or running from a past I can't face. Just complicated.

I thought my life couldn't get any more tangled in deceit and confusion. But I hadn't met him. I hadn't realized how far I could fall or what I'd have do to get free.

He has a secret.

I've never pretended to be good or deserving. I chase who I want, do what I want, act how I want.

I didn't have time to lust after a woman I had no right to lust after. I told myself to shut up and stay hidden. But then she tried to run. I'd tasted what she could offer me and damned if I would let her go.

Secrets destroy them.

About Pepper

Pepper Winters is a NYT and USA Today International Bestseller. She wears many roles. Some of them include writer, reader, sometimes wife. She loves dark, taboo stories that twist with your head. The more tortured the hero, the better, and she constantly thinks up ways to break and fix her characters. Oh, and sex... her books have sex.

She loves to travel and has an amazing, fabulous hubby who puts up with her love affair with her book boyfriends.

Her Dark Erotica books include:
Tears of Tess (Monsters in the Dark #1)
Quintessentially Q (Monsters in the Dark #2)
Twisted Together (Monsters in the Dark #3)

Her Grey Romance books include:
Destroyed

Upcoming releases are
Debt Inheritance (Indebted Series)
Last Shadow
Sins of Silver

To be the first to know of upcoming releases, please join Pepper's Newsletter (she promises never to spam or annoy you.)

Pepper's Newsletter

You can stalk her here:

Pinterest
Facebook Pepper Winters
Twitter
Website
Facebook Group
Goodreads

She loves mail of any kind: pepperwinters@gmail.com

Acknowledgements

This is going to be a mini novella, so settle back while I thank everyone.

First, I want to thank my hubby for putting up with me working fourteen hour days on this book and talking nothing but Q this, Q that. Q, Q, Q. He really is a saint.

Next, I want to thank the amazing Beta Readers who read Tears of Tess in all its misspelled glory. Skye Callahan— you were the very first, and my God, I'm sorry for putting you through that. I couldn't imagine writing every day without you on my FB page.

Ing from As The Pages Turn, Chelle Bliss, Monica Robinson, Blakely Bennett, Kyra Lennon, Kelley Lynn, and Suzi Retzlaff. Thank you so much for your suggestions and giving such encouragement and putting up with my endless *I suck moments*

A huge thank you to Ari from Cover it! Designs. I couldn't imagine any other cover for Tears of Tess and I'm in love with Q's cover! <3 I love our two a.m. conversations about all things books.

I want to thank the wonderful editors—TJ Loveless, Lindsey, and Robin for doing a great job—hopefully we caught all those hidden errors

I could never have achieved the buzz surrounding this

book without all the awesome, kickass bloggers. In no particular order: Aestas Book Blogger, Helenas Book Obsession, Breezy Books, Totally Booked, Hopeless Romantic, Dirty Books, House of Vetti, Read More Sleep Less, As The Pages Turn, Must Read Books, Swooning Over Books, Hook Me Up Book Blog, Jacqueline Reads, all the AMAZING ARC reviews—Alaina, Nishat, Nadie, Ing, Surjit, Tiffany, Susan, Amber, Tamara, Donna, Haloangel Reads, ItsyBitsy Book Blog, Stacey, Patricia, Kristina, Jennifer, Mara, and all you incredible bloggers who signed up to help spread the word. I can't thank you enough so I'll send you kisses.

Thank you to the amazing ladies who organised the promo for Tears of Tess: Ing from As The Pages Turn—your generosity and support is priceless. Giselle from Xpresso Book Tours, I'm so, so happy you were in charge of the crazy amount of blogs that signed up. And, Laurynne from CBL Book Tours—you're brilliant and thank you so much for all your hard work.

Thank you to Jenny from Totally Booked for answering all my questions about using lyrics in a book (apparently you can't—hence why I got my music writing hat on and did it myself. But please see the playlist for songs that inspired.)

And lastly, thank you to Black Firefly for handling all the publishing requirements on this thing. You were a life-saver.

Playlist

Some songs that inspired Tears of Tess

Demons by Imagine Dragons
Bring Me Back To Life by Evanescence
Arms by Christina Perri
Dark Paradise by Lana Del Ray
Undisclosed Desires by Muse
Animal by Disturbed
ET by Katy Perry
Halo by Depeche Mode
Higher Level by Beseech
My Immortal by Evanescence
Tainted Love
Familiar Taste of Poison by Halestorm
Gravity by Sara Barielles
Closer by Nine Inch Nails
Stay With Me by Danity Kane
So Far Down by Three Doors Down
SOS by Rihanna

211

Made in the USA
Lexington, KY
26 October 2016